D0343788

Six
Days

DANI ATKINS is an award-winning novelist.
Her 2013 debut *Fractured* (published as
Then and Always in North America) has been
translated into eighteen languages and has
sold more than half a million copies since first
publication in the UK. Dani is the author of
several other bestselling novels, one of which,
This Love, won the Romantic Novel of the
Year Award in 2018. Dani lives in a small
village in Hertfordshire with her husband, one
Siamese cat and a very soppy Border Collie.

ALSO BY DANI ATKINS

Fractured
The Story of Us
Our Song
Perfect Strangers
This Love
While I Was Sleeping
A Million Dreams
A Sky Full of Stars
The Wedding Dress

DANI ATKINS

An Aria Book

First published in the UK in 2022 by Head of Zeus Ltd,
part of Bloomsbury Publishing Plc

9 7 5 3 1 2 4 6 8

A catalogue record for this book is available from
the British Library.

ISBN (HB): 9781800246546
ISBN (XTPB): 9781800246553
ISBN (E): 9781800246577

Typeset by Divaddict Publishing Solutions Ltd

Printed and bound in Great Britain by
CPI Group (UK) Ltd, Croydon CR0 4YY

Head of Zeus Ltd
First Floor East
5–8 Hardwick Street
London EC1R 4RG

WWW.HEADOFZEUS.COM

To Debbie
Who reads them first

SATURDAY

1

The bedroom door still creaked when it opened. Dad had never fixed it, and I kind of liked that. He stood in the opening now, a stranger in a suit I'd never seen before.

For a long moment neither of us spoke. He was the first to break the silence. 'You look beautiful, Gemma.' His voice was gruff and oddly husky. 'If only your mum was here to see this.'

I turned in a rustle of tulle and sequinned lace to face the man I'd loved my whole life and half of his. Dad was practically unrecognisable in the charcoal-grey morning suit. The haircut he'd had the day before was so short it looked as though he might be planning on enlisting after the ceremony. And the habitual salt-and-pepper stubble had been banished by a razor so sharp I could see where the blade, in an unsteady hand, had nicked him. The two small cuts were the only splash of colour in his uncommonly pale face.

'Oh, Dad,' I said, trying to summon up the strength I'd set aside for this moment. Because I'd always known those words were going to be spoken today. The only thing I hadn't been sure of was whether *he'd* be the one to say them, or me.

He held out his work-roughened hands and I placed mine in them and suddenly I was eight years old again, falling off my bicycle; or twelve, when my pet rabbit died; or fourteen, when the boy I liked asked someone else to the school dance. Dad had been there for all those moments – but as part of a team. I could see how difficult it was for him now, to face this big milestone in my life without Mum beside him.

'You look just like her,' he said softly. It was a refrain I'd heard countless times before. Teenage me would probably have rolled the green eyes we shared and vowed to dye my hair a different shade from its natural auburn. But the me I'd become since losing Mum three years ago snatched eagerly at every similarity, as if it were a strand of a fast-unravelling rope.

I turned to the mirror and slid my hand into the crook of his arm, the way I would do in less than an hour when he walked me down the aisle. And for the first time I could truly see it. I *did* look like the woman in the silver-framed photograph in the lounge. True, our wedding dresses were totally different, and her hair had been styled in an elaborate up-do, while mine was left to curl softly in beachy waves down my back. But the expression on her face as she looked at the man standing beside her was one I recognised from a hundred Facebook posts. It was the one I wore when I looked at Finn.

With excellent timing, the door of my old bedroom flew open and the whirlwind that was Hannah Peterson stood in the frame, my wedding bouquet in her hands. Her eyes darted between Dad and me. 'No one had better be crying in here,' she warned, only half joking. 'I've only been gone five minutes.' After twenty-five years as my closest friend, Hannah had practically attained sibling privileges and would think nothing of taking either Dad or me to task if she thought it necessary. 'Remember our agreement: no tears until after everyone has said "I do", okay?'

'How does that poor husband of yours put up with you?' Dad teased, passing an arm around my chief bridesmaid's shoulders and giving her a fatherly squeeze.

'Noise-cancelling headphones, mainly,' she shot back with a wicked grin. 'The bridesmaids' car is waiting downstairs, and the driver says yours is just a few minutes behind,' she said, slipping back into her role of unofficial wedding planner. I swear if she'd found a place to squirrel away a clipboard in the folds of her magenta taffeta dress, she'd have happily carried one all day.

'Where's Milly?' I asked, looking beyond my friend for her adorable little girl. My goddaughter would be four in a few months, almost the same age her mother had been when our friendship had begun. I simply couldn't imagine having anyone but Milly as my flower girl.

'At the moment she's busy tormenting your cat,' she said, turning to my dad with an apologetic 'Sorry'. 'Then she'll probably move on to destroying the fake posy I gave her. She's not getting her hands on the real one until the moment the church doors open.'

I flashed my friend a grin. 'You really do think of everything, don't you?'

'I just want today to be perfect for you, that's all,' she said, sounding choked and for a moment very un-Hannah-like.

A squeal that could have come from either her offspring or the cat travelled up the stairs, and Hannah spun on an elegant satin shoe and turned to go.

'I'll see you both at the church doors,' she said, blowing a kiss our way and disappearing from the bedroom in a cloud of perfume.

A few minutes later, the front door closed with a reverberating shudder and the house heaved a quiet sigh of relief as it finally fell into silence. The hairdressers, the beautician and the florists were all long gone; so too were family and friends, who would be comfortably settled in the flower-bedecked pews of the church by now.

Everything and everyone were exactly where they were supposed to be. So why did I have this niggling feeling of unease? It had been there since my phone's alarm had woken me early that morning. Still half asleep, I'd lain blinking up at the ceiling, trying to work out where I was. Unthinkingly, I'd reached out for Finn, but the unoccupied half of my old double bed was cold and empty. Was this how Dad felt every single morning? It was a heartbreaking thought to begin what is traditionally billed as the 'happiest day of your life'.

I swung out of bed and finally found my smile as I looked at the ivory lace dress I'd be wearing later that day when I married the man I loved.

Unable to resist the temptation, I reached for my phone, pulling it towards me by its charger wire, as though reeling in a fish. Was it too early to send Finn a 'good morning' message? Was that considered as unlucky as seeing him, or was modern technology beyond the reach of old wives' superstitions? I decided a quick WhatsApp was worth the risk.

Good morning, Mr D. Happy wedding day! Can't wait to see you later. xxx

I spent five whole minutes with the phone cradled in the palm of my hand, waiting for him to reply, before eventually setting it aside with a small feeling of disappointment. Finn was probably already in the shower or still out on his morning run. *Or hung-over*, suggested a troublesome voice in my head. I tuned it out because I really didn't want to revisit that particular dispute.

'You do realise *no one* has a stag do on the night before their actual wedding any more? They have it *weeks* before the big day, so they have time to recover.'

'There wasn't time to fit it in,' Finn had replied, winding his arms around my waist and drawing me against him. 'I've been working flat out to make my deadline before the honeymoon.' He'd bent down and kissed me then in the way that always made my knees forget how to hold me up. 'You may not know this, but I'm about to get married,' he'd whispered into the curve of my neck.

'So I heard. She's a lucky girl.'

Finn shook his head, his eyes fixed on my face. 'No. *I'm* the lucky one.'

Dad was waiting for me at the bottom of the stairs I'd slid down, skipped down, even fallen down on occasion over the past thirty-three years. There was a proud smile fixed firmly on his face that threatened to take me down far more effectively than the staircase ever could. Through the open front door behind him I caught a glimpse of a gleaming silver Bentley decorated with ribbon streamers, waiting at the kerb.

'Before we go…' began Dad, so nervous his Adam's apple was bobbing up and down as if it were looking to escape. He cleared his throat, which settled it slightly. 'I have something I want to give you,' he said, fumbling awkwardly in the pocket of his suit jacket. 'It's from your mum and me.'

I could already feel the prickling threat of tears as I reached for the small velvet jeweller's box. The beautician's carefully applied bridal make-up, complete with 'tsunami-proof' mascara, was suddenly in jeopardy.

I took the box and held it in my trembling hands for a long moment before springing open the lid. The chain of the necklace was silver and delicate, but it was the pendant hanging from it that came close to undoing me.

'It's Mum's stone, the one from her engagement ring,' I breathed, recognising it instantly from a kaleidoscope of memories.

'She would have wanted you to have it,' Dad said, his voice suddenly gravelly and scratchy. 'I thought if we had it made into a necklace, it would feel as though she was still with us today.'

I turned to the hallway mirror and lifted the hair from my neck to fasten the chain. The pear-shaped diamond dropped like a falling star and settled on my bare skin, just above the curve of my cleavage. I felt the weight of it close to my heart as I hugged my father tightly. 'I love it. I really do. But Mum was *always* going to be here today, even without this. Wild horses couldn't keep her away.'

Dad held my hand tightly in his as he led me down the crazy-paved pathway to the car, climbing in carefully behind me and settling himself on the small section of seat my dress wasn't occupying. It felt as though we were being swallowed by suds of tulle, but it was only a thirty-minute drive to the church.

'Nervous?' Dad asked. It was the same question he'd put to me when he'd dropped me off for my first day at school, and then again, thirteen years later, at university.

This time the answer was an easy 'No'.

'Just excited for this next chapter of my life to begin,' I said, leaning across the ocean of ivory fabric to kiss his cheek.

'That's my girl,' he said, his voice laden with love and pride.

Having a big white wedding had never been high on my wish list. But life has a funny way of changing your plans. You meet someone you love, you lose someone you love, and suddenly you're trying on meringue dresses and booking a church and a venue. This wedding was very much a homage to Mum, for this had been *her* dream for me.

'She would have loved you,' I remember telling Finn. We'd left the cities and towns behind and were now streaking through the villages and hamlets towards my childhood home for his first meeting with my dad.

Finn had taken one hand from the steering wheel and warmly squeezed mine. 'If she was anything like you, I'd have loved her too. But it's your dad I'm more worried about. I have a mental image of him patrolling the hallway tonight in case I stray out of the guest bedroom.'

I'd laughed, although in reality he might not have been too far off the mark. 'Well, you know what dads are like.'

'Not so much,' said Finn.

If I'd had just one superpower, it would have been to rewind time and take back my unthinking comment.

'I'm so sorry, Finn. I—'

'It's okay,' he said, cutting me off and changing the subject, the way he always did whenever his parents were mentioned. 'So, do you think *one* bottle of Scotch will be enough to charm him or should I have gone for a case?'

'Dad's going to love you,' I'd said. 'Everyone does when they first meet you.'

Finn's eyes were on the road, but there was no mistaking the wry twist of his mouth.

'*You* didn't.'

2

THE FIRST MEETING

Seven years earlier

'Hair up or down?' I asked, walking into our flat's tiny kitchen, where Hannah was busy scrolling through something on her phone. She set it down and scrutinised not just my hair but my chosen outfit. The smart black trousers and tailored white shirt had looked good in my bedroom mirror two minutes earlier, but they weren't getting the reaction I'd hoped for.

'It's a waitress job you're going for, right?'

I pulled a face at her snarky comment and released my grip on the makeshift bun at the top of my head. My hair tumbled down over my shoulders, softening the whole look.

'Better,' declared my friend.

'I just want to look professional… and intelligent.'

'There's more to being smart than having a sensible hairstyle,' Hannah said with a grin, running a hand through the pink-tipped ends of her spiky haircut. With a Mensa-level IQ, Hannah had no trouble being taken seriously, despite a hairstyle that rivalled the plumage of a bird of paradise.

'You make a good point,' I conceded, 'but there's too much riding on this interview to blow it because I don't look the part.'

'Isn't it supposed to be the quality of your writing that gets you the job, rather than your resemblance to a 1950s librarian?' she teased, reaching for a slice of toast and demolishing it in two enormous bites. For a very small person, Hannah had a huge appetite. I wasn't sure where the calories she consumed actually went, but very few appeared to linger on her petite frame. 'And I *love* your writing style,' she declared loyally.

I flashed her a grateful smile as I reached hopefully for the coffee pot. I managed to squeeze out a cup and sipped it slowly as I once again ran my eye down the articles bearing my byline that I'd uploaded to my iPad. 'It's hard to know which one will impress them the most: the kitten that had to be rescued from the tree or the furore at the WI jam-making contest.'

'The kitten one, obviously,' Hannah said, pressing a clenched fist to her heart. 'It has "Pulitzer" written all over it.'

I snorted, and for a moment it was touch and go as to whether I'd swallow my mouthful of coffee or spray it all over myself and the kitchen.

'It's going to be seriously dull around here when you move out,' I said, which sounded more woeful out loud than it had done in my head. I wasn't trying to make her feel sad or guilty, although I saw both emotions flicker briefly in her violet eyes. After years of renting a succession of grotty flats, Hannah and

I had taken the plunge and bought a place together, somehow forgetting to consider what might happen if one of us wanted to move out and the other didn't.

I could vividly remember the night she'd come home early from her date with William, who she'd been seeing for the last six months. She'd walked into the lounge with worried eyes and a look of torment on her face, and I'd automatically reached for a bottle of wine, two glasses and a box of tissues, fearing the worst. But I was wrong; William hadn't broken up with her – just the opposite, in fact.

'He's asked me to move in with him,' she said, sounding as though she was being coerced into something illegal.

'Bastard,' I deadpanned. I was so relieved he wasn't breaking her heart, it took a few moments for me to realise that it was actually *mine* that might end up getting hurt here. 'And you said...?'

She bit her lip as though trying to stop the smile, but it found a way out anyway; it was right there in her eyes.

'I said yes.'

I spilled the wine, and we both cried and hugged and quoted *Friends* by saying it was 'the end of an era'. But the cold, hard reality of the situation only hit me later. Not only was I going to lose my flatmate, I could end up losing the flat too.

'Maybe I could just carry on paying my half – I'm sure William would understand,' Hannah suggested gamely.

'Absolutely not. That would be totally unfair,' I insisted. 'Besides, there's this magazine feature writer job coming up that I've been thinking of going for. If I get it, I'd be able to cover the repayments for this place by myself.' *As long as I cut out all unnecessary expenses, like eating*, I silently added.

Getting this job was actually an enormous 'if', because I'd

be leapfrogging up a great many rungs on the career ladder, going from humble reporter on a local newspaper to feature writer for a well-known glossy magazine. But I had to give it a shot.

Although the morning rush hour should have been and gone by then, the roads were still surprisingly busy. The forty-five-minute contingency I'd built into my journey was swallowed up with delays, faulty traffic lights and a jackknifed lorry. And to cap it all, my car's air con didn't seem to appreciate that this was an extremely bad day to decide to finally die. 'It's a September scorcher,' the radio announcer crowed delightedly. I switched him off mid-sentence.

By the time I spotted the first sign for the business park, a thin film of sweat had beaded on my forehead and was busily dissolving my foundation. I swung into the car park, panicking when I noticed the time on the dashboard clock. My interview was in fifteen minutes.

Glow's offices were in a towering blue glass-clad building, which made it look like a gigantic glacier that had somehow taken a wrong turn and mistakenly ended up in an urban setting.

I should still be okay as long as I can find a parking space quickly, I told myself as I began the first of several unsuccessful circuits of the car park. And then suddenly I spotted a car just up ahead, pulling out. I braked to a stop and flicked on my indicator. The driver took ages to reverse out of the bay, and my court-shoed foot was already hovering above the accelerator when out of nowhere another car shot into the space. Not only had they stolen the spot I'd been patiently waiting for, but they'd also driven the wrong way around the car park to do so.

I didn't do road rage, or at least I never had before, but I didn't even stop to think. 'You've got to be kidding me,' I cried out as I leant the flat of my hand on my car's horn, splitting the quiet morning with its strident scream. I saw the driver stop and do a quick 360-degree scan of the car park. As I was the only other vehicle searching for a space, it didn't take a genius to work out who had made the noise. The driver's gaze locked on to mine through our respective windscreens and I threw my hands up in the unofficial Highway Code sign language for 'What the fuck?'

Through the red mist of my anger, I saw a flash of white teeth. Was this man actually *smiling* at me? I was pretty sure I saw his lips mouthing a word that might possibly have been 'Sorry'. If so, he was wasting his time as I was in no mood to accept his apology. And then, to add further insult, he proceeded to roll down his window.

'Sorry about that, but I'm really late for an appointment.' He flashed me another hundred-kilowatt smile, the sort I suspected usually allowed him to get away with all manner of transgressions. But not today, and certainly not with me.

I too wound down my window.

'That was my space,' I yelled, sticking my head out like a dog on a long drive.

His voice carried better than mine; he didn't have to resort to such contortions to make himself heard.

'Well, technically it's not your space until you're actually in it,' he argued equably, as though he wasn't just about to ruin my chances of getting the job I desperately needed. 'Like I said, I apologise, but I'm running late, and' – he glanced down at his watch and then back towards me – 'as pleasant as this is, yelling at each other across the width of the car park, I really *do* have to get going.'

My mouth couldn't decide whether to drop open at his gall or snap shut in fury. I was still deliberating as he climbed out of his car and headed towards the glass-panelled building. His path took him almost directly in front of me, and it required more restraint than it should have done not to rev my engine menacingly. I wasn't so enraged as to *actually* mow him down, but it would have been good to startle him just enough to wipe that smug look off his face.

He glanced my way one last time before disappearing into the maze of parked vehicles, and actually had the audacity to give me a quick wave. Never, ever had I taken such a complete and instant dislike to another human being in my entire life.

3

The church came into view, and despite my assurances that I wasn't nervous, I felt my heartbeat take a tiny skip and then skitter weirdly in my chest. St Anthony's was old and traditional, with a rustic lychgate that we'd already earmarked for photos following the ceremony. There were flowers wound through its timbers, which I had expected to see, and Finn's best man Doug pacing up and down in front of it, which I hadn't.

As we approached, he hurriedly stuffed his mobile phone back into his pocket and began gesticulating. I frowned and leant forward, trying to work out what he was panto-miming. It looked an awful lot like he was miming mixing a cake.

Our driver clearly couldn't decipher the charade either, for he pulled the vintage car to a stop beside the gate. Doug looked inexplicably frustrated and this time pantomimed winding down the car window. That one we understood.

The glass slid down with a whisper that sounded vaguely ominous.

'Can you go round the block again?' Doug asked, directing the request to the driver, before looking into the back of the vehicle with an expression of false cheer that even a blind man could have seen through.

'We just need a few more minutes to get ready,' he explained with a smile that never made it to his eyes.

Something eel-like twisted unpleasantly in my stomach. 'Why? What's wrong?'

'Nothing. Nothing at all.'

I didn't know Doug well enough to realise he was worried, but I'd been a journalist long enough to know when someone was lying.

'Where's Finn? He *is* here, isn't he?' My voice was rising, as though climbing through musical scales. It had gone from middle C to the top of the keyboard with disturbing ease.

'Yeah, he is… or he will be in a minute.'

'Well, which is it, son?' My dad's question cut through the best man's bluster like a hot knife through butter.

'Finn's just running a bit late,' Doug said lamely. 'Probably forgot the rings or something.'

'But I thought *you* had the rings,' I challenged, not liking the sudden tremor in my voice. 'Finn told me yesterday morning that he'd given them to you.'

A brick-red colour flushed Doug's cheeks. 'Ah yes. So I do.' He made a big show of patting the breast pocket of his silk waistcoat, as though all our problems were now happily sorted. 'Just one more circuit around the block and then I'm sure we'll be back on track,' he added.

The driver was looking at us over his shoulder, his face

devoid of the panic that I felt sure was painted all over mine. Perhaps this was common; maybe it happened all the time. Although the muscle twitching beside his eye told a different story.

'Let's take a leisurely drive around the block and let Doug get everything sorted out here,' suggested my dad, taking command.

It was neither the time nor the place to voice my concerns about Doug's questionable ability to organise a booze-up in a brewery. He was Finn's oldest friend, and if my fiancé believed he was the man for the job, then I was just going to have to trust his judgement.

'You're sure it's just that he's been delayed?' I couldn't resist asking one last time.

'Yeah. Absolutely positive,' Doug said, straightening up from the open car window.

I would have felt so much better if I hadn't heard his quietly voiced instruction to our driver as he stepped back on to the pavement. 'Drive slow, mate.'

I was looking back as we pulled away from the kerb, so I saw the precise moment when Doug's shoulders slumped and he ran one hand distractedly through his hair. Still swivelled in my seat, I saw a man I didn't recognise jog up to Doug, shaking his head as he approached. The news – whatever it was – made the best man reach for his mobile once again.

'Do you think maybe *I* should try to call Finn?' I asked, feeling suddenly vulnerable without my own phone, which was currently at the bottom of a bag Hannah was bringing to the reception. 'Perhaps I could give him a quick ring on yours,' I suggested, already knowing exactly how my dad was going to respond.

'Why don't we just take a breath or two and see what happens after we've given them ten minutes or so.' Dad was, and always had been, a 'wait and see' and 'we'll cross that bridge when we come to it' sort of person.

I sat back in my seat, my eyes searching the route for signs of Finn, broken down at the kerbside, beside a beribboned car belching out smoke, or kicking a tyre that had picked the very worst moment to get a puncture. But he wasn't there.

'I thought it was the *bride* who's supposed to turn up late for the ceremony, not the groom,' I said, with an attempted laugh that came out too sharp, too high and too close to shattering into tears.

Dad's hands settled over mine, forcing them to be still. 'Everything's going to be fine. There'll be some perfectly reasonable explanation for all this, you'll see,' he said.

The driver had certainly taken Doug's advice. Even in my kitten-heeled satin shoes and ball-gown wedding dress, I could have jogged the route faster than we drove it. It took precisely thirteen minutes and twenty seconds – according to the Bentley's elegant dashboard clock – before the church came into view once more.

This time there were more people by the lychgate. But none of them were Finn.

'Dad...?' I asked hesitantly as we pulled up beside the gate again.

'Maybe you'd better stay in the car, Gemma,' he suggested, but his advice was directed to an already empty seat. Ignoring everyone else, I hurried straight to Hannah, who reached for my hands as I approached. She gripped them tightly, anchoring me even before I knew that I needed steadying.

'Finn's not here yet,' she said, shooting straight from the hip, which was the only position she knew. 'The guys have been trying to reach him for the last forty minutes, but it looks like his mobile is switched off.'

I frowned, as though she was speaking in a foreign language that I'd never quite mastered. Her words made no sense.

'How can he *not* be here? We're getting married today.'

This was hardly breaking news to any of the bridal party, who were now assembled in a worried circle, each one looking anywhere rather than at me.

I shook my head and felt the lace of my veil graze my cheek. I pushed it back from my face, something Finn was supposed to do at the altar right before he kissed me.

'How was he this morning? Did he seem okay to you?' I asked Doug.

Finn's best man worriedly ran a finger around the winged collar of his formal shirt, like a condemned man trying to loosen a noose. 'Erm, that's kind of hard to say,' he admitted, looking decidedly awkward. 'You see, I ended up not spending the night at his place after all. I was... somewhere else.'

Five pairs of perplexed eyes swivelled his way, but not mine. I'd already heard enough of Doug's history of one-night stands to join up the dots.

Hannah got there first. 'You hooked up with someone from the bar?' she cried incredulously. 'What the hell is wrong with you? You're Finn's best man – you're supposed to have been looking after him.'

'Finn's a grown man who is more than capable of taking care of himself. He doesn't need babysitting or bossing around by anyone.' His eyes flicked briefly in my direction. I'd always suspected Doug didn't like me very much, and right now the feeling was entirely mutual.

Out of the corner of my eye I could see that a small crowd of curious passers-by had started to gather. They were avidly watching while our drama unfolded on the pavement in front of them, as though it was an episode from a soap opera.

'Did either of you see Finn this morning?' I questioned the two men flanking Doug.

Their rose buttonholes identified them as Trevor and Pete, Finn's friends from university, who he'd chosen as ushers. In my panic I couldn't remember which was which. Not that it mattered, for they shook their heads in perfect unison. 'We came straight here from the hotel,' Trevor or Pete said, looking uncomfortable.

I swivelled to face Doug, sounding more like a journalist than a bride.

'What time did you get to Finn's flat this morning?'

Doug squirmed like a worm on a hook. 'I didn't actually go to his flat. I messaged him late last night to say I'd meet him at the church instead, if that was okay. He never got back to me, so I assumed it was. To be honest, I'm as surprised as you are that he isn't here yet.'

Of all the emotions coursing through me at that moment, *surprise* didn't even register.

'So where exactly is he then?' asked my dad.

'Something's wrong. Something must have happened to him.' My words sounded as though they were falling into a bottomless well.

We all jumped as the church doors swung open and a concerned-looking vicar hurried towards us, his cassock lifting behind him in the breeze like the wings of an agitated raven.

'Is everything all right here?' he asked. His probing gaze travelled straight past me to my father.

'We appear to be *temporarily* missing the groom,' Dad replied. I loved him for the way he made it sound as if this was just a minor glitch that we'd all be laughing at over champagne and canapés very soon.

'Something's wrong,' I repeated like a needle stuck in a groove.

'Oh dear, that is rather unfortunate,' declared the cleric in what might possibly have qualified as the understatement of the century.

'We're obviously trying to reach him,' Hannah cut in, pointedly nodding at the two ushers, who obediently extracted their phones. 'But so far no luck.'

I glanced away from the implicit sympathy in the vicar's eyes, only to find myself the focus of the crowd of onlookers, which had grown noticeably larger. It was from one of them that I heard the word for the first time. The stranger's question carried across the pavement like a poisoned dart, aimed straight at my heart.

'Poor girl. Do you think she's been jilted?'

I turned back to the bridal party, knowing they must surely have heard what had been said every bit as clearly as I had.

'Perhaps you'd like to wait inside, my dear – somewhere a little more private?' suggested the vicar kindly.

I shook my head, my veil catching on the breeze and billowing about me like a white cape. 'No, thank you. I'll wait out here until Finn arrives.'

I was still forty-five minutes away from accepting the devastating truth that Finn wasn't coming.

The books and internet pages Dad had studied on being father of the bride hadn't prepared him for this one. He could give an amusing speech and raise a toast with the best of them, but the issue of an absentee groom clearly hadn't been covered.

When Doug offered to make an announcement to our guests, advising them there'd been a slight 'delay', Dad glanced my way for approval. I nodded sadly and only hoped the best man would deliver the news without the air quotes he'd felt the need to use when running it by us.

'Why don't we get into the car, and you can try to reach Finn,' urged Hannah, pressing my mobile phone into my hand. I'm sure her suggestion was more to get me out of sight of the accumulated crowd, and I almost felt sorry for the onlookers when she glared menacingly at them over her shoulder as she climbed into the Bentley behind me. A few gawpers rapidly dispersed, leaving only a small group of die-hard rubberneckers.

'I know what you're thinking – what *everyone* is probably thinking,' I said as the car door closed with a solid clunk. 'But they're all wrong. Finn wouldn't do this to me. He just wouldn't.'

Hannah was too good a friend to point out that all the evidence currently pointed to the contrary. 'It does seem... puzzling,' she conceded.

With one eye on my phone and the other on the street, watching out for Finn's distinctive red-and-white retro Gran Torino, I called his number. The sound of his voice made the breath catch in my throat and it took a second or two for me to realise it was just his voicemail recording. The first message I left after the beep was so garbled it made no sense. Numbers two and three weren't much better, but by the time he heard the fourth one he'd probably be able to decipher what I was trying to say. I sat with the phone nestled on my lap like an unexploded grenade as I waited for him to call me back.

The silence stretched like an elastic band, the kind that was going to hurt like hell when it eventually snapped. Hannah risked breaking it first.

'Perhaps he's in a bad signal area,' she suggested.

'Perhaps he's been in an accident,' I countered.

We considered each other's suggestions. It was hard to decide which was worse.

'William should be back any minute now,' she said, checking the time on her own phone.

I smiled weakly. Hannah's husband had been despatched to travel the various alternative routes between Finn's flat and the church. It wasn't that I didn't trust that Finn's friends had checked properly, I told myself, before realising that was, in fact, *exactly* why I'd asked him to go.

Hannah glanced worriedly in the direction of the church. 'I hope your Aunt Helen doesn't regret agreeing to keep an eye on Milly while he's gone. She *can* be a bit of a handful.'

It was hard to imagine anything capable of making me smile at that moment, but the thought of my adorable goddaughter almost managed it.

'Why don't you go and check she's okay. I'll wait here until Finn turns up.'

Hannah's smile froze slightly, but she nodded and with a

quick squeeze of my hand slipped from the car. It took only a few seconds for my father to take her place.

'How are you holding up, kiddo?'

The old nickname almost toppled my self-control. 'I'll be okay when I know where he is.'

Dad nodded, but there was a set to his jaw that had never been there before where Finn was concerned. *Not you too, Dad? Surely you've seen the way we are together? You must know he'd never walk out on me like this?*

Dad looked down at his hands, finding it easier to talk to a hangnail on his thumb than face me. 'The vicar came out a while ago to say that he's really sorry but there's another wedding booked for later this afternoon and unless things get underway very soon, there won't be enough time to prepare for the next ceremony.'

I raised forlorn eyes towards the church. From behind a veil of tears that I refused to let fall, I saw Finn and me where we should have been right then: standing beside the lychgate, smiling hugely as the photographer snapped away; and then over there beneath the boughs of the sprawling old oak, holding hands and staring into each other's eyes. I knew what we were supposed to be doing every single minute of this special day. It was all mapped out, but now the compass was spinning wildly and I had no idea where we were or where to go next.

'Should we tell people to go home?' Dad suggested tentatively. He was the only one who could have asked that question without me turning angrily on them.

'No,' I said, shaking my head so hard I felt my headpiece dislodge and slide down my hair. I took a deep, steadying breath. 'No. Tell everyone to go on to the reception.'

'Really, Pumpkin?' Oh boy, he truly was bringing out all the old nicknames today. I hadn't heard that particular one in over twenty years.

'It's all paid for,' I said, trying to sound practical, which is hard to pull off when your voice keeps trying to break. 'As soon as we locate Finn, we'll join you there.'

Dad's nod was slow and cautious, but at least he wasn't saying I was crazy.

I glanced up hopefully as a car pulled into the small parking area. But it wasn't the bright red American coupe I was desperate to see but a gleaming white Rolls-Royce from which two strangers emerged, dressed in top hats and tails. They bantered and jostled each other playfully as they looked towards St Anthony's. The taller of the two men said something to his companion, who dutifully pulled a ring box from his pocket. The groom had arrived – but he wasn't mine. Soon guests I wouldn't recognise would begin to spill out of cars, eagerly looking forward to the wedding ceremony.

It was time for us to leave.

4

Dad headed into the church to deliver a vastly different speech from the one he'd spent the last month writing; the one he'd rehearsed so many times even the cat could recite it by now.

I turned back to William, who'd returned just a few minutes earlier. He was standing beside Hannah and there was something about their physical closeness that threatened to tear down the protective wall I was trying to construct around my heart. They weren't a particularly touchy-feely couple and rarely went in for PDAs, but I saw Hannah's hand reach for her husband's behind the folds of her magenta skirt, and how his was already there waiting for her. I was struck by a feeling of longing for Finn so strong it was almost physical.

'You definitely rang his doorbell?' I questioned again.

William was a Cambridge science graduate, with more letters *after* his name than I had in both of mine. But he took no offence when I queried his competence. 'I kept it pressed down long enough for some old biddy to throw open her window and give me a load of abuse about disturbing the peace.'

I nodded grimly, knowing exactly who he meant. Mrs Barnard, Finn's neighbour, was a cantankerous old woman who loved nothing more than a good argument.

'And you checked his parking bay?'

'Empty,' confirmed William. 'And it's not the kind of car you can easily miss.' His expression was apologetic. 'I'm afraid all that does is tell us where Finn *isn't*, rather than where he is.'

'Were the curtains of his flat open or closed?' I asked, my ingrained reporter instincts kicking in.

'Erm... I'm not sure. Open, I think.'

I closed my eyes and conjured up an image of the exterior of Finn's rented flat. It was in a small, unremarkable block of purpose-built apartments. Finn was on the second floor, his bedroom at the rear of the property, looking out over a modest square of overgrown scrubland that the landlord grandly called a communal garden. Unless William had scaled the six-foot brick wall behind the bin store, he wouldn't be able to answer the question of whether Finn's bedroom curtains were open or drawn shut.

I noted the mixture of sympathy and frustration on the faces of the ushers and Doug, who'd now rejoined us on the pavement. I knew I should probably be focusing on the larger question of exactly why my fiancé hadn't shown up at the church, but right then I could only focus on the minutiae, convinced the answer was to be found in the small details.

'Can I borrow your car?' I asked William, holding out my hand for the keys.

'Erm… sure,' he replied hesitantly, withdrawing them from his pocket.

My fingers grazed the keys before the bunch was roughly whipped away by Hannah.

'Absolutely not,' she declared, her fingers fastening around the ignition key as though I was about to wrestle her to the ground for it. *And wouldn't that give the onlookers an even bigger treat*, I thought, swallowing down a laugh that would have sounded dangerously hysterical if I'd allowed it to escape.

'You're in no fit state to drive anywhere. And besides, you'd never even *see* your feet beneath that mountain of tulle.'

I glanced down at my voluminous skirt and realised she made a good point.

I bit my lip in frustration and looked around for the liveried driver of the Bentley. Was he allowed to drive me anywhere I wanted to go, I wondered? It was a question I never got to ask.

'*I'll* drive,' Hannah announced, reaching up and pressing a kiss on to her husband's cheek. 'Can you go and relieve Gemma's Aunt Helen from childminding duties?' she asked, her brow furrowing for just a moment as she added, 'And tell Milly I'll be back as soon as I can.'

'You didn't have to do this,' I said when I'd finally succeeded in clipping the passenger seat belt around both me and the yards of fabric bunched beneath my legs. Hannah had been absolutely right; I would never have been able to work the pedals with that much material crowding the footwell.

'I most certainly did,' Hannah replied, waiting until she

had safely pulled out into the busy stream of afternoon traffic before turning to face me. 'It's actually a clause in the chief bridesmaid contract,' she said, hoping to elicit a smile. None materialised. 'Or maybe it's in the best friend one,' she corrected softly. That one at least brought a glimmer of a smile.

'Remind me again of exactly what we're doing?'

We'd driven in silence for five miles before Hannah asked the question that was probably on the lips of our guests as they sipped on their glasses of welcome champagne at the hotel where my reception was right then taking place – with neither the bride nor the groom in attendance.

'We're looking for Finn.'

We were stopped at a set of traffic lights, so she was able to swivel in her seat and give me her full attention. 'You think he's hiding out inside his flat?'

I didn't like the look in her eyes and glanced at the lights, willing them to turn amber, but they remained obstinately on red.

'No. Of course not. But what if he fell in the shower and is lying unconscious in a pool of blood in the bathroom? Or maybe he's sick; too weak to even make it to his phone to call for help.'

Hannah drew in a deep breath, which she trapped behind tightly pursed lips before replying. 'And Finn's car? Why would that be missing too?'

We used to do this all the time, play devil's advocate when one of us came up with a controversial theory. I'd always rather enjoyed the game, but today I had no appetite for her insightful questions. Probably because they were the ones I should have been asking myself anyway.

'There's a car park around the corner from the flat. Finn sometimes parks his car there when he's expecting visitors.'

The lights had changed while we'd been talking, and an impatient blast of a car horn cut short the Q & A before Hannah could ask why Finn might have done something so bizarre. Forgetting she was a responsible wife and mother, Hannah gave the other driver a highly unorthodox hand signal. His dumbfounded expression when he drew alongside us and saw that the occupants of the car were a bride and her bridesmaid almost made me laugh out loud.

But as we neared Finn's flat, I felt none of the excitement that usually kicked in at this point of the journey, when I knew I was only minutes away from seeing him. In place of the bubbling anticipation, a cold, sick dread slithered into my stomach and writhed there like a snake.

In a subdued voice, I directed Hannah to the small car park I'd mentioned. We drove around it in a slow circle, but it was easy to see that Finn's car wasn't among the half-dozen or so that were parked there. Hannah said nothing. She didn't have to, and yet I responded as though she had.

'This doesn't prove anything. His car could have been stolen overnight. It happens,' I declared, with more than a hint of challenge in my voice.

'It does,' agreed Hannah as she pointed her own vehicle towards the exit. 'But you have to wonder how unlucky Finn would have to be to get his car nicked on the same day that he knocks himself out cold in his own bathroom.'

She was trying to prepare me, to lead me to a place where I'd allow in other – more plausible – explanations. But it was too soon.

I took one last lingering look around the car park and felt it pull on my memories, tugging them inexorably back to the day Finn and I first met.

5

THE INTERVIEW

Seven years earlier

It had taken me a further ten minutes to find another parking space. By the time I ran across the car park towards *Glow*'s reception, my composure had melted like a polar ice cap. My hair was sticking unpleasantly to the back of my neck, and I was seriously worried my antiperspirant wasn't up to the challenge I'd unexpectedly set it. The air-conditioned reception was balm to my overheated skin, but there was no time to linger and enjoy it.

'Hello,' I gasped, scarcely waiting for the receptionist to look up from her computer screen. 'My name is Gemma Fletcher and I have an interview at *Glow* magazine.' I paused for a moment, still trying to catch my breath. 'I'm afraid I'm a bit late.'

The receptionist flashed me a professional smile and I felt my self-confidence teetering like a skittle. She was the kind of immaculately groomed woman you'd expect only ever to see on the cover of a magazine, not in real life. Even on my best day, I would have felt unkempt and dishevelled beside her, and this was definitely *not* my best day.

'*Glow* are on the eighth floor. Someone will meet you by the lifts,' she trilled, sliding a visitor's pass across the marble counter towards me.

The walls of the lift were mirrored; ideal for checking your appearance on your ascent. But I would have needed a building taller than the Empire State to repair the damage the humidity had done to my hair or subdue the flush on my cheeks, which were far too pink to be called becoming. Four flustered versions of me stared back wherever I looked. Who needed this many mirrors? It was a far cry from the offices of *The Chronicle*, where the only looking glass to be found was an ancient water-spotted rectangle in the Ladies' loo. Working at *Glow* would either make you incredibly vain or give you an enormous insecurity complex. It was worrying to recognise that even before my interview I was trying to find an upside to *not* getting the job.

A young, trendily dressed assistant was waiting for me by the lifts, and everything about her was fast: the way she spoke, the speed she walked, and the tap of her fingers on the electronic keypad to gain entry to the magazine offices. I was virtually having to trot to keep up with her as she led me down a glass-walled corridor. 'I'm afraid we're running desperately behind schedule,' she apologised in a posh-school, Home Counties voice. 'I hope you don't mind waiting.'

'Not at all,' I replied, just about managing to hide my enormous sigh of relief. 'I was really worried I'd be late myself. The traffic was terrible and then there was this total jerk in the car park...' My voice trailed away. Even I could hear I was babbling. Nerves always did that to me, and I was determined not to be scuppered by my own tongue. 'I'm happy to wait for as long as you need,' I added, hoping that would score me extra brownie points.

Her smile was as fast as a camera flash. 'We've set all the candidates up in the conference room,' she explained, coming to a halt in front of a pair of wooden doors. 'Someone will be along to collect you for your various interviews throughout the morning.' It all sounded very much like the penultimate episode of *The Apprentice*, although hopefully without the bit where they tore your CV to shreds and someone pointed at you and said 'You're fired'.

'There's tea and coffee in here, so please help yourself. And the toilets are just down the corridor.'

I smiled gratefully, already knowing which of those facilities I intended to use first.

The whole building was chilled to the point of being almost cold, but inside the toilets the temperature dipped several degrees lower. It was also incredibly dark. It took several moments for my eyes to adjust as I slipped into a stall at the end of the row. A minute or so later I heard the muted sound of another cubicle door closing.

Even the poor lighting by the row of basins couldn't disguise the ruinous state of my appearance. I rummaged in my bag for a comb, but despite my best efforts there was little to be done to reverse the effects of the humidity. I scowled back at my reflection as the unruly curls refused to be controlled. What I really needed was a shower, and not just for my hair. My worst fears about my antiperspirant had been realised and although there were no telltale damp patches on my white shirt, I really needed to freshen up. I bit my lip in indecision. There's an old saying that women don't sweat, they simply glow – and I was glowing big time. It might be the name of the magazine, but it definitely wasn't the look I'd been going for.

With a quick glance at my watch, I made up my mind. I whipped off my shirt and rapidly fashioned a makeshift sponge from a bundle of paper towels. One armpit was done, and I was just about to attend to the other when my day took an enormous turn for the worse. At the sound of a bolt sliding open, my head shot up while my stomach plummeted to new depths as a cubicle door opened and the most obnoxious man I'd ever met emerged from the stall.

To be fair, I'm not sure which of us was the more startled, but as I was the one who was semi-naked, I believe that title was mine to claim.

'What the hell are you doing in here?' I fired out.

His eyes had dropped to my lacy bra for less than a millisecond, a courtesy I didn't think to acknowledge until much later. It was chivalrous in a way I doubted any of my exes would have been. Even so, it was enough to make me abandon my ablutions and cross my arms over my highly exposed chest. 'Well, what are you doing?' I repeated.

He cast a glance behind him, where the cistern was still gurgling as it refilled. 'That's rather a personal question, don't you think?'

I blinked back at him, still too stunned to think straight. 'In the Ladies' toilets,' I said pointedly, my voice so loud it was practically ricocheting off the tiled walls. 'You are in the wrong room.'

'Actually, the loos here are unisex,' he said, shooting down my accusation as he strode to the basin adjacent to mine and calmly began to wash his hands.

'But… but why didn't they say so? They should say so,' I blustered.

'They do. There's a sign on the door.'

This time, poor light or not, I could definitely see the amusement twinkling in his eyes. He could very well be right, I silently acknowledged. I'd been in such a hurry, I hadn't stopped to examine the signage properly.

'What I find more interesting,' he continued, 'is why you're standing there, semi-naked, once again accusing me of being somewhere I have no right to be. Is that a thing with you?'

I had no words. None. I was sure that hours later, in the quiet solitude of my bed, I'd come up with at least a dozen pithy responses, but for now they were as elusive as my composure.

'Are you done?' I asked, nodding towards his hands, which he was washing with the diligence of a man about to perform surgery. 'Because if you are, I'd really like you to leave so I can get dressed. I have an interview to attend.'

An expression flitted across his face that suddenly worried me more than anything else had done so far on this very strange morning. 'Are you here for the feature writer position?' he asked.

I felt the colour drain from my cheeks as all the dots suddenly began to join up. He had to be one of the people on the interview panel, my prospective employer, and I'd done nothing so far that day except yell at him. I might as well hand back my visitor's pass and go home right away.

Five minutes later, and still rattled by the encounter, I slipped into the conference room. There were two female candidates sitting on opposite sides of a huge oval table. They both looked up from their phones at my arrival and we exchanged polite hellos, but there was a brittleness to their greetings that surprised me. Was it naive of me to have expected anything different? We were all going for the same job, after all.

I was good at reading people – their body language, and the expressions that they didn't realise gave away their secrets. It was a skill that came in handy as a reporter, even if you did only work on a humble local newspaper. Those instincts now told me that my fellow candidates had almost instantly decided I posed no threat for this job. And they were probably right. Their clothes, their make-up, and their quiet air of confidence made them look the part in a way I simply didn't, and more importantly they hadn't also verbally abused a member of the interview panel on their way in.

In an atmosphere that reminded me of a public library, where even a discreet cough sounded like a klaxon, we sat and waited to be called for the first of our interviews. Both women were summoned before I was, and as soon as I had the room to myself, I leapt to my feet and began pacing up and down, hoping to expel my nervous energy.

I cleared my throat repeatedly, trying to dislodge the pond full of frogs that had taken up residence there. 'Good morning,' I practised out loud to the empty room. 'It's so lovely to meet you,' I added, thrusting out my hand to shake that of an invisible interviewer. I was still pumping the hand of an imaginary person when the door behind me clicked open. A searingly hot blush was already on my cheeks as I turned to face whoever had come to collect me. Could there be any more ways to screw up my chances of getting this job, I wondered?

'It's good to meet you too,' a deep voice replied. 'Although technically you could argue that we've already met several times today.'

If I hadn't already blown my chances of getting this job, surely being caught out in a pretend conversation must have hammered home the last nail in my career coffin. *Unbalanced.* I could practically see the word being vigorously rubber-stamped in red ink all over my application.

My gaze, which was fixed somewhere in the region of his feet, very slowly travelled upwards. He was much taller than I'd realised from our encounters in the car park and the toilets. It took quite a while for my eyes to journey up the length of his well-cut grey suit, before pausing somewhere in the region of his expertly knotted tie. With an effort, I forced my chin to lift a little higher until my eyes were on his face. There was a smile on it that some might have called a smirk. Now that I wasn't preoccupied with yelling at him, I saw he was older than I'd first thought, maybe thirty or so, making him about four years my senior.

I blanked his smile with a look that said the loveable rogue act was wasted on me. Although none of his features were individually remarkable, combined they created something that had probably caused heads to turn his entire life. Unfortunately, I suspected he was perfectly aware of those charms, which made him far less appealing, at least as far as I was concerned.

Even so, it was impossible to ignore the way my body was reacting to him right then. My spine felt as though it was literally vibrating with tension, while my stomach had started to perform some impressive gymnastics with my breakfast. It was as though I was physically allergic to this total stranger, which I was fairly certain was impossible. Even so, I'd never had such a visceral reaction to anyone before.

'You must be here for me,' I said, forcing a totally fake smile on to my lips as I turned to collect my belongings for my interview.

'Must I?' the man replied, apparently determined not to make any of this easy for me. In natural light his eyes were probably very dark brown, but beneath the overhead fluorescents they appeared almost black. Like a shark's, I thought uncharitably.

'Before we get started, I believe I owe you an apology for the way I behaved earlier. I want to assure you that I'm not usually like that.'

'That's good to know.' His onyx eyes were curiously mesmerising. Being interviewed by him was going to be more than a little intimidating and I definitely wouldn't be trying the well-known advice to relax and 'imagine your interviewer in their underwear'.

'So how would you say you are... usually?' he enquired, tilting his head to one side, causing the overhead lights to pick out strands of copper in his rich brown hair.

I glanced around uneasily. Had our interview started already? Would he be relaying my answer to his colleagues, after no doubt first filling them in on how erratically I'd behaved earlier, and how unsuitable I was for the job?

'Well, I like to think I'm hard-working and diligent. I'm definitely not a clock-watcher, and I'm willing to work long hours to get the job done. I'm a team player and I get on really well with people,' I added, aware that everything I'd done so far that day totally refuted that last statement. 'I'd be an excellent feature writer,' I concluded, which had sounded far more confident in the privacy of my bedroom than it did now.

He was quiet for a long moment and there was a decidedly perplexed expression on his face. It was still there when the conference room door swung open and the speed-walking assistant stood within its frame.

'Miss Fletcher... Gemma. The panel are ready for you now.'

Like a spectator at a tennis match, my eyes flitted from her to the man standing before me.

'I'm afraid you have a half-hour wait until your next one, Finn,' apologised the young woman, whose entire demeanour had softened as she looked at the man standing between us. 'Let me just check there's still enough coffee in the urn.'

I waited until she was safely out of earshot before leaning in close enough to identify the aftershave he'd applied that morning. 'You don't work here,' I hissed.

'Not yet,' he replied with a grin.

Ignoring a very disturbing temptation to slap him, I leant even closer. 'Then why did you say you did?'

'I believe, if you think back, you'll realise that I didn't. You just jumped to the wrong conclusion. You do seem to be a pretty impulsive kind of person.'

It was a hugely inaccurate description of me, but I was still at the open-mouthed, goldfish stage where a perfect put-down was beyond me.

'I'm here for the same reason as you are, for the feature writer position,' he added unnecessarily, something I'd already worked out by then.

'Finn Douglas,' he said, holding out his hand. I made no move to take it.

'Are you ready, Gemma?' asked the assistant, apparently unaware of the bristling tension between two of the candidates for the job.

'Good luck. Break a leg,' my annoying rival called out cheerfully as we left the room.

'Aw, that was really nice of him, wasn't it?' declared the assistant, so smitten I could practically see a halo of tiny cartoon hearts circling her head.

'Lovely,' I muttered darkly.

'He couldn't have been *that* bad,' declared Hannah, determinedly chasing the last sweet-and-sour pork ball around the carton with a chopstick.

'No. He was worse. I have never met such a smug, conceited and obnoxious person in my entire life. Luckily, that was the last time we were alone together, but you should have seen the other candidates fawning all over him, like he was God's gift or something. And when I left after my interview, there he was, busily chatting up the gorgeous receptionist.' I shuddered as though physically repulsed.

'Ah, so he was good-looking then?' Hannah asked, giving up on her quest and harpooning the elusive morsel before popping it into her mouth.

'Why would you even ask that?' I said in despair, pushing aside the remains of the consolatory Chinese takeaway Hannah had insisted I deserved after my despondent return from the interview.

'Because,' Hannah said, leaning back against the settee and

twirling an imaginary Poirot-style moustache, 'you sound exactly like someone who has had their pigtails pulled by the cheeky, popular boy in the school playground.'

I rose from my cross-legged position on the opposite side of our coffee table with a grace that had totally deserted me earlier in the day. 'I can see what you're doing,' I said, bending to gather up the accumulation of largely empty aluminium trays. 'You're trying to turn this into something they make Netflix movies about. This was no meet cute. It was more of a meet want-to-punch-on-the-nose.'

Hannah chortled softly. 'This guy really got under your skin, didn't he? Shame you're unlikely ever to see him again, isn't it?'

It must have been a bad prawn or something that made my stomach flip unexpectedly. 'Why do you say that?'

'Well, they were only looking for *one* feature writer, weren't they? So it doesn't matter who they pick, there's no reason you'll ever cross paths with that Finn guy again, is there?'

6

Hannah parked her car in Finn's allocated bay because, as William had correctly informed us, it was empty. As soon as she'd engaged the handbrake I was out of the vehicle, heading not towards the two low steps that led to the entrance, but following a paved footpath that skirted the edge of the building. Adjacent to an area where the residents' dustbins were stored was a small section of crazy paving that bordered what might once have been a flowerbed – although I'd only ever seen it chock full of weeds and nettles.

'What on earth are you doing?' asked Hannah, her shadow falling over me when I dropped to a crouch beside the overgrown foliage. 'For goodness' sake, Gemma, get up, you're going to get your dress filthy.'

'Because *that* would be the worst thing that could possibly happen to me today,' I countered, squinting in the late-afternoon sunlight as I looked up at her.

Her face twisted at my words and she dropped down on to her haunches beside me. 'What exactly are we looking for?' She'd lowered her voice to a whisper, as though we were involved in something clandestine. Which I suppose is *technically* how illegally entering someone else's property is usually described.

The first stone on the path wouldn't budge, nor the one beside it. There was now a thick layer of dirt beneath the pale pink nails I'd spent over an hour having filed, buffed and polished the day before. Was I misremembering that conversation from months earlier? I shook my head and heard Finn's voice as clearly as if he were crouched down beside me. 'After I'd locked myself out for a second time, I decided to stash a spare key under the crazy paving,' he'd said, lifting up a loose stone and showing me his secret hiding place.

I swivelled on the heel of my wedding shoe as the memory sharpened, and reached for a stone further to my right. It lifted easily and beneath it, embedded in the damp soil like an archaeological treasure, was a Yale key to Finn's front door.

'He told me about this in case I ever needed it in an emergency,' I explained, prising up the key with my fingernail. 'I think this situation qualifies.'

'Don't you have your *own* key to his place?' Hannah asked, sounding suddenly much more like a reporter than I did.

I got to my feet, brushing the dirt from my hands. 'I do, but it's back at my place, and I didn't want to waste time going there to collect it.'

Getting into the building proved to be more of a challenge than finding Finn's hidden key. I buzzed the bells of both flats on the upper storey and then those on the ground floor. No one answered. It was a sunny Saturday afternoon, so it wasn't really surprising that everyone was out. I stared at the only bell I had yet to try.

Its owner answered with her customary lack of charm. 'Who is it?' she barked.

I leant closer to the panel to speak, ignoring a series of toots from a passing car. In the five minutes we'd been standing at the doorway, we'd attracted a fair bit of attention from motorists.

'Mrs Barnard,' I began, 'it's Gemma Fletcher. Finn's fiancée,' I added, even though I was fairly sure she'd recognise my name.

'*Whose* fiancée?' came back the disembodied voice.

Hannah's eyebrows rose in an expression of almost comedic incredulity.

I took a deep breath before replying. 'The trick is not to lose your rag with her,' Finn had once observed. It was almost as if he'd been preparing me for this moment.

'Finn Douglas. Your neighbour,' I said politely. 'We've met each other several times in the hallway, Mrs Barnard,' I reminded her, although I suspected she knew that as well as I did. 'Could you let me into the building, please.' It was hard to remain calm, knowing there was a very real risk that Finn might at this minute be lying sick or injured just two floors above me. 'I really do need to get into Finn's flat as a matter of urgency, Mrs Barnard. Please can you let me in.'

I counted the seconds. I got to eight before the door in front of us yielded with a satisfying buzz and swung open.

'Thank you,' I said into the intercom, embarrassed to hear the unexpected crack in my voice.

The foyer had a strong scent of lemons, which had always puzzled me, but today I scarcely noticed it as I gathered up fistfuls of voluminous wedding dress and headed for the stairs. I tripped twice on the treads as I raced up two linoleum-covered flights to the second floor.

Mrs Barnard's front door was directly opposite Finn's, and I had absolutely no doubt that she was watching us avidly through the fisheye peephole as we slid the mud-encrusted key into the lock and let ourselves into Finn's home.

'Finn,' I cried out, even before the front door had fully opened. It was shocking to realise I was actually hoping to hear a weak voice calling out for help, but there was no reply. There was a weird stillness to the flat that was obvious even in the hallway. The first door I tried was that of the bathroom, and the mental image I'd conjured up of an injured Finn was so strong that for a moment it superimposed itself over reality. In those initial seconds I believed I could actually see him lying prone on the floor, blood seeping from a head wound on to the smooth skin of his forehead. But a single blink reset the picture and revealed that the bathroom was, in fact, empty.

I spun around, almost knocking Hannah off her feet. We shared a look that I knew would haunt me for a long time. Finn's bedroom was next.

The first thing that struck me was that he'd stripped the covers from the bed. The familiar grey duvet set, which always smelt intoxicatingly of him, was nowhere to be seen. I glanced around the room, absently noting its preternatural tidiness. Finn was always a little messy, so this orderliness was peculiar. There were usually a few garments left draped over the armchair in the corner of the room or a lone sock on the floor that hadn't quite made it to the laundry basket. But today everything was tidy enough for an estate-agent viewing.

The only room left to search was the open-plan lounge and kitchen. But it was as empty as the rest of the flat. Wherever my fiancé was, it definitely wasn't here. I scoped the kitchen for signs that he'd been there that morning. But there were no telltale toast crumbs scattered on the worktop, no dirty plates or mugs beside the sink.

'What are you looking for?' asked Hannah, coming to stand beside me as I opened the door of Finn's fridge.

I shrugged helplessly. 'Answers. Clues,' I replied, staring at the single carton of milk sitting in isolation on the middle shelf. Its bulging sides declared it unfit for consumption. I reached for the container and dropped it into the kitchen bin, surprised to find that for once it was completely empty.

'Finn doesn't really cook, so there's never much in the fridge,' I explained, slamming the door, still unable to shake a feeling of wrongness that hovered just out of reach at the edge of my understanding.

'What now?' asked Hannah when we were back in her car once again. 'Do you want to go to the hotel?'

I wasn't sure of much at that point, but the thought of walking into my wedding reception without Finn at my side was too sad to contemplate.

'Something has happened to him,' I said, returning to the phrase that was fast becoming my new mantra. 'Do you think I ought to contact the police?'

Hannah's response was an immediate 'No'. She glanced at the clock on the dashboard. 'Finn's been AWOL for a little over three hours, hon. I think that's just called "late" rather than "missing".'

My eyes began to prickle uncomfortably, but Hannah wasn't trying to be cruel, just logical.

'Then I need to contact all the local hospitals myself, to see if he's been admitted to any of them.'

I could tell Hannah thought it highly unlikely that Finn was in hospital without anyone knowing, but she clamped her lips to prevent her objections from escaping. 'Well, there are quite a few of them around here, so calling probably makes more sense than just turning up at A & E. Why don't we go back to mine and phone them from there?' she suggested.

I swivelled in the passenger seat, or at least as far as my dress would allow. 'Do you mind if we go back to my place instead of yours?'

Hannah's eyes held mine for a long moment.

'So he'll know where to find you?' she said gently.

I nodded.

'And if he doesn't? If you don't hear from him?'

'I will,' I said with a conviction I knew no one was ever going to understand, except possibly Finn himself. The seconds ticked by, and it felt like every year of our friendship was being put to the test.

'Okay then,' she said. 'Let's go and make some phone calls.'

Strangely, I'd been unaware of the uncomfortable tightness in my chest until breathing in the familiar smells of my home released it. Even so, my senses remained on high alert as I opened doors and glanced expectantly into rooms. Finn had his own key to my place, and even though I'd tried not to get my hopes up, part of me had clung to the belief that I'd find him here, waiting for me. I even sniffed the air, like a bloodhound who'd lost the scent, but all I could detect were the aromas of an empty flat. In a moment of pure panic, I suddenly couldn't remember the smell of Finn's aftershave, as though even this was slowly fading from my memory.

'You should probably get changed first,' Hannah suggested, closing the front door behind her. I shook my head. There would be something achingly final about taking off my wedding dress. It was a step I wasn't ready to take yet.

'Later,' I said, already heading towards my desk and laptop. 'I need to find him first.'

Tulle and lace rustled in protest as I pushed the fabric of my skirt into the desk's kneehole and fired up my laptop. While waiting, I reached for a pen and an old-school reporter's notebook, the type I still preferred to use when working.

There were more hospitals than I'd expected in the city, and I hurriedly scribbled down their details while plotting their locations on another screen on to which I'd summoned a map of the local area. A hundred missing person incident rooms from films and TV flashed across my thoughts. I shuddered as I glimpsed a horrible premonition of my future, with my lounge wall plastered in photographs, 'Missing' posters bearing Finn's face, and a spider's web of Post-it note clues.

I reached for my phone and dialled the first hospital on the list.

Over the next two hours I was put on hold, got disconnected and was transferred to the wrong department more times than I could count. Whichever way the conversations went, they all ended in exactly the same place. They were very sorry but they had no patient named Finn Douglas at their hospital, nor had anyone matching his description been brought in without ID in the last twenty-four hours.

Sometime between hospitals number three and four, Hannah disappeared into the kitchen and returned with a mug of tea, which she set on the desk before me. I sipped it gratefully, despite the cavity-inducing quantity of sugar she'd added.

'It's for shock,' she whispered when my eyes widened on taking a mouthful. I couldn't really argue with her, because since the moment I'd first learnt that Finn wasn't at the church waiting for me, shock was the only word to effectively describe what I was feeling.

Pressing so hard that my pen sliced through several pages of the notepad, I scored a frustrated line through the final hospital on the list.

'So, what now?' asked Hannah, who at some point had pulled on one of my old hoodies over her bridesmaid's dress.

Surprisingly, I hadn't even noticed the falling temperature that had left my arms and shoulders covered in goosebumps. The day was fading into dusk and rapidly hurtling towards evening. Some fifteen miles away, in a five-star hotel that we'd chosen with care, our guests were being asked if they wanted the poached salmon or the beef. My own stomach rolled unpleasantly at even the thought of food.

'I have to go out again. I should visit the bar where Finn had his stag last night. Maybe someone there saw something useful.'

Hannah shook her head. 'There's no need. William and one of the ushers already went there while you were making your phone calls. They spoke to the bar staff and even found a couple of customers who were there last night.' I hadn't realised I was holding my breath in anticipation, until Hannah's next words set it free. 'No one saw anything unusual. Although they did say it was a bit odd that Finn left his own party so early.'

'Did he call for a taxi? Perhaps the cab company could track down the driver.'

'No. According to Trevor, Finn drove himself to the bar.'

I frowned as I corrected her. 'No, he's got that wrong. Finn was getting an Uber there, so he'd be able to drink.'

'I don't know what to tell you, hon. They sounded pretty certain that Finn drove there in his own car and left early without drinking anything, hardly.'

Hannah's eyes darkened in concern as the wall I'd carefully constructed around me began to crumble. I'd built it to keep out the other dreadful possibility. But now for the first time I gave the awful idea oxygen, and it drew breath, robbing me of mine. *What if Finn had changed his mind? What if he'd decided he didn't want to marry me after all?*

I ran blindly from the room, but there was no escaping this moment. Pieces of my future were hurtling through the air like shattered stained glass. Each fragment sliced me like a blade. Suddenly I was ripping at my dress, frantically trying to peel it from me like a contaminated skin, but the ribbons lacing me into it were tighter than a straitjacket. The room started to spin, and I could feel my knees weaken and then buckle as the dress came up around me, trying to swallow me whole.

Hannah's arms were there, firm around my waist, holding me up and against her. I fell gasping into her shoulder, as though drowning.

'Calm down. Breathe,' she urged. 'You're okay, Gemma. I've got you. Everything's going to be okay.' It was a lie I simply couldn't believe.

'Where is he? Why isn't he here?'

'I don't know. I wish I did.'

'Finn loves me. I know he does. You know it too.'

'Maybe it's not his love that's in question,' Hannah said carefully, her hands moving to the ties at the back of my dress as she began to undo the fastenings that she'd laced up only a short while ago. The gown fell to my feet, and I half stumbled, half fell out of it in my satin Agent Provocateur underwear, which now felt as inappropriate as balloons at a funeral. 'Maybe it's the commitment thing that Finn's scared of. I know you're not going to want to hear this…' she began, and then paused, her expression concerned.

'Go on.'

'Finn has everything he ever wanted, or so he claims. And yet it's looking increasingly obvious that he's *chosen* not to be here today. He has walked away when everything he supposedly wants is right there in front of him.'

Something very cold and ugly crawled into my soul and curled up several times, like a cat getting comfortable.

Hannah took a deep breath before saying the words that would shred my heart. 'And we both know this wouldn't be the first time he's unexpectedly walked away when things were just about to go really well.'

I wanted to scream at her that she was wrong. To tell her that nothing could be further from the truth. But I couldn't, and we both knew why.

Because Hannah was right. This wouldn't be the first time.

7

ACROSS A CROWDED BAR
Seven years earlier

'I thought you were going out?'

'I am,' I said, reaching for the second half of my sandwich and sinking my teeth into the thickly sliced bread. 'I'm lining my stomach in preparation.'

'Oh, it's going to be *that* kind of an evening, is it?' Hannah asked, crossing to the hob to stir something that smelt a great deal more appealing than a cheese sandwich.

'It's an engagement party for two journos, and it's being held in a bar with an extended happy hour,' I said between mouthfuls. 'I think it's safe to say things might get a little messy.'

Hannah took her attention from the recipe book she was studying and cast a concerned look over her shoulder. 'It'll be good for you to get out for the evening. If nothing else, it'll stop you obsessively checking your phone every two minutes.'

I couldn't argue with her. Ever since I'd received the call from *Glow* telling me I was one of two final candidates under consideration, I'd been as nervous as a turkey at Christmas. Despite assuring me that a decision was imminent, I'd still not heard anything.

'It'll take your mind off it to go out and have some fun,' Hannah said.

'I think I'd have *more* fun staying here with you and William,' I replied, laughing at her horrified expression. There were flowers on the table, candles waiting to be lit, and only two place settings. 'But I won't,' I added hastily. 'I'm sure there'll be *someone* I know there tonight.' Hannah's easy smile froze when I added darkly, 'Just as long as it isn't Nick or Christopher.'

My friend's scowl was just this side of terrifying. Hannah, who'd never had a cheating ex in her life, had a tendency to react like a Rottweiler whenever mine were mentioned.

'Do you think that's likely?'

'Journalism is a small world,' I said with a shrug. 'Sooner or later you're bound to bump into someone you'd rather not see again.'

To be honest, I was surprised to have received an invitation to Sarah's engagement party. It had been four years since we'd worked together at *The Chronicle*, and we'd pretty much lost touch over the last few.

'Perhaps you could do some networking tonight,' Hannah suggested. 'You might hear about some other magazine jobs.' Her face fell in dismay as she realised she'd caught a dose of my Eeyore-like pessimism. 'Not that you're going to need them, because I'm sure you've got the job at *Glow*.' She crossed the kitchen to give me a reassuring hug.

'Only if the other girl screwed up her interview even worse than I did.'

'Or the other *guy*.'

I shuddered. 'That doesn't even bear thinking about. You know, I'd sooner lose out to anyone in the world but him.'

The bar was dark and absolutely rammed. In black jeans and a scoop-necked top of the same colour, I felt practically invisible as I sidled through the crowd to a cordoned-off area that separated the engagement party from the rest of the customers. From the level of noise and shotgun rounds of laughter, it sounded like the celebrations were already well underway.

A waiter handed me a drink from a tray of bright yellow cocktails. It was fruity and sweet and probably nowhere near as innocent as it tasted. I sipped it slowly as I scoped the bar before finally spotting Sarah. She grinned and waved me over with the enthusiasm of someone directing planes on a runway.

'Gemma,' she cried delightedly, swaying on skyscraper heels as she set down her drink and enfolded me in an exuberant, alcoholic embrace. 'I'm so happy you came. We have so much to catch up on,' she slurred happily. 'I'll find you later. But in the meantime, you know loads of people here, right?'

'Sure,' I lied, smiling vaguely at the strangers around me as Sarah's fiancé appeared at her elbow to drag her away to greet someone else.

Twenty minutes and three cocktails later, I was wondering if it was too early to sneak away. The crowd was cliquey, and although I recognised a few faces, there was no one I knew well enough to go up to and say hi. *One more drink, then*

I'll make an excuse and leave, I decided, and then stopped in my tracks as a familiar laugh snagged my attention. I peered through the crowd and swore softly under my breath as I recognised a pair of broad shoulders and a shock of sandy-coloured hair. Had I conjured up my philandering ex-boyfriend simply by invoking his name earlier this evening? Fortunately, Nick had his back to me and his arm snaked around a pretty young thing in a tight red dress, which he'd probably successfully talk her out of before the evening was over. *Unless he's changed*, a charitable voice piped up in my head. I saw his hand slide down to his companion's bottom and squeeze it, as though testing a peach. *People don't change, not really.* I pivoted on my heel and headed in the opposite direction, towards the bar.

The free cocktails had long since run out, so I had to squeeze my way through a wall of fellow journalists to reach the bar. It took five minutes before I got close enough to even *see* the bartender, much less catch his eye. The poor man was literally under siege, with orders being barked at him from every direction. As I waited, I pulled out my phone for a quick check of my emails. Still nothing.

'A glass of white wine, please,' I ordered with a smile, when it was finally my turn. But instead of serving me, the barman spun on his heel to attend to a customer on the other side of the horseshoe-shaped bar. I leant forward and peered into the shadows, trying to identify the queue-jumper, but it was too dark to see properly.

'Sorry,' I said, sounding terribly British and affronted. 'But I think *I* was next.'

The barman turned towards me, his hands already full with the other customer's order. 'Sorry, love, I'll be right with you.'

I glared across the width of the bar at whoever had pushed in, and then gasped in disbelief. It was *him*. The man from the interview.

Surprisingly, he recognised me instantly. 'Hey, it's you again,' he declared. There was a brief pause when I saw him struggling to remember my name before abandoning the quest. It rankled, because his was still very much in the forefront of my mind.

The barman set down a beer in front of the only other man I recognised there tonight, who also happened to be the last one I had wanted to see.

'Finn Douglas,' I said in lieu of hello.

There was a twenty-pound note in Finn's hand, but before surrendering it, he nodded in my direction. 'And whatever the lady's having.'

It was a slick line that I felt sure he'd used successfully many times before. But not this time. 'No, thank you.' My voice was polite but firm. 'I'll wait my turn.'

'Ouch,' said Finn, pantomiming an exaggerated wince.

When it became clear I wasn't going to change my mind, he shrugged and turned away. By the time my drink arrived, Finn was engaged in conversation with someone on the other side of the bar.

I'd taken just one sip when I felt my phone vibrating against my hip with an incoming email. My fingers were slow and clumsy as I drew it from my pocket and slid them across the screen to the mail icon. I read no further than the sentence that began: *We regret to inform you...* before switching off the phone.

I fumbled for a bar stool and sat down heavily upon it. There would be other jobs, I knew that, but money was going to be tight once Hannah moved out, which made ordering another glass of wine even more foolish. But I did it anyway.

My eyes felt hot and scratchy as I stared unseeingly at the beaten copper surface of the bar, willing myself not to cry in public, or, more specifically, not in front of the insufferable man sitting opposite me. But when I lifted my head, I saw Finn wasn't even looking my way, for his attention was entirely on his phone. It was hard to tell, but it looked very much like he was smiling at whatever he was reading on the screen.

I reached for my wine glass, surprised to find it was already empty. The sensible thing would have been to go home right then, before I did or said anything I might regret. But I was already several drinks beyond sensible.

I didn't see Finn leave his side of the bar, so the startled jump I gave when he climbed on to the stool beside me almost toppled me from mine. Wordlessly, he slid a large glass of wine in front of me.

'What's that for?' I asked, wincing at how churlish I sounded. I'd never met anyone before who could unfailingly bring out the worst in me the way he did.

'Because I stole your parking space?' he suggested teasingly. His eyes were twinkling in a way I was sure many women would find attractive. Luckily, I was totally immune.

'That's not all you stole,' I muttered darkly before biting down painfully on my wayward tongue. *No more drinks for you, young lady*, commanded a voice in my head that sounded an awful lot like my mother.

'What else have I done wrong? Queue-jumped at the bar?'

My smile felt like cracking ice: sharp and dangerous. 'Oh, I think you know.'

To be fair, Finn looked genuinely mystified. Was I wrong? Had he been reading something else on his phone? After all, I had no proof that he'd just been given the job I wanted.

'Look, I know you and I got off on the wrong foot the other day. But what do you say we start over?' he said, offering his hand to me as though we'd never met before. 'I'm Finn Douglas.'

Sober me would not have taken his hand, but inebriated me was suddenly reckless. I shook it with the strength I normally reserved for stubborn jar lids. His eyes widened at the force of my grip, but he said nothing.

I reached for the wine he'd placed in front of me, and despite my good intentions took a large mouthful. 'If you're trying to get me drunk, it's not going to work,' I informed him. 'And there's zero possibility of me going home with you, so save your money,' I added for good measure.

'I'm pretty sure I haven't asked you to,' he replied pleasantly.

I turned towards him and felt the room waver as it tried to keep up with my head. 'Well, don't bother, because I really don't like you.'

'Fair enough,' he said, his hand reaching out, lightning fast, as I swayed on my seat. I stared down at where it rested on my arm and within seconds it was gone – and so was he. He returned moments later, with a pitcher of water jingling with ice cubes.

'Drink,' he instructed, pouring out a generous tumbler. I noticed he too had switched from beer to something non-alcoholic.

'So, are you always this grumpy, or is it only when you're around me?' Finn asked, the amusement still lingering in his voice as he watched me drain the glass of water.

'No, it's just you,' I said with an assertive nod. 'I really don't like you at all. And I *really* needed that job.'

'The one at *Glow*?'

I turned my head slowly because it still felt as though it was not quite secured to my neck. 'Of course the job at *Glow*. The one you've got.'

Was there a pause before he replied? My faculties were no longer sharp enough to be sure. 'I haven't got that job,' he said.

I searched his face, which had mysteriously grown more attractive as the evening progressed. Although, sadly, the same couldn't be said for his personality. 'You're lying.'

Finn shook his head. 'Why would I do that? I don't know who the new feature writer at *Glow* magazine is, but it definitely isn't me.'

'Oh God. Never again. Never, ever again,' I moaned, taking the paracetamol packet from Hannah's outstretched hand.

The midday sun was slicing painfully through my bedroom window, doing what I feared might be irreparable damage to my retinas. 'I am never drinking again.'

Hannah smiled knowingly.

'What time did I get back last night?' I asked, trying to put together the jigsaw pieces of the previous evening. It already felt as though several vital sections might be missing.

'The taxi dropped you off just after midnight.'

'A taxi? Oh God, I didn't have enough cash for a cab. Did you or William have to pay?' I asked, already panicking about how much I now owed them. The bar had been miles away.

'No. It was already paid for.'

'Ohhh,' I groaned, burying my head beneath my pillow, suddenly feeling sick for a great many reasons.

'You don't remember the evening?' Hannah probed worriedly.

'Bits of it,' I mumbled shamefully into the duck down.

Very gently, Hannah lifted the pillow from my face and smoothed back the tangled curls from my sweat-sticky forehead.

'I remember being pretty rude. And I think...' A memory hovered on the periphery of my recollection, and I winced as it swam into clarity. 'I think I accused him of being a liar and a cheat and of stealing the job from me.'

Hannah gulped noisily. I could hardly blame her.

'And then I told him that if I ended up homeless and living on the streets it would all be his fault.'

'Oh well, you were drunk,' Hannah said with a sigh, as though that somehow absolved me of being an idiot.

I shook my head and instantly regretted such foolishness. 'I was not a nice person last night,' I admitted sorrowfully, closer to tears than I wanted to acknowledge.

'Well, you can make up for it by sending him a congratulatory gift when he starts his new job,' Hannah suggested. 'And then—'

The ringing of my phone interrupted her. 'Do you want to take that?'

I very nearly said no, but something warned me not to.

I said very little on the call. I watched as Hannah began picking up the discarded clothes from my bedroom floor and bundling them into the laundry basket. By the time she was done, I was off the phone. I'm not sure I'd said anything other than a series of yeses throughout the conversation, but

I suspect she'd already guessed what I was about to tell her. I imagine it was written all over my face.

'That was the HR department of *Glow*,' I said. Even to my own ears my voice sounded incredulous. 'They said the other candidate has unexpectedly withdrawn their application.' I paused for a moment, still trying to absorb the news. 'I've got the feature writer job.'

SUNDAY: DAY ONE

8

'You're up early.'

I gave a start as I entered the kitchen. It wasn't as though I'd forgotten Hannah had stayed the night; it was more the shock of seeing her once again in her old seat at the kitchen table. It felt like a weird science-fiction story, where I'd somehow slipped into a wormhole and ended up seven years in the past.

She'd already made a pot of coffee, and now she got to her feet, reaching for my favourite mug.

'I could say the same to you.'

Hannah's laugh sounded carefree, and for a moment I envied her that. 'Oh, lie-ins are a thing of the past when you've got a lively three-year-old. You just wait until you—' She broke off, a look of horror on her face. The moment hung in the air like something toxic. 'Gemma, I'm so sorry. I didn't mean—'

'Don't give it a second thought,' I said, taking the coffee she was holding out as though it was an apology.

Hannah was still biting her lip as she picked up a cloth and began wiping down my already clean kitchen surfaces. 'Did you manage to get any sleep?' she asked when she'd run out of worktop to punish.

I breathed in, considered lying, and then thought better of it. She'd have seen straight through it anyway. 'A few snatched minutes here and there.'

Hannah tutted her disapproval and pulled out a chair, plonking herself back down at the table opposite me. She reached out both hands and clasped mine, as though we were about to conduct a seance. Ah, there was a means of communicating with Finn that I'd not yet contemplated. Because I'd certainly exhausted every other method. I'd stopped leaving messages on his phone because there were only so many ways you could rephrase 'Where the hell are you?' without getting repetitious.

'So, what *did* you do if you didn't get any sleep?'

I glanced over my shoulder into the lounge, where I'd dropped my laptop on to the settee. 'I spent some time looking into things.'

Hannah's neatly plucked eyebrows rose, waiting for more.

'For example, I now know the correct procedure for filing a missing person's report. I know how many unexplained disappearances there were in the UK last year, and how many of those are believed to be down to alien abduction.'

Hannah gave a snort that threatened to spray coffee all over the kitchen worktops she'd just cleaned.

'Yes, well, that one was around 3 a.m., and I was getting a little punchy.'

'It sounds like you had a busy night.'

'Well, it wasn't exactly how I'd *planned* to spend my wedding night...' I winced, realising it was much too soon for even a feeble attempt at levity. The very worst moment of the previous night had been when I'd watched the clock tick beyond midnight and realised my wedding day was now officially behind me.

I drew in a steadying breath before continuing. 'I also researched how many grooms fail to turn up on their wedding day.' I reached for my coffee mug, dismayed to see the slight tremor of my hand. 'It's surprisingly few. It would seem I'm a member of a very elite club – one that I never wanted to join.'

Hannah was shaking her head sorrowfully. 'I truly don't know what to say, Gemma. I have no words.' And for Hannah that was quite the admission.

'You don't have to say a single thing. Just being here last night was enough.'

It wasn't that I'd been short of offers of company to help me get through the worst night of my life. Dad had been particularly insistent on staying, until I'd reminded him that he needed to get back for Chester, his geriatric cat. Even my elderly Aunt Helen had offered to 'babysit' me – those had been her exact words. She'd been easier to politely turn down than Dad, especially as the last time she'd been called on to perform that particular duty had been about twenty-five years ago. But Hannah had proved to be a much tougher nut to crack.

'Milly needs you,' I'd reminded her, trying to dissuade her from staying, although admittedly with less conviction than I probably should have shown.

'William is perfectly capable of looking after her for one

night.' She'd paused as though weighing up whether she should say her next words. Apparently, they were deemed essential. 'You need me more.'

I wanted to deny it. I wanted to say I was old enough not to fall apart over this and sensible enough to deal with whatever had happened. Except that perhaps I wasn't.

Hannah had switched tactics then. 'Who was it who plucked that sting out of my bum after I sat on a bee in my bikini? Or drove like a maniac to the airport to deliver my passport after I discovered I'd left it at home? Or cried along with me when I had that miscarriage, the year before I had Milly?'

'This quiz is too easy. You need to find some harder questions,' I replied, touched by her words, and also momentarily distracted. Something she'd said had tripped a silent alarm in my head, but as hard as I tried to catch hold of the elusive thought, it kept slipping away from me.

'You've been there for me, Gemma, whenever I've needed you,' Hannah continued, sounding more emotional than I could cope with that early in the morning. 'So now I'm here for you' – she shook her arms, for her hands had once again disappeared inside the sleeves of the pyjamas she'd borrowed – 'although I may have to go home and get some of my own clothes before we venture anywhere today. Yours are far too big for me.'

'Well, now you're just being cruel,' I said, surprised to find that this time the humour came a little more naturally.

'My fiancé is missing.' My voice was a panicked ricochet, echoing off the walls of the police station reception. Even though I'd rehearsed how to deliver the information in a clear, non-hysterical way, I'd fallen at the first hurdle in response to a simple 'Can I help you?'

'Take a breath,' advised the station duty officer calmly, 'and start from the beginning. Firstly, how long has he been missing?'

'Since yesterday afternoon. When he didn't turn up at our wedding.'

The room I'd been led to was silent now, except for the sound of a pen scratching on a notepad. A different officer sat before me, his bowed head revealing a bald patch that I'd been staring at for the last ten minutes as he filled an entire A4 sheet with indecipherable notes and annotations. It didn't look particularly official, and that worried me. A lot.

Finally, the officer looked up, snapping the cap back on his pen in an 'I think we're done here' kind of way.

'Okay, Miss Fletcher, I think I've got all the details I need. But before we escalate this to an *official* missing person's report, there are a couple of things that I believe might have been overlooked along the way.'

I sat up straighter on the interview room's uncomfortable plastic chair. Despite the receding hairline, the officer could only have been ten years older than me, and yet I felt like a bewildered child in front of him.

'What things?'

'Well, you said you visited Mr Douglas's flat late yesterday afternoon but that you didn't notice if anything of importance was missing.'

'*Finn* was missing. He was the only thing I was looking for.'

Inspector Graham – according to his ID pass – nodded in an avuncular way that he was far too young to pull off effectively. 'Of course. Quite right. But I want to make sure that we don't take any missteps here, given the slightly *unusual* circumstances of your fiancé's… disappearance.' It was impossible not to notice his slight hesitation.

'Isn't every disappearance unusual?' I challenged, already fearing I knew exactly where this conversation was going.

'I've been a police officer for twenty years,' Inspector Graham said, leaning back in his chair. 'And in that time I've dealt with countless missing person reports. But I'm going to be completely honest with you, Miss Fletcher. What you've described doesn't fit a classic scenario of someone who's gone missing. Can you think of any reason at all why Mr Douglas might have *chosen* to leave?'

Suddenly I wasn't sure I liked Inspector Graham after all. 'You mean like deciding he didn't want to get married to me?'

The policeman had the grace to look uncomfortable at the directness of my response.

'Have the two of you argued about anything recently? Perhaps you've had a falling-out?'

'We were supposed to be getting married yesterday,' I said fiercely, as though my answer blew his question out of the water. 'So that's a hard no.'

'I don't want you to think we're not taking your concerns seriously. Contacting the hospitals was definitely an excellent place to start. So well done for initiating that. *My* team's first task will be to reach out to all local police stations to see if your fiancé might have spent last night in one of our custody suites.'

'You think Finn might have been arrested?'

'He wouldn't be the first groom to end up there, sleeping it off after his stag night.'

'But Finn wasn't drunk. You can ask any of his friends.'

'Or he might have been involved in a brawl,' the policeman suggested calmly. 'These things can get a bit lairy at times.' I shook my head because he was talking about someone who bore absolutely no resemblance to the Finn I knew.

'What I'd like to suggest is that you return to Mr Douglas's flat and see if there's anything there that might offer a clue as to his current whereabouts. People are creatures of habit; they do things they've done before, return to places that are familiar. Sometimes it's the things that are missing that are the most informative. So it's worth checking his clothes, personal possessions, passport, that kind of thing.'

Passport? The niggling sensation I'd felt earlier returned.

'In my experience, Miss Fletcher, people who are going through big life changes very often need to take a "time out". It doesn't necessarily mean anything untoward has happened to them.'

'A time out? From their own wedding?' I asked incredulously.

The police officer nodded in a way that suggested that nothing the general public did had the power to surprise him any longer.

'In the majority of cases, these people simply turn up again – usually within a week of disappearing, and your fiancé has only been "missing" for one day.' He air quoted the word 'missing', and I swallowed the urge to scream in frustration.

'So, what are you saying? That if I wait patiently for the next six days, Finn is likely to turn up of his own accord? What if he doesn't?'

Inspector Graham looked suddenly less comfortable. 'I suppose that all depends on why he left and how much he wants to be found.'

I left the station in a daze, regretting more than anything that I'd insisted on going alone. Would they have taken Finn's disappearance more seriously if I'd been accompanied by Hannah or my dad? Possibly. Or would it just have compounded the conclusion that I suspected even those closest to me had already reached: that Finn was simply a groom who'd changed his mind?

I drove on autopilot through the morning traffic as I replayed the interview in my head. *Six days.* Was that really how long I was meant to wait for Finn to return? What was I supposed to do after that, simply give up on him? I shook my head, unable to imagine a time I would ever do that.

You're not supposed to lie to the police. But today I had. Because there *had* been an argument recently. A big one. One I'd told no one about; not Dad, nor Hannah, because there was no need, we'd resolved it. It had absolutely no bearing on Finn's disappearance. Or was that just another lie I was telling today?

I hated how, despite everything, I still looked hopefully towards Finn's parking space as I drove into the residents' car park. I reversed into his bay, my thoughts inevitably going back to that other parking spot, the one we'd fought over on the day we met.

Fortunately, a resident from the top floor was leaving the

building just as I approached the entrance. She smiled vaguely at me as we crossed paths in the doorway. At least this time I wouldn't need to bother the irascible Mrs Barnard.

Finn's flat felt different today, as though it had been holding its breath since yesterday, waiting for me to return.

'Hello,' I called out as I pushed the front door shut behind me. Even though I hadn't expected an answer, I felt ridiculously disappointed when none came.

I glanced briefly into the bathroom before turning towards Finn's bedroom. His door was shut, and my heart dropped a beat and then hurried to catch up. Had I closed it yesterday? I couldn't remember. My mouth felt dry as I slowly turned the door handle, desperately hoping to find him there, asleep in a twist of tangled duvet on the king-size bed. But the stripped mattress was bare except for broad chevrons of sunlight shafting in through the window.

My eyes slowly travelled the room, looking for answers I still wasn't sure I wanted to find. 'See if any of his clothes are missing,' Inspector Graham had advised. My legs felt wooden, as if the joints were fused, as I walked to the bank of fitted wardrobes against the far wall. Like a magician on a big reveal, I grasped the handles and flung open the doors.

Everything was gone. Every last item that should have been hanging in Finn's wardrobe was missing. I stared at the long row of empty metal hangers dancing eerily before me.

Breathing heavily, I opened the adjacent doors and was met with another empty clothes rail above a set of deep drawers. It was the top one I went to first, because that was home to both Finn's socks and his passport.

'You keep your passport with your socks?' I heard an echo of my own voice ask with a laugh.

'Yeah. So I don't lose it, or forget where it is. This way I get to see it every week when I change my socks.'

That had been early in our relationship. I'd only stayed over at his place a couple of times by then, and I'd been easy to prank. He watched me trying to disguise an expression of horror before gathering me into his arms with a deep, rumbling laugh.

'You…' the ghost of me said, punching his shoulder even as I felt us tumbling back on to his bed. It was where most of our conversations had ended in those early days, in either his bed or mine.

Now, in the stripped-bare room, I ran my hand over the checked mattress, as though I could psychically connect with him through the memory foam. Did it remember the shape of him, the way I did? Did it hold in its fibres every moment of passion we'd shared there? Because *I* did.

On knees that suddenly felt too weak to support me, I folded like a marionette on to the bed, but this time without the man I loved tumbling beside me.

Think, I urged, my eyes transfixed by the row of empty clothes hangers. *There has to be a logical explanation for all of this.*

Obviously, Finn would have packed some of his clothes for the honeymoon, but not all of them. And anyway, who would take winter coats, ski jackets and jumpers on a trip to Australia? There was still a further two months left to run on the lease for Finn's flat, so we'd not even begun to think about packing up his stuff yet. Or so I'd thought.

Twenty-four hours earlier, I'd swept through the flat in a panic. But now I took my time, kicking myself for all the clues I'd missed. Where was the row of toiletries lined up in the shower cubicle? Or the toothbrush that should have been in the glass beside the basin?

At first glance the lounge appeared exactly as it should, but the flat was a fully furnished rental, so it took closer scrutiny to finally notice the empty spaces on the shelving unit, the missing photograph frames, and the fact that Finn's laptop was no longer sitting on the desk in the corner of the room. I yanked open the usually overflowing desk drawers, already knowing by the ease with which they skated on their runners what I'd find. Empty. Every single one of them.

Either Finn had become an overnight Marie Kondo convert, or the truth staring me in the face had a far simpler explanation. Finn had moved out.

'I don't understand. How could he have done all that without you knowing?' Hannah asked, hushing Milly, who I could hear in the background asking if she could speak to Auntie Gemma. 'How long is it since you last visited his flat?'

'Not for a couple of weeks or so. We've mainly been at mine.' Was that at my suggestion, or his? It was a suddenly terribly important question that I simply couldn't answer.

'Do you want me to come over? I could meet you there.'

I made an inarticulate sound that Hannah managed to identify as 'No'. 'There's no point. There's nothing here to see. It's all gone.'

There was a crack in my voice that threatened to split wide open. Finn had quite literally taken everything, leaving just one thing behind. Me.

★

I sat in his empty flat for a long time, watching the afternoon shadows move across the floor and finally disappear into the corner of the room as clouds darkened the sky. I made at least three abortive attempts to leave, only to get snagged by a memory that stilled my feet. There we were, dancing barefoot on the kitchen tiles to a late-night radio station, Finn's arms around my waist while my head nestled comfortably on his shoulder. The music had been slow, soft and gentle, and so were his lips as we kissed by the light of the open fridge door.

We were there in the lounge too, pretzelled together on the settee, watching a film that always made me cry. It wasn't his kind of movie, he'd said, and yet by the time the credits rolled he'd long abandoned whatever he'd been doing on his phone. 'I hope someone loves me just like that, one day,' I remember saying on a sigh. 'They already do,' Finn had said softly, pulling me closer against him. It was the first time either of us had mentioned the L-word. It was one of my best memories.

'This place is an emotional minefield,' I muttered into the bathroom mirror as I washed my hands at the basin while a flickering reflection of our naked, soap-slicked bodies was replayed in the shower cubicle behind me, re-enacting the night we broke the soap dish (which was bad) and ticked several fantasies off my bucket list (which was very, very good).

But not all the memories were so happy. The worst one came hurtling back as I reached into the kitchen cabinet for a drinking glass. My hand rested on the tumbler as I looked at the diminished stack of dinner plates; four instead of the six there should have been. That was all it took to transport me back to the disagreement I'd denied had ever happened.

It had been a perfectly ordinary, unremarkable evening. I'd

been banished to the settee while Finn happily dirtied every pot and utensil in his kitchen making his 'famous' spaghetti bolognaise. *One of only two dishes I know how to cook*, he claimed, refusing to acknowledge that beans on toast didn't count as the second.

Music was playing softly from his Alexa, which effectively masked the sound of his footsteps. I didn't realise he'd left the kitchen and was standing directly behind me until it was too late. I rapidly clicked off the property page on my laptop, trying to convince myself that the lighting had been too dim, or the angle all wrong for him to have seen what was on the screen.

Finn was quiet, too quiet, I now realised as we ate. It was only when I got up to begin clearing the table that I knew that however fast I'd been, I hadn't been fast enough.

His fingers gently circled my wrist, stopping me.

'How often do you do that?'

Damn. So he *had* seen. I considered lying or playing dumb, but that felt even worse than telling the truth.

'Every now and then. I'm just surprised that he put it on the market after all.' My words felt like arrows because he flinched when I said them. 'But it doesn't *mean* anything. I'm just curious, that's all.'

My heart was thumping uncomfortably in my chest, so hard I could practically see it through the fabric of my T-shirt as I turned towards the dishwasher. He crossed the room silently and I jumped as he gently turned me around, his hands covering mine on the plates.

'But you're still thinking about it... and all that it represents?'

I shrugged, trying to look as though this wasn't the most important conversation we'd had in a very long time.

'I haven't changed my mind, Gemma,' he said gently.

My throat felt dry and tight, as though it was trying to stifle the words I was about to say. 'I've never asked you to.'

His eyes flicked to my laptop on the kitchen counter. It felt as dangerous as an unexploded bomb. 'Not in so many words, maybe.'

I shook my head so hard my ponytail slapped each cheek, as though it was trying to bring me to my senses. To stop me before I said anything else. But these words had been bottled up for a long time.

'I know what we agreed last summer. But how can you be so *sure* you'll never change your mind? People do. Look at me. I once said the last thing I'd ever do was fall in love with a writer. That it was impossible to trust a man who told stories for a living. And just look at us now.'

It was supposed to be the comment that defused the situation, but it had the exact opposite effect.

'Yes. Just look at us. I'm not being fair on you. We want totally different things.'

I was crying now. 'We want *each other*,' I insisted. 'Please, Finn, let's not do this again.'

'If I don't say it now, then when should I? In six weeks, on the day we get married? On our first anniversary? Or in ten years' time, when you hate me for standing in your way?'

I jerked free of his hold, so sharply that the plates slipped from my hands, shattering noisily around our feet. Neither of us moved. We stood inches and a thousand miles apart, our chests heaving as though we'd run a race and still didn't know who'd won.

An imperative knocking on his front door broke the spell. 'Finn? Is everything okay in there? I heard a commotion.'

The voice was surprisingly loud through the thickness of the door.

Finn swore under his breath and strode to where his neighbour, Mrs Barnard, was rapping on the door. He opened it just a crack, using his body to block her view of the kitchen, where I was picking up broken plates as though clearing up a crime scene. By the time Finn had managed to assure her it was a noisy TV programme and a minor kitchen mishap, I had calmed down.

Finn still looked troubled when he returned to the kitchen, but my thoughts were clear. I reached for his hands, winding my fingers through his, like a network of vines. 'I never knew a love like this before I met you,' I said shakily. 'A love so big it fills every corner of my soul. There are many things I can live without in my life... but you're not one of them. So please don't ever ask me to do that.'

Finn nodded, his eyes bright with tears as he pulled me, finally, into his arms.

It had been our worst disagreement, but we'd got through it. It was done. Only now I wasn't so sure whether we'd actually resolved anything.

I strode from the kitchen, but the memory followed me. 'I need to get out of here,' I told the haggard-faced woman in the hallway mirror, who looked even worse than my passport photo. Which was saying something.

As I turned to leave, the hall was suddenly cast into stark relief as strobe-like lightning flashed through the window, followed by a clap of thunder. The summer storm, which the weather forecasters had predicted, perfectly suited my mood. But confusingly, long after it should have faded, I could still hear the low, almost rhythmic rumble of thunder. It was there when I turned off the lights in Finn's flat and opened his front door to leave.

The noise was even louder in the communal hallway, only now I realised it wasn't the sound of thunder but of wheels trundling over linoleum as Mrs Barnard dragged a shopping trolley loaded with two enormous bags of rubbish. She hadn't got very far, just a dozen steps from her front door. I must have startled her, for she jerked and then seemed to sway alarmingly for a moment. The stick she usually relied on was nowhere to be seen.

Her eyes narrowed suspiciously as I shut Finn's door behind me, as though I might be robbing the place. *Truly, there's no need to worry*, I almost assured her. *He's left nothing behind to steal.*

'Can I help you with those?' I asked, my eyes going to the large bin bags, which looked precariously balanced.

'Do I look like someone who needs help?' Mrs Barnard's reply was the snap of an angry terrier.

'Actually, yes. You do,' I said, crossing the space between us and reaching for the bin bags. 'I'm going downstairs anyway, so it's really no trouble. Besides, it's pouring out there. You'll get soaked.'

I glanced down and noticed her footwear. She was in slippers, the old-fashioned granny type, although I could remember Finn saying she had no children. There was a stain on the left slipper that she'd probably be mortified I'd spotted. Perhaps that's what softened me. 'Please, Mrs Barnard, it's horrible out there. There's no need for you to get wet.'

If I was expecting a miraculous change in attitude, I was in for a long wait. 'Well, I wouldn't normally have to do this myself. That young man of yours usually takes out my rubbish on the day before the bin men come.'

'Does he?' I said, wondering why he'd never mentioned it. How unfortunate it was to find something new to love about Finn while he was currently busy falling out of love with me.

'Well, as he's not here… right now' – *or ever*, added a cruel voice in my head – 'I'm happy to do it for you.'

She stepped back, as though bestowing her two overfilled bin bags into my care was doing me an enormous favour. I wound my hands through the plastic tie handles and headed towards the staircase. My foot was hovering over the topmost tread when her words halted it.

'I shall miss him popping round with those fancy coffees he kept wanting me to try. What was it he brought me last week, a late mucky something or other.'

'A latte macchiato,' I said softly. It was one of Finn's favourites. For just a moment it felt as though he was standing right there in the hallway with us. The bags were suddenly too heavy to hold. They dropped to the floor, landing at my feet with a resounding thud.

Mrs Barnard tutted expressively. 'If those bags split open, young lady, I hope you don't think *I'm* cleaning them up.'

Despite her tough carapace, I'd always believed Mrs Barnard had a soft spot for her neighbour. She'd want to help if she knew he was missing, wouldn't she?

'I know this might sound a little strange, Mrs Barnard, but you haven't heard from Finn in the last day or so, have you?'

The older woman's eyes were beginning to cloud with cataracts, but they bored into mine with the intensity of a laser.

'No. Why would you even ask that?'

'Because Finn never showed up at the church yesterday.'

I couldn't imagine there were many things that left Mrs Barnard without a cutting retort or render her speechless. But that certainly did.

I paused before leaving the building, trying to decide if this was the kind of intense rain that would peter out in a minute or two or whether it was going to continue pounding the pavement like artillery fire for a while yet.

Tightening my hold on the two enormous rubbish bags, I went for it, running head down through the rain towards the bin store. My vision was blurred by the deluge, making it hard to read the faded numbers daubed in paint on the sides of the bins. But I finally spotted the one allocated to the residents of the second floor and flung open the lid. I gave a small grunt of irritation when I saw it was already almost full.

It couldn't have taken more than a minute or two, but by the time I'd pushed down the contents of the bin to make room for Mrs Barnard's bags, my top was plastered against my back like a second skin. Arm-deep in other people's rubbish felt like an appropriately awful way to end my visit to Finn's flat.

My shoes made weird squelching sounds as I ran back to my car, but instead of leaping straight into the driver's seat, I hesitated. Despite the downpour, I turned back to look at the wheelie bins, feeling oddly troubled. Something there wasn't quite right, but I had no idea what it could be.

I shook my head, spraying water in every direction, but the elusive concern was as hard to catch hold of as the raindrops around me. It would come to me, I decided. If it was important, it would come.

MONDAY: DAY TWO

9

There was soap in my eye, or maybe shampoo. I'd been in the shower long enough to turn my fingertips into prunes and had probably used up at least half the hot water in the tank. I lifted my face to the jets cascading from the shower head and was transported back to standing in the rain outside Finn's flat the previous day. And just like that, with no logical train of thought, the niggling concern that had eluded me yesterday presented itself. Like a gift.

The bins.

The ones for the second-floor flats.

They had been full. But Mrs Barnard's refuse had yet to be taken down. So the bulging black plastic sacks filling the wheelie bin had to be Finn's.

I half stumbled, half fell out of the shower cubicle, uncaring that there were still soap suds in my hair. Today was the day the bins were emptied. If there *were* any clues to be found in the rubbish bags, they would shortly be disposed of or incinerated, or become part of a landfill somewhere. Unless I got to them first.

Pulling on jeans over damp legs wasn't something I'd ever tried before or would particularly recommend, because it was surprisingly tricky. The T-shirt I yanked on was inside out, which I only realised when I flew past the mirror in the hallway on my way to the front door. I didn't stop to change it; I just swept up my car keys and ran from the flat as though being chased.

The traffic was appalling. Rush hour should technically have finished by then, and yet every road had queues at junctions and traffic lights that changed three times or more before they let me through.

I had no idea what time the bins were collected in Finn's area and was trying hard not to focus on the very real possibility that his might already have been emptied by the time I got there.

I drove badly, coming close to scraping the wing of a car in the next lane, and if any of the speed cameras I passed were working, I could expect a flurry of fines in the days to come. But none of that mattered. I was focused only on finding out what was in the bags that I'd stupidly overlooked the day before.

I pressed my foot down harder on the accelerator, heedless of another fine, and offered up a silent plea. *Just one lucky break, that's all I need. Just one tiny lucky break.*

Whenever something went my way, either at work or personally, I liked to think my mum was behind it. It was a stupid notion that I'd never shared with anyone except Finn, for fear it would sound as crazy to them as it did to me.

But Finn hadn't laughed. 'I think that's a lovely way of looking at it,' he'd said, drawing me closer against him. Perhaps it was because he understood how hard it was to lose a parent. At any age. And he'd lost both of his so young. 'If someone has looked out for you all your life, it makes sense they'd want to carry on doing that – wherever they are now.' It was a comforting thought that I took with me into dreams at night. And it helped. It really did.

So when I finally pulled into Finn's road and saw the grey refuse-collection vehicle up ahead, my first instinct was to whisper a grateful, 'Thank you, Mum.'

The refuse vehicle was blocking the road, and I was in a queue at least ten cars deep, waiting for it to move. As I peered beyond the line of cars, I saw a man emerge from the side of Finn's building, trundling two wheelie bins in his wake. I was too far away to read the numbers painted on them.

My fingers drummed an anxious tattoo against the steering wheel as I stared through the windscreen. The driver of the truck leant out of his cab and shouted something to the crew, which seemed to immediately galvanise them. Suddenly everyone began moving faster. The man in the high-vis vest, wheeling the bins from Finn's building, moved to the back of the truck.

At the head of the queue of cars, someone had found a gap to squeeze through, but there were still nine cars ahead of me. I wasn't going to reach the dustcart in time. With a crunch of mechanical gears, one of the bins was lifted from the pavement.

'No!' I shouted, too late to stop the rubbish from cascading into the gaping mouth of the truck. In frustration, I smacked my hand on the steering wheel, startling myself and everyone around me as my car's horn turned every head my way. It bought me a few extra seconds, and I didn't waste them.

Without bothering to switch off my engine, I threw open the car door and began running towards the dustcart. I was shouting as I pounded along the pavement, but from that distance no one could make out what I was saying.

The second bin was now lined up, waiting its turn. Sweat trickled into my eyes, stinging them like acid. I wiped them clear just in time to witness a wheelie bin with Finn's flat number on it begin its upward journey.

'Stop! Wait! Don't empty that bin!' I screamed.

All eyes were on me. I could only imagine that a deranged woman hijacking a wheelie bin wasn't a regular occurrence. Just when the angle of the bin meant gravity was about to take over, one of the dustmen reached out and thumped a button on the back of the truck. Finn's bin, which might or might not be holding the answers I was looking for, froze in mid-air and then slowly returned to the ground.

'For the record, I want it noted that I'm really not enjoying this.'

I looked up, brushing the hair out of my eyes with my forearm, making sure to keep my rubber-gloved hands clear of my face.

'You didn't have to join in. You could have just watched,' I said, sitting back on my haunches. We were in the middle of Hannah's lawn, in her pretty suburban garden. At least it had been pretty, until we'd upended four huge bin bags on to the grass. In hindsight, we should have put something down to collect the rubbish instead of tearing into the bags like a pair of rabid dogs. Although that description probably applied more to me than Hannah.

She had actually been remarkably sanguine when I'd turned up on her doorstep carrying a collection of decidedly pungent bags.

'Are those for me?' she asked sweetly, looking too clean and wholesome for dirty work in her denim shorts and sleeveless top. 'Aww... you shouldn't have.'

'They're rubbish bags,' I explained needlessly. The heat of the day was already helping in their identification.

Hannah blinked at me from her doorstop for several moments. 'I feel bad now for not getting *you* anything.'

'Ha ha,' I said, bending to pick up the bags. 'I thought maybe we could go through them in your garden?'

'I can't think of anything I'd rather do on a lovely summer morning,' she said, softening the sarcasm with a twisted grin. 'Bring them round the side. You're not trudging that lot through the house.'

To be fair, after I'd explained their potential importance, Hannah was much more on board with the plan. She even dashed back into the house and returned with two pairs of sturdy rubber gloves.

By the second bag, our enthusiasm had waned considerably. By bag three, I was seriously regretting my so-called brainwave. So far, the bags had yielded only the expected domestic waste. Hannah's frown was leaving furrows on her brow as she ploughed through the rubbish. 'Has Finn never heard of recycling?'

'I'll be sure to ask him, as soon as I'm done finding out why he failed to show up at our wedding.'

'I'm sorry, hon,' Hannah said with an apologetic smile as she turned back to the pile of garbage on her lawn.

'Hey. What's this?' she exclaimed a few minutes later, plucking two screwed-up balls of paper from the pile of detritus.

I recognised the lined yellow paper instantly. They were sheets torn out of the legal pad Finn liked to use for making notes when writing.

I took the balls from her outstretched hand and with the care of a forensic scientist carefully unfurled them. Seeing his handwriting made my stomach contract as though from a blow. I scanned the sheets, my throat tightening as I read his words.

'What is it?' Hannah asked, getting to her knees to take back the sheets.

Forgetting for a moment where they'd come from, I clutched them tightly against me. They were a tangible link to Finn, the first I'd found in days.

It didn't start well.

'"Gemma, this is without doubt the hardest thing I've ever had to write,"' I read out loud, my voice shaking almost as much as the hand holding Finn's note.

Hannah scowled but nodded encouragingly for me to continue.

'There's quite a lot of crossing out, so it's hard to work out what it says. Most of it seems to be just random words and phrases that he's circled.' I looked up and saw Hannah's brows had risen meaningfully. 'He's underlined "disappointment" several times, and also "change of plans".'

Hannah scrabbled across the grass on her knees to come and sit beside me. Her arm went around my shoulders as we sat on the sun-warmed lawn, reading the disjointed thoughts and half-formed sentences.

'"It's hard not to feel overwhelmed right now,"' Hannah read, taking over the narration.

She turned to look at me. 'I suppose these *could* be notes for his latest book?'

I shook my head. Finn had allowed me to read several chapters from the thriller he was writing. This didn't sound like anything to do with it.

'No,' I said, feeling a little sick. 'Besides, it starts off with my name.'

Hannah's mouth was a grim line that looked like it had been tattooed on to her face.

'I'm going to kill him. I will fucking kill him.'

Hannah was neither violent nor given to swearing. I had truly never seen her so incensed. She took my hand before speaking, as though physical contact would lessen the pain of her words. 'You do know what this is, Gemma, don't you?'

I shook my head, my eyes beginning to water as her words cut me to the bone.

'It's a "Dear Jane" letter.'

There wasn't a drawer I didn't open or a cupboard I didn't search. I found my missing sunglasses, a ten-pound note in a jacket pocket, and a pair of earrings I didn't even know were lost. But nowhere did I find the letter Hannah was convinced Finn had written and left in my flat for me to find.

'He'll have put it there when you went to stay at your dad's,' she said, convinced in her theory. 'It would have been easy enough for him to let himself in and leave it somewhere prominent.'

But the letter wasn't prominent; it wasn't even hidden. I'd pulled out settee cushions and even looked behind pieces of furniture. But the final version of whatever Finn had been composing on those yellow sheets of paper was nowhere to be found in my home.

'Because he never wrote any such letter. Hannah's wrong,' I said, worryingly talking to myself as I surveyed the mess I'd made, looking for something I'd known I would never find.

Then he must have sent it in the post, Hannah texted back when I messaged her later that day. *What a dick, getting the Royal Mail to do his dirty work*. It was, I realised, just as surprising to read her new-found vocabulary as it was to hear it.

Fortunately, our text exchange had clashed with Milly's lunchtime, so I didn't have to defend Finn yet again or argue that he'd never break up with me in such a cowardly and callous manner.

With a heavy heart, I began the task of tidying up the mess I'd created in my search for the letter. Once done, I surveyed my bedroom, my eyes settling on possibly the only place I'd not thought to check. Resting against the wall, where it was meant to have been easy to grab after the wedding we never had, was the leather holdall that I always used for carry-on luggage.

Would Finn have slipped the letter in there, I wondered? Would it be nestled up against the folder of Australian currency and my passport wallet? It seemed unlikely, but even so I carried the bag to the bed. It was heavy, probably way over the weight limit, but the flight it had been packed for *was* to have been the longest I'd ever taken. My fingers had fastened on the zip tag when suddenly a conversation to which I'd assigned no importance a few weeks ago floated back with perfect clarity.

'Why don't you give me your passport to hang on to, and I'll stick it with mine in my carry-on bag?'

Finn had stopped whatever he'd been doing and turned to me. He seemed to take a long time to answer, and his reply when it came was unexpected.

'No. If you don't mind, I'll just hold on to it.'

'But why? Isn't it easier to keep all our travel stuff for the honeymoon in one place?'

Again, he'd paused before replying, as though he was running through several replies in his head before finding the one he liked best.

'I just prefer to keep hold of my own passport, that's all. It's no big deal.'

He'd kissed me then, and all thoughts of his slightly odd response had melted under the warmth of his touch.

Until now.

Now, I was asking the questions I should have been asking back then. Why was it so important to Finn to keep hold of his passport? It really wasn't rocket science, so why had it taken me so many false starts before I finally landed on the reason? Finn hadn't wanted to surrender his passport, because he needed it to travel.

Just not with me.

It was getting late, and more from habit than hunger, I wandered into the kitchen. But after staring disinterestedly at the contents of my fridge and larder for several minutes, I realised the emptiness inside me had nothing to do with lack of food. Although, if I carried on like this, my wedding dress was going to have to be taken in – assuming I ever had reason to wear it again.

Before closing the cupboard, I plucked Finn's favourite blend of coffee from the top shelf, even though it was far stronger than the one I preferred. I was forever teasing him about being a coffee snob, which he took with unfailing good humour. The aroma of the familiar blend quickly filled the flat, strangely making Finn seem closer and at the same time further away than ever.

10

THE COFFEE SHOP

Four years earlier

There was something about the coffee shop that drew me in. It was more than the enticing lure of roasted beans filtering through the open door. It was more than the decor, although that was certainly appealing, with its exposed brickwork, bleached wooden beams and low-hung copper lamps. It was because it felt comfortable and familiar the moment I walked in, which was weird because it was in a road I'd never set foot on before, in a part of the city I didn't know well.

Perhaps we'd featured it in one of those 'Trendiest Places to Eat' articles in *Glow*, I mused as I took a seat in an empty booth beside the window. I waited for a moment for my eyes to adjust to the change in light, before reaching for the menu. It would probably have been easier to read if I'd taken off my sunglasses, but they were in place to conceal my tired, red-rimmed eyes rather than for UV protection.

I leant back against the padded leather banquette and looked through the coffee shop's plate-glass window. Beyond the row of boutiques, artisan bakeries and bars, a single building dominated the skyline. Squinting slightly, I tried counting the floors, but from that distance it was impossible to make out which was the seventh, much less which was the window beside Hannah's hospital bed.

'What can I get for you?'

I hadn't heard the approach of the barista and jumped nervously. 'Just a latte, please.'

'Can I tempt you with a cupcake to go with that? The banana ones are to die for.' The woman was slight, and her fashionably ripped jeans hugged her slender frame as though they'd been sprayed on. She didn't look like a cupcake eater to me.

Although I shook my head in refusal, my eyes travelled to the cake display cabinet at the counter. A male employee who had his back to us was wiping down surfaces and polishing a gleaming espresso machine that looked more like a modern art installation than a device for making coffee.

'Just the latte, thanks.'

The pretty young barista didn't need to know that I'd eaten nothing that day. She'd have little interest, I was sure, in hearing the reason why. Although, with the hospital so close by, she'd probably served scores of worried friends and family just like me in the past.

I watched her walk back to the counter, heard a low rumble as her colleague said something, and saw how she laughed in reply and leant towards him, laying her hand lightly on his arm. They looked like a couple, I thought absently, or if they weren't, then she'd like them to be. As a journalist, my curiosity would normally have been piqued enough to watch them, observing the ebb and flow of their body language as they slipped past each other behind the counter. But my thoughts were elsewhere. They were winging back in time to earlier that day.

I'd missed the first wince, being too busy rummaging through dresses on the sale rack.

'This would really suit you,' I said, turning around with a vibrant red shift dress in my hand. I held it up for Hannah to consider. Her frown – which I now realised was a spasm of pain – I stupidly mistook as a commentary on my taste.

'Or not,' I said, replacing the dress with a shrug. I'd always hankered after wearing clothes in that particular shade of crimson and kept forgetting that with an ash-blonde tint currently masking my natural auburn, I could probably pull it off.

On impulse, I plucked it from the rail and added it to the others already draped over my arm.

'Aren't you going to try anything on?' I asked, noticing for the first time that Hannah's hands were empty. She was wearing a pair of oversized sunglasses, even though we were inside the shop. Perhaps if she had removed them, I would have seen the concern in her violet eyes or the way they tightened in almost perfect synchronicity with the spasms in her abdomen.

It was warm in the shop, and I naively thought *that* was the reason for the tiny beads of perspiration my friend wiped off her upper lip before replying.

'There's not much point in buying anything if it doesn't have an elasticated waistband. In another three months or so, that's all I'll be able to fit into.'

I grinned excitedly. 'I can't wait.'

'Varicose veins, stretch marks, and a strong possibility of haemorrhoids,' she said, trying to sound wry. But even at that moment, as she tried to ignore the first warning pains, I could tell what she really meant was 'Bring them on'.

Hannah and William had travelled a bumpy road to become a family, and after the tragedy of having a miscarriage the previous year, Hannah was happily embracing even the unlovely aspects of pregnancy.

'Look, it's probably going to be hot and stuffy in the changing room,' I said. 'Why don't you find a seat somewhere while I try these on.'

Her lips formed a tight line as she nodded. I cursed myself afterwards for not realising why.

Fifteen minutes later, I was queued up at the tills with three dresses over my arm. Even in the sale, they were going to make a sizeable dent in my take-home that month, but working at *Glow* had changed the way I dressed. While my new style might have looked great in the mirror, it was considerably less pretty on my bank statements.

Even though I was tall enough to see over the heads of my fellow shoppers, I couldn't spot Hannah anywhere. The seat where I'd left her outside the changing room – the one where women usually parked long-suffering partners – was currently empty. That might have been the moment when I felt the first twinge of anxiety.

I kept scouring the shop for her, before finally asking the woman at the till if she'd seen my friend.

'There *was* a woman sitting by the fitting room,' chirruped her colleague at the next till. 'But she left the shop about ten minutes ago. I heard her say something about needing some air.'

My throat tightened, and suddenly Hannah wasn't the only one requiring that particular commodity. The assistant was folding my purchases with painstaking care, in a Rowan Atkinson, *Love Actually* kind of way, but I was suddenly overcome with the urgent need to leave.

'Just shove them in the bag,' I said, leaning across the counter and doing it myself when she looked back at me with horror. I snatched up the receipt and hurried out of the exclusive boutique and into the hot July morning.

The shop was on a large piazza landscaped with trees and numerous seating areas, and in those first few scary moments I wasn't a capable twenty-nine-year-old woman with a responsible job; I was a child who'd just lost her parent.

And then I saw her. She was in a far corner of the piazza, bent low over a water fountain. I hurried to join her, the heels of my sandals clipping on the cobblestones.

'There you are,' I declared.

Hannah was still bent over the water fountain, her arms braced on either side of the large stainless steel bowl.

'You will never guess how much I've just spent,' I said, revealing the figure that still made me wince.

Hannah lifted her head slowly, and this time there was no mistaking the pained expression that I knew had nothing to do with my extravagance.

'Hannah. What is it? What's wrong?'

'Nothing. I'm just a bit hot and bothered, that's all.'

It *was* unseasonably hot. The barometer had been hitting the mid-thirties for the last week, and in hindsight perhaps it wasn't the weather for traipsing around the shops. But we'd had this date in the diary for weeks now. William was away on an overseas business trip, and I had annual leave to use up, so it had seemed like the perfect time to arrange a girly day out.

'Do you want to go home?' I asked worriedly, already trying to work out how long it would take us to get back to my car, which I'd left at the park-and-ride.

Hannah straightened and shook her head. These days she wore her dark, silky hair in a precision-cut bob that fell back into place like a swinging pendulum.

The tightness around her jaw had slackened enough for her to smile.

'No. We've not even been out for an hour yet. Maybe I'm just hungry,' she said, sounding as though she was trying to convince herself more than me.

'Well, we could go for brunch now if you like, rather than wait.'

Hannah nodded gratefully and I was happy to let myself think everything was okay, even though the arm she slipped through the crook of mine felt as though it was seeking support rather than expressing affection.

We'd made a reservation at a popular hipster eatery, and it should only have taken us ten minutes to walk there from the piazza. But Hannah kept stopping to look in every other shop window, even the boring ones – and I still didn't twig why.

'Mountain climbing?' I laughed as she stared intently at an outdoor activity display. 'I don't think you and your bump are going to be doing much of that in the foreseeable future,' I joked.

Hannah's free hand came down and cradled the only just visible swell of her stomach. She kept her hand there, as though in comfort, as we walked the rest of the way to the restaurant, and I never even thought to question it.

'Outside, but definitely in the shade,' Hannah said decisively when the waiter asked us where we'd like to sit.

I stole several surreptitious glances at her as we were led to a table beneath the boughs of a flowering tree.

As though we'd just crossed the Sahara, Hannah drank greedily from the glass of iced water placed before her.

'Hannah. Something *is* wrong. I can see it is.'

She shook her head, still trying to deny what her body must surely have been screaming at her in no uncertain terms.

It was only when I reluctantly picked up the menu and began to run my eye down the brunch choices that Hannah reached across the table and grasped my wrist in a grip tight enough to leave white fingertip imprints on my skin.

'I think it's the baby,' she said in a frightened whisper.

The blood drained from my face in panic. If there was a contest to see which of us was the paler right then, it would have been a close call.

I pulled my phone from my bag.

'What are you doing?'

'I'm calling for an ambulance.'

The grip on my wrist tightened further, like a manacle of torture.

'No,' she hissed. 'No ambulance. Just get us a cab and get me to the hospital.'

Within minutes I was helping her into the back seat of a taxi. I directed the driver to take us to the nearest hospital, but Hannah once again overrode me. 'No. I want to go to St Thomas's. That's where the consultant I'm under is based.'

'Hannah, that's miles from here. We'd have to drive past God only knows how many hospitals to get there.'

'Please, Gemma,' Hannah pleaded. 'They have all my

medical notes and details about what happened last time. Please take me there.' There were tears on both of our cheeks as I relayed her instructions to the cab driver.

The clanging of the bell above the door brought me abruptly back to the present. Behind the counter, the female barista's attention had been claimed by a sudden influx of customers grabbing takeaways for their journey home. They were dressed in hospital tunics, and it was hard to reconcile the laughing, rumbustious group with the dedicated professionals who were right now working to save Hannah's baby.

The barista called out something to her co-worker and he responded with a nod, moving back to the espresso machine as he began to fill my order. I switched my gaze from the medics and watched as the man poured a shot of espresso into an oversized cup and then, with an expert flourish, swirled foaming milk on to it from a height.

As fascinating as it was to observe, it wasn't only his coffee-making skills that had snagged my attention. With Hannah lying in hospital less than half a mile away, it seemed inappropriate to have noticed the breadth of the man's shoulders or the way his thin grey T-shirt had been washed so many times, it clung to every muscle on his back as he moved. But it was only when he reached over to grab something to his right that a slumbering memory began to stir. There was something about the way the overhead lights had caught glints of copper in his dark brown hair that reminded me of something – or someone.

He straightened up as the girl behind the counter said

something and nodded in my direction. Inexplicably, my heart started to beat super-fast. The man still hadn't turned around, so I'd yet to see his face, but there was something about the way he stood and the way he walked that was slowly turning a key in a lock. For one crazy moment, I wondered if I had time to dash from the coffee shop before he turned around. It was ridiculous, because of course it couldn't be him. It couldn't be the man who'd once had a curious habit of showing up in places where I least expected to find him. That man had been a journalist, not a barista.

I eyed the distance between my seat and the door, like a shoplifter who was about to get caught. It wouldn't be him. But then he picked up a tray and pivoted away from the coffee machine, stepping out from behind the counter and walking towards me. It was Finn Douglas.

He seemed taller than I remembered, but perhaps that was because I was currently doing my best to shrink into invisibility in the leather upholstery of the booth.

'Your latte,' he said with a smile that thankfully seemed to hold no recognition. He set the full-to-the-brim cup before me, without spilling a single drop, something I imagined I was unlikely to achieve when drinking it.

'And a cupcake,' he added, placing a plate before me.

'Oh, I didn't—' I began, before he cut me off with the same dazzling smile I could remember him using so effectively three years ago.

'The cupcake's on the house. Tasha suggested it.'

I looked beyond him to the girl with the wavy blonde hair, who glanced up from the till she was operating and flashed a toothpaste-ad-worthy grin my way. I tried to remember the correct facial muscles required to return it.

Finn's eyes were on my face, but there was still no flicker of recognition within them. My hair was a completely different shade and style from when we'd met, and half of my face was currently hidden behind darkly tinted sunglasses. I certainly hadn't wanted him to recognise me, so the flash of irritation I felt when he failed to do so was totally irrational.

'That was kind of her,' I said, my voice not quite as steady as I would have liked. I wasn't usually so emotional, but it had been quite a day, and a random act of kindness from a stranger could easily have become my kryptonite. I drew the plate closer, eyeing the cupcake as though it was an eating challenge on *I'm a Celebrity*.

'Well, I'll leave you to enjoy your coffee in peace.' Finn straightened and yet still made no move to walk away. I could feel his eyes searching my face. Thank God I'd put on the sunglasses, I thought, confident he'd tried but failed to place me. He was probably sifting through a list of conquests from his past, trying to remember if I'd ever been one of them.

Just go back to the counter, I silently telegraphed, dropping my eyes to my coffee and the frothy heart shape he'd created in the foam. I picked up a spoon and stirred it vigorously away.

Finn continued to linger, clearly puzzled. 'Well, I'll be going then,' he said, still not moving. Perhaps he was waiting for me to tell him not to.

'Okay,' I said with relief.

Finally, he turned and began walking away, but he'd taken no more than four steps when he suddenly froze. Perhaps he'd heard something in the timbre of my voice that made him pause, for he tilted his head to one side in an oddly avian way. Very slowly, he turned back around with a look of triumph on his face, which was probably at odds with the one of dismay on mine.

'It's Jenna, isn't it?'

Typical. Of course he'd misremember my name.

'Gemma,' I corrected, my voice tight for reasons I would explore another time.

'Sorry. Yes, of course,' he said, covering the distance between us in a couple of strides. 'How the hell are you?'

I'm not sure which of us was more shocked when my response to that perfectly innocent question was to burst into extremely noisy tears.

'That was incredibly embarrassing. I'm so sorry,' I said as I reached for yet another serviette from the pile Finn had placed in front of me to wipe away my tears. Half the stack was already gone.

'Not at all,' he said, replacing my now cold latte with a fresh one. 'Happens all the time. Although usually it's when customers get the bill.'

I got closer to a laugh than I thought I'd be able to.

Finn had surprised me. I had no idea how most people would have reacted to such an outburst, but his response had been totally unexpected. He'd stalled Tasha's approach with a decisive shake of his head and then dropped into the seat in front of me, his broad-shouldered silhouette effectively shielding me from the remaining customers in the coffee shop.

The tears seemed to come from a bottomless well, and the strength I'd had to summon up to support Hannah washed away like a dam built of matchsticks. By the time the sobs had become hitching, hiccupping gasps, the coffee shop had emptied.

'I'm sorry. I'm not very good for your trade,' I said when I finally looked up and noticed the deserted shop. The lights over the counter had been switched off, and Finn's co-worker Tasha was nowhere to be seen. With a start of surprise, I saw too that the sign on the door had been flipped to 'Closed'.

'Won't the owner be annoyed that you've shut early?' I asked, finally gaining enough motor control to risk lifting the coffee to my lips without spilling it.

'Well, he *is* a grumpy old sod, but I think it'll be all right,' Finn replied, reaching for his own coffee.

'*You?* You own this place? You don't just work here?'

There was admiration in Finn's smile, and even though he represented everything I knew I disliked in a man, something peculiar happened in the region of my stomach.

'I'd forgotten how sharp you are. Not much gets past you, does it?'

To be perfectly honest, that he'd managed to place me at all was a complete surprise.

'I'm amazed you remembered me,' I said, cringing a little because that sounded horribly like I was fishing for compliments. Just to make sure he knew there was nothing remotely flirtatious going on, I reached up and removed my sunglasses. There are women who cry prettily, whose eyes don't disappear into red, puffy pockets of flesh when they're upset. But I'm not one of them.

'It's hard to forget someone who takes such an instant and visceral dislike to you,' Finn said smoothly. 'I was enormously impressed. Most people need much longer to decide I'm a complete dick. But you got there almost immediately. You definitely left an impression, *Jenny*.'

'Gemma,' I said with a flicker of a smile, because this time I knew the slip had been deliberate.

The sun was slowly shifting, casting elongated shadows on the pavement beyond the window. I checked my watch. The ward sister had politely suggested that while Hannah was undergoing the various tests she needed, I might like to take a walk for an hour or two. As a journalist, I'd been diplomatically ejected from enough places to know when I was being booted out. And yet I'd resisted leaving Hannah alone, especially as William still hadn't returned any of the urgent messages I'd left for him.

'I'll be fine,' Hannah had said, which would have been easier to believe if her complexion hadn't been the exact same shade as the pillow beneath her head.

'Come back in two hours,' the sister had advised, her hand pressed gently against the small of my back. With the skill of a nightclub bouncer, she steered me away from Hannah's bed.

'I'll reach William,' I promised my friend as I walked with reluctance towards the exit.

'And did you?' asked Finn now. I had no idea how he'd managed to extract the entire story of the day's events from me so easily. Presumably there was still more journalist than barista running through his veins. Either that or I was so overwrought, it had taken only the slightest glimmer of interest to get me to spill my tale to a total stranger. Which, in effect, was what Finn was. I mean, it wasn't as though I knew the man. And the history we did have wasn't exactly comfortable. *And let's not forget that what you did know of him, you didn't particularly like*, Past Me took pains to add as a reminder.

My phone pinged and I lurched towards it, my fingers clumsy as I hurriedly opened the message.

'William's at the airport,' I said, a small, shaky smile – the first I'd allowed myself in hours – curving my lips.

'That's fantastic news,' Finn said, and although he didn't know Hannah and William from Adam, he did sound genuinely delighted. 'What time will he get here?'

I scrolled back through the message. 'His plane doesn't land until nine, so I suppose the earliest he'll be at the hospital will be ten thirty.'

I sighed.

'Hey, but at least he's on his way,' Finn said.

I nodded, still finding it hard to reconcile Mr Glass Half Full with the man I'd quietly disliked for years. Either I'd read him wrong when we first met or he really had changed out of all recognition.

I glanced again at my watch. 'I should get back to Hannah and let her know the good news,' I said. I hadn't been away for as long as the hospital had asked, but every minute that I wasn't with her felt like an act of betrayal.

'Feel free to stay here for as long as you want. I'm not chucking you out.'

The offer produced my second smile, this one less of a surprise to me than the first. I glanced beyond Finn towards the display of confectionery at the counter. 'Actually, if they're not already spoken for, could I buy the rest of those cupcakes from you? I'd like to take something back for the staff on the ward, as a thank you.'

'Of course,' Finn replied easily. 'I'll box them up for you.'

And then in a move that made my breath catch oddly at the back of my throat, he reached across the table and patted my hand. It was an innocent gesture, companionable rather than intimate, but when Tasha unexpectedly emerged from the back office, I snatched my hand back as though it had ventured too close to a flame. My cheeks felt warm as I met the gaze of Finn's colleague, slash employee, slash something else that was really none of my business.

'There's a phone call for you,' she told him, her eyes dropping for just a moment to the tabletop. She'd surprised me on two counts: by still being here, and by looking less than pleased about Finn's hand resting briefly on mine.

'Can you take a message?' he asked.

She shook her head, her blonde pony swishing like the tail of an agitated palomino.

'You should probably take it. It's the solicitors.'

Finn got to his feet with a degree of urgency I'd not seen in him before. 'Sorry, this shouldn't take long.'

He paused for a moment to say something to Tasha, in a voice too low for me to catch, as he squeezed past her. She glanced my way and nodded.

I waited until Finn had disappeared into the back room and then quickly gathered up my belongings. I was pretty intuitive when it came to reading atmospheres, and it suddenly felt as though I was the last guest at the party and had embarrassingly outstayed my welcome.

I pulled out my purse as I approached the counter, where Tasha was busily transferring the entire tray of cupcakes into an enormous cardboard box.

'Are you leaving right now?'

From somewhere unseen I could hear the deep rumble of Finn's voice on the phone. 'Yes. I want to get back to my friend. She's been admitted to St Thomas's.'

With practised speed, Tasha flipped the box lid shut and slid it across the counter towards me.

'How much do I owe you for the coffee and the cakes?'

'Finn said there's no charge.'

My mouth dropped open in a small O of surprise. 'No, really, I'd like to pay for them.' I wasn't sure why it suddenly felt so important not to be beholden to this man, I just knew that it did.

'He's the boss. You'll have to argue it out with him.'

I glanced back towards the doorway through which Finn had disappeared and then out through the window towards the hospital. It was rude to leave without at least thanking him in person for his generosity, but Hannah would be back from her tests soon and I couldn't bear the thought of her facing the possibility of bad news without someone who loved her beside her. In a battle of loyalties, there was really no contest.

'Could you please thank him for me. For everything,' I said, rearranging my shopping bags so I could hold the box of cakes more securely in my arms.

Tasha crossed to unlock the door, and I stepped back outside into the still-warm afternoon, as though emerging from a particularly surreal dream.

'Good luck,' Tasha said as she pushed the door shut behind me. It was a curious thing to say, but I took it at face value and assumed she was referring to Hannah. It was only later that I wondered if she'd actually meant something else entirely.

11

The Ride Home

Four years earlier

William arrived on the ward in a cacophony of pounding feet and rumbling suitcase wheels. He wove past anyone in his path, like an American footballer on the way to a touchdown. *This is what love looks like*, I thought, as his face transformed when he spotted Hannah in her hospital bed. I'd never had that; I'd never even come close. I wanted someone who saw me and only me; who didn't scan every room we entered looking for a newer, shinier, prettier upgrade, like the men I'd dated in the past. My track record of picking the wrong guy – the one *guaranteed* to break my heart – was painfully impressive. But this was what I wanted. I wanted a partner who'd run like a man possessed to reach my side.

Hannah, who'd been drifting into sleep, pinged instantly awake at the sound of her husband's voice. I slipped from my chair beside her bed, giving him free access to her arms, which were already outstretched towards him.

'I got here as fast as I could,' he cried, his voice breaking as tears of relief began to trickle down his cheeks. I'd never seen William cry before, and I was so moved, it started me off again. Hannah joined in, for good measure.

'How are you? How is… everything?' he asked on a terrified whisper, his eyes going to Hannah's stomach. Beneath the bunched hospital blankets, it was impossible to detect if their hopes were still intact.

'Everything is still okay, for now,' Hannah said, her face awash with tears and a smile.

William's knees buckled, and he sort of folded into the chair I'd just vacated. He laid his head on Hannah's bed, and her hand – the one without the drip attached to it – gently stroked his hair. William looked as though he was praying, and perhaps he was.

'They say I'll have to stay on bed rest for a while.'

'I don't care if it's for the next six months,' William declared, his words muffled, spoken as they were against Hannah's abdomen. 'Just as long as you're okay.' His hand came up to run lovingly over her tiny baby bump. 'Both of you.'

I suddenly felt like an intruder, peeking through a curtain I had no business parting. This was their time, and I wasn't needed there any more.

'Erm, guys, I'm pretty sure they'll only allow you to have one emergency after-hours visitor, so I'm going to make tracks now and leave you in peace.'

They turned towards me, wearing matching expressions of gratitude. I dismissed their chorus of thank yous as totally unnecessary.

'You were here for me when I needed you, Gemma,' said Hannah as I enfolded her in my arms and hugged her carefully, as though she were made from glass. She hugged me back, hard, as though to prove that she wasn't.

'There are no words for what you've done today,' she whispered against my shoulder. 'You've been a rock, and I truly don't think I'd have got through any of this without you.'

'Phwah,' I replied, somewhat inarticulately for a woman who used words to earn her living. 'It's no more than you'd have done for me. It's what friends do. I know you'd be there for me in a heartbeat if I needed you.'

'You can count on it,' Hannah said.

I crept as silently as I could through the quiet ward, mindful that the darkened bays meant most of the patients were already asleep. I paused to check the time on the clock beside the nurses' station, smiling when I saw that the box that had once held almost two dozen cupcakes now contained just a scattering of crumbs. At almost eleven o'clock, it was much later than I'd thought. I had no idea what time the last park-and-ride bus ran, but I was pretty sure it would have left several hours ago.

The deserted hospital corridors felt eerie as I followed signs for the lifts that would take me back down to the main foyer. I travelled down to ground level with an elderly gentleman dressed in a hospital gown that gaped revealingly at the back. In his hand was a packet of cigarettes, which he politely proffered my way.

'No, thank you,' I said, trying to avert my gaze from the mirrored walls of the lift, which unfortunately revealed everything he'd been trying to conceal by keeping his back to the wall.

'After you,' he said chivalrously when the carriage eventually pinged to announce we were on the ground floor. I smiled and strode swiftly ahead.

The foyer felt totally different to how it had done several hours earlier, when I'd returned from the coffee shop. All the merchandising outlets were now closed, their entrances secured behind metal grids and shutters. There was no longer a queue by the vending machine, nor at the enquiry desk. Even the chairs in the waiting area were empty. Or so I thought, until I got closer. There was one in use, but its occupant was partially hidden behind a huge yucca plant. All I could see were two extremely long legs clad in faded denim, and a pair of slightly scuffed boots.

The owner of the legs courteously drew them in as I approached, and I murmured a word of thanks without looking, until a voice I instantly recognised stopped me in my tracks.

'Hello.'

I halted so abruptly, my lift companion in the ill-fitting hospital gown almost collided with me. He slipped past me and went through the revolving doors, his gown lifting in the evening breeze. But my attention wasn't on the inadvertently mooning patient; it was on the man who had been waiting in the hospital foyer. Waiting for me.

'Finn,' I said, turning his name into a cry of surprise.

'Jemima,' he said, getting to his feet. I was too shocked at seeing him there to play along with his running gag this time.

'What on earth are you doing here?'

Finn Douglas was full of surprises, and his reply was typically not the one I was expecting.

'You didn't pay for the cakes.'

The blush ignited my cheeks like a flash fire. 'Oh, God. I'm so sorry,' I began, already scrabbling in my bag for my purse. 'There must have been a misunderstanding. Tasha said—'

I broke off as his hand covered mine and gently pushed my purse back into my bag.

'I'm joking,' he said, his eyes twinkling with devilment.

'I... oh, I thought...' I shook my head, indignant and also more than a little embarrassed. 'That wasn't very nice of you.'

His face softened then, and devilment changed to remorse. 'I'm sorry. I was just trying to make you laugh.'

'Ha ha,' I said drily, taking a step towards the spinning doors that were beckoning me to leave.

Finn reached down and took the large glossy carrier bag from my hand; within it were the dresses I'd bought what felt like weeks earlier.

'What are you doing?'

'Carrying your shopping for you,' he said, falling into step beside me.

'No. I mean, what are you doing *here*? At the hospital. At this time of night.'

'I'm guessing investigative journalism wasn't ever your specialism, Gina,' Finn said smoothly, inserting a ticket into the parking machine. I saw from the amount displayed on the screen that he'd been at the hospital for more than two hours. It silenced my snarky reply.

'You've been waiting a long time for me.'

There was a seriousness in his eyes that even the low-level lighting couldn't conceal.

'I really have,' he said solemnly.

I was still attempting to decipher his meaning when he took the mood and flipped it. 'Besides, you slipped out of the coffee shop without saying goodbye.'

I was glad the hospital grounds were dark enough to conceal my blush. 'I'm sorry about that. I know it was rude of me, but I was anxious to get back to Hannah.'

Finn's expression turned serious once more. 'I'm sorry, I should have asked that first: how is your friend doing?'

'I think she and the baby are going to be fine,' I said, feeling as though a heavy weight I hadn't even known I was carrying was suddenly lifting from my shoulders.

'Well, that's terrific news,' he replied with a grin. Something happened to Finn's face when he smiled, or maybe it just happened to the people around him. Either way, it ignited a sensation I'd never experienced before. It made me inexplicably want to run both to and away from him.

His fingers lightly touched my elbow, guiding me towards a pathway that I could already see would take us to the multi-storey car park. 'I remembered you saying earlier that you'd left your car at the park-and-ride, so I thought you might like a lift back to it.'

'That's really kind of you, but I can just as easily call an Uber.'

Finn came to a stop, his face half hidden in the shadows thrown by the boughs of a tree. 'I'm sorry. I'm an idiot. I shouldn't have just assumed you'd be happy to get into a car with someone you scarcely know. The last thing I want to do is make you feel uncomfortable.'

He did. For a great many reasons. But none of them were the ones he was worrying about. He'd probably have been truly shocked to know that far from being someone I hardly remembered, he'd actually lived on in my memory for a very long time.

'No, it's not that at all,' I said, and even to my own ears I could hear how flustered I sounded. 'I just don't want to take you out of your way this late at night.'

'You don't know that it will,' he argued reasonably.

He was right. I had no idea where he lived. Or anything else about him, come to that. And yet he felt so much more than a stranger to me.

'Why don't we just call this part of the service the coffee shop extends to all its best customers?'

I laughed then, as with unspoken agreement we headed into the shadowy car park. 'Except that I didn't *pay* for the cakes, remember?'

'Well then, you can buy our first dinner together,' he said easily, as he pointed his key fob into the car park and a dark-coloured sedan squeaked back at him. He made it sound like a foregone conclusion that we'd share a meal at some point in the future, but I couldn't see that happening somehow.

Even so, my pulse was skipping along faster than usual as I buckled myself into the passenger seat of his car. This man was no stranger; I knew his name, I knew where he worked, and I'd already told Hannah that I'd run into him that afternoon. All things considered, accepting a lift home with Finn was a fairly low-risk activity. So why did it feel as though I was doing something incredibly dangerous?

Fortunately, journalists aren't known for long or awkward silences, and with two of us in the car it was inevitable that before long we'd both come out with questions blazing.

'So how have things worked out for you at *Glow* magazine?'

'What prompted your change of career?'

We laughed as our questions collided.

'You first,' Finn said, his eyes on the road as he moved into a stream of fast-flowing traffic.

'What makes you think I got the job or that I still work there?'

Finn didn't strike me as the type who was easily fazed, but he looked momentarily thrown by my reply. I studied his profile and swear I caught the moment when the lie he was going to tell me was suddenly discarded.

'I've read a few of your pieces over the years. You're good.'

I fidgeted in the passenger seat. I was normally better at accepting compliments, at least those about my work, but his praise made me uncomfortable.

'I wouldn't have had the job at all if you hadn't walked away from it. Why *did* you do that, anyway?'

'Hey, I thought I was the one asking the questions first.'

I said nothing, knowing from experience that was the surest way to get someone to open up. Finn really ought to have remembered that from his previous career.

'I have no idea what you're talking about,' he said eventually. 'The job at *Glow* was never mine.'

I didn't believe him. Plus it ruined a secret narrative I'd happily indulged for years. Whenever I was overwhelmed by work or crippling deadlines, I'd silently curse him for having dropped this job in my lap. *Boy, you sure knew what you were doing, walking away from this one, didn't you?* I'd say to the Finn who lived in my head, who was a far more convivial individual than the one I'd actually met. And conversely, when the job was going well and some praise or plaudit had come my way, I'd silently ask if *he* could have done it so well. It was a weird relationship to have with someone I didn't even know, but unlike our real-life encounters, in those conversations I always managed to get the last word.

I looked at him now, his handsome profile illuminated by the lights of the oncoming cars, and knew there was no way I would ever tell him how he'd lived on in my head long after the expiry date for our brief encounter had passed.

I chatted about my job for a while, unconsciously slipping into a speech I'd given several times to groups of university students or at school career days. It freed my thoughts and allowed them to wander. Finn was an enigma; that was where my fascination with him began and ended, or so I tried to convince myself. It was only natural for my curiosity to be piqued by a man who'd oddly never disappeared from my thoughts the way he should have done. For years I'd thought it was because he'd been so downright annoying – and he had been. But I was honest enough to admit now that it might have been something more than that.

Being intrigued by his massive career U-turn didn't explain the way my eyes kept straying to his hands, which were resting lightly on the steering wheel. Nor how curiously safe I felt with him. Even a dangerous manoeuvre from a taxi, which would have earned a blast on the horn from anyone else, hadn't riled him. Finn drove with a relaxed, confident competence that I suspected he applied to everything he did. He was probably an excellent kisser. The observation escaped from a deep well of totally inappropriate thoughts and shocked me so much, I completely forgot what I'd been saying and began stammering like an idiot. Desperately hoping that telepathy wasn't something else he was good at, I hastily turned the questions back his way.

'My turn now. Why a coffee shop?'

'Why not?'

I digested that one for a moment or two. 'It just seems like a million miles away from working in journalism.'

Something flickered in Finn's eyes for a moment. I caught it briefly in the twin headlights of a lorry, but it was gone before I could properly identify it. 'Maybe that was the idea,' he said. And then with a skill I envied, he effortlessly redirected our conversation down a completely different path.

For years I'd imagined Finn was the kind of man who'd like nothing better than to talk about himself. But that clearly wasn't true. It made me wonder what else about him I'd got wrong.

We wove through the still surprisingly heavy traffic while a playlist from Finn's phone provided a quiet backdrop to our conversation. His musical tastes were eclectic, ranging from soft rock and country to classic old-school jazz. The picture of him I was trying to compile in my head kept shifting, like smoke caught in a breeze. Finn was a conundrum, and as much as I didn't want to be, I was intrigued.

When I spotted a signpost up ahead for the park-and-ride exit, my knee-jerk reaction of disappointment surprised me. I wasn't ready for the night to end yet. But when we sailed straight past the slip road, I sat bolt upright in my seat.

'You've just missed the turn-off.'

Nobody likes a back-seat driver, but Finn responded with a relaxed smile. 'It occurred to me that you must be feeling hungry,' he said. 'I bet you've not eaten a thing since that cupcake this afternoon.'

He was absolutely right, I hadn't, but I immediately denied it. 'Actually, that's where you're wrong. I grabbed something earlier from the hospital cafe,' I lied.

'Oh, okay.' He flicked on his indicator and changed lanes. I glanced up ahead and saw the familiar yellow logo of a well-known burger chain. 'Well, do you mind if we stop here for a moment so I can grab something, because *I'm* absolutely starving.'

'I wouldn't have figured you for a dirty burger kind of guy.'

Finn pulled into the queue for the drive-in and swivelled in his seat towards me.

'Why's that?'

I could feel the flush creeping up from my throat. I'd blushed more in his presence than I'd done with anyone else I'd ever met. It was almost as though I was pheromonally allergic to him.

'You seem more like a sushi or steak tartare kind of person.'

He chewed over my words for a moment. 'It's interesting that you imagine my preferred choice of food is raw. I wonder if that means you think of me as some sort of barbaric caveman.'

'I don't think of you at all,' I said, knowing instantly that neither of us believed that particular lie for a single second.

Fortunately, my awkward interrogation was brought to a halt as a disembodied voice from a crackly speaker asked for our order. Finn hadn't been kidding about his love of fast food. He ordered everything designed to make his arteries regret his choices in about thirty years' time.

'Are you sure you don't want anything?' he asked solicitously.

The 'No, thank you' was ready and waiting on my lips

when the smell of fried onions and greasy burger wafted in through his open window. My stomach growled, and not in a ladylike way but with the ferocity of a rabid dog.

'Make that two of everything,' I told the speaker beside his window. I'm surprised the woman taking our order managed to hear me above the sound of Finn's laughter.

I got the last laugh though – or at least I thought I did – a few minutes later, for while Finn was reaching to take our bags of food, I leant across him to swipe my debit card on the payment screen.

He made a sound of protest, and I looked up, shocked to find his face so close to mine. 'You did say I should buy dinner,' I reminded him, which had sounded much sassier when I'd been silently practising it while we waited for our meals. What I'd failed to factor in was that leaning so close to his body would cause a lot of me to brush against him. The hairs on my bare arm stood to attention as they grazed the skin of his. How could I have known how easily I'd be derailed by the warm smell of him, mixed with the lingering aroma of whatever he'd used in the shower that morning?

My body was reacting dramatically to the nearness of him. *Hello*, it murmured, waking sleepily from what had admittedly been a long, dry spell. I could practically see it lazily stretching as it emerged from its prolonged slumber. There'd be no getting it back to sleep now.

For the sake of my dignity and my pale, cream-coloured top, I was glad when Finn suggested parking up to eat our takeaways. I wasn't sure what would have mortified me more, spilling dollops of ketchup down myself or dropping them all over his upholstery. Finn struck me as the kind of man who thought a lot of his car.

The long, hot days were slow to cool, so when Finn suggested pulling away from the drive-through and sitting on a grassy slope on the side of the road to eat, I happily agreed. Finn had been wrong about one thing: I wasn't just hungry, I was absolutely ravenous, and while we jumped easily from topic to topic, I somehow managed to demolish every last morsel of food. He even caught me looking hopefully in the corners of the empty bag for any straggling fries. He grinned at that and offered me his final few. It wasn't quite the same as giving me the last Rolo in the packet, but it was close enough for me.

I had no idea it was so late until I heard the chimes of a distant church clock striking midnight, the sound travelling easily over the moonlit open fields.

'It's late,' Finn said, getting to his feet and offering me his hand. The slope was steep and I got up too quickly, forcing him to take a tighter hold on me to stop us both from toppling backwards. The clock was still chiming, I could hear it, but it seemed to be happening in another dimension, because the one I'd slipped into contained no one but Finn and me. The moonlight was bright enough for me to see from the look in his eyes that he felt it too. I could feel the pounding of his heart against my own, their tempos perfectly in sync.

I looked up. Even though we probably both smelt of fast food, I had never wanted someone to kiss me as much as I did right then, and for a very long moment it seemed as though he was going to. My disappointment when he finally took a step back and widened the gap between us felt truly crushing.

'I should get you back to your car,' he said, his voice huskier than it had been just moments before. 'You must be exhausted. You've had a pretty full-on day.'

We were only a few minutes' drive from the park-and-ride depot, and although I tried out several sentences in my head to recapture our earlier banter, none of them made it past my lips. It was only when we pulled up beside my car that the inexplicable frisson between us sparked back into life.

'Does it sound totally crazy to say how much I've enjoyed myself this evening?' Finn asked.

I shook my head, my voice momentarily AWOL.

'Can we do this again?' he asked, and although I couldn't see very well in the dark, I thought I'd glimpsed a slightly worried expression on his face.

I immediately forgot every article I'd ever read – or written, come to that – about not appearing too keen too soon.

'I'd like that. I'd like that a lot.'

'Tomorrow?' said Finn, smiling at my reply.

A little late, I decided a degree of nonchalance might be in order. 'Umm... maybe *not* tomorrow. I don't know if Hannah will still be in hospital and...' I trailed away, not really sure where I was going with that thought.

There was real disappointment in his voice. 'I'm sorry, but tomorrow is the only day I can do.'

'Okay. Tomorrow it is,' I said, ignoring the imagined protesting screams of a thousand feminists.

Finn climbed out of the driver's seat and waited until I was settled in my own car. I'd lingered long enough while getting in and yet he still hadn't kissed me. *But he will tomorrow*, a voice in my head whispered. Despite the warmth of the night, I shivered.

'I'll pick you up tomorrow,' he promised, taking a step back from my car window with what I told myself was reluctance.

'It's a date,' I said, managing to squeeze in one last blush before we went our separate ways.

He couldn't have seen in the dark, and yet I swear he knew. His voice was warm as he replied.

'It is.'

12

THE DATE

Four years earlier

Hannah foraged eagerly in the carrier bag I'd set down on her hospital bed, like a child with a Christmas stocking. With a triumphant flourish, she plucked out a smoked salmon sandwich and then a tub of her favourite moisturiser.

'You know me so well,' she said gratefully, already ripping the cellophane from the sandwich. 'The toiletry bag William brought in from home this morning contained a box of ancient hair dye and some verruca-removal cream.'

I laughed with relief at hearing my friend sound so much more like herself than she'd done just twenty-four hours earlier.

'I wasn't sure if you'd make the afternoon visiting session. I thought you might come tonight,' Hannah observed, sinking her teeth into the sandwich.

I absently twisted a grape off the obligatory bunch I'd brought in and popped it in my mouth, buying myself a moment or two of thinking time. 'I thought you and William might like to have some alone time this evening,' I said disingenuously.

Hannah chewed rapidly, her BFF sixth sense already on high alert. If she'd had antennas, they'd have been twitching like crazy. 'Gemma Fletcher…' she began, setting down the rest of the sandwich. The use of my full name and the abandonment of her favourite treat from Pret told me there would be no escaping the interrogation. 'Is there something you're not telling me here?'

I had no idea how Hannah unfailingly saw through my smokescreens. It was like a superpower. My eyes dropped to the Boots carrier bag on the bed, filled with items I'd sourced on a shopping trip that morning. Everything I'd bought was for her, except the tube of bright red lipstick and the bottle of expensive perfume sitting at the bottom of my handbag. They were for me.

Hannah cleared her throat meaningfully and narrowed her eyes, causing her eyebrows to join in a single line that brooked no nonsense.

I caved so easily, it was almost embarrassing. 'Okay. I might have plans for this evening,' I said. The eyebrows rose, demanding more information. 'All right, if you must know, I have a date. I'm going out with Finn Douglas.'

'I knew it!' Hannah declared in triumph, thumping the mattress with her fist before picking up the sandwich again. 'I absolutely knew this would happen.'

'What? When exactly did you know? Because *I* didn't even know until last night.'

Hannah shook her head impatiently. 'I knew it years ago, when the two of you first met. I knew then that it was only the first chapter of your story together.'

'Oh, you did, did you?' I said, hoping to sound sceptical when what I really felt was intrigued.

'No one takes that much of an instant dislike to a total stranger without there being more to it.'

Part of me wanted to buy into Hannah's fairy-tale-romance story, but it was so full of holes, it was practically a sieve.

'You like him, don't you?' Hannah pushed, her voice full of glee now that I'd finally relented and given her a blow-by-blow account of everything that had happened after I'd left the hospital the night before.

'He's okay,' I said with a feigned nonchalance that did not cover the flotilla of butterflies that kept taking off and landing in my stomach whenever I thought of the evening ahead. 'He might not be as bad as I first thought,' I added, hoping to put her off the trail, but she was part best friend and part bloodhound.

'I can see exactly how this is going to end,' she said delightedly, actually clapping her hands in glee in a way I'd always thought no one ever did in real life.

Except she couldn't know, of course. Not really. How could anyone?

He brought me flowers. It was the first surprise in an evening that turned out to be full of them.

I'd been lurking in my hallway, never straying too far from the doorbell intercom, and yet I still jumped when the buzzer sounded beside me.

'Hi. I'm here. Can I come up?'

I gulped, which I hoped the occasionally dodgy intercom system hadn't picked up. My usually tidy flat looked as though it had been burgled or struck by a twister. I'd left quite a trail of devastation in my attempt to be ready on time. Thankfully, the worst of the mess was confined to my bedroom, and Finn certainly wasn't going to be invited in there – well, not tonight, at least. The thought brought a flush to my cheeks that I didn't even bother trying to fan away.

'Sure, come on up. I'm on the fifth floor.'

The lift was always slow to respond to a summons, and for once I was grateful as I studied my reflection one last time in the hallway mirror. My hair had gone better than I could have hoped. I'd styled it in soft, tousled curls, which was a nice contrast to the simple lines of my new red shift dress. Even after eighteen months, it still occasionally took me by surprise when I saw a blonde-haired me staring back from the looking glass. Did Finn even remember I'd been a redhead when we'd met years ago or wasn't that the kind of thing men noticed?

He'd probably be much more likely to have spotted if you'd had a boob job, a voice in my head couldn't resist pointing out. I scowled, because that wasn't entirely fair. I'd dated my share of men who would happily conduct an entire conversation with my cleavage, but my instincts told me that the man currently travelling up to my floor to take me out for dinner wasn't like that.

At least, I assumed taking me for dinner was the plan. Finn had been intentionally vague in the messages we'd exchanged during the day.

Pick you up at 5.30? I know it's early, but we've got a bit of a drive.

Intriguing. Can I ask where we're going?

No. It's a surprise.

I could hear the sound of approaching footsteps on the other side of my front door. I did one last quick check in the mirror to make sure the glossy bright red lipstick hadn't strayed to my teeth. Sunlight from the adjacent window glinted off the glass and caught the silver hoops at my ears. They were the only jewellery I was wearing. Anything else would have detracted from the dress, whose scooped neckline showed off the column of my throat and sat just below my collarbones. In contrast, the back of the dress was a little more risqué, with a deep, plunging V that ended just millimetres above my bra strap.

I grinned at my reflection, acknowledging that I was more excited about the evening ahead than I'd been about anything in a very long time.

It was neither cool nor sophisticated to feel the breath catch in my throat when I opened the front door and saw Finn leaning casually against the frame. In the summer the public areas of my building were frequently as hot as a greenhouse, so he'd slipped off the jacket of his light grey suit and it now hung over his shoulder, swinging from one finger by a loop. He looked like an advert for something very masculine and expensive. My stomach gave a lurch, probably colliding with several other internal organs that I imagined were twisting and turning inside me. Never, ever had I reacted in such a visceral, physical way to a man. It was as if my self-control was already slipping away. There was a very real possibility that whatever he asked me to do, I'd agree to without stopping to think. And that wasn't like me at all.

With no trace of awkwardness, which probably meant he'd done this many times before, Finn passed me the bunch of flowers he'd been holding in his free hand. They were a riot of reds and golds and didn't look like the kind you picked up as an afterthought from a petrol station forecourt or at the checkout of a supermarket. I couldn't remember the last time anyone had brought me flowers on a first date, and I dipped my face into the blooms, inhaling their sweet fragrance.

'They're gorgeous, Finn. Thank you.'

His smile was devastating and did little to stop my heartbeat from reading like a seismograph during an earthquake.

'I'll just pop them in some water,' I said, leaving him in the hallway as I disappeared into the kitchen. As I waited for the vase to fill, I practised a few deep, cleansing breaths.

'I like your flat.' Finn's voice floated in from the front door, where I'd rudely abandoned him.

'Thanks,' I called out in reply, before muttering in a private stage whisper to my distorted reflection in the kettle, 'For goodness' sake, Gemma, get a grip.'

I emerged from the kitchen with a smile that I hoped hid my inner turmoil.

'Are you ready to leave? You might want a jacket; it can get a little breezy where we're going.'

'Curiouser and curiouser,' I said, reaching for my black leather jacket and draping it over my shoulders. I was no longer bothered about not knowing where we were heading. Wherever it was, I was safe with Finn. I had no reason to be so certain, and yet I'd willingly have bet everything I owned on it being true.

We shared the lift down to ground level with a group of my neighbours, which pressed pause on all further conversation until we left the building. The late-afternoon sun was still surprisingly strong, and I blinked in its glare like a dazzled mole before reaching for my sunglasses.

'Where did you park?' I asked, looking up and down the street but still not spotting Finn's dark blue car. I rocked on to my tiptoes, trying to see a little further, but my view was blocked by a long black limousine idling at the kerb, taking up twice the space of a normal car. It was the kind of vehicle from which you expect a Hollywood A-lister to emerge.

'This is us,' Finn said, his hand lightly cupping my elbow to bring me to a stop.

Stupidly, I continued to look around for the car we'd travelled in the night before. One of the limo's dark-tinted windows slid open with a whisper, and behind the wheel I saw a man in a dark suit preparing to climb out. Finn bent down and said something to him through the open window. The driver stayed where he was.

'You have a limousine,' I told Finn, just in case he hadn't noticed.

He laughed, his hand resting lightly on the car's gleaming roof.

'It's only mine for the evening,' he said with a grin as he reached for the rear door handle. 'I thought it might be nice for us to travel in comfort.'

'Your car was perfectly comfortable,' I said, too wrong-footed to realise my comment might have sounded churlish. 'I mean, this is great, don't get me wrong, but you didn't need a different car.'

'Actually, I did, because I sold mine this morning.'

He opened the back door and all my objections dissolved as I peered into the luxurious interior. There was a back seat that appeared wider and more comfortable than my own settee, and a champagne bucket with a bottle of something that I suspected was expensive chilling on ice. But most appealing of all was the blast of icy air from the car's air-conditioning system, which I could feel even from the pavement. Grinning like an idiot, I climbed into the car, wondering if this was what it felt like to win the lottery.

'You should have told me you'd got rid of your car,' I said as Finn climbed in behind me. 'I'd have been happy to drive us.'

'But then you wouldn't have been able to drink tonight,' Finn reasoned.

My eyes flashed to the waiting ice bucket. 'True. But you already know what a lightweight I am. If I drink half of this before we reach our destination, there's every chance I'll be completely hammered before we get there. Incidentally, where is that again?'

He laughed and shook his head.

'Nice try, Ginny,' Finn teased, slipping easily back into his game of not knowing who I was. Only this time I felt as though I might be playing too. Because I wasn't sure that *I* knew who I was any more either.

I certainly wasn't the woman who forty-eight hours earlier would have referred to Finn Douglas as an unpleasant, egotistical individual who I'd hopefully never see again. And yet here I was, sitting beside him, already wondering if this might be the best date I'd ever been on. And it had only just started.

Just like the night before, the conversation flowed so effortlessly it was easy to forget how little we knew of each other. Long before we'd left the city traffic jams behind and joined the motorway, I realised I could happily have stayed there for the rest of the evening, without ever bothering to get out of the car at all.

The world outside continued to flash past at seventy miles an hour, only intruding now and again when a passing motorist blasted out a greeting on their car's horn. 'I wonder if people think we've just got married,' I mused.

Finn's raised eyebrows spoke volumes. 'I'm all for whirlwind romances, but I prefer to leave it a little longer than just one date before I propose.'

He was joking, I realised that, but there was something in his words that sobered me up more effectively than a gallon of black coffee.

'Have you?' I asked, very deliberately placing my champagne flute back in its holder. *No more alcohol for you, young lady*, I told myself sternly.

'Have I what?'

'Ever proposed.' It was galling to realise I'd been only too happy to assume that the absence of a ring meant Finn was unattached. Had that been wishful or simply ostrich-like thinking? I'd been lied to in the past and yet I still appeared to have learnt nothing. Why was I so willing to trust Finn?

'No, Gemma, I have never proposed. I've never met anyone I've wanted to spend forever with.'

I waited for a totally inappropriate 'until now' to be added to the end of his sentence. But obviously it never came. I cast a blameful glance at my glass of champagne. *This is all your fault*, I told it silently. It was only much, much later that I realised that for once Finn had called me by my correct name when answering my question.

As the car ate through the miles to our mystery destination, Finn steered our conversation away from all things personal with the skill of a hawk riding a thermal current. I never saw the movement of his wings, but we swooped seamlessly between innocuous topics on an invisible slipstream. He really must have been an excellent journalist, because his interviewing technique put mine to shame.

'We should be there in about five minutes,' said the driver's voice, making me jump when it came through on the car's intercom.

I swivelled in my seat to peer out of the window again, this time catching my first glimpse of a long slice of blue on the horizon.

'We're at the coast,' I declared in surprise, amazed to find we'd got there so quickly. But a quick glance at the clock set into the limo's leather upholstery revealed that we'd actually been driving for a couple of hours.

I don't think I had ever wanted time to slow down as much as I did right at that moment. *Make it go backwards, or at least make it go slower*, I wished like a child. I wanted there to be no yesterday and no tomorrow, just one long, endless tonight.

Within minutes of leaving the motorway, we were deep in a maze of twisty coastal lanes that seemed to grow ever narrower the closer we got to our destination; I began to fear for the limo's immaculate paintwork as hedgerows reached out with thorny fingers. We squeezed down lanes so tight, I had no idea what would happen if we met an oncoming vehicle. Thankfully, before we had the chance to find out, the driver flicked on the indicator and we drove through a brick-pillared entrance.

'The Manor House,' I said, reading the name on the discreetly positioned signage. Below the name of the hotel was an impressive number of Michelin stars that had been awarded to its restaurant.

The driveway was lined with tall poplar trees, lit by spotlights that would come into their own in the next hour or two when the sun finally went down.

The building itself was hidden from view for the first few curves of the gravelled approach road, offering just occasional tantalising glimpses through the branches of the majestic poplars. I caught sight of a window, ablaze in the low evening sunlight, a hint of gabled roof, and then a towering chimney stack. Finally, the building finished its game of peek-a-boo and revealed itself as we swung on to a circular forecourt.

It was the kind of place people booked for their wedding venue. People who didn't have to worry about how many zeros were on the end of their invoice, that is. Perhaps even more impressive than the period property were its immaculate grounds. In a spell as hot and dry as the one we were currently experiencing, I was truly mystified how everything was still so green and lush, when every single plant on my tiny balcony was now a crispy brown version of its former self.

'This place looks amazing,' I said, turning towards Finn with an expression of delight.

'You've not seen the best bit yet,' Finn declared as the limo came to a stop in a flurry of gravel chips. He climbed out of the car first and then turned back to give me his hand. Even though I'd been successfully getting in and out of vehicles unaided for the last twenty-five years or so, I happily took it, because I liked the feel of his fingers curled around mine.

I took in a slow 360-degree panorama of The Manor House's grounds, breathing in an intoxicating combination of newly mown grass and the smell of the sea. I couldn't see it, but I could definitely hear the subtle swish of waves above the chorus of evening birdsong. Finn was busy giving the driver instructions while I continued to drink in the perfection of our surroundings.

I turned at the sound of the engine starting up, in time to see the limousine heading down the driveway. With a blink of brake lights, it was gone.

'Is he coming back?' I asked, surprised to discover how little I'd have cared if Finn's reply was 'No'.

'Of course he is,' Finn said, trying to look wounded at my lack of faith. 'You really do have a very warped opinion of me, don't you?'

Unexpectedly, the conversation had suddenly turned serious. 'I did. Once. A few years ago,' I admitted. 'But I have to be honest – I'm revising it pretty rapidly right now.'

The smile that brought was the kind I wanted to photograph and put in a frame.

'Come on,' Finn said, holding out his hand to me once more. 'Let me show you the real reason I brought you all this way just for dinner.'

My fingers slipped easily into his grip, as though they were puzzle pieces that had finally found the place they were meant to be. I shook my head in disbelief at my own thoughts. That's the Bollinger speaking, I told myself. And that was true to a degree, but it wasn't the only reason.

I had imagined that Finn would lead us towards the enormous double doors at the front of the hotel, which were thrown wide open, welcoming in the warm July evening, but instead we crunched through the deep gravel to one side of the building. Long before we emerged from the shadow of the hotel, I could hear the sea again, much louder now as it crashed somewhere below us on to what I assumed was a rock face.

'Close your eyes,' said Finn, slowing his pace.

'I'll trip,' I warned him, having already found the deep gravel chippings a little challenging in my heels. 'Have we covered the fact that I'm congenitally clumsy yet?'

He chuckled softly. 'No, I don't believe we have. But don't worry, I won't let you fall.'

'Or push me off a cliff,' I added, trying to revive some of the banter that was evaporating into something that had begun to feel serious. This was ridiculous. Feelings didn't grow this fast. They took time to develop and mature. And yet I felt like I'd been torpedoed into a relationship that had been building for weeks or even months.

'Close your eyes, Genevieve,' Finn instructed, trying and failing to pull off a long-suffering tone.

We took a dozen steps, and Finn was as good as his word. His right hand gripped mine firmly, while his left moved to my waist, ensuring that even if I did stumble, he'd be there to catch me.

'Okay, you can open them now,' he instructed.

I did so slowly, savouring the moment. *Wow* seemed inadequate for a journalist to use as a descriptor, but I truly couldn't think of another word to capture the beauty of what I was seeing.

There was so much to take in, it was hard to know where to look first. A deep, flagstoned terrace was set with tables elegantly draped in snowy-white cloths and topped with gleaming silverware. Tall candles flickered on every table, their glow in competition with the thousands of LED lights twinkling from the branches of the trees and nestled within the foliage. But as magnificent as the outdoor dining room was, it was the backdrop that made this place truly spectacular. Beyond a low wall, the only thing to be seen was the sea, glinting in a kaleidoscope of blues, greens and gold as the rippling waves captured the sunlight.

'Oh. My. God. This might literally be the most beautiful place I've ever seen,' I said, gushing like an idiot. Ridiculously, I could feel the smart of tears springing to my eyes as I turned to the man beside me. 'Thank you for bringing me here.' Finn looked inordinately pleased at my delight. 'How did you ever discover this place?' I asked as we walked in unspoken agreement towards the wall that looked out over the water.

'I covered a conference here several years ago as a journo,' he said, leaning against the waist-high wall and breathing in deeply as though recalibrating. 'I remember thinking at the time that it would be the perfect place to bring someone for a special occasion.'

'Do first dates count as special occasions?' I asked, my voice husky.

Finn turned away from the sea and stared deep into my eyes, making it impossible to look away. Not that I had any desire to do so.

'I don't know. You tell me.'

I could have found a quip then, defused the moment into something trivial, and yet I did the exact opposite. I was already holding one of his hands, but now I reached for the other, as though we were exchanging vows.

'It feels pretty special to me.'

★

Our table was ready, Finn informed me, after checking in with the maître d', who resembled the captain at the helm of a ship as he stood on his podium, surveying the diners and the sea beyond them.

'We could eat now, or if you prefer, we could grab a cocktail and take a wander around the grounds before the light fades.'

'Option B, please,' I said happily, more because I knew he'd take my hand again as we walked through the hotel gardens than from a burning interest in horticulture.

I was right, Finn did reach for my hand. In the other I held my cocktail, chosen from the menu chiefly because it was one of only a few I could order without blushing like a teenager. The night already felt sexually charged, without choosing a drink with a side order of double entendre.

There was a warm, sweet smell in the air, emanating from either the climbing honeysuckle, the concoction in my glass or the anticipation that something was happening tonight that was so deliciously combustible, it could ignite at any moment. With previous boyfriends, desire had always been a long, slow burn, but this felt as though we were under a giant magnifying glass beneath the heat of the sun.

One circuit around the garden proved that Finn knew even less about trees and shrubs than I did.

'Do you have a garden?' I asked, aware that I still knew so little about his life.

'No. Not even a window box,' he said with a rueful shrug. 'I rent a flat with a couple of other guys. It's fair to say the only thing we successfully grow is mould from the occasional plate that never makes it to the dishwasher.'

'Ugh.' I shuddered. 'And you in hospitality too.'

Finn grinned. 'The coffee shop has a glowing bill of health,' he said proudly, and then added as a teasing afterthought, 'Three years, and I've not poisoned a single customer.'

'It's the little things,' I agreed soberly, loving the way I could make him laugh, and loving even more the way his arm had somehow snaked around my waist as we walked.

Excitement was thrumming quietly through me, like a low-grade electrical current. Later it would spark into life, I knew that with a certainty I'd never experienced before. It was there in Finn's eyes when he looked down at me, burning like twin flames. Delaying the gratification of feeling his lips on mine was only going to make it even more intense when we eventually surrendered to the moment.

'Hungry?' he asked, his voice low.

I had to remind myself he was asking about food. I nodded.

Finn began leading us back towards the terrace, taking a leisurely route beneath the trailing boughs of some weeping willows. Surprisingly, the sun was still playing games with the light, turning the glass in a couple of the hotel's ground-floor windows into fiery portholes.

'They do an amazing salmon dish here that's—'

'What's that smell?' I asked, interrupting him.

Finn paused and inhaled deeply, before checking the soles of his shoes in case we'd found one of the 'gifts' left by the hotel's wandering peacocks. He flashed me a beam when he saw they were clean. It was the last natural smile I'd see from him for a while.

I sniffed the air again, like a tracker dog, aware that the smell was even stronger now. 'No. It's not that. It's kind of pungent, almost acrid.'

I didn't register Finn's hand falling away from mine, but it must have done, for it was now raised to his eyes, acting like a visor. His other was curiously clenched at his side.

'I think it smells like there's a—'

'Fire!' cried a voice from the hotel's entrance, completing my sentence. Moments later, this was confirmed by the continuous pealing of the fire alarm.

'Oh my God,' I cried, realising the flickering red light I'd seen in the downstairs windows had actually been flames.

I began hurrying towards the hotel in case help was needed, with Finn half a step behind me. Before we were even halfway across the manicured lawns, we were met by a tide of diners and hotel guests who'd been evacuated from the building and were being guided to safety by hotel employees. Like well-trained border collies, the staff were rounding up everyone to a fire assembly point in the grounds.

There were several worried faces among the guests, but none looked quite so concerned as the man standing beside me. We were nowhere near the heat of the flames and yet I spotted tiny beads of perspiration on his forehead.

'Are you okay?' I asked, already aware that whatever was bothering him was being hastily concealed behind impenetrable shutters.

'I'm fine,' he said, twisting his lips into an approximation of a smile that didn't reach his eyes.

The hotel staff were busily checking off guests and staff on registers and clipboards. They bustled around us, to a backdrop of rumours and speculation.

'I heard someone say it started in a storeroom but was quickly confined and put out in minutes.'

'Let's hope they let us back in soon, because my entrée was about to arrive.'

'Hey, I bet they comp our meals,' someone added gleefully.

The general level of anxiety seemed fairly low-key, although it spiked slightly at the sound of approaching emergency vehicles.

'Ladies and gentlemen,' began the hotel manager, shouting in a way that seemed out of character as he struggled to make himself heard above the crescendo of fire engine sirens. 'I sincerely apologise for the disruption to your evening's enjoyment. As some of you might have heard, we experienced a very small fire in one of our storage rooms, which was quickly extinguished. However, the fire service will need to fully inspect the building before we're permitted to return inside. Again, please accept our apologies and a glass of complimentary champagne that we'll be offering you in a moment.'

There was a rather bizarre round of applause from the crowd on the lawn, which could have been for the manager, the champagne or the firefighters, who were now leaping down from their appliances and unspooling hoses they'd have no need to use.

I turned to Finn, but his focus was fixed on the three fire engines and the teams who were about to enter the building. The sirens had been deafening, and even after they'd been turned off, it felt as though I could still hear them, like a ricocheting echo bouncing off the trees.

Waiters were now circulating among the crowd, carrying silver trays loaded with champagne. One headed towards us, but I shook my head and motioned him away. Finn had said nothing since the fire alarm first sounded, but I'd have had to be blind not to see the tension thrumming through him. It was totally different to the kind that had arced between us just a short while ago.

My thoughts were spinning, like wheels in mud, as I tried to think of a way to recapture our earlier relaxed mood. 'I imagine it'll take them some time before they can give the building the all-clear,' I said, slipping my hand into the crook of Finn's elbow. It was like trying to snuggle up to a statue. 'Why don't we go for a walk while they sort things out here?'

Journalists are pretty good at trusting their instincts, and mine were telling me that Finn wouldn't be able to fully relax until we'd put some distance between ourselves and the fire. It seemed to take a real effort for him to tear his eyes away from the three appliances at the front of the hotel. I wondered if he'd ever had to cover a story about a fire; one that hadn't ended as harmlessly as the one this evening. That kind of thing could leave a scar on even a hardened journo. Could that be the reason he'd abandoned the profession and opened up the coffee shop?

'There's a pathway to one side of the grounds that leads down to the seafront and a small promenade,' Finn said, jerking my thoughts back from my musings.

'That sounds perfect,' I said, pleased to feel a noticeable relaxation in his rigid stance.

It wasn't really surprising to find we were the only guests who wanted to leave. The combination of free bubbly, firemen and a smidgen of drama was clearly enough of a draw for the other patrons to want to hang around.

We were stopped by a solitary hotel employee who happily informed us that our meal tonight would be on the house, just as the hopeful guest had predicted.

'We'll be back in a little while,' Finn informed him.

13

THE BEACH

Four years earlier

We were several hundred feet down the narrow pathway that led to the seafront before Finn spoke again. We might have left the lingering smell of smoke far behind, yet it still seemed to hang over our heads like a dark cloud.

'I'm sorry about the way I reacted back there,' Finn said eventually, inclining his head in the direction of The Manor House.

For a moment I considered pretending that I hadn't noticed anything peculiar, but lying seemed like a very poor way to start whatever this thing between us might turn out to be.

'I'm not usually in the habit of freaking out like that.'

'You didn't,' I assured him. 'And if you think *that's* bad, you should see me when there's a spider in the bathtub. I've been known to phone friends at all hours for emergency assistance.'

His face was definitely relaxing now, and I saw with relief the glimmer of a smile. 'Well, you can add me to the list of potential rescuers, if you like. Spiders don't bother me. I spent the first ten years of my life in the country that made the huntsman famous.'

I raised my eyes from the pathway, which was proving more and more tricky to negotiate the further we got from the hotel. 'Australia? I didn't know you grew up there.'

A memory flickered in his eyes. It looked like a happy one. 'My mum was Australian, and my dad was English. We moved back to the UK for my father's work when I was a kid.'

Finn's use of the past tense when he spoke about his parents hadn't escaped me. But I knew better than to ask about them. If he wanted me to know more, he would tell me.

'You don't sound much like an Aussie,' I said, determined to keep things light.

'The accent comes and goes,' Finn said, with an easy shrug. 'It'll probably return with a vengeance when I spend time there.' His jaw hardened, as though he'd accidentally revealed a secret.

The pathway had been getting steeper, and the heels I'd chosen for the evening were proving totally inadequate.

'Are you okay to walk in those shoes?' asked Finn when a loose stone nearly felled me. 'We're almost there now,' he continued, offering me his hand for assistance, 'but I could give you a piggyback for the rest of the journey down.' His smile was broad, and his eyes were finally twinkling again.

For a millisecond I imagined myself on his back, my thighs clamped fast around his torso, his hands clasped beneath my bum for support. A totally inappropriate dart of desire shot through me, leaving a scorched trail that started in my stomach and ended between my legs.

'I'm fine,' I said on a gulp, dropping to a crouch and

spending far longer than necessary unbuckling my sandals. I didn't risk standing up until I was one hundred per cent certain every trace of my wayward thoughts had been erased from my face.

The sun was continuing its low slide towards the horizon, bathing the area in that particular hue photographers like to call the golden hour. I'd never appreciated that expression quite as much as I did right then, as I placed my hand in Finn's once again.

The colours grew even more intense when the pathway ended its meandering course and spilled us out at the end of a seaside promenade. I smiled as my gaze travelled along a row of pastel-coloured beach huts that stretched as far as I could see. 'They look like tiny Monopoly houses,' I confided to Finn, laughing at his wry comment that you'd need to pass 'Go' a great many times to be able to afford one.

'Beach walk or seafront?' he asked, reaching over to take my shoes and carry them for me.

There was an ardent feminist deep within me who was probably wondering who the hell I was right now, but I was happy to ignore her.

'Seafront.'

Most of the beach huts had been closed up for the day, but there were a few diehard owners who were determinedly squeezing the last moments from the warm summer's evening. They were sitting outside their miniature buildings on folding deckchairs, with plaid blankets spread across their knees to ward off a chill I couldn't even feel.

Almost everyone we passed called out a greeting; some even raised their cup of tea or can of soda in an unspoken toast to the end of the day. There was a charming, quintessential

Britishness about the huts, with their peeling, weather-worn paintwork and their cheery occupants. I was totally enchanted – which was how I'd been feeling about almost everything that evening.

We'd almost reached the end of the promenade, and as spectacular as The Manor House was, I was in no real hurry to return. The Finn walking at my side was a far more laid-back version than the one we'd left in the hotel grounds, and I wanted to keep hold of him for as long as possible.

Finn heard the music before I did. He paused on the pathway, his head tilted, to catch the faint strains above the sound of the waves lapping at the shoreline. There were only a few beach huts up ahead, and it was fair to say they all looked a little more shabby than chic. The one playing the music had long corkscrews of faded yellow paint curling on its clapboard front.

The music was surprisingly loud and crackled in a way that made me think it was an old vinyl record. I vaguely recognised the song as one more likely to live in my parents' music collection than mine.

We slowed down and then came to a stop as an elderly man emerged from the yellow beach hut's open doors. I don't think he even saw us standing to one side in the shadows, for his attention was focused only on the elderly woman two steps behind him. He held out a liver-spotted hand, and she placed hers within it. The thin band of gold on her finger gleamed among a concertina of wrinkles.

The man's spine was stooped, but he was still taller than the slight woman with the wispy white hair. He gave her a smile full of dentures and love as he placed his hand at her waist. He paused for a moment, listening for the beat, and then swept her into a dance that my years of watching *Strictly* reliably informed me was a waltz.

Beside me, Finn was smiling warmly as his eyes followed the elderly couple while they danced on the pathway as though it were a ballroom. They were lost, not just in each other but wherever it was the song had taken them. They moved with the ease of a couple who'd been held in each other's arms for decades. There was a beauty in their somewhat clumsy, stumbling movements. This song was theirs; this moment theirs; and their love was so tangible, it brought tears to my eyes.

I glanced at Finn, surprised to find him looking down at me with an unreadable expression on his face. Someone would be there in *his* future, when his eyesight was fading, his jaw less firm, and his back bent with age. How crazy was it to want so badly for that someone to be me?

'I'm so sorry, do you want to get past?' called out the old man, attempting a twirl in true Fred Astaire fashion.

'No. Please carry on,' said Finn, his eyes crinkling at the edges with the warmth of his smile.

'It's lovely watching you both,' I added.

The old lady's smile was beatific as she looked at us over her husband's bony shoulder. 'It's our anniversary. Sixty years today. We danced to this song at our wedding.'

'Congratulations,' I said, aware that Finn's arm had now moved to my waist.

We stayed on the pathway until the song had ended, giving the couple a small round of applause when the music finally came to a close. The woman responded with a girlish blush, and the man bent low in a formal bow.

I had no idea who they were or what their backstory was,

but as we turned to retrace our steps along the promenade, I felt strangely honoured to have shared the precious moment with them.

'We should probably think about heading back to the hotel,' Finn said with what I thought was a trace of regret in his voice.

'We should,' I agreed, my gaze going towards the beach, which was now largely deserted. 'Although part of me would like to stay right here.'

'Aren't you hungry?' he asked, no doubt thinking back to the way I'd devoured my takeaway the night before.

'Starving,' I said with the kind of fervour that made him laugh so loud, several heads turned our way. 'But perhaps not for haute cuisine. Not tonight,' I added, crossing my fingers as I revealed how much I hoped there'd be other nights in our future for that kind of evening.

'So, what do you fancy?'

For one dreadful moment I thought my tongue might betray me by saying 'you'. Thankfully, I had enough control to stop it.

'Can't you guess?' I said, my eyes lighting up as a man walked past us carrying a bulging white carrier bag.

'Fish and chips?'

'Is any trip to the seaside complete without them?' I countered.

Finn was shaking his head ruefully, as though I'd totally surprised him yet again, but he didn't look entirely displeased with my suggestion.

'I must admit that my plans for this evening were a little grander. I guess I wanted to make it a night we'd both remember,' he said. There was a hint of sadness in his voice that made me want to kiss him so much, it actually hurt to hold back.

'It already is,' I assured him.

There were at least four outlets we could have ordered from, but in the end we simply chose the closest. The aroma of battered cod had billowed out through the shop's open doorway, and I was practically salivating by the time we reached the front of the queue.

We passed an off-licence on our way back to the beach, where Finn picked up a six-pack of craft beers to go with our food – my suggestion of beverage, not his.

He held my hand as we descended the steep stone steps that led down from the promenade to the beach. We wove past half-demolished sandcastles, whose construction teams were sure to be tucked up in bed by now, before eventually settling on a spot halfway between the towering tidal wall and the water's edge.

Without a second thought, Finn laid his suit jacket down on the sand to act as a makeshift blanket. It didn't look like a cheapie high-street purchase, but he dismissed my aghast expression with an easy shrug. 'It's not important,' he said. 'I don't imagine I'll be needing it for a while, anyway.'

My eyebrows rose in curiosity, but Finn was busy opening two of the beers. It was yet another question he'd neatly avoided.

He offered me one of the bottles and an apology. 'I'm sorry, I should have asked the guy in the shop for a couple of plastic cups.'

'Nah,' I said, pressing the bottle to my lips and drinking thirstily.

I lowered my drink to find Finn looking at me with an expression that made the blood fizz in my veins.

'Do you know, there isn't one thing about you I don't like, Miss Gwendoline Fletcher.'

I could have corrected my name, could have made a joke or simply stayed silent. But it wasn't that kind of night.

'Ditto,' I replied.

We chatted easily as we ate, and I regaled him with amusing stories from my childhood.

'Are you an only child?' Finn quizzed.

'Yes. If you don't count the imaginary brothers and sisters I used to play with when I was little. I wasn't a lonely child, but I really longed to be part of a big, messy, hectic family. I think that's why Hannah has always felt more like a sister to me than a friend. How about you? Any siblings?'

'No. It's just me.' There was something in his reply that further confirmed his parents were no longer alive.

'Well, you definitely couldn't have picked a better place to have brought me tonight. The beach has always been one of my favourite places,' I said, smiling broadly as he held out his styrofoam food container. It was empty except for the longest, fattest chip I'd ever seen. He'd left it for me.

I held his eyes as I picked the fry from the tray and bit into it. I was shocked: who knew eating fried potato could be that erotic?

'I suppose the beaches you knew as a child were very

different to this,' I observed, realising that although we'd talked non-stop all night, I still knew very little about him.

'They were definitely warmer,' Finn said, leaning over to drape my jacket around my shoulders.

He must have spotted the goosebumps covering my bare arms and assumed I was cold. I chose not to correct him. It was safer than admitting I was so turned on by him, I could easily have ended up getting us arrested for doing something highly illegal on a public beach.

'For me, it was all about Saturday Nippers school, and snags on the barbie,' Finn said.

'*Now* you sound Australian,' I said with delight. 'I have absolutely no idea what you just said.'

There'd been so many times during the evening when I'd thought Finn might kiss me for the first time. That he did so then, while I was laughing, was completely unexpected. I was so surprised, it took a few moments for me to respond. My lips were just beginning to explore the contour of Finn's when he pulled back.

The sun had almost set, and it was hard to read the expression in his eyes. They looked practically black in the fading light.

'I'm sorry. I've been wanting to do that since the moment you opened your front door. But I shouldn't have assumed it was what you wanted too.'

Was he kidding me? Did he really think my slow response meant I hadn't wanted it just as much as him?

I could have wasted countless words putting him straight, but it was far easier to let my actions speak for me.

We were both breathing heavily when we eventually broke apart.

The desire in Finn's eyes dissolved as he caught sight of something behind me. 'Look,' he said softly, placing a finger beneath my chin and gently turning my face towards the horizon.

While we'd been kissing, the sun had become a huge fiery ball slipping rapidly out of the sky. I sighed softly as together we watched the sea tug it beneath the surface and swallow it whole.

'This really is turning out to be a perfect first date,' I admitted on a whisper. I'm not sure how I was expecting Finn to respond, but it certainly wasn't with a look of anguish.

'It *is* an amazing first date,' he said, biting his lip as though he really didn't want to complete his sentence. 'But there's something I should probably have told you before now. You see, it's also our *last* date.'

I stiffened in his arms and struggled to pull free, but he wouldn't let me.

'You're breaking up with me?' I said, trying for flippancy and missing by a country mile. 'Well, that's new for a first date.'

'I'm so sorry, Gemma,' Finn said. I knew then, by the use of my proper name, that he was serious. 'I know I should have told you this straight away, but I didn't want to put a downer on this evening, especially if it was going to be the only one we had.'

'You make it sound like you don't have a choice in the matter.' My voice was small and confused.

'I don't. Not really. I'm going away. To Australia. I leave tomorrow.'

Relief flooded through me. 'Do you mean for a holiday?'

He shook his head, and the relief was sucked out again, as though by an incoming tsunami.

'I have a one-way plane ticket.'

'But… but what about your business, the coffee shop?'

'I've sold it,' he said, his voice flat. 'The new owners made me the kind of offer you don't walk away from. They've got big plans for opening a second branch.'

'Couldn't *you* have done that? If they can make it a success, surely you would have been able to as well?'

For the first time, Finn looked uncomfortable. I'd clearly touched an exposed nerve.

'It was time to move on.'

He turned to me then, his hand gentle as it cupped my cheek. His voice was so low, it was hard to hear him above the sound of the waves. 'What I couldn't have imagined was meeting someone who'd make me regret that decision.' His lips were soft as they kissed me. 'I can't help thinking this thing between us could have gone somewhere – if things had been different.'

'And your plans are fixed? There's no possibility you'll change your mind?'

'I have a feeling I'll be wanting to change it every single mile between here and Sydney, but I have to do this. I have to go.'

'What will you do in Australia? Open another coffee shop?'

Finn looked a little hesitant before replying. 'Actually, I'm going to try my hand at writing a novel. I've been thinking about it for a while, and selling the business has given me the financial security to actually try it.'

I bit my lip on the comment that writing was just about the most portable job in the entire world. You could do it practically anywhere. Clearly, Finn had made up his mind to return to the country of his birth. Whatever this was between us just wasn't meant to be.

'I guess you and I were right people, wrong time,' I said, determined not to ruin our first and last evening together by being miserable.

I slipped my hands behind his neck and drew his head towards me. All thoughts of getting arrested had worryingly disappeared from my head as we fell back on to the sand.

If one single, perfect night was all we had, I wanted to make it count.

14

I was sitting on the floor of my hallway with my back propped against the front door. Waiting. My attention was split between the letterbox and checking through the emails in my phone's junk folder. It was almost 3 p.m., which was when the post was usually delivered to my building, and I'd spent the last fifteen minutes lying in wait for the mail, like a postman-hating Rottweiler.

Even so, when the flap eventually rattled and a handful of letters landed in my lap, I had a moment of pure panic. If Hannah was right and Finn *had* decided to post me a letter before leaving the country for who knew where, today was when it would logically arrive.

My neck felt stiff as I forced myself to look down. Never had I been so pleased to see a pile of junk mail and a collection of bills.

I got to my feet just as my phone pinged with an incoming message. Trepidation and hope fought an interesting battle within me. I desperately wanted to hear from Finn, but only if he was going to say the things I wanted to hear and not what Hannah was convinced he'd been drafting on those screwed-up pieces of paper.

It was a relief to open the message and discover it hadn't come from Finn after all but from my airline, reminding me that I still hadn't completed the online check-in for my flight to Sydney later that day.

'That's because I'm not going,' I told my phone screen. 'You don't get to go on the honeymoon when the wedding didn't happen.'

Or do you?

I froze, hearing my words as though they'd been spoken by someone else. Had Finn just received exactly the same message as me? Or was the advice redundant, because he'd already checked in?

The idea was so overwhelming, I sat back down on the hallway floor with a resounding thump. We'd booked our flights separately, as Finn had a load of air miles he'd wanted to use. And while I had absolutely no intention of getting on the flight to Australia that day, could I honestly say the same for Finn?

Had I done this? Had I been so focused on creating the wedding my mum would have wanted me to have that I'd somehow pushed Finn into doing something so desperate? Too late, I remembered him saying more than once, 'It's not the wedding day I'm looking forward to, it's the lifetime of days that will follow it.'

The wedding plans had been all mine, down to every last small detail, but Finn had totally owned the honeymoon arrangements. He had a passion for Australia. He'd lived there as a child, and then later for several years as an adult. He'd certainly made no secret of the fact he hoped our visit would make me fall in love with the idea of living there one day. With the benefit of dual nationality from an Australian mother, Finn was technically able to move back there whenever he wanted. Was today the day he intended to do that?

Suddenly, the notion of Finn choosing to live in any other country seemed ridiculous. If he wanted to leave the UK – *if he wanted to leave me*, a voice in my head quietly corrected – the country he'd choose would be Australia. Especially as he already had a ticket booked for a flight in – I glanced at my watch – three hours' time.

If I stopped to think it through, I'd find a hundred reasons why I should immediately abandon this plan. Keeping moving seemed the best way of staying two steps ahead of the many objections queued up in my head.

I hopped around my bedroom on one leg, pulling on a clean pair of jeans and searching for sandals. I tugged a comb through my hair, but there was no time for make-up. It wasn't the way I'd wanted to look the next time I saw Finn. But he'd chosen to miss the excellent job the hairdresser and beautician had done on our wedding day, so this was going to have to do.

I grabbed a cardigan because it could get chilly inside the cabin of a plane. A bubble of almost hysterical laughter escaped me. Was I seriously contemplating getting on the plane if Finn was there at the airport? If he wanted me to, then I would, I told the flushed woman staring back at me in the bedroom mirror. All the rest could be sorted out later. There was only one thing I knew for sure. If Finn Douglas was going to Sydney today, then I wanted to go with him.

⋆

The terminal was crazy busy. It was only to be expected in the middle of summer. I immediately became that annoying person who loiters just inside the doors and then stops dead, creating an obstacle for suitcase-hauling travellers and kamikaze trolley pushers. I was possibly still stunned after working out how much my daily parking tariff would be if I really did get on that plane and didn't come back for three weeks.

During my drive to the airport, I'd somehow managed to convince myself that Finn was going to be there, waiting hopefully for me to show up. But now, in a voice that sounded uncomfortably like Hannah's, the alternative was presented to me like a dish I really ought to consider sampling. What if Finn *was* there, right now, eyes on the airport doors, desperately hoping I *wouldn't* turn up?

I stepped further into the concourse, my gaze travelling a full 360 degrees, looking for a man who stood a little taller than most in a crowd, with red glints in his dark hair. I couldn't see him. Undeterred, I crossed to join a mass of travellers beneath an overhead arrivals and departures board. I studied it for a minute, my stomach performing a pancake flip when it finally displayed the flight Finn and I were booked on.

The check-in desks were already busy, and I wheeled my overnight bag – the only luggage I'd brought with me – to join the queue that chicaned back and forth between the bollards. I shuffled with my fellow ticket holders towards the bank of counters. As I got closer, I studied the four airport check-in officers on duty. I really hoped I'd get the woman at the end, because she looked around my age and was very smiley and friendly with the customers she dealt with. The two in the middle looked okay, although their sober expressions might mean they'd be less sympathetic to my situation. The person I didn't want was the irritated-looking man working at the far counter; the one with the perma-scowl on his face.

I got Mr Perma-Scowl.

'Passport,' he said, holding out his hand without lifting his eyes to make contact with mine.

I fastened my grip on the burgundy-coloured passport that I'd taken from my bag only because everyone else appeared to be holding theirs.

My hesitation clearly added to the woes of his day. 'Passport,' he repeated, hitting every consonant of the word as though I might not speak English.

'Hi,' I said, giving him what Finn had once called 'the very best smile in the entire world'. It must have been a subjective observation, for I could instantly tell it was going to get me nowhere with this man.

'I'm booked on flight QA32 to Sydney.'

'I'm going to need your passport, madam.'

'Ah. The thing is, I don't know if I want to go or not.'

His eyes flickered behind his glasses, and I could practically read his thoughts. *Out of all the counters you could have ended up at, it had to be mine.*

At least I had his full attention now. I continued in a rush. 'I need to find out if another passenger has checked in already for this flight.'

'Are they on your booking?'

I shook my head regretfully. 'No.'

He shook his own, mirroring me. 'Then I'm afraid I can't divulge information about other passengers. It would be a contravention of airport security.'

Would it? I wondered, or was that just an easy way to make me go away, something I sensed couldn't happen a moment too soon for this man.

'Look, can I be perfectly honest with you? The passenger I'm looking for is my fiancé. Well, he should actually have been my husband by now, but...' The man's eyes were starting to search beyond me, probably seeking some airport official to frogmarch me away from his counter. 'Finn Douglas,' I said with urgency in my voice. 'I just need to speak to him for a few minutes. Isn't there anything you can do to help me?'

Perhaps there *was* a heart there, beating deep beneath his airport uniform, but I wasn't reaching it. If there was any sympathy at all in his expression, I had a feeling it was directed more towards Finn than me.

'Madam, my only job is to check in passengers for the flight to Sydney. If you have a valid ticket and a passport, then I can do that for you, otherwise I'm going to have to ask you to step aside so I can deal with all the people who *do* want to get on the flight today.'

Unable to believe I was actually doing it, I surrendered my passport and watched as the man rattled my details into his computer. That the information I wanted about Finn was probably right there on the screen in front of him was beyond frustrating.

He slid my boarding pass and passport back towards me and then finally, as I was about to walk away, he turned into a human being. 'Everyone on that flight will ultimately end up at the same place. If you're looking for your fiancé, I suggest you go straight to the departure gate.'

*

It was the first time I'd ever been at an airport and not felt the lure of the designer shops or the duty-free emporium. I strode straight past them all, as well as the collection of eateries. The gate was now listed as 'Open' on the information boards, and with my heart thumping uncomfortably in my chest, I began the long walk towards it.

The idea that I might be the first person waiting for the flight quickly proved ridiculous. Even with almost an hour to go until boarding, there were hardly any vacant seats at Gate 47. The passengers were an eclectic mix: older couples poring over travel documents, and younger ones hefting backpacks so large, they'd never fit in the overhead bins. There were more families than I'd expected too.

There was a buzz of excitement from the holidaymakers and travellers, who were either venturing somewhere new or going back home. I fell into neither category, and I felt lost as I stood on the edge of the crowd, scanning every face for the one I hoped to see.

It took less than a minute to find him. It was the red glints in his dark hair that tugged my gaze back after it initially travelled past him. He was sitting on the furthest row of chairs, facing away from me, with his head bowed as though looking at something on his lap. It was probably his phone.

I'd spent two days waiting for this moment, wondering how I'd react and what I'd say, and now that it was finally here, the urge to turn and flee surprised me. My feet felt leaden, as though they were encased in heavy walking boots rather than the summer sandals I'd slipped on.

The question 'Why?', which had haunted my every waking moment since Saturday, was about to be asked. But I'd never imagined I'd be doing it here. No one in their right mind would choose to have such a private conversation in such a public place.

My breathing was fast, each exhalation a shaky gasp as I closed the distance between us. The sound of the crowd faded and then disappeared beneath the throbbing beat of my pulse.

I stopped behind his seat and reached out a hand towards him; the left one, the one he'd slipped a diamond on to just nine months ago. The stone caught the light shafting through the enormous window beside him and radiated an arc of colours as my hand settled on his shoulder.

'Finn,' I said, my voice surprisingly steady.

Several things seemed to happen at once then. All of them in slow motion. He lifted his head and I'm not sure what surprised me most, the infant cradled against his chest, or the fact that the man with Finn's hair had a completely different face.

'They didn't have any KitKats, babe, so I got us some—' A young woman in fashionably ripped skinny jeans and an oversized T-shirt came to an abrupt stop as she saw a total stranger with her hand resting on her husband's shoulder. It was still on his shoulder, I realised, long after I should have withdrawn it.

I did so now, as though I'd been electrocuted. 'I'm so sorry. I thought you were someone else. I thought you were my husband.' I had no idea why I'd elevated Finn to a position he'd not actually achieved and possibly didn't even want.

The woman seemed much happier now that I'd removed my hand. 'Nope. This one's mine.'

The couple shared a look and I stepped back, babbling an apology. Those close enough to have observed my embarrassing mistake were looking at us over the top of their freebie newspapers and their phones. It was, admittedly, an interesting diversion during the mundane wait before take-off.

I continued to back away, my face so hot it was as if it was sunburnt. I stumbled over someone's walking stick and almost fell flat on my backside, which would have just about completed my total humiliation.

I found myself a seat as far away from the couple as it was possible to get and sank down on to it, trying to make myself very, very small. I spent the next fifteen minutes staring at the moving walkway as it carried new passengers to the gate and then tipped them off at the end, like a factory conveyor belt. Finn was not among them.

The check-in officer who'd issued my boarding pass had relocated to staff the departure gate, which meant there was little point in asking again if anyone could check the computer for me. I doubted his stance on airport security would have changed in the last hour. I also had a strong suspicion that he'd pointed me out to his colleagues, because the back of my neck was prickling in that uncomfortable way it does when you know that someone is staring at you. I turned around and they both jumped guiltily while making a big show of looking the other way.

The sheer number of passengers at Gate 47 made it difficult to say for sure that Finn wasn't somewhere within the crowd. Forty minutes before take-off, boarding eventually began. The crowd thinned slowly: first class and business made a sizeable dent in it, as did families with young children. I waited as, row by row, passengers were summoned to the plane. They called my row and I glanced down at the boarding pass in my hand before slipping it into my pocket. There were now only thirty passengers left queuing patiently to board.

My head jerked up at the sound of footsteps. Some late arrivals were pounding down the travelator, duty-free bags banging against their legs as they ran. Sadly, I looked around the almost empty waiting area and then back towards the main terminal.

I'd seen this scene – or versions of it – in more films than I could remember. At the last moment, with just seconds to spare, someone would come tearing through an airport to save the day, say goodbye, say I love you or beg someone not to leave. Hell, I'd even been in one of those scenes myself.

I closed my eyes and the airport disappeared, to be replaced by another one, four years in the past.

I wasn't going to go. It was crazy. This was no big love story. One date – admittedly a contender for the best I'd ever had – did not make this a love affair. I still wasn't even sure how much I liked Finn. I definitely hadn't liked the first version of him that I'd met, but this new, improved one was an entirely different proposition.

But that didn't make him boyfriend material, and I wasn't looking for one of those anyway. I'd told myself I was done for the time being. I was taking a break, giving my heart a chance to recover from yet another bruisingly bad choice. So why was I now staring at the alarm clock, running calculations through my head? If I ran to the train station and then caught the Gatwick Express, I might – just might – be able to get to the airport in time to… *To what?* asked the sensible version of me. *To do a big romcom farewell scene in the terminal, kissing passionately in the middle of the concourse before Finn went through airport security? And why? Because he'd looked at me with eyes the colour of melted dark chocolate and asked me to see him off? Who did that anyway, outside the pages of a Hollywood script? No one, right? No one except me, it seemed.*

I'll let fate decide, I told myself as I left my flat and hurried towards the station. *If I am 'meant' to go to the airport, if I'm 'meant' to see where this thing could go, the trains will all be with me today. But if they're delayed or cancelled, then it's a sign that this was a stupid plan, and I should just go back home and do something far more sensible with my Saturday morning. How many people are dumb enough to allow the transport authorities to dictate their love life*, I wondered? But, just this once, I was willing to give in to an impulse in a way I'd never done before.

The train was at the platform, its doors open as though in invitation. I jumped on and they immediately slid shut behind me. The connecting express train for the airport was similarly ready and waiting for me. Was it a sign or was this just my lucky day? I resolved to buy a lottery ticket later, just in case.

He will not be there. Of course, he won't be. I repeated the words like a mantra as I rode the escalator up into the airport terminal. I glanced at my watch. I'd checked his flight details while on the train. It would surely already be boarding by now. Finn would have long since gone through security and be airside; he was probably already at the departure gate.

But he wasn't. He was there, in the terminal, looking unbelievably fresh on the short amount of sleep I knew he'd had.

His smile split my resolve like a coconut. Almost as though I was watching someone else, I ran towards him in true movie fashion. He dropped the bag he was holding, and I had just long enough to think *I hope there was nothing breakable in there* before his arms were around me. He lifted me off the floor, something no man had ever done before, and spun me around. It was unclear whether my sudden head rush came from the carousel-like motion, or the nearness of him.

'You came,' he said, his lips tantalisingly close to mine.

'I know,' I said stupidly. 'I have absolutely no idea why.'

His eyes were twinkling as they looked into mine. 'I think I do.'

Somewhere in the back of my mind, sensible Gemma was beating her fists in frustration on an unbreakable window while yelling at me to stop this madness. I tuned her out.

'I think maybe I do too.'

He kissed me then, and if anything it was even better than the ones of the previous night.

'Come with me,' he said, his voice low and husky.

Two beats, maybe three, made me actually consider his words, as though it was a sensible suggestion and not an act of total insanity. Reality kicked in, and it hurt, it really did.

'I can't. I have my family, my job, commitments.'

He nodded, his eyes suddenly sad. 'I know.'

'Stay,' I breathed, shocking myself as much as him. 'Cash in your ticket and stay.'

I liked the way he paused much longer than I had, before sadly shaking his head. 'I can't. I have plans, commitments.'

Brown eyes that I could have lost myself in for ever locked on to mine.

'Our timing sucks.'

I nodded, suddenly far closer to tears than I realised.

'It does. It really does.'

His arms tightened around me as the PA system burst into

life with a message that sounded urgent. 'Will passenger Finn Douglas, travelling to Sydney via Singapore, please proceed immediately to Gate 28.'

I stiffened in his arms. 'They're calling for you.'

He nodded, and there was a sadness on his face as he bent his head and kissed me harder this time, with an urgency that left my lips tingling.

'I have to go.' I nodded, suddenly unsure if my voice was up to the task of replying. 'This isn't over. I don't even know what it is, but it's not over.'

And then, without another word, he scooped up his bag and ran towards the entrance to Security. He never looked back and yet I stayed there, in the middle of the terminal, for a very long time, hoping that he would.

'I'm sorry, but they're about to close the doors on the plane.'

I was jerked back to the present. Standing before me was the kind-faced check-in lady, the one who'd clearly been told my story by her colleague.

'If you're going to get on the flight, you have to do it right now.'

I shook my head sadly. 'I'm not going anywhere.'

She nodded and spoke briskly into the walkie-talkie in her hand. She turned as though to return to the desk, then paused, a look of sympathy on her face.

'He didn't show up then?'

For a moment I wasn't sure if she meant for the wedding or for the flight. It didn't much matter. It was the same answer either way.

'No. He didn't.'

★

'Come back home, Gemma.'

I smiled sadly, cradling my phone against my ear. 'This is my home, Dad.'

He cleared his throat several times, as though searching for and then discarding a variety of persuasive arguments. The one he eventually selected was a weapon so sharp, I didn't see it coming.

'Finn's not coming back, sweetheart.' How was it possible for the words of someone I loved to wound so deeply? 'You have to accept that. He's left.'

'I can't, Dad. I won't.' But even to my ears, it sounded like the denial of a child.

Dad's sigh was raw, almost painful. 'I don't know what else to say to convince you. Finn's cleared out his flat. He's not answering his phone. None of his friends have heard from him. He's done a runner, and if he knows what's good for him, he'll keep on running.'

My dad, the saviour of spiders, the rescuer of half-mauled rodents, the man who didn't have a single aggressive bone in his body, sounded ready to kill my fiancé should he ever reappear.

The room felt suddenly several degrees colder, and I snuggled deeper into the folds of Finn's thick, fleecy sweatshirt. I'd been wearing it almost constantly since finding it on the floor of my wardrobe. 'You missed one,' I'd said sadly as I reached for the forgotten garment and slipped it over my head. My senses had filled with the smell of him that lingered on the fabric. Would I still be wearing the sweatshirt days, weeks, even months from now, when the smell of my own body had erased his? What a tragic thought.

Dad was saying something about the police, which I'd clearly missed.

'Sorry, Dad, what was that?'

'I was just asking what that policeman chap said when you told him what you'd found.'

Or what I'd not found, if we were being strictly accurate.

'He said it seemed clear Finn had left of his own volition and that as he wasn't classed as vulnerable or at risk in any way, there was very little they could do.' I sighed heavily, much as I'd done during my conversation with Inspector Graham. 'Basically, their attitude is that Finn is a grown man who appears to have changed his mind and taken the easy way out by choosing not to face the backlash following his non-appearance at his own wedding.'

I'd almost laughed at that, wondering what about this situation Inspector Graham had thought was remotely easy.

'I'm so sorry this has happened to you, my love,' Dad said sadly. 'You didn't deserve this.'

'This isn't what you all think it is,' I said, perfectly aware that by now I was sounding like a broken record.

'Why don't you come for lunch tomorrow,' urged Dad, clearly happier with a change of subject. 'I'll make us one of my famous roasts. It'll be like old times.'

Except Mum wouldn't be there. And now neither would Finn.

'Okay. I'll see you then.'

TUESDAY: DAY THREE

15

If someone had asked me where the bundle of postcards was, I truly wouldn't have been able to tell them. Which made it even more eerie when they tumbled out of the top of my wardrobe as I stowed away my carry-on bag. I retrieved the stack from the bedroom carpet, where it had landed face up. The colours of the topmost image had faded over the years. The colour of the Australian sky was less cerulean, the water of Sydney harbour looked more grey than aquamarine. But the Opera House still looked good. The rubber band holding the collection was four years old and had perished, snapping painfully against my fingers like a warning as soon as I touched it.

I crossed to the bed and laid out the postcards on top of the duvet. I didn't need to read the postmarks to know in which order they'd been sent – I could plot the course of the locations as though they were pins on a map. A map showing a route I'd never travelled, but one that Finn had.

The first postcard had been sent from Sydney and had landed on my doormat about three weeks after I'd bidden Finn goodbye at the airport. I'd scarcely paused to study the picture in my eagerness to reach his message. Journalists are taught to be succinct, but Finn had written nothing other than his name on the postcard, taking brevity to a whole new level.

The cards had continued to arrive; a new one every two or three weeks. They ranged from the Great Barrier Reef to the Twelve Apostles in Victoria and detailed Finn's comprehensive Australian road trip. But whether the cards featured the majestic stark beauty of Uluru, lovable kangaroos and koalas, or the breathtaking scenery of the Great Ocean Road, he had never written a single message on any of them.

I had no address to reply to. His UK mobile phone number no longer worked, and he hadn't given me his new Australian one. If it wasn't for the constant trickle of postcards, Finn Douglas could be said to have completely disappeared from my life. Although never from my thoughts.

I must have replayed our last evening together a thousand times, and as so often happens with a happy memory, it just kept on getting better in my imagination, until I began to wonder why the hell I *hadn't* got on the plane with him when he'd asked me to. It was a dangerous line of thinking.

'I'm thinking of taking a holiday,' I said in a whisper to Hannah.

'That's nice,' Hannah whispered back, glancing into the bassinet beside her to make sure our lowered voices hadn't woken her newborn infant, who was perfect in every way apart from her belief that sleep was something other babies did, but not her. 'Where are you thinking of going?'

I paused, not for fear of waking Milly, but because I already knew how my answer was going to be received.

'Australia.'

'What?' Hannah cried, loud enough to make her baby murmur restlessly. 'I thought you were going to say somewhere in Europe.'

'Well, I've got over three and a half weeks' holiday that I need to use, so it just makes sense to go somewhere further afield.'

Hannah gave a derisive snort. 'Oh right. And this has nothing at all to do with a certain journalist, turned barista, turned who-knows-what, who just happens to live there?'

I blushed. There was little point in lying to Hannah; she'd see straight through it in a heartbeat.

'I thought it might be nice to pay Finn a visit.'

'But I thought you didn't have his contact details – or even know where he lives, except that it's somewhere in Sydney.'

'I don't,' I said, aware that my cheeks were still flushed.

Hannah stayed quiet for a long moment. 'Not exactly a perfect plan then, is it?'

I got to my feet, too uncomfortable to remain seated as she went into full prosecutor mode.

'I thought you said you were happy when Finn and I went out together? You told me you'd always known it would happen.'

'Did I? I can't remember,' Hannah said, conveniently feigning a case of baby brain. 'I mean, obviously I want you to be happy, Gem, but Finn hasn't exactly kept in contact since he left, has he?'

'He sends postcards all the time,' I countered, seriously regretting this entire conversation. 'They're kind of like an invitation for me to go out there... in a way,' I finished lamely.

Milly stirred again and Hannah gently rocked the bassinet until she had settled once more.

'So, what are you planning on doing? Catching a flight and hoping you'll just randomly bump into him somewhere in the city?'

'Don't be ridiculous.'

We'd been friends long enough to call each other out when needed without causing offence, but her reply still stung. '*One of us is being ridiculous here, but I really don't think it's me.*'

I did have a plan, of sorts, and to her credit Hannah listened to it without further interruption.

'I'm going to send him a message on Instagram,' I said. 'Something breezy and casual.'

'Uh huh.' It was almost as if Hannah already *knew* how many hours I'd spent trying to compose the supposedly innocent request. I glanced down at my phone, not needing to click on the Notes icon, because every word of the draft message was indelibly imprinted on my brain.

Hi, Finn. How are you? Just wanted to say thank you for all the postcards you've sent me over the last eight months. I've loved getting them and they've really made me want to see Australia in person! So, here's an idea. I've got over three weeks holiday owing to me and was wondering if you fancied having a house guest next month? It would be so great to see you again. Message me back and we can hopefully fix something up. Love Gemma x

Fortunately, before Hannah could add any further objections to the ones she'd already put forward, Milly woke with a start and immediately began crying for her next feed.

It wasn't as though Hannah could have said anything I hadn't already considered myself, I acknowledged, as I drove home from her house. The postcards from Finn were a conundrum. On the one hand they suggested that I was still very much in his thoughts, but if that was truly the case, why hadn't he bothered picking up the phone to speak to me, or sent me a message? It didn't make sense. Was he simply giving me enough time to miss him, because if that was the intention he need wait no longer: I already did.

Hannah might believe Finn was just my 'one who got away', but late at night, in the quiet of my bedroom, I relived the passion of his kiss, the warmth in his expression, and the sincerity in his voice when he'd told me at the airport that *this wasn't over*. I was banking on the reliability of those memories, despite my friend's scepticism.

I stared down at the postcards on the duvet now, as though they held a hidden clue. Was Finn already on the other side of the world? Was my search for him fruitless because one of the locations spread out before me had presented a more attractive proposition than spending the rest of his life with me?

I swept the cards angrily to one side, watching as they fell to the floor in a kaleidoscope of colours, before collapsing on to the carpet beside them, my shoulders heaving in silent sobs. Because as much as I had told myself the postcards proved that Finn wanted me, the truth four years ago had been a little harder to swallow.

*

It was a full week before Finn replied to my Instagram message. I'd sent a second message by then, giving him my phone number in case he'd lost it. But in the end he opted not to speak to me in person, which even I had to acknowledge didn't bode well. Seven days after reaching out to him, his reply landed. Or rather – as Hannah so eloquently described it – crash-landed.

Hey G, it began. Great to hear from you. Hope all is well in rainy old England. I totally understand why you'd like to escape to the Aussie sunshine. But I'm afraid next month isn't good for me.

I'd seriously debated not telling Hannah about Finn's reply because no one likes to hear 'I told you so', but to her credit Hannah never actually said those words out loud, although her body language yelled it from the rooftops.

She read the message several times before handing my phone back to me. 'What kind of crappy excuse is that? *His building is being fumigated and he has to move out?*'

Instinctively, I leapt to Finn's defence, and I really had no idea why, because she was only saying what was in my head. 'Insect infestation is a real problem out there. Getting buildings fumigated is a regular thing. You don't want roaches running all over the place.'

Hannah's expression was grim. 'There's only one cockroach in this story, hon, and it's not the type with six legs and bug eyes.'

I sighed sadly. 'It could be a genuine reason.'

Hannah shook her head. 'And what about the bit he wrote after that?'

I looked back down at my phone, reading the last words Finn Douglas was probably ever going to say to me.

I'm going to be moving in with a friend while they fumigate the unit and then do some major renovations, and unfortunately she only has *one* spare room so I wouldn't be able to offer you anywhere to stay. Maybe another time? Finn

There would be no 'other time'. I knew it. And as though to prove me right, the postcards had stopped after that. Finn had clearly moved on and with reluctance I'd realised I had to do the same.

I knocked on the door and waited to be let in. At my feet, Chester, my dad's crabby and overweight cat, did the same. He rushed through the door first, no doubt heading straight for his food bowl. My manners were a little better, although I did sniff the air appreciatively as the smell of roasting beef wafted down the hallway. For the first time in days, I thought I might actually be hungry.

'How are you doing, kiddo?' Dad asked, enveloping me in the kind of hug that made me long for the time when there was no problem he couldn't fix, no monster he couldn't slay.

'I'm okay,' I lied into the cotton of his shirt front. I made sure there was a passable smile on my lips before I stepped out of his hold. 'I'm hanging in there.'

Dad nodded. 'One day at a time, Gem, that's the only way to cope with this kind of thing.' He was treating Finn's disappearance like a bereavement, one I had to grieve my way through, while Hannah was treating it like a crime, whose only fitting punishment was castration. It amazed me how they could both be on my side so wholeheartedly and yet still be completely wrong.

I followed Dad into the kitchen, glancing at the banister post to see the tie that I knew he'd have discarded there. I fingered the silky fabric as I passed, my eyebrows lifting at the vibrant psychedelic pattern.

'It's getting harder to find new ones. I've pretty much cleaned out every charity shop in the area.'

Dad wore a new tie every Tuesday, without fail. The crazier the better. He was a jeans and T-shirt kind of man, through and through, but Mum used to love getting dressed up and would try to get him to wear a shirt and tie when they went out on Tuesdays, which had always been their 'date night'. He always resisted, with an obstinacy I never understood. In retaliation, she'd buy him a new tie every single birthday, Christmas and anniversary. He'd never worn any of them until the day of her funeral. Each week since then, he'd pulled a new one from the dresser drawer and worn it to visit the place where she lay in one half of a double plot, patiently waiting for the day he'd join her.

'It's his way of saying she was right and showing her how much he still loves her,' I'd told Finn, trying to explain my father's Tuesday pilgrimages. 'Each week he irons a shirt, puts on a new tie and goes to sit on the bench beside her grave. He tells her all about his week, what's new with me, what the neighbours have been up to, and anything else he thinks she might like to know.'

I'd waited for Finn to back away or say something about it being a little unhealthy – an observation one of my exes had foolishly made. But Finn wasn't like that. He'd mulled over my words for a moment before nodding slowly.

'That makes sense. I can see why he'd do that. It's nice for both of them.'

That might have been the moment when I first realised that everything I'd ever hoped to find in a partner was standing right there in front of me. Finn was the unexpected miracle I'd almost stopped believing in.

Dad went straight to the kettle without bothering to ask if I wanted tea. The room felt comfortable and welcoming as I sat down at the same table where earlier versions of me had created finger-painting masterpieces, made cakes with my mum and struggled for hours over my maths homework. I breathed in the memories like Entonox pain relief.

'Any news today?' asked Dad, placing a steaming mug of tea in front of me before sitting down with one of his own.

'No. No news,' I replied, taking a sip from the scalding brew.

'What did the police say this morning?'

'"Please stop calling us three times a day, Miss Fletcher."' I'd meant it as a joke, but it was too close to the truth to be funny.

'Do you think they'll ever launch a proper investigation?'

I shrugged. 'According to them, there's still nothing *to* investigate. They refer to Finn as being absent rather than missing. I guess it's all about the semantics.'

Dad looked pained, and I could only imagine how much he hated not being able to help me.

'Inspector Graham is keeping his eye on the hospitals and

his ear to the ground, or so he says. I don't think he has any other body parts spare to look for my missing fiancé.'

We did well for the next twenty minutes, managing to switch topics and successfully ignore the elephant in the room. But it came trumpeting back as Dad busied himself at the sink. Some questions are easier to ask when you're not looking into someone's eyes.

'What are you going to do now, Gemma?'

My hands were in the cutlery drawer, but somehow I didn't think 'Lay the table' was the answer he was looking for.

'I'm going to keep looking for him.'

Dad dried his hands on a tea towel and turned to face me. I could sense a question coming and knew it was the kind that demanded eye contact. 'For how long?'

The tines of a fork were pressing into my palm, but they didn't hurt as much as his words.

'For as long as it takes. I won't stop, because if this had happened to *me*, if *I* was the one no one could find, Finn would never give up until he found me.'

Dad's sigh needed no words. It spoke volumes.

'Lunch is almost ready.'

It was a relief to escape from the look in his eyes as I crossed the hallway to the dining room. There was a large oak tree in the garden that kept the room permanently in shadow, so even though it was summer, I automatically reached for the light switch. The bulb glowed with unexpected brilliance for a moment before expiring with a small ping. I dumped the cutlery on the dining room table and headed for the stairs.

'I'm dishing up,' warned Dad from the kitchen.

'I'm just getting a new bulb from the cupboard in the spare room,' I replied, taking the stairs at a run.

'Okay. Oh, no. Actually, hang on, Gemma. Let me get it. Please.'

'I'm there now,' I called down from the upstairs landing, frowning at the inexplicable anxiety in his voice. Except it wasn't inexplicable for long. I opened the door to the spare bedroom, which had admittedly become a bit of a dumping ground over the last few years. And never more so than today.

'Oh,' I said, my voice a soft exclamation as I rocked on my heels just inside the doorway.

My eyes scanned the room. There was a small double bed in there. It was where Dad had insisted Finn slept, that first time I brought him home. Only I couldn't see the bed now, for it was lost beneath a mountain of wrapped gifts. All of them unopened. Dad hadn't mentioned the wedding presents, and I'd certainly not thought to ask what had happened to them. It must have taken him ages to carry them all up there, which I now realised he must have done so I wouldn't be confronted with yet another reminder of the wedding that never was.

There was a curious sweetness in the air that I could practically taste on my tongue, and even before I turned around, I knew where it was coming from. I heard the slow thud of Dad's footsteps climbing the stairs and had just enough time to swipe a hand beneath my eyes to brush away my tears. His hand felt warm on my shoulder as he drew me against his side.

It was the first time I'd seen my wedding cake in real life, and it looked even better than it had in the catalogue we'd picked it from. The presents I could deal with; they were just prettily wrapped packages. But coming face to face with the three-tiered creation covered in delicate run-outs that made it look as though it was draped in lace was just too much.

'Why is this here? Why didn't it get eaten at the reception?'

Dad's voice was thick. He was clearly hoping to have avoided this one today.

'No one could face cutting it, sweetheart, much less eating it. It seemed... wrong somehow.'

I swallowed several times, until the lump in my throat was small enough to let me speak. 'Well, I hope you still like fruit cake with your tea, because it looks like you'll be eating it for the next couple of years.'

The hand resting on my shoulder squeezed it warmly. I didn't need to turn my head to know he was shaking his.

I drew in a deep breath and took one last look at the bride and groom standing side by side on the top tier in a way Finn and I had never got to do. I'd declared the figures too cheesy, but Finn had said it wouldn't be a proper wedding cake without them. I reached out a finger and gently touched the groom figurine.

'Can you arrange for this to go to that care home on the edge of town?' I asked softly. 'It's a shame for it to go to waste.'

My appetite had gone, but I still ate every last morsel on my plate, because Dad was worried enough about me and didn't need to add 'potential eating disorder' to the list. We got as far as the apple crumble without venturing on to any conversational quicksand. When we did, it came from a chance comment I made about the bunch of bright orange gerberas Dad had placed in a vase in the middle of the dining room table.

'Those are gorgeous.'

'I took your mum a bunch this morning, and they looked so nice, I bought a second one for here.'

'Was it quiet there this morning? I imagine you must have had quite a lot to tell Mum this week.'

Dad's smile was tender, the way it was whenever he spoke of his weekly visits. 'It's always quiet that early. There's seldom anyone else—' He broke off suddenly, as though he'd almost stepped into a yawning chasm. He blinked several times, the way people do when they can't quite make out what they're looking at. As the only thing in front of him was his empty dinner plate, I assumed that whatever he was seeing was in his head, rather than the dining room.

'What is it, Dad? Is something wrong?'

He took several moments to come back from wherever it was his thoughts had led him. 'No,' he said, shaking his head back and forth. 'It's nothing.'

It clearly wasn't nothing. But it was just as obvious that he wasn't going to share whatever was bothering him with me.

'Really. It's nothing,' he repeated, getting to his feet so quickly he almost tripped over Chester, who was never far away from a table full of food. 'Let's take our coffees into the garden, shall we? It's a lovely afternoon.'

I was being steered – none too subtly – away from the topic, but because I loved him, and because he was all I had left right now, I allowed him to do it.

16

Right now, we should have been strolling hand in hand through Sydney's botanical gardens or preparing to climb the famous Harbour Bridge or sipping cocktails at the bar by the water's edge outside the iconic Opera House. Our itinerary for the first few days of our trip had been full of tourist must-dos.

But instead of that, I was standing outside my office building, trying to find the courage to walk through the doors. I'd parked my car in the exact same spot Finn and I had fought over the first time we met. It had been curiously vacant today, even though the rest of the car park was packed. I wasn't superstitious, I never had been, but I took that as a sign.

Dad had been astounded when he'd asked me what I was doing for the rest of the day and I'd replied, 'Going into the office.'

'To work?' he'd queried incredulously. 'But you've still got almost three weeks left from your h– holiday.' We both politely pretended not to notice he'd done a very poor job of substituting the word 'honeymoon' with 'holiday' at the last moment.

'I'm not going in to *work*. I want to use the big colour photocopier. I'm going to print up flyers of Finn's photograph and then distribute them to as many places as I can during the rest of my time off.' I sighed wearily. 'If the police aren't willing to do this kind of thing, then I'm just going to have to do it myself.' I sat up straighter in my chair, braced for his objections. But none came.

'That sounds like a really good idea to me.'

I'd told no one I was coming into the office. I was hoping to slip in unobserved, make the copies I wanted and then leave as unobtrusively as possible. I wasn't sure I was up to explaining why I was still in the UK and not honeymooning on the other side of the world.

What I'd failed to factor in was that there would be no need to tell anyone what had happened to me – because they already knew. I'd invited a handful of close colleagues to the wedding, and news travels fast in offices, particularly in that industry. We'd doubtless been the number one topic of conversation at the water cooler this week. I shuddered, knowing only too well how some of those exchanges had probably played out.

There's an unpleasant culture of bitchiness in some magazines, and *Glow* was as big a culprit as any. I doubt it would have taken long before someone's claws were unsheathed and comments of sympathy digressed into something entirely different.

The girl behind the reception desk clearly knew all about what had happened, and she was so new to the company I didn't even know her name yet. Her face journeyed through at least five different expressions of amazement as she watched me swipe into the building, nod briefly in her direction, and stride towards the lifts.

Avoiding my desk, I took a circuitous route to the print room, hoping to find it empty. Sadly, it wasn't. Jacqueline, the MD, looked up as I entered the room. Her latest Botox injections were too effective to allow the astonishment she was clearly feeling to show, but her mouth dropped open in a huge O of surprise.

'Gemma, darling, whatever are you doing here?'

Jacqueline was impossible to age, but from the number of years she'd been in publishing, popular opinion placed her somewhere in her mid-fifties. She wore the years well, and today I looked and felt at least twenty her senior.

'I've come in to use the copier,' I explained, my hold tightening on the tote bag slung over my shoulder. Inside it was a photograph of Finn. Too late, I realised I should probably have asked permission to use the company's facilities rather than just telling her. 'If that's okay with you?' I added hastily. 'I'd like to print out some "Missing" posters.'

Jacqueline's eyes widened and then narrowed, as much as her cosmetic surgery would allow.

'I'll obviously pay for whatever supplies I use.'

She shook her head, her immaculately cut bob falling instantly back into place. 'You'll do no such thing. Feel free to use whatever you need. We're all here for you, Gemma. I hope you know that.'

I nodded vigorously, afraid that my voice would crack if I attempted to use it right then.

'Pop into my office and see me before you go.'

It was a directive rather than an invitation.

I nodded again, waiting until she'd left the room before drawing out the envelope with Finn's photograph from my bag.

I'd probably taken hundreds of photos of Finn during the time we'd been together, but most of them lived in either my phone or his. As much as I loved our many selfies, what I needed for the flyer was a front-facing shot of Finn by himself, preferably one where he wasn't pulling a goofy face at the camera.

In the end, there was really only one I could pick. It was my favourite of all the photographs I'd ever snapped of him, which was why it lived inside a silver frame on my bedside table. It was a great photo, taken late the previous summer, just as the sun was setting. Finn had been looking straight at me, and somehow I'd managed to capture in pixels the excitement we'd both been feeling at that moment.

People say you're in charge of your own destiny, but sometimes fate steps in and takes over. How could we have known that getting lost on a summer's evening in the middle of nowhere would change the course of our future?

From the first moment I saw it, I knew Mushroom Cottage was my dream home – Finn's too, or so he said.

It was only much, much later that I came to realise we'd been dreaming two completely different dreams.

I considered stopping at five hundred sheets but found myself reaching for a second ream and feeding it into the paper tray.

What if flyer number 1,000 was the one that succeeded in jogging someone's memory; what if that was the one that shed some light on Finn's disappearance?

It was oddly hypnotic, staring down at the rapidly growing pile, as Finn's image shot out fifty times a minute. It was hard to look away from his face, although, to be fair, the building in the topmost corner of the photograph drew my attention every bit as much. Mushroom Cottage. Just thinking about it made my heart beat a little faster.

It's impossible to say how much more of *Glow*'s stationery I might have depleted if there hadn't been a sudden rush of legitimate users for the photocopier. I quickly slid my printing into a box, aware that someone from Accounts – whose name I'd forgotten – was staring with interest at the word 'Missing' emblazoned across the top of the sheet. I rammed the lid on to the box and made a rapid retreat before someone asked me a question I wasn't prepared to answer.

Jacqueline's office was on the other side of the open-plan floor, and a quick look at my watch confirmed it was almost the time when many of the *Glow* workforce took a trip up to the rooftop cafe for a break. Silently congratulating myself on my excellent timing, I turned instead towards the Ladies', which had dropped its unisex access several years earlier.

My luck was definitely on a roll, for the room was empty. Even so, I chose the furthest cubicle from the entrance. I heard the swish of the door opening and closing several times in the minutes that followed and realised there was probably little chance of avoiding every single person I knew on this visit. Sooner or later I'd either have to face everyone or find somewhere new to work. Oddly, the latter option didn't sound entirely unappealing. Was it time to move on, I wondered?

I could hear a low buzz of conversation, but over the hum of the hand dryer and water splashing into the basins it was difficult to identify who was in the Ladies' with me. There were three or possibly four different voices. I drew in a steadying breath and had just placed my fingers on the bolt, ready to slide open the cubicle door, when I heard my name.

I froze.

'Did you guys see that Gemma was here today?'

I frowned, trying and failing to identify the voice.

'Nooooooo,' replied one of her companions, with more 'o's than I'd thought it possible to add to that word.

'Yeah. God, if it was me, I'd be sitting in a darkened room somewhere with a tub of ice cream and a bottle of vodka.'

They laughed, and my jaw tightened, which at least prevented me from saying what I was thinking.

'She must feel awful, though,' added someone, who I was pretty sure was Melanie, one of the junior staff writers.

I should make a move, let them know that I'm here, I thought. *Before it gets too awkward to emerge from the stall altogether.* And yet instead of sliding open the bolt, my hand dropped to my side.

'Lucy was there, you know, at the wedding on Saturday. She said it was excruciating. Apparently, Gemma kept insisting that something dreadful had happened to him.'

'Like what?'

There was a silence, which I imagined was filled with an expressive shrug of the speaker's shoulders.

'I dunno. It's a shitty thing to do to someone. I mean, fair enough if Finn had changed his mind and didn't want to marry her any more, but he shouldn't just have buggered off and done a runner.'

'What makes you think he did?' asked the person who I was now positive was Melanie. If *she* hadn't asked that question, it would have been an excellent moment for me to have emerged from the stall and done so. But I'd missed my moment, and what I heard next made it unlikely I'd be going anywhere until they'd all left the room.

'Do you really need to ask that? You've seen Finn, haven't you? I mean, Gemma's pretty enough, in a girl-next-door kind of way, but surely she must have known that she was batting. Big time. A friend of mine went out with Finn a couple of times a few years back and said it was like dating a film star. And that was before he became a successful author. Women are always going to be falling all over him. Guys like that aren't the settling-down type.'

A fourth voice piped up for the first time.

'I don't think you can dismiss other people's relationships purely on who's more attractive than who. And I always thought Gemma and Finn were kind of cute together.'

The other woman, who'd clearly been the inspiration behind the original *Mean Girls* concept, gave a decidedly pig-like snort. 'Well, if you'd seen what I saw a couple of weeks ago, you might want to rethink that idea.'

My heart dropped like a broken lift into the pit of my stomach, as though it fancied trying out a new location.

From the girls at the basins, I could sense an excited clamour, like crows picking at the unfortunate remains of something that never made it to the other side of the road. It felt very much like the thing they were pecking at was my heart.

'What? What have you heard?' someone asked.

'It's not what I heard, it's what I saw.'

I felt sick, literally physically sick. As I was in close

proximity to a toilet, that was handy, but the need to stay very, very quiet was never more important than it was right then.

Too late, I remembered my mother once telling me never to listen in on other people's conversations, as eavesdroppers rarely heard anything good about themselves. What she'd failed to mention was that they never heard anything good about the people they loved either.

'I saw Finn getting into a car with a very attractive woman with long blonde hair a couple of weeks ago. They looked pretty "up close and personal", in my opinion.'

'That doesn't prove he was fooling around.'

'I dunno. There was just something about how it looked – sort of shifty. The woman was driving, and I was in the car behind them, and it was easy to see the way she kept leaning towards him and laughing, and how he kept looking all around whenever they were stopped at the lights, as though he didn't want anyone to see them.'

'Why didn't you say anything to Gemma?'

Again, that was my question, screamed silently from the privacy of my cubicle.

'It was none of my business. Anyway, like you said, there might have been some perfectly innocent explanation. I wouldn't want to be accused of spreading gossip.'

Too late, I thought bitterly, as, having casually decimated my relationship, the women walked out, completely oblivious to the devastation they had left behind.

'Close the door,' instructed Jacqueline.

I turned and did as she asked, dismayed to see there was

still a slight tremor in my hand. What I'd overheard in the Ladies' had rattled me, and the only thing stopping me from immediately fleeing the building was my promise to drop by and see Jacqueline.

Once the room had emptied, I'd spent several minutes splashing copious amounts of water on to my flushed cheeks. It hadn't done much to tone down the redness, and I still looked like someone who'd been repeatedly slapped. That wasn't a bad analogy, because the words of my unseen colleagues had certainly felt like an assault.

It wasn't the identity of the mystery woman in the car with Finn that bothered me, because we both had plenty of friends of the opposite sex who we saw regularly. It wasn't even their verdict that I was punching above my weight, because what Finn and I shared was too secure to let that kind of nonsense worry me. All that proved was that no one ever really knows or understands the dynamics in someone else's relationship.

But what did bother me, much more than I cared to admit, was that the person telling the story had been so certain that Finn hadn't wanted to be seen.

My eyes looked odd, suddenly too big for my face, as I'd patted my cheeks dry with a handful of paper towels from the dispenser. What was it that Finn had been doing that he was so anxious no one should know about?

'Did you manage to do your printing?' Jacqueline asked as I entered her room, her eyes dropping briefly to the box balanced on my hip.

'Yes. Thank you again for that.'

Jacqueline smiled and nodded towards the chair on the opposite side of her desk. Reluctantly, I sat down, my hopes of making this a flying visit rapidly disappearing.

'How are you doing, Gemma?' my boss asked, leaning further towards me with her chin resting on her cupped palms. It was a classic 'I am really listening' pose, and it instantly made me uncomfortable.

'Okay. Well, you know, not okay. Not really.'

'If there's anything at all we can do to help, you only have to ask.'

I didn't imagine for a moment she was volunteering to join me in tacking flyers to tree trunks, but suddenly I realised there was a way she could help me – very significantly, in fact.

'Actually, there is something.'

Jacqueline bristled in the way of someone who hadn't really wanted – or expected – her offer to be taken up.

'Would you be able to post one of these on the *Glow* website?' I asked, my fingers clumsy as I pulled the lid off the box and passed one of the 'Missing' posters across the desk to her.

Jacqueline looked down at the sheet for a long moment, as though it was a piece of copy that required a great deal of work before it could go to print. After what felt like an uncomfortably long silence, she set down the flyer and met my anxious gaze.

'Finn's an extremely attractive man.' I wondered what the appropriate response was to that observation. Thank you? I know? 'It must have been very upsetting to have been left at the altar.'

Unconsciously, my hands tightened on the wooden arms of the chair. 'That wasn't exactly what happened.'

Botox allows for only limited eyebrow movement, but Jacqueline gave it her best shot.

'I mean, yes, Finn didn't turn up at the church, but not in

the way that everyone seems to think. He didn't leave me. He's missing.'

'Of course.'

My answer was there in those two words, and yet I pressed on. I had no idea why. 'So, would you be able to put this up on the website?'

Jacqueline pretended to consider my request, but after working at *Glow* for seven years, I already knew when her mind was made up. 'As much as I would love to, it's not really… appropriate. It's not the kind of thing we *usually* do.'

'Well, perhaps that's because this isn't the kind of thing that *usually* happens,' I countered, too angry to notice her slight recoil of surprise.

Jacqueline drummed a set of perfectly gelled nails on her desktop. 'I suppose we could run a piece about how it feels to be in your current… predicament.'

I almost laughed at her careful choice of words, as though losing your fiancé on your wedding day was a terrible inconvenience, right up there with your Uber not turning up on time.

'You mean a piece about being jilted,' I challenged, getting to my feet as I spoke.

Jacqueline had the grace to look momentarily uncomfortable, but little shook her equilibrium for long. You needed to be sure-footed to climb as high up the publishing ladder as she had. It made me suddenly realise that I had absolutely no head for heights.

'No, Jacqueline. Thank you for the offer, but I really don't think I'll be writing that piece.' I wondered if the distant thumping noise I could hear was my heartbeat or the sound of me hammering the first nail into my career coffin. 'But thanks for the paper and the use of the copier. I'll see you in three weeks,' I said, turning towards the door.

She didn't try to stop me, and it really wouldn't have done her any good if she had.

'You should leave,' Finn said. It was six months before our wedding, and we were lying in bed on a lazy Sunday morning, which I'd just ruined by thinking about the amount of work waiting to be dealt with in my inbox the following day. 'You're too good for that job, Gemma.'

I laughed and pulled him closer, breathing in the warm smell of his skin. If I could have bottled it, I swear I'd never buy another fragrance for as long as I lived. 'I think you might be biased,' I said, wriggling my hips until we were skin to skin, heartbeat to heartbeat. His was getting faster, and mine wasn't far behind.

'And what would I do if I left?' I asked him, finding it suddenly hard to concentrate as his body began to react to my closeness. 'And anyway, it seems ungrateful to walk away from the job you patently gave to me.'

He laughed, a low throaty chuckle. 'Not that again. How many times do I have to tell you, the job at *Glow* was never mine.'

It was an old bone of contention that I dug up from time to time. Finn had never once admitted to turning down the job so I could have it, and I'd never once stopped believing that he had.

His hands were on my hips now, and with a practised skill I didn't like to examine too closely, he effortlessly lifted me so that I was now positioned on top of him. I gasped and knew that thirty seconds from now, this conversation would be the furthest thing from my mind.

'You could do anything you want. Find another magazine, or another newspaper, or jack it all in and write a book.'

I laughed, but his last suggestion had piqued my interest.

'What about? I don't have a story to tell.'

'Everyone has a story,' Finn replied, his breath warm against my throat. 'You just haven't found yours yet. Taking a gamble and writing a book was the best decision I ever made.' He shook his head then, as though he'd just said something ridiculous. 'Nah. Make that the second-best decision. Coming back to you will always be my number one.'

He looked up at me, his expression warm and growing hotter by the moment.

Leaving *Glow* was something that would need careful consideration, but with Finn's hands slowly travelling up from my ribcage and cupping my breasts, coherent thought had never seemed further away.

17

THE BOOKSHOP

Eighteen months earlier

'I'm sorry! I'm so late!' Hannah cried as she raced across the slippery pavement towards me.

'Not really,' I lied, because I didn't want her to feel bad, and also it wasn't *her* fault that my toes were so cold I'd lost all feeling in them fifteen minutes earlier. That was entirely down to me having chosen thin-soled fashion boots rather than something sensible. 'I only just got here myself,' I added for good measure.

'Well, that's just a big, fat lie,' Hannah said, linking her arm through mine. 'Because your bright red nose says you've been waiting for me in this snowstorm for quite a while.'

I grimaced at her words. A shiny red nose was definitely not the look I'd spent so long in front of the mirror trying to achieve.

'It's cute. It makes you look kind of Rudolphy,' Hannah said consolingly. 'Although admittedly you're a bit early for Christmas.'

She wasn't wrong there. It was only mid-November and the unexpected miniature blizzard had caught everyone by surprise. The roads weren't gritted yet, public transport was ill-prepared, and the trains were all running late. Even more annoying, the 'see what you've been missing' look I'd been aiming for didn't work nearly so well when you resembled someone suffering from hypothermia.

I shivered and burrowed deeper into the thick white scarf I'd wound tightly around my neck. Waiting at the busy intersection, I'd been transfixed by the window display in the bookshop on the opposite side of the road. The bookshop where, right now, a man I hadn't seen for two and a half years was holding the final event of his book tour.

'Do you think it will have started already?' Hannah asked worriedly as she pressed the pedestrian-crossing button.

'Probably,' I said, my eyes going once again to the glossy photograph in the bookshop window. Below Finn's face, a banner had been pasted, which read: *Book Signing Here Tonight*.

Like a portrait in a scary movie, Finn's eyes seemed to follow me as we waited for the green man to allow us to cross. I could still feel them on us as we stepped on to the crossing.

'William got held up at work,' Hannah explained apologetically, 'which meant I missed my train, and now *you've* missed the start of the event.'

'It's really not important,' I assured her, because she was already doing me a favour by swapping our monthly girls' night out of pizza and Prosecco (which she loved) to attend an author talk by Finn Douglas (who she most definitely did not love).

'You want to go to his book signing?' she'd asked incredulously, several weeks earlier, when I'd shown her the screenshot on my phone advertising the tour.

'Erm… yes,' I'd said, bracing myself for what I knew would surely come.

'For a man who has effectively ghosted you for the last two and a half years?'

I shifted uncomfortably on my chair. 'I think it's fair to say I ghosted him every bit as much as he did me.'

Hannah gave an angry snort. 'He could have kept in touch. At the very least he could have messaged you after your mum died.'

I swallowed the mouthful of coffee from the cup I'd been enjoying until that moment. It tasted suddenly bitter. 'Finn wouldn't have known anything about Mum unless he was following me on social media – which he wasn't.'

With a vicious tug, Hannah tore a strip from the Danish pastry on her plate. It felt symbolic of the strip she'd quite like to tear off the man who'd disappeared from my life and shown no interest in re-entering it.

'Okay, I'll come,' she said, chomping down on the sweet pastry. 'But for the record, I would like it noted that a man who walks away first from a great job, and then a successful business, and finally from the best woman he's ever likely to meet, is most definitely not a keeper. He's a bloody idiot.'

'You be sure to tell him that at the signing,' I said, giving her a grateful hug.

An old-fashioned bell tinkled above our heads as we eased open the bookshop door and slipped inside. Almost immediately, a woman appeared out of nowhere, carrying a clipboard and looking important.

'Are you here for the Finn Douglas event?' she asked in a stage whisper that seemed unnecessary, as the shop appeared to be completely deserted. Was the event over so soon? Or had no one bothered showing up? If so, it was probably the first time Finn had ever been stood up.

'I'm afraid you've missed the bit with the wine and the canapés,' the woman whispered regretfully as she led us past tables displaying all the latest bestsellers.

'So people did turn up?'

She looked at me as though I'd said something totally crazy.

'In their droves. Mainly women, of course, but then it's been that way at every stop of the tour. There aren't too many thriller writers with such universal appeal, and of course it helps that Finn's great in front of a live audience.'

He's pretty amazing one on one, too, a tiny voice in my head piped up. I ignored it, the way I'd taught myself to do very effectively over the intervening years.

'His latest book is brilliant,' continued the woman, who I guessed must be his publicist. 'It made *The Times* bestseller list this week, you know.'

I did know. And I also knew how good it was, having blagged an early proof copy from *Glow*'s book editor several months ago. I'd read it three times. Finn's career was clearly on the ascent, and in a way that made his decision to prioritise it over a potential relationship with me slightly more bearable. Finn had followed his heart, and you really couldn't blame someone for doing that, even though my own might have sustained some collateral damage as a result.

'There should still be a couple of spaces in the back row,' the publicist whispered as she ushered us towards the rear of the shop, where I could now see how ridiculous my question about poor attendance had been. There had to be at least twenty rows of chairs set out, and pretty much every one was occupied.

I hunted along the back row until I found two vacant seats. It was only when we were settled on them that I finally allowed myself to look towards the front of the room, where on a raised dais sat the man I'd come there to see.

Finn was sitting on a wing-backed armchair, his long legs stretched out in front of him, crossed at the ankles. He looked relaxed and confident and so achingly familiar that my mouth immediately went dry, while my eyes threatened to do the exact opposite.

He was dressed entirely in black, which made him look intriguing and also a little bit dangerous. I ignored the part of my brain that wanted to add 'sexy' to that description, even though I knew it to be true. Finn was smiling at the female interviewer sitting diagonally opposite him on the stage. She introduced him with an abundance of compliments and a squawk of feedback from the microphone. With gentle self-mockery, Finn thanked her for the warm welcome and politely declined the offer of a microphone.

'Can you hear me okay at the back?' he asked the audience. I sank a little lower in my chair, desperately hoping he wasn't looking our way. 'I prefer not using a mic if I can avoid it. It feels more intimate without one.'

The notion of being 'more intimate' with Finn seemed to go down a storm with the largely female audience. Under cover of the crowd's laughter, Hannah leant closer towards me.

'Your Finn might be a dickhead, but I have to admit, he's every bit as hot as you said he was.'

'He's not *my* Finn,' I hissed back. 'Or a dickhead.'

Hannah sat back in her seat with a knowing smile.

It took me a moment to realise I hadn't refuted her third observation: that Finn was hot. Probably because it was a truth that was impossible to deny.

The interview was surprisingly entertaining. Finn was both amusing and engaging, and as a former journalist he seemed to instinctively know what the audience wanted to hear. He was good at this and seemed happy and relaxed when they opened up the session to questions from the floor.

'You could ask him why he never bothered keeping in touch,' Hannah suggested, not nearly sotto voce enough for my liking. I shot her a look that promised a slow and painful death if she said another word.

Finn's eyes were travelling along the rows of audience members as he sought out those with raised hands. I could feel his gaze coming towards me, like a spotlight swooping through the crowd at a concert. I braced myself for the moment of recognition, for when his voice faltered or he lost his train of thought on seeing me.

My heart was beating so hard it was impossible to hear what he was saying as his eyes travelled past the stranger sitting beside me and finally found my face in the audience. But he didn't hesitate or stumble or even miss a beat. With a smile that was pleasant but entirely bland, his gaze continued its journey down the row of seats.

'Well, as much as it pains me to admit it, that was actually quite interesting,' Hannah declared some twenty minutes later. Finn had followed the audience Q & A with a short reading from his novel, and you could have heard the proverbial pin drop as he held the room spellbound. With his eyes focused on the book in his hands, I could finally study him without worrying that he'd unexpectedly catch me doing so.

He looked, if anything, even better than I remembered. He was perhaps a little leaner these days, his jaw more chiselled, although it was hard to tell beneath the shadow of dark stubble. His skin was evenly tanned to the colour of summer honey, and despite the current cold snap, he'd rolled back the sleeves of his shirt. My eyes kept straying to his forearms, covered with hair that my fingertips remembered was soft to the touch. That was the trouble. I'd forgotten nothing, and he'd remembered none of it.

'Do you really think he didn't recognise you?' Hannah asked, firing an arrow with deadly accuracy that went straight to my heart.

'I don't know,' I said, glancing across the room to where Finn had now been ushered. He was sitting at a table beside two towering, Jenga-like piles of his book, with a Sharpie at the ready. A long, snaking queue had already formed of people who wanted their copy signed by its author.

'Perhaps it's my hair that's throwing him. It was blonde last time he saw me,' I said, running my fingers through my auburn curls, which seemed to have lost some of their usual bounce.

'You may have a bit of a hat-hair situation going on there,' Hannah said, in a way that only an old friend could have got away with.

I hurriedly scoped the shop for a Ladies' room.

'So I take it we're not beating a hasty retreat,' she guessed wryly. 'You really are determined to take this all the way, aren't you?'

'It would be rude not to say hi,' I replied, finally spotting a sign for the loos.

'No ruder than ignoring you for years,' Hannah batted back.

I said nothing as I hunted in my purse for a twenty-pound note, which I held out to Hannah.

'You're bribing me to stay?'

'Ha ha. It's for a copy of Finn's book. Can you get me one while I fix my hair?'

The mirror in the Ladies' sadly confirmed my worst fears: without a set of straighteners or a qualified hairdresser, there was little that could be done. I spent several minutes trying to make it look less like someone had accidentally sat on my head, fluffing up the damp curls until they fell around my face in copper tendrils. It was only when I turned away from the mirror that I realised how much I looked like the first version of me Finn had met, on the day of the job interview. My hair was awry and I was flustered and more than a little out of my depth. It felt like serendipity.

Hannah was waiting beside the till with not one but two copies of Finn's book tucked beneath her arm.

'You didn't have to do that.'

'I know. But that extract sounded pretty interesting,' she admitted grudgingly. 'Although that still doesn't mean I like him.'

The queue for the signings had alarmingly grown even longer. As well as a personal dedication, most people appeared to be having a selfie taken with Finn. It was a request I definitely wouldn't be making.

Finn's publicist was positioned behind him at the desk, looking for all the world like a personal bodyguard. Not that Finn appeared to be in need of protection. Had he been that muscular before leaving for Australia? An image of us on a moonlit beach surfaced from its locked vault. I swallowed down a memory of my hands travelling over his skin beneath his untucked shirt before it caught in my throat and choked me.

The line was moving slowly as Finn chatted amiably with each customer. Between signings, I saw the publicist lay her hand on his shoulder and whisper something in his ear. A dart of something that felt an awful lot like envy caught me by surprise. Finn and the publicist glanced at the wall clock and then at the row of customers still waiting in line.

In a move to speed things along, an assistant began travelling down the line, passing out Post-it notes for customers to write their chosen dedication.

'At least this way he'll remember your name,' Hannah said darkly, looking at the small yellow square on which I'd neatly printed: *GEMMA*.

My smile felt weak, because the possibility of Finn not remembering me at all was no longer even remotely amusing.

We were three customers from the table. Close enough to hear Finn's conversation as he scribbled the same words on the title page of each book.

Thank you for coming tonight. I really hope you enjoy the book.

Below the message was his signature, illegible enough to be at the bottom of a prescription.

As we inched closer to the table, the tiny hairs at the back of my neck tingled in anticipation. My palms felt damp, which was going to be really embarrassing if we shook hands.

'If we could just hurry things along,' said the publicist.

'Sure,' Finn replied with an easy smile, turning his head towards the next person in line.

Me.

Here it was. The moment I'd been waiting for. My legs felt like spaghetti, and I was sure that if I looked down, I'd be able to see my heart thumping through the soft wool of my dress.

'Hello,' Finn said pleasantly. He held out his hand and, sweaty palm or not, I went to place mine within it, before realising at the last moment he was waiting for me to pass him my book.

Like a well-oiled machine, the publicist plucked my Post-it from the front cover and stuck it on the desk where Finn could easily read it, while a shop assistant stood on his other side with a bookshop carrier bag at the ready. Finn glanced at the yellow square for less than a second before looking back up at me. Time seemed to stop, and I felt myself unconsciously holding my breath.

'Thank you for coming out on such a filthy night. I do hope you'll like the book,' Finn said, his hand already reaching for the Sharpie.

I wanted to run from the queue, or, worse, to lean across the table and grab him by those ridiculously broad shoulders and force him to look at me. *Really?* I wanted to challenge him. *It really meant so little to you, you've totally forgotten me?*

He was writing now, his eyes bent to the title page. I caught a glimpse of movement from the corner of my eye as the publicist glanced down at the book and gave a small frown, but Finn had already snapped it shut, slipped it into a bag, and was passing it back to me, with a pleasant 'Have a lovely evening'.

*

'Can I call him a bastard now?' Hannah said with uncharacteristic venom.

'I thought you didn't want me to have anything to do with him again,' I argued, lifting my hand to get the attention of a passing waiter. 'Is red okay?' I asked, setting down the menu of the wine bar we'd ducked into after leaving the bookshop.

'I care more about the quantity than the colour,' Hannah said, so indignant on my behalf it was almost funny. Except that realising you've spent two and a half years with a memory so faulty it was practically broken wasn't anything except incredibly sad. How was it possible that one night could end up meaning entirely different things to the two people who'd shared it?

'Well, I don't think I'm going to bother reading his pathetic little book now,' Hannah said, drawing her own copy out of the bookshop carrier bag. She paused as the waiter arrived with our bottle of house red and a plate of olives, which didn't look up to the job of soaking up the alcohol.

Hannah set the book on the table, moving it into a pool of light from the overhead lamp to see it better. Her lips pursed as she read Finn's handwritten inscription. Absently, she flicked through the next few pages; two were blank, but when she reached the third, she paused. She tilted the book in order to read the printed words better, as though her twenty-twenty vision had chosen tonight to fail her.

There was an entirely different expression on her face when she set the book back down on the table and slowly inverted it.

'Have you seen who he's dedicated this book to?'

'No,' I said, pulling the copy closer. 'There wasn't a dedication on the proof copy I read.'

'Well, there's one now,' Hannah said.

I read it to the accompaniment of my pounding heart, which was trying to see how many extra beats it could squeeze into a minute.

'"To G",' I read out loud, my voice not quite as steady as I would have liked. '"For the best night ever."'

'Do you think he means you? Is he referring to your date?'

I reached for my wine glass, hoping it was dark enough in the bar for Hannah not to notice the slight tremble of my hand.

'Of course not. He didn't even recognise me, remember? That dedication is clearly for some other woman whose name coincidentally also begins with G. There's a twenty-six-to-one chance of it happening to be the same letter as mine. Maybe Finn just likes dating people with the same initial. Probably makes it easier for him when he forgets their name.'

Hannah was shaking her head. 'Firstly, that's not how probability works, and secondly... I don't know. Where's your copy of his book?'

I didn't want to give it to her. I didn't even want her to take it out of the carrier bag. There was only so much disappointment a person should have to go through in one evening.

Hannah snatched the carrier bag from me while I was still dithering. She plucked out the book and flicked straight to the page covered with the distinctive strokes of a message written with a Sharpie. She frowned, in exactly the same way the publicist had done on glimpsing what Finn had written.

'"To Geena"?' Hannah exclaimed in disgust. 'Is the man

blind? You printed your name clearly enough for anyone to see. What? What is it?' Her head jerked up at the sound of my laughter. 'Why are you laughing? I don't get it. What's so funny?'

I took the book from her hands. The words were difficult to read because there were tears in my eyes, but they were happy ones.

'"To Geena",' I read out loud. '"Thank you for coming tonight. I really hope you'll call me."'

Below the message, where everyone else's book had Finn's signature, mine had his phone number.

18

LONDON

Eighteen months earlier

'Do you think, years from now when we look back on this, we'll call this our first date or our fourth?'

For a moment I wasn't sure if the sip of wine I'd just taken was going to be lost in a startled coughing fit. Somehow, I managed to swallow it down without anyone having to save me from choking. Even so, I needed to clear my throat several times before I managed to say, 'Pardon?' There was, after all, so much to address in Finn's question.

First was the fact that he was referring to tonight as an actual date, rather than a casual evening shared by two acquaintances (which was the only way I'd allowed myself to think of it all day). And second, it was his careless – almost throwaway – assumption that we'd be together years from now to debate the number of times we'd been out together. That one seemed the safest to challenge.

'How did you manage to get to *four* dates?' I asked, setting down my glass and smiling at him across the restaurant tabletop. 'At best this can only be our second.'

'Well, there was the night of the engagement party at the bar, then the McDonald's takeaway at the side of the road, and then our fish and chip supper on the beach.'

A flush warmed my cheeks as Finn's eyes held mine while the memory of the night before he left for Sydney filled my head. That he remembered each of our past encounters as vividly as I did was something I'd be spending a lot of time thinking about later; for now, I was happy just to bask in the happy glow that it gave me.

'I think you're confusing random occasions when our paths have crossed with dating per se.'

Finn's lips twitched in amusement. 'I'm not dating anyone called Percy – and I'm really hoping you're not either.'

My laughter was loud enough to turn nearby heads our way, but it was silenced as though a switch had been abruptly flicked when Finn reached across the table for my hand. 'And I'm not confused. In fact, I don't think I've ever been able to see anything more clearly than I see this.'

His words affected me more potently than the strongest alcohol. They were like pure adrenaline, already travelling halfway to my heart before I could stop them. But this time, when the voice in my head screamed out 'Too fast!', I knew I had to listen.

Perhaps Finn saw it on my face, for he steered the conversation back on to neutral territory so quickly, I'd later question if I'd actually imagined that brief moment of intensity.

★

The decision to call Finn, after discovering his phone number in my copy of his book, had never been up for debate. But Hannah had still given it her best shot.

'He's a bit up himself, isn't he, to simply assume you're currently single? Or that you've been sitting around for the last two and a half years measuring every guy you meet against him and finding them all wanting.'

'Exactly like I have done, you mean?' I asked wryly, my eyes unable to shift from Finn's handwritten message.

'Finn Douglas doesn't know a damn thing about what's going on in your life right now. It's not like the two of you kept in touch or made any ridiculous promises to wait for each other. Thank God,' she added fervently.

'I know all of that. And I also know that everything you're saying is coming from a place of love—'

'Why do I sense a "but" is on its way?'

I smiled at my old friend, who wanted to save me from something I wanted no protection from. She was trying to stop me from walking into a fire, but I could already feel the warm flames beckoning me.

She sighed deeply, knowing me so well I didn't even have to argue my corner. 'Just promise me you'll take your time before calling him. Don't be *that* keen. Wait a week – or maybe even two.'

But from the look on her face, Hannah already knew I'd be dialling Finn's number much sooner than that.

I called him the morning after the book signing. It was early, just after eight, and it was only when I heard his voice, still croaky from sleep, that I stopped to consider there might be such a thing as looking too eager. But in my head the reasons I'd given Hannah for not delaying were all still true. I had no idea how long Finn was going to be in the UK. I could waste days on playing it cool, only to find that he was about to disappear off to the other side of the world yet again.

'Hi. Good morning. It's me,' I said on a rush. 'Er... Gemma, that is.'

'I'm not sure if I actually know anyone of that name,' Finn said, his voice clearer now as he shook off the last hold sleep had on him. It was disconcerting, as though he was waking up beside me.

'You found my note,' he continued, and I could tell from his tone that he was smiling.

'No. I've just been dialling random numbers for the last two and a half years, and you won't believe it, but today I got lucky.'

Finn's laughter was low and rumbling but not quite loud enough to mask the female voice I heard in the background.

I closed my eyes and saw it with a clarity so sharp, I wondered if I might be clairvoyant. A gorgeous blonde (they were always blonde) would be emerging from his bathroom, her long, bronzed limbs still damp from the shower, with something the size of a hand towel draped around her. Or worse, no towel at all.

How could I have been so stupid?

'Over there is fine,' said Finn, sounding momentarily distracted.

'I'm sorry, you sound busy. I can call back later,' I said, already knowing that I never would. This would be our last conversation.

'No, don't go,' said Finn. Surprisingly, his voice sounded panicked. 'It's just room service with my breakfast.'

I heard him mumble his thanks and was very glad he couldn't see the colour embarrassment had painted on my face. 'Well, I should probably let you eat it in peace before it gets cold, or something.' Dear God, did I really earn my living from finding just the right words to use at any given time? Why was it suddenly impossible to find any that didn't make me sound like a total idiot?

'It's only fruit and yoghurt. It can wait.'

I smiled, for no other reason than that he'd ordered exactly what I would have chosen from the room service menu. It was hardly proof of lifelong compatibility, but I was building a dream out of fragile glass bricks here and was willing to take a win wherever I could find one.

'It was really good of you to come to the book signing.'

'You already said that last night,' I replied, determined to keep the tone of the conversation breezy, but then went and took the wind out of my own sails by adding, 'I really thought you didn't recognise or even remember me.'

Finn's indrawn breath sounded genuinely shocked. 'What on earth made you think that?'

I fanned my face with my hand, but it did little to douse the flames engulfing my cheeks. 'You looked right through me, not just once but several times.'

There was a long pause before he replied. 'I didn't want our first conversation after all this time to be overheard by a roomful of strangers. And as far as looking right through you goes, well, that couldn't be further from the truth. I've been looking *for* you at every stop on this book tour. I've searched every face that's come through the door, telling myself I had no right to expect you'd want to see me again, much less come and find me.'

'But if I hadn't turned up last night, would that have been it? Would you have got on a plane and gone back to Australia without ever bothering to make contact with me?'

'No, Gemma Fletcher. That most definitely is not what would have happened. I'd already cleared my diary for today, with the sole intention of tracking you down. I was going to turn up at the *Glow* offices, and if you didn't work there any more, or they wouldn't tell me where you were, I planned to sit outside your flat until you came home or your neighbours called the police.'

'Oh.' It was an incredibly small word in response to such a huge admission.

'Which leads me to an important question: are you by any chance free today?'

I spent longer than I should have done considering whether I could pull a sickie, for I could already hear a soundless clock ticking away the time Finn and I had before he left again. But I had commitments, not just to my job but also to my colleagues. I was due to travel to London to interview a family for a major feature *Glow* would be running in next month's edition. I couldn't just blow it off for a man who'd probably be long gone before my article was even in print.

To be fair, Finn understood perfectly when I explained.

'I've got an idea. How about I come to London and meet you after your interview is over? I can check out of the hotel where I'm staying now and find myself a room in London instead.'

I should have paused. I should have made it sound as though I was weighing up all the options. At the very least I should have made it clear that I hoped he was talking about a hotel room for one and not two. But I did none of those things. He'd had me at 'I've got an idea', even before I knew what he was about to suggest.

Arranging to meet beside Covent Garden's sixty-foot Christmas tree was a bit of a cliché and, in hindsight, perhaps not one of my brightest ideas. It might have helped if I'd remembered that the Christmas lights had only just been turned on, so the area was even more crowded than usual.

While I might not have picked the easiest spot for a rendezvous, if I was looking for a magical location, this one was hard to beat. There were Christmas decorations everywhere, thousands of twinkling lights, and huge mistletoe chandeliers suspended from the market's arches, which quite a few couples were putting to good use.

I said 'Excuse me' more times than I could count, and inadvertently appeared in several tourist snaps as I made my way towards the giant Norwegian spruce. I peeled away from the surging crowd just once, lured by an intoxicating aroma of warmed wine and spices. On impulse, I bought a couple of mulled-wines-to-go from a vendor's cart at the edge of the market. Two hot drinks and high-heeled boots on slippery cobbles is a dangerous combination, but somehow I made it to the base of the Christmas tree without mishap.

I was early, and while I hadn't exactly rushed through the interview, I certainly hadn't lingered after it was done. I only hoped, when I played it back on my phone, that no one would realise that for once my mind hadn't been entirely on my work.

A clock chimed the quarter hour, and the excitement I'd been trying so hard to suppress fizzed in my veins. In less than fifteen minutes I would see Finn again, and my emotions kept swinging like a pendulum between being nowhere near ready for this to so eager it was frankly embarrassing. For so long I'd wondered if I'd simply imagined the strength of the connection between us before he'd left for Australia. It would be good to finally find out – one way or the other – if it really had been all in my head.

As much as I'd tried to tell myself this wasn't an actual date, my actions kept betraying me. In my bathroom that morning I'd reached for the ridiculously expensive shower gel, the one I kept for special occasions, rather than the supermarket cheapie I usually used. I'd skipped straight past my normal workday clothes and pulled a dress from my wardrobe that hugged the bits of me I liked and was kind to those I didn't. My hair had behaved perfectly, my make-up was subtle but flattering. I was ready for this.

Except when I finally spotted Finn weaving his way through the crowds towards me, with a smile that whipped my breath away, I realised I was nowhere near ready. I was lost, even before his first hello.

'Snap!' he said, his eyes crinkling warmly at the edges as he held up two styrofoam cups of mulled wine. There were too many hot drinks and no free hands to allow us to hug, which took away the awkward 'should we or shouldn't we' dilemma. Instead, Finn bent his head to graze my cheek with a fly-by kiss.

'Shall we get out of this throng?' he suggested, taking the cups from my hands and balancing them effortlessly on top of his own.

'Old skills,' he said with a smile, noticing my impressed expression.

'Do you ever miss the coffee shop?' I asked, which seemed a safer way of asking if he missed living in the UK – or anyone he might have left behind there.

'I miss seeing people every day,' Finn said thoughtfully. 'Writing a novel is a pretty solitary way of earning a living.'

We just happened to be walking past a bookshop at that moment, with a window display featuring his latest.

'You seem to be doing very well at it. I really loved this book, by the way,' I said.

'You must have stayed up all night reading it.'

I shook my head. 'No. I managed to get hold of a proof copy a few months ago.' Finn smiled. I was giving myself away with every sentence that came out of my mouth, and I didn't even care.

Somehow, without dropping our drinks, Finn had managed to loop an arm around my shoulders, protecting me from the crowd that we now appeared to be walking against. He steered us towards the edge of the piazza and set the four cups on a low wall. He prised the lid off two of them and passed one to me.

'Cheers,' he said, bumping his cup gently against mine. 'To old friends and second chances.' I looked up at him. His toast was confusing. We weren't really old friends, just two people whose lives had briefly collided. Was this his way of saying he wanted to keep things purely platonic? I couldn't tell, so I ignored the first part of his toast and focused instead on the words I preferred.

'To second chances,' I said softly.

*

The restaurant was amazing. Set on the twenty-eighth floor of a top London hotel, it overlooked Hyde Park – and the Queen's back garden, or so it cheekily claimed. The cuisine had won numerous awards, but to be honest the food could have tasted like cardboard and I'd still have said it was the best meal I'd ever had. Part of that was due to the spectacular view from the window beside my chair, from where the city looked like a tray of sparkling gems set out beneath us. The other reason this night would live on as one of my favourite memories ever was down to the man sitting across the table from me.

After finishing our mulled wine at Covent Garden, I would happily have walked the three miles to the restaurant. But a few intrepid flakes of snow had begun to fall, and so too had the temperature.

'I'm still acclimatising to the change from blistering Aussie summer to snowy UK winter. Shall we get a cab?'

Before hailing one, Finn took our two unopened drinks and placed them on the pavement beside a homeless man and his dog. 'Try and get yourself somewhere warm for the night, mate,' he said, his words so quiet they were practically swallowed by the city's soundtrack. I suspected I wasn't supposed to have heard them or seen him pressing something into the man's hand before ruffling the dog's head and straightening up.

Finn closed the distance between us and held out his hand to me. I'd never felt more sure that I was doing the right thing as I placed my own within it.

He flagged down a taxi with the ease of a city dweller and

gave the driver our destination, adding a request that we drive 'via the Mall'. 'It's a more scenic route,' he explained as he joined me on the cab's bench seat, 'and I've really missed London these past few years.'

Just London? I really wanted to ask.

It was easy to fill the fifteen-minute cab journey with talk of Finn's life in Sydney, but the burning question of when he was going back sat on the tip of my tongue and never managed to make it past my lips.

'There's something very special about London, particularly at this time of year,' Finn said, although his eyes were on my face rather than the capital's distinctive landmarks flashing past the window. 'But nothing comes close to the feeling of driving over Sydney Harbour Bridge at sunset or sipping a cold one beside the Opera House.'

'It sounds like you can't wait to get back,' I said, trying to sound chipper.

The cab grew darker as we passed beneath Admiralty Arch, making it impossible to see his eyes, which was frustrating, because we'd unexpectedly reached an important point in the conversation.

'There are good reasons to go back and good reasons to stay,' Finn said quietly.

I swallowed, perhaps not quite as soundlessly as I would have liked.

'Here you go,' said the cab driver, shattering the moment as we pulled up in front of our destination. I couldn't decide if I was disappointed or relieved by the interruption as Finn paid the fare and we entered the hotel.

Tables beside the windows were obviously at a premium in the restaurant, but Finn had secured us one. Like an excited tourist on their first trip to London, I spent a good ten minutes trying to identify various city landmarks from a chart placed on each table. I could feel the warmth of Finn's eyes on me as he watched me incorrectly identify several buildings.

'What?' I said, his gaze like a torch that had the power to set my cheeks on fire.

'Nothing. It's just very good to see you again, Ginny Fletcher.'

I smiled, because two and a half years was a long time for no one ever to teasingly call you by the wrong name.

Don't go back. Stay here in England. With me. Those words were so dangerously close to escaping, I had to reach for my glass of wine to swallow them back down.

Over a shared platter of starters, we skipped lightly from topic to topic. From Finn's side of the table, we covered the life of an author, Australian creepy crawlies, and surfing; while I contributed with life at *Glow* magazine, my delight at becoming godmother to Hannah's daughter, and my new hobby of Argentine tango dance lessons.

'Are you any good?' Finn asked with interest.

'Terrible. Absolutely appalling. Suffice to say, no one wants to partner me when we get to the bits with the kicks and flicks. Apparently, I'm considered dangerous.'

'I'd brave it,' said Finn, his eyes holding my own captive.

My laugh came out a little too high and fragile, because suddenly I wasn't sure if we were still talking about ganchos and ochos or something entirely different.

'And do you have one – a regular dance partner, that is?' Finn's attention was on my wine glass, which he was now refilling. It prevented me from reading his expression.

'What exactly are you asking me, Finn?'

He set the bottle down with a smile. 'I'd forgotten how direct you can be.' He shook his head as though he'd disappointed himself. 'I know I have no right to ask this question, but I'm asking it anyway. Is there someone important in your life right now? Are you seeing anyone?'

The time for playing games was over. And I was glad.

'No. No one. How about you?'

Very slowly, Finn shook his head. 'I wouldn't be here with you now if I were. That's not who I am.'

My smile was slow, but it just kept on growing.

Somewhere between the entrée and the dessert, the conversation grew serious when Finn asked about my family and I told him about losing Mum fifteen months earlier. Sometimes I could say it without getting emotional, without the tears coming to my eyes or my voice cracking. This wasn't one of those days.

'I'd always thought that by the time people reached their thirties they probably didn't need their mum so much. But d'you know what, you do. You really do.' My eyes were stinging, and tears were only a blink away.

'I'm so sorry, Gemma,' Finn said, reaching out to me across the table. His fingertips grazed the back of my wrist and my pulse went crazy. I willed it to slow down, because it wasn't fair that he should know how much he affected me when I still had no idea what we were doing here.

'How is your father coping alone?'

My sigh was sad. 'He's doing a little better now, but it's been tough.'

A silence fell between us and I saw an opportunity, although the window was closing rapidly with each passing second.

'You… your parents aren't around any more?'

Finn stiffened. Every single fibre, muscle and sinew reacted to my question, or rather overreacted to it. My words had such a visceral effect on him, I honestly didn't expect him to answer me. But he did.

'No. They're not. They died in an accident shortly after we came back to live in England.'

'When you were only ten years old?' I asked, remembering our conversation from two years ago.

If Finn was surprised that I'd recalled the exact details, he didn't show it. 'Yes. It's not something I talk about often.'

I stayed silent, because as a journalist you know that is the tipping point when people will tell you more.

'My grandmother took me in afterwards.' Finn reached for his wine, as though this part of his history was best told with alcohol on standby. 'She wasn't exactly the most maternal woman in the world; not to my father, and then, years later, not to me. Boarding school actually felt more like home to me than her house ever did.'

The tears were back in my eyes, this time for him and not me.

'Oh, Finn. That's really sad. I'm so sorry. You must have felt terribly alone, losing both your parents and being in a strange country.'

His mouth, which had been smiling pretty much since the moment the date began, was now a tight line. 'It was a long time ago.'

I might have asked more, but when I glanced up I saw a waiter heading towards our table, carrying the indulgent dessert I'd ordered. There seemed to be an in-house ritual with the chocolate bombe that involved molten sauce being poured from a height and a round of applause once the sparklers set into the dish had fizzled out. By the time the ceremony and interest from the surrounding diners was over, Finn had corralled his memories back into a steel-doored vault, from which I suspected they were seldom released.

I tried steering the conversation back to his family, but he was having none of it.

'I'm sorry, but do you mind if we change the subject?'

Of course, I told him that was fine; how could I say anything else? Although I couldn't resist adding, 'But if you do ever want to talk about it...' I let my words trail away on the offer.

Finn's smile looked wry. 'Thanks, but over the last couple of years I've talked about my past more than enough.' There was something about his words that hinted this might be more than just idle chatter with his new Aussie mates.

He blew out a long, slow breath. 'Well, I believe this officially counts as one of the best ways of putting a damper on an evening. Any minute now you'll probably remember a pressing prior engagement, or you'll hotfoot it to the loo and never come back.'

Behind the humour, there was something in his eyes that broke the tiny bit of my heart that hadn't already started to fall for him.

'I'm not going anywhere,' I said.

We lingered so long in the restaurant that we were among the last diners to leave. Finn took my hand as we walked towards the bank of lifts, and I happily curled my fingers around his.

'I've had such a great time tonight, Finn. Thank you,' I said as we stepped inside the waiting carriage.

Four smiling Finns looked back at me from the lift's mirrored walls. 'It doesn't have to be over just yet.'

His hand was hovering over the control panel, and I felt a shard of disappointment pierce my mood. Finn was staying at this hotel; I knew that because he'd charged the meal to his room. Was he suggesting we went there now? Was that where we'd been heading all night? And if so, why was it so disappointing? *Because you don't want this to be another meaningless one-night stand*, an inner voice that I could no longer ignore reminded me. *You want this to go somewhere.*

Unaware of my hesitation, Finn firmly pressed his forefinger on the button marked 'G'. 'Because I was wondering if there was time for a walk in the park before we have to get you to the station. What time is your train, by the way?'

'The last one leaves at midnight,' I said happily. Never in my entire life had I been so delighted to have totally misjudged someone's intentions.

'Okay, Cinderella,' he said with a smile. 'We'll get you there before the clock chimes twelve.'

The lift spilled us out into the marble-floored foyer, and while Finn retrieved our coats from the cloakroom, I pulled out my phone and rattled off a quick message to Hannah.

Having the best night. Ever, I wrote, tagging a few heart-eyed emojis on to the WhatsApp for good measure.

She replied immediately with an eye-rolling GIF that made me giggle like the lovestruck teenager I was apparently morphing into.

With the kind of impeccable good manners that would have seriously impressed my mum, Finn held out my coat and carefully lifted my hair free from the collar. I shivered as his fingers briefly scraped against the sensitive skin at my nape.

Perhaps it was just as well we were going somewhere public. Maybe I was the one who couldn't be trusted if we were to find ourselves alone together, not Finn.

The November night air bit hungrily at our exposed skin as we headed towards the nearest entrance to the park. I cinched my coat a little tighter around me.

'Too cold?' asked Finn, who was already buttoning up his own thick wool coat.

'Not really. It's you Aussie guys who can't hack the British winter.'

He grinned back at me. 'That sounds like a challenge. And as I'm only half Australian and lived in the UK for over twenty years, I'm pretty sure I can take it.'

'Great,' I said, tucking my gloved hand into the crook of his arm. 'Then how about an ice bar for our next date? My shout. Let's see how well you do at minus five degrees, where even the seats are made of solid ice.'

We were paused at a pedestrian crossing, and in the seconds before a van stopped to let us cross, I caught the hint of a smile as it played over Finn's lips. 'That's assuming you're not about to disappear back to Sydney in the next week or so,' I added hastily. There. I'd finally asked it. Not particularly subtly or casually, and with absolutely no degree of finesse, but at least I'd now know how things stood, one way or the other.

'I'm planning on sticking around for quite a while, actually.'

As much as I tried not to look delighted, I was pretty sure my emotions were plastered all over my face.

'Oh, really?' I said in an attempt at nonchalance no one would have bought. 'I didn't realise your plans had changed.'

'It only happened recently. Just this minute, in fact,' Finn replied, his hand squeezing mine. And even though we were both wearing gloves, I swear I could feel the warmth of his touch straight through the leather and suede that separated us.

It was gone eleven o'clock at night, yet there were still plenty of pedestrians on the streets. Among them was a cluster of people who appeared to be queuing for something beside the park gates. They were stamping on the pavement, trying to restore feeling to feet that had probably long since gone numb, and when they spoke, clouds of vapour floated above their heads like silent speech bubbles.

As we got closer, I noticed that the group appeared to be comprised mainly of couples. I still had no idea what they were queuing for, until I heard a noise that sounded like sleigh bells, quickly followed by the trundle of heavy wooden wheels on tarmac.

The group fidgeted and sprang to attention with palpable excitement as three old-fashioned horse-drawn carriages emerged from the shadowy park. They drew to a halt in front of the queue with a stamp of impatient hooves and a chorus of whinnies from the horses.

I laughed as passengers in the carriages scarcely had time to disembark before their seats were filled by the next customers waiting in line.

'Ever been on one of those?' Finn asked, looking down at me with a quizzical smile.

'No,' I said, shaking my head from side to side, making the ends of my scarf flutter like sails. 'This kind of thing is just for the tourists.'

Finn nodded as though in complete agreement, before observing, 'Of course, you did just call me a tourist.'

I slipped my hand back into the crook of his arm and drew

us one step further away from the queue. 'I meant overseas ones.'

Finn nodded wisely, paused for a moment, and then innocently remarked, 'Although last time I looked, Australia was overseas.'

'Are you saying you want to go on a carriage ride, Finn Douglas?' I challenged.

He was grinning as he shook his head. 'No. Not really. But I rather suspect that you do.'

'Nope. Not at all. Crazy idea,' I said, tugging him further down the footpath. 'It's way too cheesy, and it probably costs a fortune. These things are always a rip-off,' I said, as though I was doing an in-depth exposé on the best way to fleece foreign holidaymakers of their cash.

'Fair enough,' said Finn with a shrug.

We couldn't have gone more than twenty steps down the pathway before Finn came to an abrupt stop. 'You really want to go on one, don't you?'

'More than anything,' I admitted sheepishly.

We were in luck; a fourth carriage had just returned, and miraculously the queue was now gone.

'Have we got time for this?' I worried belatedly as I climbed into the carriage and tucked the thick plaid blanket the driver had handed me over our legs. It felt curiously intimate to be beneath the cover with Finn, even though we were both fully clothed and wearing winter coats to boot.

'It's a thirty-minute ride,' said Finn, sliding closer towards me on the padded leather banquette and putting his arm around my shoulders. 'We're just about okay for time.'

It was cheesy. Maybe even a little tacky. And I suspect our driver might have made up his 'interesting London facts', because some of them sounded dubious to me. But I absolutely loved every last minute of it.

I leant back and looked up at the clear, star-strewn sky as we clipped our way through the London park. Held tightly against Finn's side, I could smell the cocktail of him, and I inhaled it deeply, wanting to commit the aroma to memory. Whatever might happen in the days, weeks and months ahead, this would remain a moment I'd cherish for ever.

I caught the train by the skin of my teeth. The taxi we'd hailed for the station must have been driven by a cabbie who'd needed numerous attempts to pass the Knowledge.

'How did he not know the way to one of the major train stations in the city?' I gasped as Finn bundled some notes at the driver and took my hand as we raced together up the steps towards the concourse.

An overhead clock confirmed we had less than four minutes until my train left, and although my ticket was clasped in my hand, I had no idea which platform I needed. We wove at speed through the milling crowd as though it was an obstacle course.

'What if I miss it?' I gasped, aware that only one of us was seriously out of breath. My New Year's resolution was now definitely to join a gym.

'If you do, then you'll just have to spend the night with me,' Finn reasoned.

My steps faltered and I very nearly stopped altogether because, suddenly, missing my train sounded like a pretty good idea after all.

Finn bit his lip, looking every bit as torn as I felt, before eventually shaking his head. 'As tempting as that idea is, we should at least try to catch it.'

We found the platform, which came into sight just as the station clock clicked away one more minute. With just two to go, we thundered up to the barrier. Without a platform ticket, this was where I had to leave Finn.

There had been so many opportunities for him to kiss me throughout the evening, and yet we'd foolishly let them all slip past us. I wanted so much for it to be a moment we'd both remember. It should have happened under the starry night sky in the horse-drawn carriage, or even in the back of the taxi. But not here. From the rueful look in his eyes, I knew Finn was thinking exactly the same thing.

In my head scrolled a montage of vintage black-and-white films featuring passionate, forbidden embraces on station platforms, where couples locked lips surrounded by billowing clouds of steam from the train's engines.

My hand hovered hesitantly beside the automatic barrier, which was waiting to snatch the ticket from my fingers. Oblivious to the other late-arriving passengers flying past us, Finn took his time as he reached for the trailing ends of my scarf and tugged me closer towards him.

There was no time for a long, lingering kiss, but the moment his mouth joined mine the booming tannoy announcements, the whistle of the guards, and the station chaos disappeared. My lips had only just parted beneath his before the kiss was over.

Finn took my ticket, slid it into the slot, and then gently propelled me through the barrier as it sprang open.

'Run,' he urged, as the clock clicked over to midnight.

'Will I see you again?' I asked ridiculously.

His smile, I knew, would stay with me for the entire journey home. 'Of course you will,' he assured me, calling out to my retreating back. 'I'll call you tomorrow.'

I had literally only just thrown myself on to my seat when the train began to pull out of the station. My breathing was still erratic, perhaps from the run to the platform or from the kiss. Maybe both.

I closed my eyes, but they flew open just moments later when my phone rang.

'Hello,' I said, uncaring that the rest of the carriage could easily overhear me.

'It's tomorrow already,' said Finn, and even though the train was pulling me ever further away from him, I knew he was smiling. 'So, when can I see you again?'

19

THE PARTY

Eighteen months earlier

'I feel really bad about leaving you, Gemma. Perhaps I shouldn't go after all.'

I'd been expecting this objection, or something very similar. They'd been coming thick and fast ever since I gifted Dad a Christmas cruise holiday. I shut the boot of my car in case his last-minute jitters prompted him to remove his luggage from where we'd stowed it.

'Of course you should go. You're going to have an absolutely amazing time.' My enthusiasm was a little over the top; if I'd had a pair of pompoms, I could have passed for a cheerleader. I dialled it back down. 'Honestly, Dad, I'll be fine.'

'I just don't like the thought of you being alone for the holidays,' he said, one foot in the car but the other still firmly planted on the pavement.

'Don't worry about me. I'm looking forward to having a wonderful, long, relaxing break from work,' I assured him, neatly skirting his point about being alone. I climbed into the car, hoping that if he wanted to continue our conversation, he'd follow suit. He did.

'And remember I'm not going to be alone on Christmas Day; I'll be spending it with Hannah, William and Milly.'

Dad's smile was wistful, and I knew without asking that his thoughts were travelling back to Fletcher family Christmases of the past. 'I suppose it really is all about the children,' he said on a sigh. His eyes appeared a little misty as he looked at me, making me wonder who he was seeing. Was it the grown woman who was about to drive him to the train station or the tomboy five-year-old I'd once been, who'd always been far too excited to fall asleep on Christmas Eve?

'I love you, Dad,' I said, leaning across and pressing a kiss on his weathered cheek before switching on the engine.

Last Christmas had been awful. We were only a few months past losing the woman who had held our family together, and neither of us had felt like celebrating. Which was why it seemed so important to do something completely different this year. We needed a Christmas reset. So Dad was off to the Azores, and I was going to be spending some quiet time at home. Dad wasn't wrong about that; I would be at home – although not necessarily alone.

'Big night for you tonight, isn't it, sweetheart?'

For a moment I stiffened, and the car juddered as I messed up changing the gears. I made a sound that came out a little strangled.

'It is your magazine's Christmas do today, isn't it? Aren't you off to that swanky party tonight?'

'I'm not sure people still say "swanky", Dad,' I said, hoping he hadn't noticed the tightening of my hands on the steering wheel or the pulse fluttering wildly at the base of my throat.

I did have plans for that night. Big ones. And while some of them involved attending *Glow*'s annual Christmas extravaganza, there were others that were definitely not appropriate for sharing with my parent.

For the last four weeks, I'd been swept up in a whirlwind. The jury was still out as to whether this was a heady romance type of whirlwind or a devastating tornado that was tearing through my life. I still didn't know which was the more accurate description of what was happening between Finn and me.

From the moment he'd kissed me goodbye at the train station barrier, I knew I was in trouble. I was falling for a man who might yet disappear from my life as unexpectedly as he'd dropped back into it. It was something, to be fair, that Finn had never denied. He had a home and a life in Australia, but as far as I knew, no one waiting there for him. In England, all he had was an open-ended Airbnb booking. And me, of course.

Everything was exciting and new between us. We were building something made out of a thousand firsts, without knowing if the foundations we were standing on were strong enough to hold them.

On the plus side, Finn had cancelled his flight back home; on the negative, he'd changed his booking to an open-ended return rather than cashing it in. It was indicative of where we saw this thing heading. We simply didn't know.

'Slow and steady' had become our mantra. To minimise travel time, Finn had checked out of his London hotel and found temporary accommodation in town, close enough for us to see each other as often as we wanted.

'But that doesn't mean I want to crowd you,' Finn said. 'I

don't want you to feel like I'm invading your space. You're under no obligation here. If you want to see other people, well… that's perfectly okay.'

I imagined that was the point where I was supposed to say 'You too'. I stayed tellingly silent.

After a moment, he smiled and pulled me into his arms. 'Thank God. I was hoping that would be your response.'

We weren't exclusive… but I wasn't seeing anyone else and would happily never do so again.

We weren't calling it love… but it felt an awful lot like it to me.

We weren't talking about the future… but I could no longer visualise one without him in it.

We weren't sleeping together yet… but I hoped that after tonight we would be.

'Is that Aussie friend of yours going to the party tonight?' Dad asked as he hefted his case from my car and prepared to enter the station.

I'd told him very little about Finn, because since Mum's death he'd had a habit of 'worrying for two'. I'd always thought my mother was the more observant of my parents, better able to read between the lines and decipher the invisible writing hidden there. But now I found myself wondering if Dad was every bit as astute.

'Probably,' I said, pulling Dad in for a hard hug, because it would be the first time we'd ever spent Christmas apart, and it hid my face nicely from his scrutinising eyes.

'You've seen quite a bit of him, haven't you, over the last few weeks?' he asked innocently.

A far from innocent image of Finn with his shirt unbuttoned by my impatient fingers came into my head and refused to budge. I feigned a sudden interest in a notice outlining the station's parking restrictions until the unfortunate double entendre had faded away.

'Yeah, I guess,' I said with a shrug. 'But he'll probably know loads of people at the party tonight. He used to be in the business.'

The *Glow* Christmas party was legendary in the magazine industry. Somewhere in the past, long before any of the current employees worked there, a gauntlet had been thrown down by one of the glossies as to who could throw the flashiest Christmas bash. Each year, *Glow* prided itself on being the undisputed winner.

I usually flew solo at industry events, which were often just thinly veiled networking opportunities. But this year was different. When the MD's secretary approached my desk and asked if I was bringing a plus one, I gave a decisive 'Yes', even though at that point I hadn't asked Finn if he wanted to come.

'Are you ready to go public?' he asked me when I eventually broached the subject.

'Is there something here to go public about?' I countered.

He pulled me into his arms then and kissed me. 'Remind me never to play chess with you. You'd slaughter me.' And then he kissed me again, and I kissed him back with a fervour I didn't try to hide. 'You do slaughter me,' he said breathlessly when we finally broke apart.

There was really only one dress I wanted to wear for

the party. It had been sitting in the shop window of a small boutique near my flat, the kind of place that didn't price the items on display. Even on a cold December day, scurrying past with my head pulled into the neck of my coat like a turtle, I could hear the dress calling out to me.

'What's it like?' Hannah asked.

'Imagine if a glitterball and a red-carpet gown had a love child,' I replied.

'Wow,' she said with an impressed whistle. 'Can you afford it?'

'Probably not.'

'Will that stand in your way?' she asked with a smile.

'Probably not.'

Hannah shook her head. 'Poor Finn. The man doesn't stand a chance, does he?'

After spending half of my monthly take-home pay on the dress, I really hoped she was right.

I'd never actively set out to seduce anyone before. And for all my bluster and bravado, I needed that dress for ammunition. In the beginning, I'd rather enjoyed the fact that Finn didn't want to rush the physical side of our relationship. Until I realised that waiting for the fourth date was fun and kind of exciting, but waiting four weeks actually wasn't.

'I don't want you to end up having regrets about anything,' Finn had said on one of our earlier dates. 'I never want you to look back and wish that we'd waited or wish that it had been something more than just lust.'

To be honest, I could see nothing wrong with good old lust, but I also knew that Finn was in new territory here.

'I've slept with people I probably shouldn't have, people I didn't care enough about.' He looked directly into my eyes.

I wasn't sure if I was supposed to be shocked by his admission, but it was hardly breaking news. It was, after all, what I'd suspected about him from the first time we met. He was the type of man who'd probably never had to try that hard. I imagined women had been happily jumping into bed with him for years, and the fact that he wanted things to be totally different with us was possibly the highest compliment he could pay me. It was also the most frustrating thing to accept.

'I don't want to make love to you and then disappear out of your life. I don't want to be that guy any more.'

'Then why not make the first move yourself?' suggested Hannah with the confidence of someone who curled up each night in the arms of a man who adored her and who'd never look at anyone else. 'You're a millennial woman. You don't have to sit around and politely wait for a guy to ask you out or invite you into his bed. You can do it yourself.'

So I'd taken a deep breath and asked Finn to come to the *Glow* Christmas party with me. As for the second part of the challenge... well, I was just going to have to see how my nerve held out.

There was a gratifying moment of stunned silence when I opened my front door. The look on Finn's face confirmed that every penny I'd spent on the new dress had been worth it – even if it did mean I'd be eating nothing but beans on toast in January. I especially liked the way that despite the dress's plunging neckline – which was lower than I usually dared to go – the place where Finn's gaze lingered longest was my face.

He smiled, his eyes warm as they met mine. I wasn't the only one who'd made an effort tonight. Finn was wearing an inky-black suit that I'd not seen before, teamed with a shirt so dazzlingly white it had to be brand new. He wore no tie – it wasn't that kind of a party – so the top two buttons were left undone, revealing a tantalising glimpse of a tan that I knew went all the way down to the waistband of his boxer shorts. I had no idea if it continued any further south.

'You look absolutely incredible,' he said. 'That's quite a dress.'

'What... this old thing?' I teased.

I turned to get my bag, but Finn's hand encircled my wrist and drew me towards him. The graze of his fingers on the bare skin of my back made me shiver, although his hands were warm. They were gone a moment later as he stepped back with a small square of card clasped between them.

'That "old thing" still had its price tag on,' he said, passing it to me.

I laughed, a little embarrassed. 'Well, that's gone and ruined my plan of taking it back tomorrow.'

'Don't even think about returning it,' Finn said. 'It'll always remind me of tonight, every time I see you wear it.' There it was again, Finn's subtle, unshakeable certainty that there was a future of tomorrows for us.

As we turned to leave, I caught a final glimpse of our reflection in the hallway mirror. My dress sparkled like crushed diamonds under the artificial lights, but my eyes shone even brighter. Finn had ignited something within me, an inner flame that had never burnt before. I could see it on my face, and tonight I thought I could also see it on his.

The party was in full swing when we arrived. The converted Victorian bathhouse had been decorated to within an inch of its life with fairy lights and poinsettia garlands. It all looked incredibly festive.

'Great venue,' said Finn, taking my hand in his as we descended the short flight of stairs and entered the reception room.

'Last year it was at the zoo,' I said, leaning in and speaking close to his ear so he could hear me above the steady throb of music coming from the far end of the room, where a DJ would later lure partygoers on to the dance floor.

A few heads turned our way when we arrived, and a couple of my work colleagues lifted an arm in greeting, but our entrance had largely gone under the radar, or so I thought. Gradually, though, I became aware of a curious buzz humming through the room, generated not by me but by the man standing at my side. I'd thought some people there tonight might remember Finn from his journalist days, but I hadn't factored in that even more would recognise him as the author whose latest novel was currently on every bookshop and supermarket shelf.

I saw several people peeling away from the groups they were with and heading towards us and realised too late that my hopes for a romantic evening together were disappearing even faster than the free cocktails.

An old drinking buddy of Finn's was the first to reach us, clapping a hand so heartily on his back, I felt the slap ricochet down the entire length of my arm. In a cloud of alcoholic fumes – the kind that needed to stay far away from a naked flame – Tim, Terry, or whatever his name was, attempted to drag Finn off to join the group he'd just left.

'Maybe later,' Finn said, his fingers squeezing mine in silent reassurance.

'You should go and say hi,' I said. 'I don't mind.' Because I'd never been that girl, the one who needs to hang on to a man's arm all night, and I was far too old to be starting now.

'See, you've got permission,' said the guy. I had no idea why Finn had ever befriended him.

'We've only just got here, so like I said, maybe later.' Finn's less than enthusiastic response somehow filtered through the tequila haze and his old friend disappeared into the crowd, muttering something that sounded suspiciously like 'ball and chain'.

It was a brief victory because as we wove our way through the crowd towards a group of my friends, a perfectly manicured hand with an exceedingly large diamond ring upon it descended on to Finn's shoulder. I knew who it belonged to without having to look up.

'Finn Douglas. What a wonderful surprise to see you here.'

I didn't know if Finn had ever met our slightly terrifying MD in the past, but he was way too professional not to have done his research.

'Jacqueline Carstairs. It's a real pleasure to meet you,' he said, releasing my hand and extending his to my boss for a formal greeting. But she was already halfway in for an industry double kiss.

'I had no idea you knew our Gemma,' Jacqueline said,

trying – and I believe failing – to hide her astonishment that he was here as my guest.

'We're very old friends,' Finn said, turning to give me a warm smile.

My lips felt sticky from the oversweet cocktail I'd snagged from a passing waiter as I forced them to smile back. *Old friends*. It felt like the words had been written in neon and blasted out through the DJ's enormous speakers. He could have said, or at least hinted, that we were something more than that. So much for his desire to go public.

'You don't mind if I steal him away for a while, do you, Gemma?' And before I could commit career hara-kiri by saying that actually I did, she added, 'I'm sure our CEO would love to meet you, and there's something I'd really like to discuss with you.'

Finn's eyes met mine, full of apology, which I answered with a quick shake of my head. Business was business, and there was a very good reason why people always told you not to mix it with pleasure.

'Go,' I urged him. 'You can find me later. I'll be the one slaying them with my tango moves on the dance floor.'

At least I sent him away with a laugh, I told myself proudly.

I had a good time. It just wasn't the good time I'd planned on having. It seemed that no sooner had Finn managed to break away from one conversation than he was immediately sucked into another. As I laughed, joked, and drank a few too many free cocktails with my friends, I could feel Finn's eyes searching for me across the room. When I met them, all my senses sprang to attention. My fingers itched to touch him; I wanted to hear his voice whisper in my ear, smell the aftershave I'd forever associate with him or savour the taste of him as his mouth claimed mine. Finn had a unique and disconcerting ability to affect every single fibre of my body.

I lost sight of him for a while, which didn't concern me until I eventually spotted him in a dark corner of the room with Felicity, *Glow*'s book editor. The sane part of my brain said she was probably discussing a feature for the magazine, but every time I glanced their way, Felicity seemed to have closed the distance between them. I'd always quite liked her and had paid little attention to her reputation for seeing every man as a potential conquest, but I was rapidly revising my opinion as I saw her repeatedly laying her hand on Finn's forearm whenever he spoke and laughing uproariously. I mean, Finn was amusing but not *that* funny. I wasn't used to feeling jealous, and I didn't like the way I was suddenly comparing Felicity's laugh to a hyena's cackle or noticing that her blood-red acrylic nails looked an awful lot like talons.

Enough, I told myself firmly. 'Anyone fancy a dance?' I asked, knocking back the last of my cocktail. It was a little worrying to realise I could no longer remember exactly how many I'd had.

'Sure,' replied my friends.

I deliberately didn't look across to Finn and Felicity's corner of the room as I headed to the dance floor.

The area was crowded, and sufficient alcohol had flowed for inhibitions to have loosened and for people to be performing moves they'd be hoping wouldn't get uploaded on to social media in the morning.

We found a spot on the far side of the wooden dance floor, not too far from the DJ desk for making requests but out of the way of the more exuberantly flailing limbs. The music was a mixture of nineties pop and disco, a soundtrack guaranteed to appeal to all ages.

The strains of a Bee Gees song were fading away as the DJ's voice spliced into the gap between songs. 'And here's one I don't get too many requests for.'

Like a herd of antelopes, everyone paused, heads tilted as they waited for the music to begin. All around me, people hesitated as they tried to identify the song and then decide how to dance to it. But not me. I'd recognised it from the first few chords.

I waited, and a moment later felt the touch of a hand on my shoulder. It tapped lightly as though he was cutting in. I turned around with a smile and nodded my head towards the DJ.

'I take it that was you?' I asked, as the *Moulin Rouge* version of 'Roxanne' throbbed out through the speakers.

'Guilty,' admitted Finn, his hands reaching for mine. 'It was the only tango song I could think of.'

'I am *not* going to tango,' I warned him.

In response, Finn pulled me against him, lifting my arms to gently position them around his neck, while his hands slid down to my hips. We began to dance, following a beat, although not the one the musicians were playing.

We swayed together on the dance floor, which had emptied considerably due to his unusual song request. I could feel the strength of him as we moved in infinitesimally small circles under the neon lights. Someone's heart was beating really strongly in their chest; it could have been mine or his. What was harder to ignore was the effect we were having on each other. My breathing was fast, coming in excited, snatched gasps, while Finn's body was reacting to our closeness in a way that made me extremely grateful for the low lighting.

'This *isn't* how you tango,' I whispered, tilting my face towards him, so close that he could have kissed me if he wanted to – and I could tell from the look in his eyes that he really, really wanted to.

'It's how *I* do it,' he said, his voice far huskier than usual.

We made it almost to the end of the song, and although the suggestion could have come from either of us, I was really glad that he said the words before I did.

'Do you want to get out of here?'

I had only a hazy memory of leaving the party and tumbling into a taxi that had fortunately been passing as we emerged into the cold December night. I expected the sudden change in temperature to act like a bucket of cold water being thrown over us, but we were beyond burning by then. We were molten.

Finn kissed me in the back of the taxi in a way I'd never been kissed before. It was a real struggle to remember there was a driver with a rear-view mirror just a few feet away, because my hands were only just under my control.

Finn peeled a note from his wallet without even looking at the denomination. From the grateful 'Thank you' from the driver, I suspected it might have been a fifty.

We kissed by the lifts and then tumbled into the carriage with his arms still firmly clasped around me. We were alone for the first time since leaving the dance floor, and as our kisses deepened in intensity, we fell back against the wall of the carriage. I inadvertently selected every button on the control panel with my back, and the delay as we stopped on each floor before reaching mine felt like torture.

It took me four attempts to line up my door key with the lock, and that had nothing to do with the alcohol I'd consumed earlier. I was drunk, but not on anything that had come out of a bottle. I was higher than I'd ever been on desire and had long since crossed the point where stopping was even a consideration.

I only hoped Finn felt the same.

He pushed my front door shut, and it was as though a starting pistol had sounded in my head. My hands were tugging off his jacket and fumbling with the buttons of his shirt. To my shame, I heard at least one ping softly against the wooden floor.

And then came the moment I'd been dreading. Finn's hands reached up and fastened around my wrists, stopping me. I groaned against his mouth, but there was a strength and control in him that I couldn't fight.

'I don't want to stop. Don't make us stop,' I pleaded.

'Are you sure, Gemma?'

'Do you really need to ask me that?' I replied, aware I wasn't exactly playing fair as I pressed myself against him.

This time it was his turn to groan.

I felt weak and yet at the same time more empowered than I'd ever felt in my life. 'Do you want me?' I asked with a confidence I'd never felt with a man before.

'More than I've ever wanted anyone or anything,' Finn said, lifting me so all that separated us were a couple of annoying layers of fabric.

I wound my arms and legs tightly around him as he carried me to the bedroom.

20

THE NIGHT BEFORE CHRISTMAS

Eighteen months earlier

We must have got out of bed at some point in the days
following the *Glow* party. There would have been
essential bathroom breaks and occasions when we'd have
had to perform such necessary tasks as eating, drinking or
showering. Yet all I can remember of those days is being held
in Finn's arms, and the feel of his body on top of mine, or
mine on his.

We were leisurely, and we were frantic, taking our time and
then crazily cramming in every experience and sensation as
though they might suddenly be snatched away from us. We
spoke in a nonsense language that only new lovers are fluent in.

It was the best weekend of my life.

'I don't want tomorrow to come,' I whispered into his
shoulder, tasting the salty tang of perspiration that glistened
on his body from our lovemaking. 'I'm scared that when we
let the real world back in, it'll break the spell,' I confided in
the darkened bedroom.

Finn twisted to prop himself up on one elbow beside me. 'It won't, not if we don't let it,' he said softly. He kissed me then with a tenderness that made the words 'I love you' incredibly hard to suppress. They'd threatened to escape more than once over the last two days, until I could no longer trust my tongue to safeguard my secret. It was ridiculous to be talking about love this soon, but the words were hovering on the other side of a very thin curtain that kept wafting open whenever I looked into Finn's eyes.

He reached down to brush back a damp strand of hair from my forehead. 'You've no idea how scared I was of doing this.'

'Why? Did someone tell you you're bad at it?' I teased with a smile I knew he could see in the moonlit room. 'Because I have to tell you, you're really not.'

Finn's chuckle was low and throaty and ignited a chain reaction between my legs. Practically everything he did turned me on.

He sobered then, his eyes fixing on mine in the shadowy half-light. 'I didn't want to screw this up. And I have a long track record of doing exactly that.' For a man who outwardly appeared to have the Midas touch, it was a curious confession that made no sense. I waited for more, but instead he bent his head and nuzzled his lips against my throat. It was a distraction technique, but even as my body arched instinctively towards him, I realised there were secrets in his past he wasn't yet ready to share.

The sound was low and long, perforating my dream and tearing me from my sleep. It was the moan of the wind, the call of a gull, the cry of a child.

'Dad...' The word echoed in the darkness.

I sat bolt upright in bed, pushing aside the tangle of sheets that Finn's thrashing limbs had tugged free from the mattress. He was still writhing beside me, his head twisting on the pillow so violently, whiplash felt like a real concern.

'Finn?' My voice was hesitant.

He moaned again and then spoke clearly. 'Dad!'

I'd seen people have nightmares before, but nothing like this. This was real night-terror stuff, and for a moment I panicked. Was it dangerous to wake him, the way they said it was with sleepwalkers? Should I just let the dream run its course?

'No, Dad!' Finn cried again, and I acted without thinking, not for the thirty-five-year-old man sharing my bed, but for the child he'd once been.

I touched his shoulder, shocked to find it drenched in sweat even though the room was cool. 'Finn, wake up. You're having a bad dream.'

I shook him, surprised at how long it took to free him from wherever his subconscious had taken him. He looked startled and disoriented as he stared up at me. Something was glistening on his cheek, and while it might have been sweat, it looked more like tears. He swiped a hand across his face, and it was gone.

'Are you okay? You were having a nightmare.'

'I'm fine,' he said brusquely, sitting up and swinging his legs out of bed in a single manoeuvre.

'What was it about?'

'Nothing. I can't really remember it,' he said, getting to his feet. I wondered if he knew that the muscles of his back had tensed with the lie. Finn was halfway across the bedroom, heading for the door. 'I'm just going to grab a glass of water. Go back to sleep.'

I flopped back on to the pillows, staring with unseeing eyes at the ceiling. Part of me realised Finn probably wanted to be alone, to decompress from the horror of his dream, but I could still hear his words echoing from its depths. He'd cried out for help and it had something to do with his father, and that felt too important to ignore.

I glanced at the illuminated display on the bedside clock. Three a.m. The middle-of-the-night hour when things always seemed far worse. It was Christmas morning. All over the world there'd be children struggling to sleep, but my concern wasn't for the ones waiting for dawn so they could tear open their stockings. It was for a child I'd never meet, who still called out for a father who'd died more than twenty years before.

I crossed the bedroom, shivering in the early-hours chill, and reached for the first thing my hand fell on to cover my nakedness. It was Finn's T-shirt, which had been thrown carelessly over the chair – by me, I now recalled. I slipped it over my head, revelling in the softness of the fabric that still smelt of him. It reached the top of my thighs, just long enough for modesty.

The flat was in darkness. I looked first in the kitchen and then padded silently into the lounge. He was sitting on the very edge of the settee, as though poised for flight. He glanced up as I entered but said nothing. His hair looked dishevelled, as though fingers had recently raked roughly through it. I debated turning on the light but imagined Finn would prefer darkness. I compromised by reaching for the plug socket and switching on the Christmas tree lights. They twinkled in cheery defiance of the mood.

I decided against joining him on the couch but dropped instead to my knees before him. 'Are you okay?' I asked again.

Finn's lips twisted. I think he was trying for a smile, but they couldn't quite manage it. 'Yeah. I'm fine.'

He didn't look it, but this wasn't the time to disagree. In fact, it wasn't the time to say anything at all, so I reached for his hand, and waited.

The minutes ticked by. Ten passed before he spoke.

'I'm sorry if I freaked you out. It's been a long time since I had that dream.'

'Is it something you want to talk about?'

He shook his head. 'No. Not really. It feels like I've spent hundreds of hours and thousands of Aussie dollars doing that already.' He looked down at me in the glow of the twinkling LED lights. 'But you do deserve an explanation.'

'Only if you want to give me one.'

He lifted his head and nodded slowly.

'I'm guessing this is something to do with your parents' accident,' I prompted.

'Yes and no,' he replied mysteriously. 'And it wasn't an accident, not in the true sense of the word. My parents died trying to rescue me from a house fire.'

'Oh my God, Finn. How terrible. I had no idea.'

His eyes were fixed on our joined hands as he continued. 'They'd been out for the evening and returned home before the emergency services got there. The babysitter had managed to get out of the house and raise the alarm, and there was a crowd of neighbours gathered below my bedroom window yelling up at me to jump. But I was too scared. When Dad realised I wasn't going to be able to do it, he ran into the building to get me. Five minutes later, when he hadn't come back out, Mum followed him.'

Finn finally lifted his head, and his face was awash with tears. 'They died trying to save me, because I was too fucking scared to jump.'

I was trying to wipe away his tears with my fingers, but they were falling faster than I could keep up with. As I pulled him close, I had a sudden flashback memory of Finn's reaction to the hotel fire at The Manor House on our first proper date. Now, horribly, it all made sense.

'How did you get out in the end?'

'The fire eventually reached my bedroom. Everything was going up in flames around me. And that's when I climbed out on to the windowsill and finally jumped. If I'd done it just ten minutes earlier, my parents would probably both still be alive today.'

'You can't blame yourself. You were just a child.'

Finn gave a long, shuddering sigh. 'I thought I'd dealt with the grief. But really all I did was bury it. I genuinely thought the quitting thing I kept doing was totally unrelated.'

'"Quitting thing"?'

Finn's hand gently cupped my face, his thumb running over my cheek as he spoke.

'Whenever something – anything – in my life was going great, I'd find a way to sabotage it.'

I blinked up at him. He wasn't making any sense; Finn was one of the most successful people I'd ever met. My head was filled with a million questions, but this wasn't the time to ask any of them.

'I was predicted a first at uni, but I dropped out halfway through finals. I threw everything I owned into a backpack and bummed around Europe for a year. Even without a degree, I managed to get a great job – several great jobs, in fact – but I found a reason to leave every single one of them when I was at the top of my game.'

'Or you chose to walk away and give the job to the only other candidate in the running,' I said softly.

Finn's thumb brushed across my lower lip in a soft caress. 'You were always the best man for that job.'

'And is that why you sold the coffee shop rather than expand the business like the new owners did?'

Finn nodded. 'I found reasons each time to justify my decision to move on: I was bored; I needed a new challenge...' He paused as though considering how best to continue. 'And I did it with relationships too, over and over again. As soon as anyone got too close, I pulled the pin on the grenade.'

'Or caught a plane to the other side of the world,' I said quietly.

'To be fair, I did already have a ticket for that one.' Finn paused, as though hearing his excuse for the first time. 'But you're right. I could have stayed. I could have written anywhere. I guess it was easier to tell myself I *had* to go.'

He was baring his soul to me in a way that left him vulnerable and exposed. That had to mean something, didn't it?

'There's a name for this thing I do. It's actually a recognised condition. They call it achievemephobia.'

'That doesn't even sound like a real word.'

'That's exactly what I said – right after the therapist told me I was suffering from it.' My heartbeat quickened, already terrified of anything that could harm this man. 'Basically, it's a fear of success, and many people who suffer from it don't even realise they've got it. It's feeling that you don't deserve to be happy or to do well, and so you sabotage it. They say it can be caused by several things – and a childhood trauma is one of them.'

'What made you finally seek help in Australia after so many years?'

The first genuine smile I'd seen so far lit up Finn's face.

'You. You did. I realised I'd found something I didn't want to run away from. I found something worth staying for.'

He dipped his head, and his kiss was soft and warm.

'Two and a half years is a long time to wait before realising you miss someone you left behind,' I said quietly.

Finn shook his head. 'I was missing you before we were even wheels-up on the runway.'

'I thought you'd changed your mind, that you weren't interested in me any more. The postcards confused me; I thought they meant more than they did. But when I invited myself to stay and you knocked me back, I assumed it was because you'd found someone else.'

'Never. I can see now that sending the cards wasn't fair, but I wanted to let you know that I was still thinking about you. Even though it was too soon for me; I wasn't ready then. I was still trapped in a cycle that I couldn't seem to break. I had to work out why I kept pushing the self-destruct button. Because I couldn't ever risk doing that to you – or to us.'

It was a lovely thing to say, but the thought of him suddenly changing his mind and disappearing out of my life filled me with genuine terror. Was it possible to be cured of this achievemephobia thing, or would it always be there?

'What would you have done if I hadn't been free when you came back?'

Finn's eyes darkened, and I could see it was a fear he'd

already faced. 'If you were happy, then I'd have walked away, even though it would have killed me. But something kept telling me that our story wasn't over yet. All I could do was hope that you felt the same way.' He gently touched my cheek. 'You were always going to be the one I would never get over; the one I'd never forget.'

His hands slid down to my waist, drawing me towards him.

'I'm in this, Gemma. All the way in. Fair warning, I have no intention of going anywhere. In fact...' Was that a blush staining his cheeks? '... the only way I see this thing going is when you agree to change your name to mine.'

My heart flipped in my chest. 'Is that so you'll finally be able to remember it?' My smile was impossibly wide.

He grinned back. 'You have no idea how much I love you,' he said, stealing my line just seconds before I could say it.

WEDNESDAY: DAY FOUR

21

'Here you go,' I said, placing a still-fizzing Prosecco in front of Hannah. She reached for the glass and held it up to mine and then paused, suddenly uncertain.

'I was going to say "Cheers", but maybe that's not really appropriate.'

'Let's toast to friendship then,' I said, clinking my glass against hers. 'Because only a true friend would have volunteered to tack up posters with me on the hottest day of the year.'

'*Volunteered?*' Hannah queried, her eyes twinkling in the midday sunshine of the pub garden. 'I think you'll find "press-ganged" is a more accurate description.'

I smiled, leaning back on the wooden bench I'd managed to snag for us. I was treating us to lunch after we'd spent the last four hours plastering 'Missing' posters all over town. Finn's face could now be found in petrol station forecourts, on supermarket noticeboards, and nailed on to the bark of countless trees.

Hannah kicked off her flip-flops and absently rubbed the soles of her feet, which I was dismayed to see looked red and sore. I wasn't surprised; we'd clocked up an impressive number of steps that morning, yet we'd still only covered a fraction of the locations on the list I'd compiled. It was all about pacing, and while I was happy to keep going until the sun went down, I suspected Hannah might very well be done for the day.

'Two brie and bacon baguettes, and a portion of chips,' announced the barman, who'd crossed the pub garden and set down a tray of food before us.

Hannah's eyes lit up. Much might have changed over the years, but my friend's love of fried potatoes remained a constant. She was already diving into the basket as the waiter turned towards me.

'I've put that poster you gave me up in the bar, and one of our regulars was wondering if you're offering a reward.'

I set down my glass of Prosecco so abruptly, I lost half of it over the rim. 'Do they have some information?'

The barman looked apologetic. 'No. Sorry. I think he was just being hopeful.'

'Bloody cheek, expecting a reward,' Hannah said when the man was safely out of earshot. 'That makes it sound like Finn's a lost labradoodle or something.'

'No, I should have thought about offering a reward,' I said, annoyed the idea hadn't even occurred to me.

'Why?' Hannah challenged, still fired up with indignation. 'It shouldn't be about money, and it's not like Finn's been kidnapped and you have to come up with the ransom to get him back.'

I bit my lip and turned away from her gaze, feigning a sudden interest in the pub's bouncy castle.

'Oh, Gemma, really? *Kidnapped?*'

'It was fairly low down on my list of possibilities,' I mumbled, reaching for my sandwich before she could ask me what other outlandish theories I was still harbouring rather than face the one everyone else thought was obvious.

'I suppose a financial incentive *might* help,' Hannah conceded, after chewing over both the idea and her lunch for a moment. 'But it would need to be a large enough amount to make it worthwhile. You don't have that kind of money lying around, do you?'

There wasn't much about my life Hannah didn't know, but on this particular issue she wasn't entirely correct.

'Actually... I might be able to lay my hands on some money.'

'Please tell me you're not thinking of doing something illegal,' she pleaded, only half joking.

I gave a small laugh. 'Of course not,' I replied, reaching into my bag for my phone. 'Well, it might be a tad immoral, but it's definitely not illegal.'

Hannah set aside her plate, her expression suddenly serious. 'Go on,' she urged.

I twisted on the bench, using my body to cast a shadow across my phone's screen. 'Finn and I opened a joint bank account after we found that cottage last summer.'

'The Toadstool place, the one that fell through?'

'Mushroom,' I corrected her, surprised to feel a sting of disappointment still at finding and then losing our dream home. 'We pooled our savings for the deposit, and then when it all fell apart, we just left them in the account.' I sighed sadly. 'We were going to start house-hunting again after the wedding.'

There was a long pause, which, good friend or not, Hannah

didn't know how to fill. I used the time to log in to our account and key in the passcode. Two more taps of my fingertips and the page opened before me.

Hannah craned forward in her seat. She was way ahead of me on this one. She'd already guessed what I'd find.

My frown was the first giveaway, quickly followed by a confused shake of my head.

'There must be some sort of mistake,' I said, buying a few more precious moments before I was forced to acknowledge what I was seeing.

Hannah's voice had hardened. 'Has he taken it all?' I'd never heard her sound so cold.

'No. Not all of it. Just fifty thousand. He left three for me.' I gave a small broken sound. 'Oh, and the interest. He left me that too.'

There was a brandy in my hands, and I had absolutely no idea how it had got there. Hannah must have gone into the bar to buy it. It was hard to say which burnt more: the fiery liquid scorching my throat or my eyes from staring unblinkingly at the page displaying the recent transaction on the account.

'When did you last check it?' Hannah asked.

'A week or so before the wedding.'

'And you've not thought to look since then, not even after everything that's happened?' The tone of her voice and the look in her eyes said: *Because I sure as hell would have done.*

'No,' I lied. Because of course I'd thought of looking. In the middle of the night, when every worst fear seemed like a real possibility, of course I'd thought of checking the account. But it would have unravelled me. I couldn't allow myself to stop believing in Finn. I still couldn't.

Hannah's nostrils flared as she exhaled heavily. If she was a dragon, she'd have scorched half the garden by now.

'You have to get back in touch with the police. Maybe now they'll actually do something to find Finn. Now that a crime has been committed.'

I put down the brandy. There was still half a glass left, but I couldn't finish it, not if I wanted to drive home. 'Finn hasn't done anything illegal.'

For the second time that day, Hannah's anger surprised me. 'You have to stop doing this, Gemma. Stop defending him. The bastard left you at the altar and robbed you blind and yet you're still making excuses for him.'

If Hannah had been even slightly on the fence about Finn's guilt, she was now coming down, feet first, on the side of him being just one step up from the Antichrist.

But she was wrong.

'When we needed the deposit money for Mushroom Cottage, we each put whatever we had in savings into the account,' I said. 'Finn still had a sizeable amount left over from the sale of the coffee shop. I didn't have nearly as much to put in the pot.'

'So how much of the money was his?'

'Fifty thousand,' I said with a sigh. 'Finn's taken out only what he put in. No one's robbed anyone here. There's been no crime.'

Unless breaking someone's heart was a criminal offence. If it was, then I was now closer to finally admitting that Finn just might be guilty after all.

22

Mushroom Cottage
Twelve months earlier

'This car is insane.'

Finn's eyes briefly left the road as he turned to me. 'Do you mean in a good way?' he asked with a grin.

'No, I mean in a crazy "Who on earth buys a car like this?" way.'

'Me. I do... I did,' Finn said with a happy shrug of his shoulders. And for a moment I didn't see a thirty-six-year-old man sitting behind the wheel of a head-turning American Ford, I saw an irrepressible, mischievous little boy. With a start, I realised I was glimpsing the face of the son we might one day have. Perhaps that's why I softened.

'It's certainly not the kind of car that slips under the radar, is it?'

Finn's hand left the wheel and briefly squeezed my thigh, making me momentarily forget all about the classic red-and-white Gran Torino he'd picked up that afternoon.

'At least it'll be easy to spot in a car park,' he said, as though that was the only reason he'd bought it.

I shook my head in amusement. 'Probably because it'll be taking up two spaces.'

'Only if you park it,' he teased, and we shared a look no one but us would ever understand. Any conversation about parking always transported us back to the day we first met, six years earlier. It was a curious trigger, but it never failed to remind me how much I loved this man.

We were on our way to an early evening cocktail party at his editor Tom's house. Tom lived in a remote village 'at the arse end of nowhere' – his words, not ours. The roads we were travelling were narrow, and the car was wide, and for all his banter I could tell Finn was having to concentrate hard on his driving. I, on the other hand, had the luxury of being able to enjoy the scenery, and I had to admit it was spectacular. I'd grown up in a hilly rural area, but here the land was low and flat, turning the fields around us into an enormous green patchwork quilt.

'It's so pretty around here,' I said.

'It is. It reminds me of Australia, in a way; there's space to breathe here. I can see us living somewhere like this one day.'

'You can?' I said, twisting happily in my seat towards him. I loved it when Finn did this, spoke about future us, as though it was the next chapter in a book we were writing.

'Sure,' he said, his fingers drumming lightly on the steering wheel in time to the music on the radio. 'We'll find an old, cosy place to do up, with a garden large enough for a couple of dogs to run around in.'

I was like a child hearing her favourite bedtime story for the hundredth time. I knew every word, and yet I still never tired of hearing it.

'Dogs?' I queried. 'In the plural?'

'That's negotiable,' Finn said, throwing me a look that melted something inside me.

I sat back in my seat with a happy smile, imagining a pair of lively border collies and a little boy, who looked just like Finn, running gleefully behind them.

We were happily following directions on my phone when we suddenly fell into a signal black hole. We drove on for a while, trying to remember the next bit of the route, which had now disappeared from my screen, but it wasn't long before we realised we'd taken a wrong turn somewhere.

Finn seemed totally unconcerned, but it was beginning to worry me that it had been quite a while since we'd passed the last village, and I hadn't seen a signpost in ages.

'We're going to be very late,' I said, trying not to panic that we had absolutely no idea where we were.

'Try my phone again,' Finn suggested, pulling it from his pocket and dropping it on to my lap.

I wafted his iPhone about, trying to trap a signal. I even stuck it out through the open car window, which would have been disastrous if I'd dropped it, for the narrow road we were travelling on was bordered on both sides by gullies so deep, I couldn't even see the bottom of them through the dense, overgrown foliage.

'Up there,' declared Finn, pointing to something he'd glimpsed through a thick bank of trees. 'I saw sunlight glinting off glass, the way it does off a window. There must be a property up ahead, on the left.'

I pulled a face, preferring the idea of turning around and going back the way we'd come rather than showing up at someone's home in the middle of nowhere.

'It'll be fine,' Finn said, already turning down a dirt track that would lead us who knew where. 'What's the worst that could happen?'

'For a man who writes psychological thrillers for a living, you seem to have a remarkably poor imagination,' I said darkly. 'I bet you wouldn't catch Stephen King saying that.'

Finn laughed and took my hand once again.

The cottage stood on an enormous plot. The grass was overgrown, and there were weeds sprouting in the driveway. Ivy was creeping determinedly around every window, as though trying to peek in. Nature was definitely on a mission to take back this solitary dwelling, but despite its dilapidated appearance, the cottage was holding its ground.

It was the kind of house little children draw when you give them a sheet of paper and a handful of crayons. It was perfectly symmetrical, with four windows on either side of a front door that might once have been a deep forest green but was now faded to the colour of a vegetable smoothie. A single chimney rose from a roof that was missing several tiles but otherwise looked sound. Like an old lady who'd once been beautiful, this house had excellent bones. They shone through the patina of age and neglect.

I'd never believed in love at first sight, because – if anything – the exact opposite had happened between Finn and me. So it was startling to find myself falling head over heels not for a person but for a collection of bricks and mortar. We pulled up at the foot of the driveway to Mushroom Cottage and for a moment neither of us spoke. I turned to Finn with a look of barely reined-in excitement and saw the same expression reflected back at me.

If this had been a film, there would have been a 'For Sale' sign hammered into the front lawn, but the overgrown grass held nothing except a sprawling oak tree and a lot of weeds.

The property wasn't for sale, and, more than that, it was clearly occupied. There was an old car parked on the driveway, and flowery drapes bordered the lacy net curtains at the windows. One of those nets twitched several times as we idled at the end of the drive.

'Have you got any signal yet?' asked Finn, after checking his own phone.

I shook my head as Finn unclipped his seat belt and prepared to climb out of the car.

I glanced all around. We were quite literally in the middle of nowhere and although the house looked delightful, we couldn't be sure that the same would be true of its owner.

'I don't think you should read any more of my books,' Finn teased as he took my hand and began leading me down the path to the front door.

We passed beneath the overhanging boughs of the oak, and something made me look up. The remains of an old rope swing, looped around a sturdy branch, were still visible through the leaves. At some point in its history, this had been a family home, and for some reason that comforted me.

We were just a few yards from the front door when my phone suddenly connected with a nearby mast. The frozen screen sprang back to life and our route was once again displayed. I nudged Finn's arm, but it was too late. Behind the green front door, I could hear the rattle of a security chain sliding on its track.

I gripped Finn's hand a little harder, and he squeezed mine back reassuringly.

The front door creaked ajar, plaintively crying out for oil or more visitors. The same might also have been said for the wizened elderly man who stood in its opening.

'Hello,' he said, peering forward like a tortoise emerging from its shell. 'I don't know you, do I?'

'No, sir, you don't,' said Finn, extending his hand to the elderly gentleman. 'My name is Finn Douglas and this is my girlfriend, Gemma Fletcher. I do apologise for bothering you, but I think we might be lost.'

I glanced up at Finn and then meaningfully back down at my phone screen, but Finn responded with an infinitesimal shake of his head.

'We're trying to get to Hodgeson Creek. Do you happen to know where that is?'

The old man smiled, revealing a set of dentures that I suspected were even older than Finn's Ford.

'Mercy me. You are definitely on the wrong road. But don't worry, I can give you directions.'

My vote was still to offer an apology for disturbing him and let Google Maps do what it did best, but Finn clearly had a different plan in mind.

'Would you two youngsters like to come in for a moment and have a glass of lemonade while I draw you a little map to put you back on the right road? My name is Walter, by the way. Walter Simpson.'

'That's very kind of you, Walter. We'd love to,' said Finn with such shocking lack of self-preservation, I decided we'd be having a little talk later on the subject of 'stranger danger'.

Walter had already turned around with a cheery 'Follow me' and disappeared down the hallway.

'Is this wise?' I hissed at Finn as we crossed the threshold. 'What if he's dangerous?'

We both looked at Walter, who'd stopped to pick up a walking stick to aid his journey from front door to kitchen.

'If things get iffy, I think I can take him,' Finn said, his lips twitching in amusement.

The kitchen was circa 1970 and instantly transported me back to my grandparents' home. Despite the dated units and elderly white goods, it was a bright and sunny room and looked out on to an enormous back garden.

Walter was rummaging in a cupboard for glasses while I was scouring the room for a pot plant I could surreptitiously tip my drink into. Almost as though he was reading my mind, Finn gave me an enormous wink.

Surprisingly, Walter produced a jug of old-fashioned homemade lemonade from the fridge. He set it down on a vintage Formica kitchen table that would probably have fetched a fortune on eBay.

'You'll like this,' said Walter confidently, pouring out three glasses. 'It's my Alice's recipe.'

He took one of the lemonades and lifted it to his mouth, gulping it down with old-man, lip-smacking enthusiasm.

'Is Alice your wife?' I asked, looking around the kitchen as though his elderly partner might be hiding somewhere.

'She was,' Walter said, setting his glass back down on the

table, his hand trembling in a way it hadn't just moments before.

'She took ill last year. She got the cancer.' He shook his head sadly, as though he was still struggling to come to terms with the tragedy. 'I always thought it would come for one of us. There isn't a day that passes when I don't wish it had been me.'

'I'm really sorry to hear that, Walter,' said Finn compassionately.

I reached for my glass, ashamed of my foolish suspicions, and took a sip. It was just the right amount of sweet and sour.

I smiled across the table at our unexpected host. 'Alice certainly knew how to make good lemonade.'

Walter smiled. 'Aye. She did.'

We chatted to the old man about the house while he drew the most detailed and convoluted directions map I'd ever seen. He put Google to shame.

'Have you lived here a long time?' I asked Walter's bent head as he laboriously filled in landmarks we had no need of on the sketch.

'All of our married life,' he said with a sad smile. He glanced towards the front door. 'I carried her over that threshold as my bride fifty-five years ago and then helped them carry her back over it in a mahogany casket last year.'

Unexpectedly, I felt my eyes fill with tears. Beneath the table, Finn reached for my hand and squeezed it.

'It's a very beautiful old house,' Finn said.

Walter looked up with a new brightness in his rheumy eyes. 'Would you like a little tour?'

I don't think I'd ever felt so torn. We were already horribly late for the party, but I sensed the loneliness in the elderly widower. How many visitors did he get, I wondered? And hidden less nobly beneath that thought was a burning curiosity to look around his wonderful house.

'We'd love to, if it's not putting you to too much trouble,' said Finn.

Walter needed his stick to get to his feet, and I felt Finn tense in readiness as the old man wobbled briefly before somehow managing to locate his centre of gravity.

'My daughter worries about me living alone in this big old place since her mum passed,' he explained, walking in slightly jerky steps. 'She thinks I'll take a fall and lie here for days with no one to help me.' Walter's gait seemed to improve the further we progressed across the quarry-tiled kitchen floor. 'I keep telling her I'd be fine if it wasn't for arthritis.' He pronounced it 'Arthur Rightus', as though the condition was a particularly troublesome neighbour he had to contend with. I hid a smile and knew, without even looking, that Finn was doing the same.

It was a slow tour through the house, covering not only the downstairs rooms but also all four of the generously proportioned bedrooms. I was glad of our snail-like progress, for it gave us more opportunity to appreciate every last detail of the house. It was a sweet torture, because it was clear from his commentary that every room held beloved memories of Walter's late wife, Alice. Of course he'd never want to leave it.

'I can see how much you love this place, Walter,' said Finn when we'd eventually finished the tour and were once again in the hallway, preparing to take our leave.

'My daughter, Chrissie, keeps saying I should move in with her.' Walter sighed as he looked around the hallway, as though searching for something – or someone. 'But as lovely as it would be to spend more time with the grandbabies, I can't see me ever leaving this house.'

I reached for Walter's hand, holding it warmly rather than shaking it. 'I understand. I think I'd feel exactly the same way if it was mine.'

'On the very small chance that you do ever think about selling up, Walter,' Finn said, reaching into his wallet for a business card, 'we'd love to be the ones to take care of this house for you.'

Finn made no mention of how much we'd be willing to pay, and I think that impressed Walter almost as much as it did me.

At the doorway I impulsively kissed our host on the cheek, and he looked so delighted, it made me wonder how long it had been since anyone had done that.

'Thank you so much for showing us around your home,' said Finn, shaking the old man's hand. 'But, please, Walter, be careful in future. You really shouldn't go inviting total strangers into your home. It isn't safe.'

Walter gave a cackle that only those on the wrong side of eighty can pull off effectively. 'Bless you, lad. I know that. It wasn't my idea to let you in, I can tell you. But Alice said you looked like good folk, and I still trust her judgement.'

We waved Walter goodbye from the bottom of the path, before climbing back into the car. I kept my eyes on the house until the trees and bushes once again swallowed it from view.

Even with Walter's slightly worrying final words, Mushroom Cottage had lost none of its charm.

'We could do something really amazing with that place, if Walter ever decides to sell it,' I said, my head already filled with ideas. 'Did you notice that cute little room beside the master bedroom, the one with the deep bay window?' I asked, summoning up an image of how it would look with an antique rocking chair in the bay and a crib in the corner of the room.

'I did,' Finn said with a happy grin. 'It would be a perfect spot for a desk. I could just see myself writing there the moment I walked in.'

I bit my lip, momentarily worried about our conflicting ideas. But as the cottage wasn't currently for sale, it was a moot point.

But two days later, a number Finn didn't recognise appeared on his phone screen. It was Walter. Apparently, he'd been thinking about it very carefully, and if we were genuinely interested, he'd like to sell us his home. In all the excitement, the small second bedroom seemed unimportant. It was only later that we came to realise it was actually the most important room in the whole house.

23

We didn't put up any more flyers that day. To be honest, given the mood Hannah was in, placing a hammer in her hands didn't seem a particularly good idea right then.

Instead, we stayed in the pub garden, talking in circles that carefully skirted anything to do with weddings, empty bank accounts or missing fiancés. It was only when I dropped her at her car that Hannah gently steered the conversation back towards the topic we could no longer avoid.

'What will you do now?'

I looked through the windscreen. The temperature outside was high; so hot, the air seemed to shimmer like a mirage, or maybe that was just the tears that had sprung to my eyes at her gentle tone. I held back a blink, to keep them hidden behind my sunglasses.

'I'll carry on,' I said simply.

I didn't expand on whether I meant carry on posting flyers or carry on looking for Finn or carry on holding a torch for the man everyone believed had left me. In truth, I was probably going to do all three.

I filled what was left of the afternoon with chores and errands. To any casual observer, no doubt everything appeared entirely normal. But I spent fifteen minutes at the supermarket meat counter, trying to decide if I should buy one piece of steak or two. And then another ten deliberating whether Finn's favourite chocolate biscuits deserved a place in my trolley. They came in and went out four times, before I defiantly placed not one but two packets on top of my other shopping.

I stopped at the dry cleaner's to collect a couple of my work dresses that I wouldn't be needing for a few more weeks, completely forgetting that a suit of Finn's was also on the ticket. I was quite proud of the way I held it together in the shop, but considerably less so of my behaviour back at the car, when I ripped open the protective plastic cover and pressed my nose against the lapel, searching for a lingering trace of his familiar smell. All I got was a strong hit of perchloroethylene and a strange look from a woman passing by.

'Enough, Gemma, enough,' I told myself firmly as I got back into the driving seat and headed towards home.

I didn't see his car in the car park. It wasn't in my designated bay, where he sometimes parked, or even in my visitor one, which to be fair could sometimes be a bit of a free-for-all. He wasn't waiting for me by the lifts. So it threw me completely when I rounded the corner and saw him sitting on the floor of the communal hallway beside my front door.

He got to his feet with the kind of stiffness that told me he'd been waiting there for some time. I immediately dropped the dry cleaning and the supermarket bags and hurried to help him up. His arms tightened around me in the kind of hug I needed most right then. He'd always given the very best of hugs.

'What are you doing here, Dad? Why didn't you phone and let me know you were coming?'

He gave a shrug, looking shamefaced. 'It was a bit of an impulse decision. I was halfway here before I realised my phone was flat, so I had to take a chance that you were home.'

He gave a small chuckle, the kind that featured in a thousand childhood memories. 'I guessed wrong.'

I retrieved my abandoned belongings and slid my key into the front door. I'd got into a silly habit of calling out a hopeful 'Hello' into the empty flat every time I returned, and it was a real effort not to do so right then with Dad beside me. Would there ever come a time, I wondered, when I stopped believing that one day I'd walk in and find Finn sitting in the kitchen, patiently waiting for me. Only after I'd finally given up and changed the locks, I realised sadly.

Dad looked hot and flushed, which could have been from his wait in the fusty, poorly ventilated hallway. Instead of flicking on the kettle in the time-honoured Fletcher family way, I went instead to the fridge and pulled out one of Finn's bottles of beer. I made a mental note to replace it, which I immediately crossed out with an invisible red pen, even though I knew I'd do it anyway.

'So, what's with the unexpected visit?' I asked, throwing my perishable items haphazardly into the fridge and grabbing a can of ice-cold soda for myself.

I popped the ring pull and sat down opposite my father, noticing for the first time the twin dark circles beneath his eyes. Those same eyes were clouded with a grave expression that panicked me.

'Are you okay, Daddy?' I asked, slipping unconsciously back to the name I hadn't called him in years. 'You look really tired.' *And older*, I added silently. *Way older than you did yesterday.*

'I didn't sleep very well last night,' he began, his hands restless as he picked at the label on the beer bottle.

The panic that had started as a spasm in my stomach was beginning to rise inside me, like a sickness that I might embarrassingly expel at any moment.

'Are you ill? Is that it?'

In the single beat before he answered, I threw down a defiant gauntlet to a God I'd not had a proper conversation with since Sunday School days. *Oh no you don't. Not Dad. You've taken away too many people I love. You are NOT getting him too.*

It was disconcerting to realise I was including Finn in the same category as my mum. Did I truly think he was 'gone' from me in that way? Now I really did feel sick.

'Something's been troubling me, really troubling me, ever since I saw you yesterday.'

'Something physical?' That was not the voice of a thirty-three-year-old woman. It was the voice of a frightened child.

Dad stopped trying to destroy the beer label and reached for my hands. 'No, sweetheart, it's not an illness. But it's been like the world's worst itch that I simply couldn't scratch.'

I frowned, still no closer to understanding what was wrong.

'Erm, I've got some calamine lotion in the bathroom cabinet,' I offered hesitantly.

His laughter released the tension, allowing me to dial down my concern from 'raging panic' to 'quietly concerned'.

'Not a physical itch, Gemma, honey. A mental one.'

'Oh,' I said, nodding as though this was suddenly all making sense to me. Which couldn't have been further from the truth.

'There was something we said at lunch that I couldn't shake off. It kept quietly nibbling away at the back of my mind, you know, like mice gnawing through a wall. And then today, I finally got it. And I had to tell you.'

'And you couldn't have done it on the phone?' I asked. 'You had to drive all the way here?'

He shook his head, his eyes solemn.

'No. This thing I have to say is too important for me not to be here with you when I tell you.'

The fear was coming back, but it was swept away, just moments later, on a tide of incredulity.

'I think you may be right, Gemma. No. It's more than that. I know you're right.'

My heart was beating fast, because unless I was reading this wrong, I was about to hear something I never thought anyone would ever say.

'You're right about Finn. I think something may have happened to him.'

My hands were shaking. It was a miracle that the can of soda hadn't puddled all over the table. Dad reached across, gently removed it from my grip and folded my hands within his.

'It was the gerberas that did it,' he said.

I nodded fiercely, still with no idea what he meant but happy to wait for the fog to clear.

'We were talking about the flowers I'd taken to your mum that morning, and you asked me if it had been quiet at the cemetery.'

I nodded again, wondering if my apparent inability to vocalise a response was permanent or if my tongue was simply as shocked as the rest of me right then.

'Do you remember what I answered?'

This time I shook my head, just for variety.

'I said it was always quiet that early in the morning. And that was what started me thinking. That was the first domino to fall over.'

Head movements simply weren't going to cut it any longer. 'I'm sorry, Dad. I'm not following you.'

His hands were warm as they gripped mine more tightly. 'I have something I have to tell you, and I want you to hear me out without interruptions. Okay?'

'Is it something bad?' I whispered. My heart was racing as though I was running to reach wherever it was my dad's revelation was leading us.

Dad's smile was gentle as he shook his head. 'No. It's not. Let me tell you what happened…'

'It was a Tuesday morning in late September. There was a nip in the air and a thick mist on the ground, the kind that hangs around for hours and makes you drive with your head-lights on.

'It was no surprise to discover mine was the only car in the cemetery car park. When you get there at eight o'clock in the morning, you can pretty much guarantee you'll have the place to yourself for an hour or two.

'I made my way to your mum's plot – it's a walk I swear I could do blindfolded; I know every bend in the path, every uneven paving stone.

'I probably did the same as I do every week when I get there: I'd have said hello and then chatted away about my week while I tidied up around her plot. At that time of year there are always leaves to clear away or the odd piece of litter blown there by the wind.

'I'm always struck by how strangely peaceful it is there, which I know sounds like an odd thing to say. In the early days, visiting her grave just about broke me, over and over again. It took a while to recognise that it was actually a comfort just being near her again.

'So there I was, sitting on the bench, wittering on about something or other, when out of nowhere I suddenly feel a hand resting on my shoulder. Now, I don't spook easily, but when you're sitting in a misty, deserted cemetery, the last thing you expect is that. I jumped up like I'd been shot, and probably shocked a few of your mum's neighbours with some pretty colourful language. I'm not sure who – or what – I thought I'd see when I spun around, but the last thing I expected was to see your Finn standing there.

'"Christ, Ted, I'm really sorry," he said, and I have to say he did look genuinely apologetic. "I thought about calling out to you as I approached, but I was worried it might startle you."

'"So you thought laying a hand on my shoulder in an empty, misty graveyard was a better plan?" I said, trying not to look like someone whose heart was still going like the clappers.

'Finn apologised again and when he was finally done, I asked him what on earth he was doing there. I mean, it was obviously not a random coincidence. I don't know how many times I'd met him by then, or how long you two had been going out – you know me, I've always been terrible with dates. But I have to say, I knew Finn well enough to realise he looked on edge – not nervous exactly, but more jumpy than I'd ever seen him before.

'Also, it was early in the morning, but he was wearing a shirt and tie and a smart jacket. It made me wonder if he was off somewhere important afterwards. Anyway, before answering my question he holds out a bunch of exotic-looking flowers and then turns to your mum's plot.

'"Is that Catherine?" And I know it sounds daft, but I liked the way he said her name, without asking if it was her grave or anything.

'I said that it was, and Finn looked down at the flowers and then back at me. "May I?" he asked, and of course I nodded and said it was fine. He walked over to the headstone and crouched down beside it. He took a moment or two to read the engraving, and there was a real sadness on his face when he got to the bit about being a beloved wife and mum.

'"Hello, Catherine," he said. "My name is Finn, and I wish more than anything this wasn't the way I got to meet you for the first time." He set down the flowers, really gently, and before getting to his feet he added, "In case you're wondering, I'm the man who's fallen in love with your daughter."

'I don't mind admitting that got me a little choked up. I sat down on the bench and Finn crossed over and joined me. I could tell he was working up to say something important, and I think a part of me already suspected what it might be. But he'd clearly got this speech worked out in his head, and it wasn't up to me to jump the gun.

'"I know it might seem a bit strange to have hijacked your private time together like this," Finn said, his eyes going from me to your mum's headstone, like she was really standing there, instead of a big slab of marble. "But there's something important I want to ask both of you."

'I bet if your mum had been there in the flesh at that moment, she'd already have been crying. To be honest, I felt a little that way myself. I nodded encouragingly for Finn to carry on.

'"I love Gemma," he said. "I love her more than I thought it was possible for anyone to ever love another human being. I can't imagine a life, a world or my future without her in it. And I know that a lot of the credit for how unbelievably amazing she is comes down to both of you."

'My voice was a bit gruff then, as I looked down to the plot beside us. "Most of the credit for that has to go to her mum, Catherine, not me."

'Finn reached over and set his hand over mine for a moment, which should have felt all kinds of odd, but actually it didn't. "I see you in her, Ted, all the time," Finn said gently, and I truly don't think anyone has ever paid me a higher compliment than that.

'Finn was smiling now; I guess the hard part for him was already over. "And the reason I'm here today is to ask if you'll both give me your blessing, because I'm going to ask your daughter to marry me."'

★

'Oh, Dad,' I said, reaching for a fistful of tissues from the box on the table. 'Why did you never tell me? I had no idea Finn had done that.'

Dad rubbed a hand roughly over his cheek. 'Finn asked me not to. I think he just wanted to keep it a private thing between him, me and your mum.'

I nodded, too choked to say anything right then.

'It takes a lot to surprise me, Gemma, but your Finn managed to do it that morning. He'd got up early, put on a smart outfit – not because he was off somewhere fancy afterwards, but because it was an important occasion and he wanted to do it right. He was respectful, kind and thoughtful, and obviously crazily in love with you.

'A man like that – a man who does something like that – isn't the kind to walk out on you on your wedding day. I'm sorry, sweetheart, that it took me so long to realise you've been right all this time. But I believe you now, I really do.'

'Oh, Dad,' I said sorrowfully, 'if you'd told me that just a few hours ago I'd probably be dancing around the kitchen right now.'

Dad sat up straighter in his seat. 'Has something happened today?'

I nodded and between gulps, hiccupping sobs and a great many tissues, I told him about the missing money.

Dad's jaw tightened, and by the time I finished talking he looked like a man carved out of granite.

'I don't know what to say, Gemma, I really don't. I thought what I came here to tell you today would make everything better, but instead I'm afraid it's just made it worse.'

I reached for his hand again, missing on my first swipe, for my eyes were blinded by tears. 'Every day there's another revelation that I can't explain away: missing belongings, mystery women and empty bank accounts. If I was hearing this story about anyone else, I'd tell them to wake up and face the facts. But this is Finn we're talking about here, Dad. *Finn.*'

He nodded.

'And then you go and tell me about how he was at the cemetery, and I can see him doing that *so* clearly, it's like I'd been there with you. My head is telling me to give up, but my heart just won't listen.'

'Because you love him,' Dad said simply.

'I do,' I said, my heart contracting at the irony of using the words I never got to say at the altar. 'But that doesn't mean Finn didn't change his mind about wanting to be with me. Am I being the world's biggest idiot here? How long do I keep trying to find a man who doesn't want to be found?'

'Only you know when it's time to give up, sweetheart. That's a decision only you can make.'

I made it at 2 a.m. to the accompaniment of the chimes of a nearby church. I would stop. Finn had disappeared from my life once before, it had hurt like hell, but I'd gotten through it. And now I had to face the fact that he'd done it again.

But by four o'clock I'd changed my mind again. I had eighteen months of evidence of how much Finn loved me, against just five days' worth that he didn't. It didn't add up.

But I couldn't do this to myself for ever. It would destroy me. At some point – some point soon – I was going to have to stop looking for him. *A week*, Inspector Graham had said at our first meeting. *If someone chooses to disappear, and they haven't been found in seven days, then they probably don't want to be found.*

Abandoning all hope of sleep, I padded through my silent flat towards the kitchen, but my need for answers was stronger than that for tea. My feet took me on their own detour, leading me into the lounge and to my desk. Almost of their own volition my hands began rummaging through my files of electricity bills and council tax statements until they found what they'd been looking for. The grey folder was tucked into the back of the drawer. I'd long since deleted the emails from my inbox, but I'd not been able to bring myself to throw out the property details and the initial paper chain of correspondence concerning Mushroom Cottage.

I pulled the sheaf of papers from the folder, pausing for a moment to look at the photograph of the chocolate-box cottage with an 'Under Offer' sign hammered into its lawn. Walter's daughter had insisted he place the sale of the property in the hands of an estate agent, but in the end it had been an unnecessary expense. Because the purchase of Mushroom Cottage hadn't 'fallen through' last year, the way I'd told everyone. The owner hadn't simply changed his mind at the last minute and decided to stay. Walter had been perfectly happy to sell his beloved home to us.

We were the ones who'd pulled out of the sale.

Or more accurately, *I* was.

I'd been slow to realise there was a problem. Slow to recognise that the dark circles that had appeared beneath Finn's eyes weren't due to a tricky plot issue in his latest book.

We'd decided not to sell my flat, but to rent it out instead, so there was nothing slowing down the purchase: no chain of buyers above or below us to jeopardise the sale. 'It should all go through really quickly,' the estate agent had advised us. Surveys and paperwork were almost complete, and I *still* hadn't realised the look in Finn's eyes had become that of an animal caught in a trap.

One evening, shortly before we were due to exchange, I'd been messaging Hannah on WhatsApp while Finn finished the chapter he was working on. With a tired sigh, he saved his work and turned towards me. It was only as he moved away from his desk that I noticed how drawn and weary he looked. Was there more worrying him than just his book, I suddenly wondered?

'Sorry I've been so preoccupied lately,' he said, stretching as he got up from his chair. He came to sit beside me, lifting an arm for me to snuggle against him. I happily obliged.

'Why don't we try to get away somewhere this weekend,' he suggested.

'I'd love to,' I said regretfully, 'but I've just this minute promised Hannah I'd babysit Milly on Saturday night. Not that she's a baby any more, of course,' I added wistfully. Like a fool I plundered on, unaware I was digging a hole I was about to fall straight into. 'You should have seen me with her when she *was* really tiny. I didn't have a clue what I was doing. Maybe they should have another one, so I can get in some more practice.'

Finn didn't move, not a muscle, and yet I felt an almost gravitational pull as he drew away from me. The seconds stretched until they felt like minutes, and then hours.

I heard the sadness in his voice before I saw it in his eyes. 'We need to talk, Gemma,' he said.

He held my hand as he spoke, as though that could save me from the pain, but his words were like tiny razors, each one cutting me deeply. 'I don't think this is going to work,' he said, shaking his head sorrowfully. The air went out of my lungs as though I'd been punched. 'You want children,' he said.

'Well, not right this minute,' I replied, desperately trying to lighten the mood, and failing abysmally.

'But one day you will,' he said, before delivering his coup de grâce like a reluctant executioner. 'And I don't. Not ever.'

'But why not? You're great with kids.'

Finn's smile was full of sadness. 'That doesn't mean I want any of my own.'

It wasn't breaking news. There'd been hints and clues dropped over the nine months we'd been together. I'd just chosen to ignore them. It was a conversation for 'future us', I told myself, for when we were living together, or even engaged; there was plenty of time. Until suddenly there wasn't.

'This is my fault,' Finn said with obvious regret. 'I should have made my feelings clearer long before now.'

I shook my head, unwilling to let him shoulder all the blame. 'No. Don't say that. I think part of me has always suspected how you felt.' I raised my tear-filled eyes to his face. 'I just hoped that you'd change your mind... in time.'

Finn got to his feet and that simple action opened a chasm between us that I was terrified we would never breach. 'You had an amazing childhood, Gemma, filled with love and thousands of wonderful memories. I understand why you want to replicate that.' He was pacing now, as if pleading his case to a jury of one. 'But you have to know that recreating mine is the *last thing* I'd ever wish on a child.'

'Finn, what happened to you and your parents was a

terrible tragedy. But you can't shut yourself off from loving someone because you're scared of losing them.'

'It's not *me* I'm trying to protect. I cannot and will not inflict what I went through on a child of my own.' He was talking about hurting someone who I was suddenly terribly afraid I'd never get to meet.

'Couldn't you talk to someone about this, a counsellor, like you did in Australia?' It was a desperate suggestion, but Finn loved me too much to allow me even a sliver of hope to hang on to.

He crouched before me and held my face tenderly between his hands. 'You're going to be a wonderful mother, Gemma. You've got so much love to give.'

'I love *you*,' I said desperately.

His eyes were bright with tears. 'I know you do. And I love you. So much that I'd rather walk away from you now than make you live without something you truly want. If you stay with me, I'm scared there'll always be something missing from your life. That's why I've been so freaked out about buying this house.'

'What? But I thought you wanted the cottage as much as I do.'

Finn shook his head sadly. 'I want it, but not for the same reasons as you. You see Mushroom Cottage as a home to fill with children,' he said sadly, 'and you're right, it really is. But I'm not the man to have them with you.'

'Then I don't want them either,' I declared fiercely. 'You don't get to decide what's right for me, Finn, or what I'm prepared to give up. Those are *my* choices. And I'm making them now. I've already lost one person I love, and I don't think I could get through losing another. I choose you, Finn. I will *always* choose you.'

I phoned the estate agent the next day to pull out of the purchase, without consulting Finn first. He was right. Mushroom Cottage *was* a family home; it should go to a couple who wanted to raise their children there. It felt wrong to deprive someone else of that dream. And besides, I had a feeling I'd never be able to look at that small bedroom beside the master without feeling the pain of losing something I'd never had.

Was the mystery of Finn's disappearance tangled up within these memories? Could he be so misguided as to believe that 'freeing' me to find someone else was the ultimate way of proving how much he loved me?

Through the window, I watched as the night sky dissolved to grey, then pink and finally blue.

It was the dawn of the fifth day.

THURSDAY: DAY FIVE

24

My phone was ringing on the front seat of my car. I could hear it through the rolled-down passenger window. I removed the nail I had clamped between my teeth and quickly hammered it into the bark of the oak tree. I was getting better at this now: faster at putting up the flyers, and far less likely to hit my thumb with the hammer.

The number of posters in the box had diminished. I counted how many were left before leaving my flat, unable to understand why the six hundred and thirty I'd already distributed hadn't yielded a single response.

Finn had gone up crookedly; I could see him looking down at me from a forty-five-degree angle. The jaunty tilt made him look almost quizzical, as though he too was beginning to doubt how effective this plan would be. 'It's better than doing nothing,' I told him as I leant through the car window and plucked up my phone.

'It's me,' Hannah announced unnecessarily, as my phone had already identified her. 'Where are you?'

'By Southland Woods, tacking up flyers.'

'That's only about twenty-five minutes from here. Can you come round?' There was something in Hannah's voice that I couldn't identify. Which in itself was odd, because after a lifetime of friendship I was pretty much fluent in every nuance.

'Is something wrong? Is it Milly?' My stomach did a little flip of anxiety. I'd accompanied Hannah on two trips to A & E courtesy of her daughter, and while Hannah had gone into a curiously Zen coping mode, I'd panicked out of all proportion to a nastily twisted ankle and then a tumble from a climbing frame that hadn't even needed stitches. I was going to make a terrible mother. *If I ever get the chance*, a voice in my head commented silently.

'It is and it isn't about Milly,' Hannah replied mysteriously. 'I need to show you something – well, ask you something, really. Look, I don't want to get into this on the phone. Can you come round?'

'I'll be there as soon as I can,' I said, feeling considerably more relieved when I heard the sound of Milly's laughter in the background. Whatever it was clearly didn't involve broken bones or projectile vomiting, a phenomenon I'd never seen outside of a horror film until my friend had a baby.

I forced my right foot to keep within the speed limit as I headed towards Hannah's house. I'd got very little sleep the night before, and the paltry amount I'd snatched had been interrupted by disturbed dreams. Unsurprisingly, after my dad's revelation, quite a few of them had involved graveyards, which never makes for a good night's rest.

It was impossible not to feel as if something momentous

had happened, now that Dad believed me. It should have been such a big turning point, and yet in the morning nothing had changed. I'd phoned Inspector Graham at the police station, and he'd listened to my father's anecdote as though it was a charming little story that he might possibly relate to his family that evening, but it didn't change his stance on declaring Finn an officially missing person.

'It goes to proof of character,' I said, perfectly aware I was lifting that phrase from a hundred courtroom scenes I'd seen in films.

There was a moment of silence from the policeman's end of the line. 'It does. But doing something nice twelve months ago doesn't necessarily change what happened last week.'

What shocked me far more than his casual dismissal of what I'd hoped was a break in the case – I really had watched too many police shows – was the realisation that Finn had indeed been missing for almost a week now. If there was a trail, it was quickly growing cold. And if there was any hope of jogging anyone's memory with one of the 'Missing' flyers, it had to happen soon, before someone came along and plastered an advert for a car boot sale over Finn's face.

At least now there were two people in the world who believed Finn would never have abandoned me at the church. It wasn't much, but it was a start.

I pulled into Hannah's drive, slotting my car in behind her Mini. She answered my knock on the front door so quickly, she must surely have been looking out of the window waiting for me to arrive. The twinge of concern returned to take another nibble at my peace of mind.

I caught a hit of the sunscreen Hannah had probably smothered Milly in as she leant in to kiss my cheek. Today was the first day of the nursery school summer holidays, and if the weather stayed as good as this, I imagined Milly would be spending most of it outside.

'Come into the garden,' Hannah said, already heading down the hallway and into the kitchen. Her legs were shorter than mine, but for the first time ever I was having to hurry to keep up with her.

'What's this all about, Hannah?'

'There's something I want to show you,' she said over her shoulder.

Their kitchen was bathed in sunlight and, as always, was in a state that teetered on the edge of chaos. I loved it for its comforting, unfussy charm. The painted wooden chairs around the table deliberately didn't match, and neither did the crockery, and the fridge could scarcely be seen beneath a gallery of Milly's latest masterpieces.

Hannah threw open the patio doors and the sunlight hit me like a blast wave as we stepped through them. But it wasn't the heat that rocked me to a halt as I looked across the garden. Beneath the shade of their sprawling eucalyptus tree, I saw Milly kneeling down before something that definitely hadn't been there on my last visit.

'You didn't!' I exclaimed. 'You got Milly a rabbit! I know you said you were going to let her have one this summer, but I didn't realise you were doing it so soon.'

Hannah had also come to a stop on the lawn. She turned towards me with an unreadable expression. 'William and I didn't buy her a rabbit,' she said carefully.

I frowned as I looked at my goddaughter, who had a

Christmas morning expression of pure delight plastered across her face. For as long as I could remember, Milly had made no secret of wanting a pet. And now, nestled on her lap was the cutest silvery-grey rabbit I'd ever seen. Its tiny black nose twitched delicately as Milly bent down and kissed it squarely between its long, droopy ears.

'Well, if *you* didn't get her the pet rabbit, then who did?' I asked, totally confused.

'You did.'

I stared at my friend, her daughter, and then the rabbit, who'd apparently arrived complete with a hutch that was surely the bunny equivalent of a mansion. The delivery had also included a run, several months' worth of food and enough toys to amuse even the most discerning rabbit. I seemed to have thought of absolutely everything. The only problem was... it hadn't been me.

'Hannah, there's been a mistake somewhere. I mean, I knew Milly *wanted* a rabbit; she's always talking about it. But I didn't buy her one.'

'According to this, you did,' Hannah contradicted, pulling a small gift card from the back pocket of her denim cut-offs.

I took the card from her, and even pushed my sunglasses on to the top of my head, so I could read it better. The handwriting was unfamiliar, but it was the wording that stunned me most of all.

To Milly,

This is to thank you for being the best flower girl in the world at our wedding.

303

This little rabbit needs a name and someone to love him. He's very lucky to have you as his new owner.
Lots of love, Auntie Gemma and Finn xxx

'I'm assuming by the shocked expression on your face that you knew absolutely nothing about this?'

I shook my head, reading and then rereading the card. I could hear Finn's voice in every word of the message, as though he was standing right there beside me.

'We said we'd get her a special gift, but I thought we'd pick up something like a cuddly koala toy from Australia.'

'Fluffy is the best present I've ever had, Auntie Gemma,' declared Milly, carefully setting down her new pet and running towards me to wrap her arms fiercely around my legs.

I bent down and kissed her head, my eyes still locked on Hannah's.

'Let's talk in the kitchen,' Hannah said, as Milly raced back to the newest member of the family.

I pulled out one of the brightly painted kitchen chairs and positioned it where I could watch Milly playing delightedly with the rabbit.

'I called the pet shop,' Hannah said, pouring a coffee and setting it before me. 'They confirmed that the order was placed by a Mr Finn Douglas last Friday.' She paused before adding unnecessarily, 'The day before the wedding.' She shook her head as though the truth was a troublesome wasp buzzing around her.

'I've been going over and over it in my head all morning, and none of it makes sense. Why go to the trouble of picking out a present to thank a child for being your flower girl, twenty-four hours before the wedding, if you know full well you're not going to go through with the ceremony?'

She was looking at me as though I had the answer to that one. She should have known better.

'I don't know why he did it,' Hannah said, and I could see how hard it was for her to stop hating Finn, having already decided he was the villain of this story. She pointed to the gift card that was still in my hand. 'But that changes everything.' She gave a troubled sigh. 'I still have no idea what happened last Saturday – I wish to God I did. But it's starting to look more and more like Finn did have every intention of marrying you.'

She took a huge swallow of her coffee, as though the admission had left an unpalatable aftertaste on her tongue. 'I'm sorry it's taken me a while to get here.'

I smiled at her across the table as she swam in and out of focus through my tear-blurred vision.

Two believers had now become three.

25

FINN

The birds had woken him again. He couldn't see them, but he could hear them. Too large for starlings, too angry for blackbirds; he was convinced they were crows. And they sounded hungry. It had been a horrible thought to wake up to on this, his fifth – or was it his sixth – morning? The days were beginning to run into each other, and without the benefit of sunlight, which scarcely penetrated the darkness, it wasn't always easy to tell night from day. There were other things he was struggling with too. Reality was slowly disintegrating. He could hear things that made no sense, and voices of people who he knew couldn't be here with him. And yet sometimes they were.

The pain had been constant to begin with, but that too had started to fade. That should have been a good thing, but the loss of sensation in his right leg was terrifying. His head made up for it though, pounding with a headache that had been there from the moment he'd come round, and had never left. It was his only companion.

Hours must have passed again. He knew that, because it was hotter in the car. His body was drenched in sweat. It would stay that way until the sun went down, and then the perspiration would dry like liquid ice on his skin. He'd shake for hours, so violently his teeth would rattle in his head. It made the headache a million times worse.

The stench in the car was becoming unbearable. For the first day or two he'd smelt nothing but petrol. It had dripped steadily into the passenger compartment from the tank he'd filled shortly before the accident. Logically, he knew cars rarely burst into flames the way filmmakers would have you believe. But fire was his nemesis. He'd escaped it once as a child, but if the spilled fuel ignited while he was trapped in his mangled vehicle, he wouldn't escape again.

As the hours and then the days passed, other smells had filled the car. His sweat was pungent and acrid, so strong it made him gag. And the urine he'd eventually had to release had stung his wounds and the stupid remnants of his pride that told him he should have somehow managed to hold on to it. But those odours were easily eclipsed by the hot, coppery tang of blood. He couldn't see his leg, but he knew it was still bleeding, for it continued to drip down on to his torso in slow, lazy tributaries.

Finn had no recollection of the crash. He had no idea how his car had ended up on its side, tilted upwards, at the bottom of a steep-sided gully, hidden beneath a dense cover of bushes.

He'd waited for the sirens and flashing blue lights. But they never came. He could only assume his car wasn't visible to passing motorists. There could be no skid marks on the road, no signpost bent askew. The foliage in the gully had simply swallowed him up.

Sometimes, in the distance, he could hear the sound of a passing vehicle. Then he'd cry out so loudly, he'd make himself physically sick – another joyous smell to add to those already clinging to him. But there'd been no sound of braking. No voice frantically calling down to him from above, telling him to hang on, that help was on the way.

Surely they must be looking for him? Gemma would be frantic with worry by now. Thoughts of her were a double-edged sword. In the middle of the night, in almost total blackness, tears leaked from his eyes as he allowed himself to remember the warmth and the softness of her as she lay in his arms. Her smile filled his head, and he could almost hear the sound of her voice begging him to hang on, that she would find him. At other times, he was wracked with despair, knowing how terrified and alone she must be feeling.

His lips were cracked and sore, and he looked longingly at the bottle of water he'd wedged behind the sun visor. The litre container, that miraculously hadn't punctured in the accident, had been almost full when he'd driven away from the stag party. The urge to drink rabidly from it now was getting harder to resist. What did it matter if he rationed himself to just two sips, four times a day, or drank the whole thing in one greedy swallow? It would all be gone soon anyway.

His body was covered in cuts and abrasions, and while they throbbed and stung, Finn knew they were mostly insignificant.

More worrying was his right arm, which was hanging at a weird angle that limbs weren't meant to achieve. His right hand and fingers twitched pathetically when he instructed them to move. Anything else was beyond them.

He'd cracked a couple of ribs once, while playing rugby at university, and the sharp pain he felt now whenever he breathed in deeply made him think he'd done it again – only more spectacularly this time.

But the worst of his injuries was the one to his leg. Suspended in the driver's seat, Finn couldn't assess the extent of the damage, although his first tentative exploration had terrified him. When his trembling fingers had encountered the long piece of metal skewered through his thigh, he'd drawn them back in panic. He'd stared in shock at his left hand, which looked like it was wearing a single crimson glove that dripped like something out of a horror film. Finn knew just enough first aid to realise he shouldn't be attempting this again, but what else could he do? He had to try.

His hand shook as he reached for the water bottle and stole a quick swig, wishing – as he did every single time – that it was Scotch or brandy.

His breathing was already ragged, and all he could do was hope that this time he wouldn't pass out. The shard of metal was slippery and his fingers struggled to find purchase. He gripped it awkwardly as he began counting down. Three. Two. He closed his eyes before reaching 'one' and summoned up Gemma's face. He pulled on the metal with all his strength, feeling the hot gush of fresh blood coursing down his thigh, but the metal refused to budge. His scream of agony was swallowed by the darkness of the gully that came up and washed over him, as he once again lost consciousness.

*

He came round the way he always did, panicked and disoriented. There was a drumming in his ears and he was slow to realise something was trundling along the road. Whatever it was, it was heavy, for the wreckage shook in the ditch and the metal shrapnel in his leg stung like hell as it dug a little deeper into the meaty flesh of his thigh.

Finn quickly moved his hand to cover the horn. Timing was everything. His previous over-eager attempts had all been too hasty. The passing cars' own engines had muted the feeble bleat of his Ford's horn.

'Hold your nerve,' he instructed himself. It had taken too many failed attempts for him to realise he needed to let the passing vehicles drive beyond him before leaning on the horn. He reckoned that three seconds should be just about right. 'One Mississippi, two Mississippi, three Mississippi,' he gasped hoarsely, before slamming his good hand on the horn. Nothing. Not even a pathetic squeak. He hit it again and again, practically punching it in his frustration, even though he knew that by now the van, tractor, or whatever it had been, would be too far away to hear him. The car's electrics had finally given out.

It was a miracle that they hadn't shorted out in the accident. It had been his one and only stroke of luck, and now that too was gone. In hindsight, he realised he'd wasted too much juice in the first few days, switching on the radio, convinced he would hear a news report about his disappearance. After several bulletins, he'd felt the first touch of his own mortality. There had been nothing about him being missing on either the local or national announcements. Why was no one looking for him?

His secret wedding gift now seemed like the most stupid idea he'd ever had. Why had he told no one about his plan? How ridiculous to have been so worried that someone might accidentally ruin the surprise. There were only two people who knew anything about it, but unless the media was reporting him as missing, neither of them would think to come forward with information. And no one else had any reason to suspect he was in this area.

To the rest of the world, it must look as though he'd walked away from his wedding and the woman he loved – from his whole life, in fact. And how could he blame anyone for thinking that, when he'd done something similar so many times before? But surely Gemma would know he'd never have done this to her, to them? She knew how much he loved her. She knew that he'd changed. Didn't she?

26

I phoned Inspector Graham again, gripping Milly's card so tightly I was in danger of crushing it. To give him his due, the policeman heard me out, and even though I suspected there might have been some eye-rolling at his end of the line, none of it was evident in his voice.

'Miss Fletcher – Gemma – I know how much you don't want to hear what I'm about to say.' He might as well have stopped right there; I already knew what was coming. 'What I need, what police regulations require, is cold, hard, tangible evidence that Mr Douglas hasn't simply decided to take himself away from the… situation.'

By 'situation', he meant me.

'I know you think you've found it in this gift your fiancé sent from the pet shop, but it still isn't enough for us to proceed.'

My frustration finally erupted. The only surprise was that it had taken so long.

'You want evidence that this man wouldn't have left me on the day of our wedding? I can give you hundreds, no, thousands of pieces of evidence.' I was breathing hard now, as though this speech could only be completed at a full-pelt run. 'But none of it is your kind of evidence. You can't drop it into a sterile plastic bag, you won't be able to produce it in a court of law when someone asks for Exhibit A, and you can't transcribe it into any of the boxes on your bloody missing person report.'

Inspector Graham drew in a breath as though he was about to interrupt me, but I spoke straight over him.

'My kind of evidence isn't tangible – you can't pick it up and hold it in your hand, but it's still one hundred per cent solid. It's in the way Finn will watch *The Notebook* with me, even though I've seen it a hundred times and it's not his sort of film. It's when he passes me the tissue box at just the right moments, because he knows which bits make me cry. It's how he puts way less chilli into a curry than he'd like, because he knows I can't take it hot. It's there when we sleep under a fifteen-tog duvet, even though he's sweltering, because otherwise my feet get cold.' I drew in a shuddery breath. 'And it's how he'll buy me flowers on my mum's birthday, even though she died long before we got together. That's my evidence. That's how I know how much this man loves me. And that's why I know without a single doubt that something terrible must have happened to stop him from being at the church last week.'

Inspector Graham sighed, and I thought I could hear a trace of sadness in the sound.

'Are you married, Inspector Graham?' I asked suddenly.

The question clearly threw him. 'Erm, I'm not sure how that's relevant.'

'It's not a hard question. Is there a Mrs Graham?'

He paused, and I imagined there was probably some rule prohibiting police officers from divulging personal details to members of the public.

'Yes, there is.'

'Then you already know what I'm talking about. There are things only you and your wife know about your relationship. The behind-closed-doors things. Things that no one else looking in from outside would ever understand. It's the DNA of your love story: the history, the secrets, the memories, even the silly jokes that only the two of you share. They're your evidence. And every couple has them.'

There was a long moment of silence. Was he wavering now?

'I need more, Gemma. Give me just one tangible fact so I can get this thing started.'

'I'll find one,' I vowed.

Hannah persuaded me to stay for lunch, which Milly insisted had to be a picnic on the lawn so that Fluffy didn't feel left out.

'That big storm they keep banging on about is supposedly on the way,' Hannah said, looking up doubtfully into a clear, cloudless sky. 'So we might as well take advantage of the sunshine while we've got it.'

She was busily tipping a bag of carrot sticks into a bowl, even though Milly would probably sneak them to Fluffy, when a thought suddenly occurred to her. 'Silly question, but I suppose you are still checking all of Finn's social media accounts?'

I nodded. 'Only just this side of obsessively,' I admitted. Hannah's smile was wry, but I could feel the subtle shift of her changing sides. 'There's been nothing on Finn's Instagram, and he hasn't been online on WhatsApp either since the day before the stag,' I said.

'It's hard to know what else we can do.'

The pronoun she used was enough.

I carried a tray into the garden and settled myself on the grass beside a clearly besotted Milly.

'That fiancé of yours is very lucky that we'd already agreed on getting a rabbit or he'd have been in real trouble,' Hannah muttered darkly as she passed me the plate of sandwiches. I took a cheese and pickle with a smile. Hearing her refer to Finn as my fiancé again lifted my heart.

'Don't you remember, you and William were talking about it when we were here for Sunday lunch a few weeks ago,' I reminded her. I bit into the soft bread as my thoughts flew back to the four of us sitting on that very lawn, drinking tall glasses of sweet, sticky Pimm's. I could practically smell the newly mown grass William had cut that morning and hear the lazy buzz of circling bees as Milly continued her ongoing campaign for a pet. Finn had been sitting in a deckchair beside me, casually leafing through the local paper, his attention seemingly focused on the property section. It was an inconsequential memory, one of thousands we would surely have made as a foursome over the years, but this one had me suddenly pausing mid-swallow.

The coughing fit that ensued was lengthy and painful, making my eyes water and Hannah rush to thrust a glass of water into my hands.

'You okay?' she asked eventually, when the worst of it had subsided. She peered at my red face with concern. 'I thought I was going to have to do the Heimlich for a minute there.'

'You should have asked Mummy to cut the crusts off, like she does for me,' Milly said wisely, from her position beside the rabbit hutch.

My throat still felt sandpaper-raw from the coughing as I drained the water and jumped to my feet.

'I have to go.'

Hannah looked down at my uneaten lunch. 'What? Right now?'

I nodded as I hurriedly thrust my feet back into my sandals, my fingers clumsy as they attempted to work the buckles.

'I'm sorry to rush off,' I apologised, glancing at my watch with a worried frown, 'but if I hurry, I might just be able to make it.'

'You do realise you're not making any sense,' Hannah declared, trotting after me as I swept through her kitchen looking for my bag.

I snatched it up from the back of a chair and spared a few vital seconds to explain. 'There are still a couple of hours until they go to press. If I'm lucky we might be in time to get something in tomorrow's edition.'

'Of *Glow*?' Hannah asked, clearly confused.

I was at her front door, hand on the latch, but in my head I was already halfway towards my old place of work. 'No. *The Chronicle*. I don't know why I didn't think of it before. They could run a full-page feature on Finn's disappearance. It'll reach far more people than the "Missing" flyers ever could.'

I didn't wait around long enough to discover if Hannah thought this was an excellent or totally foolish idea. But as I backed out of her driveway, I'm fairly sure I heard her calling out something to my retreating car.

It sounded an awful lot like 'Hold the front page'.

27

The smell took me right back. I likened it to the way stepping into a school building immediately transports you back through the years. Admittedly, there was less of the cooked cabbage odour at *The Chronicle* offices, but it was still an olfactory time machine. The local newspaper offices had a warm, musty smell that over the years I'd separated out into overheated office equipment, stacks of old papers, and nose-wrinkling BO from a few colleagues who still believed that deodorant was optional and the best way to measure hard work was from the oval sweat stains beneath your armpits.

Unlike at *Glow*, there was no fancy reception desk or state-of-the-art ID entry system. There was simply a bell on the door, which I pressed. I was immediately buzzed into the office with a shocking lack of security.

The drive from Hannah's home to the newspaper offices had been just long enough for me to worry if I'd still know anyone who worked there. It was an unnecessary concern, because apart from a couple of unfamiliar faces – who had most probably still been at school when I was employed by the paper – I recognised practically everyone.

If the world of magazine journalism has a reputation for cattiness, then that of local newspapers is the polar opposite. 'We're one big happy family,' I was told at my interview. And in truth I always looked back on my years at *The Chronicle* with nostalgia. Somehow, I'd managed to erase the memory of the antisocial shifts assigned to the newest reporters, and the feeling of dread when you handed in a piece to the sub-editor only to have it thrown back with so many corrections, you wondered if you'd even managed to spell your own name correctly.

'Gemma Fletcher,' cried Marjorie, the office manager, jumping to her feet with a speed that surprised me. Marjorie was impossible to age. I'd have put her in the retirement age bracket back when I was a cub reporter, and yet here she still was, larger than life and just as exuberant as I remembered. She enfolded me against her bolster of a bosom, and the need to maintain an airway took my mind off the fact that she'd hesitated for just a moment before saying the surname that should no longer have been mine.

'How are you, lovey?' It was hard to read her eyes through her impossibly thick spectacles to see if she knew what had happened to me. But then she gave me an extra tight squeeze before setting me free, and I realised that of course she knew. In truth, there was probably very little that escaped Marjorie's gimlet eye, both within *The Chronicle* offices and outside them. It was a loss to the world of investigative journalism that she'd been content being the custodian of the stationery cupboard keys instead of moving to the news desk.

'Are you holding it together?' she asked now, as succinct as ever.

'As best I can,' I replied, glancing around the open-plan office, where the dozen or so employees were all doing a poor job of pretending to work. Some smiled vaguely in my direction, and a few chanced a wave before drawing their hands back down as though questioning too late if that was appropriate.

I turned back to Marjorie. 'Is Bill in? Is he free?'

She gave me a warm smile. 'For you, he will be.'

Bill had been the editor of *The Chronicle* since dinosaurs had walked the planet. He'd given me my first job, taking a chance on me when all I'd had to offer was some limited experience working on the university rag and far more enthusiasm than style. I'd left *The Chronicle* for bigger and better things, in the manner of an ungrateful child. I only hoped that, like a forgiving parent, there was still enough affection banked in my account to ask Bill for a favour. A big one.

His hug was less all-consuming than Marjorie's but no less heartfelt. 'Well, I hope your father is hunting down that man of yours with a shotgun.' His greeting was as non-PC as ever. I wondered how I could have forgotten Bill's peculiar brand of irreverent humour. 'Seriously, sweetheart, both Frannie and I were gutted to hear what that bastard put you through.'

I gave a sad smile and shook my head. 'Come on, Bill, you know better than to believe everything you read in the papers.'

Fifteen minutes later and I still wasn't certain I'd swung it. Bill was pulling the kind of faces that could have won him prizes in a gurning contest but which those at *The Chronicle* knew only too well meant that he wasn't sure about something.

'It's press day,' he said, nodding meaningfully at the oversized clock on his office wall. 'We've got less than forty-five minutes to get things sent over to the printers, and you're asking me to change the splash.'

I smiled at the old familiar term for the front-page story.

'Mine might sell more copies than the town hall debate you were planning on running,' I said, trying very hard not to sound as desperate as I was beginning to feel. I glanced up at the second hand ticking inexorably from one notch to the next.

'I don't know if I've got anyone free on the news desk to write it up in just three-quarters of an hour.'

That objection, at least, was one I was prepared for. '*I'll* write it up. Just give me a desk and a computer and I'll have it in your hands in thirty minutes.'

There were so many more arguments I wanted to put forward, but I knew Bill well enough to know when my best chance of success was to stay silent.

'And you've got some decent photos we can use with it? Not just of Finn but also of that fancy Yankee car of his, and maybe one of his latest book, so we can capitalise on the author angle?'

I lifted up my phone. 'All on here.'

It felt like my entire future was tied up in his sigh of resignation.

'On my desk in thirty minutes,' he barked, which was totally ruined by the breadth of his smile.

I was already on my feet and halfway out the door. 'Got it.'

★

My fingers had flown over the keys. I hadn't done this sort of journalism in years, but it was like riding a bike. The skills might have been rusty, but they were all still there. If I'd had four times as long to write up the story, I couldn't have done it any better. I printed it out, because Bill was old-school like that, and to save valuable time I also emailed it to both the sub and news editors.

I left them perusing the piece as I scrolled through my phone looking for a photo of Finn's car. The red-and-white Gran Torino was a head-turner of a vehicle, even in its country of origin. I could remember Finn saying there was only a handful of similar models in the UK. If someone *had* seen it at any time in the last six days, surely they'd remember it.

'Gemma,' called Bill from his office doorway. For a moment I forgot this man was no longer my boss about to haul me over the coals for missing a deadline. I hurried to the office, where my piece sat on his desk. Amazingly, I could see no red ink upon it. Not a single correction.

'You've got the splash,' he said.

28

FINN

His phone was ringing, which was ridiculous because Finn knew perfectly well the mobile was irreparably broken, its shattered pieces scattered in the wreckage of the car.

'Aren't you going to get that?' He jerked in his seat and turned to his right, where Gemma was sitting beside him. She was wearing a wedding dress, conjured up from the depths of his subconscious. He had no idea if it bore any resemblance to the one she'd been wearing as she stood at the church last week, waiting for him to show up.

'Phone's broken,' he said, the words sounding croaky, as though they'd been dragged reluctantly past his parched throat.

She nodded and the gossamer-thin veil bobbed up and down with the movement. She looked so beautiful that tears sprang to his eyes. He couldn't afford to lose any more bodily fluids, but he let them run down his cheeks unchecked.

He reached out with his right hand – the one that could no

longer move – and gently touched her face. She leant into his cupped palm, the way she always did.

'You're not really here, are you?'

She shook her head sadly. He'd known it anyway, but it still hurt.

His mobile was still ringing, but he tuned it out. He wanted to focus on Gemma, on the feel of her hand as she reached out and stroked his face, the smell of her perfume, which obliterated the odours in the car, and the love that shone from her eyes.

'I'm so sorry,' he told her brokenly. 'I had this big, incredible surprise planned for you and I've totally fucked it up.'

'Hush, hush,' she soothed, leaning over and pressing her soft, warm mouth on to his cracked lips.

'I had something to tell you. Something really important. And now you're never going to know.'

'Know what?'

'That you were right. About you and me, about our future, about everything,' he said brokenly. 'And the worst thing about all of this is that I'm going to leave you without you ever knowing that I changed my mind. I've let you down so badly, Gemma.'

His hallucination shook her head fiercely. 'Don't you ever think that. The only way you'll let me down is if you stop believing you'll get out of this.'

'I won't,' he vowed. 'I'll never stop trying to get back to you.'

The sound was loud. Like an explosion. Finn opened his eyes, but at first it made little difference. He blinked and waited for a moment as the darkness gradually separated into discernible shades of black and grey. This was what the middle of the night looked like at the bottom of the gully.

The noise came again, and he flinched, as though dodging artillery fire. It had been excruciatingly hot in the car all day, and yet at night the temperature still plummeted to a desert-like chill. Despite the cold, it felt muggy and airless in the wreckage. The rumbling sound was directly overhead now, and this time he identified it. Thunder.

In the weeks leading up to the wedding, they'd been keeping a watchful eye on the long-range weather forecast. Getting married in the middle of a heatwave carried with it the risk of summer storms, something that had admittedly worried Gemma far more than it had him. Finn would happily have married her in the middle of a monsoon.

'We're in luck,' she had declared happily, looking up from her laptop screen. 'It looks like the weather won't break until the week after the wedding.'

He'd bent low to peer at the Met Office web page, getting momentarily sidetracked by the scent of her perfume. 'By then we'll be an old married couple, enjoying the weather on the other side of the world,' he'd said with a smile.

A sudden flash of lightning scythed through the foliage in a way the sun's rays had never achieved. It allowed Finn to see the cramped, mangled space he was entombed in with a brief and horrible clarity. It looked like the kind of photograph you might find in a coroner's report.

How on earth did he ever manage to get out of there alive?
He didn't.

The voices in his head sounded so real that when the lightning flashed again, he glanced over his shoulder to check the back seats. He saw nothing but lacerated leather and twisted metal.

It was a tomb. His tomb. He wasn't sure when the realisation had finally forced its way to the front of his thoughts, but it was there now. All the time.

It wasn't just the seat belt he couldn't release or the metal lance through his leg that imprisoned him; the car itself was a massive steel trap that had sprung shut on impact. Without the benefit of acetylene cutting torches, the so-called jaws of life, and a whole team of rescuers, there was no way he was getting out of there.

Morbidly, he wondered how long it would take for them to find the car. He really hoped, for Gemma's sake, that it would stay hidden for years. He wanted the discovery to happen far into the future. *Let it be when there's another man's ring on her finger*, he thought. *Let the phone call come when she's surrounded by small red-haired children who look just like her.* Perhaps that way it wouldn't hurt quite so much when the news she would have been waiting so long to receive was finally delivered: 'They've found Finn's car.'

FRIDAY: DAY SIX

29

I showered with my phone on the glass shelf above the basin. It nestled among the make-up in my cosmetics bag while I swept mascara across my lashes. And it was propped up between the jar of marmalade and the butter dish as I ate my breakfast.

I'd been on the newsagent's doorstep at 6 a.m., impatiently waiting for them to open. I truly don't think I'd been that nervous or excited to see something I'd written in print since my very first article.

Finn's face looked up at me now from the front page as I chewed on my toast and marmalade. Even as a compilation of slightly fuzzy pixels, he still had the power to make my heart beat faster. Beside that picture was one of Finn and me together, smiling like idiots at the camera, blissfully unaware that the route to our happy-ever-after would be littered with landmines. Below those two images was the clearest photo I'd been able to find of Finn's car. It was a model that had attained cult status in a US police show that aired before I was even born. I wasn't particularly into cars, vintage or otherwise, but even I could see why this particular one had earned its celebrity status. I only hoped the American design with its striking paintwork – tomato-ketchup red with a broad white stripe – was unique enough to have stuck in the memory of anyone who'd seen it.

Too late to do anything about it, I realised that including my personal phone number on the 'Missing' posters and in the newspaper might not have been such a great idea. A cheapie pay-as-you-go mobile with a disposable number would have been a better plan. It wasn't yet ten o'clock, but I'd already had a handful of crank calls, as well as a sad one from a lonely old lady who freely admitted she hadn't seen Finn but was desperate for someone to chat to.

Screening calls was clearly the way forward. But in truth, each incoming message had me pouncing on my phone like a cat who'd spotted a mouse. The last caller had been a woman who'd sounded so hesitant and unsure as I played back her message, I was already afraid it was going to be yet another wild goose to chase after.

'Hello. I do hope I'm through to the right person. I'm phoning about the article in today's *Chronicle* – the one about the man who's gone missing. I'm not sure if this is relevant or not, but I thought I should call just in case. You see, last Friday night at a little after eleven, I was pulling out of my local petrol station when a big American car drove in. It was dark, and I'm sorry but I don't know if the car was red or not, as I didn't get a very good look at it. I didn't even see who was driving it. But... well, it did strike me as a bit odd at the time. You see, it's pretty rural around here and it's unusual to see *anything* on the road that isn't a four-by-four or a tractor. Anyway, I'll leave you my number, although you might have more luck phoning the petrol station direct. It's called Foxton Garage, and even out here in Hicksville they should have CCTV coverage on their pumps.'

I replayed the message three times before getting to my feet. My hands were busy stacking the plates and utensils I'd used for breakfast, but my mind was somewhere entirely different. *Foxton?* Why did that sound so familiar? I didn't know anyone who lived in a place of that name, nor did I think I'd ever been there myself. *Foxton. Foxton. Foxton.* The name rang in my head with the persistence of a clanging bell.

I crossed to the sink like a sleepwalker, no longer in my humid kitchen but lost in a tangle of memories. I closed my eyes and saw a long road, bordered on either side by trees and foliage, and half hidden by the overgrown hedgerows was a signpost with the name of a village. *Foxton.* An almighty crash snapped me rudely out of my semi-trance. The plate had slipped from my fingers and shattered into the sink, taking out my favourite mug and two glasses in the process, and yet I smiled as I looked down at the breakages.

I knew now why Foxton had sounded familiar, but what Finn was doing in that area – if indeed it had been his car – was still a mystery.

Leaving the broken crockery for later, I returned to the table. I've always found it easier to think things through with pen and paper before me, so, ignoring the toast crumbs and ghost rings from my coffee mug, I reached for a notepad.

Fifteen minutes later, there were several sheets covered with more doodles and question marks than tangible ideas. Why would Finn have been in an area where we knew no one except for the owner of a cottage we'd ultimately not bought and the estate agent who'd been handling the negotiations?

I glanced down at one of the many doodles my subconscious had summoned up while my thoughts had been busy blue-sky diving. I'd drawn the figure of a woman who, even in caricature, was clearly the estate agent. My pen had perfectly recreated her doe-like eyes, which had always lingered a little too long on Finn's face while simultaneously looking straight through me, as though I was a ghost halfway to being exorcised. At the time it had been funny, only now it felt considerably less amusing.

I'd exaggerated her long wavy hair in the sketch, giving her a Medusa-ish appearance, but in reality those curls had been softer and ash-blonde in colour.

My subconscious could do no more; it was practically screaming out to me from the notepad.

I saw Finn getting into a car with a very attractive woman with long blonde hair a couple of weeks ago. They looked pretty 'up close and personal', in my opinion.

I pushed the notepad roughly aside, like it was contaminated, as the overheard conversation in the Ladies' room at *Glow* came back to me. Had the unknown woman in Finn's car, the one he clearly hadn't wanted to be seen with, been the flirty estate agent?

After all the agony of the last week, could Finn's mysterious absence turn out to be this tawdry? When we'd almost had it all, had Finn himself sabotaged us? Those demons were in his past, or so he'd repeatedly told me. But now I wondered if they'd always been there, waiting in the wings, to take him down again.

'Hello. This is the manager. You wanted to speak to me?'

I drew in a deep breath before launching into my

explanation for a second time. The mechanic who'd initially answered the phone had heard me out and then exhaled heavily, as though about to deliver a truly horrendous repair estimate, before admitting the question was 'above my pay grade'. I was hoping for more success with his boss.

'I'm sorry, love, but I don't think we can do that.' He sounded genuinely regretful after hearing my plea. But I'd had enough time between looking up the number for Foxton Garage and waiting to speak to someone in charge to fine-tune my request.

'I understand that you have a responsibility to protect your customers, and I wouldn't ask you to share any sensitive information. All I need is for someone to look at the CCTV tapes for last Friday night and tell me if my fiancé's car came in for petrol. I can give you the make, model and registration number. You just have to say if he was there or not.'

It sounded so simple when summarised like that. I only hoped the garage manager would think so too. Sadly, he didn't.

'It's not a data protection issue – although now you mention it, I might be on thin ice with that one.' I bit my lip, annoyed that I'd accidentally shot down my only good idea. 'What I meant was that we only keep the tapes for a week before recording over them. I don't even know if the one for the night you're talking about still exists.'

'Could you just check,' I pleaded.

The garage manager was silent for so long, I honestly thought he'd hung up on me.

'I'll look,' he said eventually, 'but I'm not promising any more than that.'

My thank yous were so effusive, I'm not sure who I embarrassed more, him or me.

30

FINN

He'd halved his water rations, but, even so, it would soon be gone. With each passing hour Finn could feel his thoughts becoming blunter, clumsier. Ideas were fragmenting and twisting out of his reach, like images in a kaleidoscope. Were these the first symptoms of severe dehydration, he wondered? He knew just enough about the condition to be terrified of what might follow.

His mind kept trying to spin him out of there to another place and time. Somewhere happier. With a feeling of inevitability, Finn knew that soon he might stop fighting quite so hard to stay there.

Weak and exhausted, Finn drifted into a troubled sleep but was abruptly jerked awake by a sensation of pressure on his cracked ribs, and a hot foetid smell that somehow eclipsed the other foul odours in the car. It took a moment for him to realise this wasn't just another horrible hallucination, there really *was* something on his chest. Something with a hot, throbbing body, and sharp, scratching claws. Finn screamed in revulsion as his vision sharpened and he saw the largest rat he'd ever encountered just inches from his face.

His useless right arm was incapable of knocking it off, but his startled cry had dislodged the creature's hold. For one dreadful moment the rat skittered even closer to his face before he managed to bring up his left arm and knock it roughly back out through the window it had presumably just crawled in through.

The rat was bold, and hungry perhaps, for it didn't instantly disappear into the jungle-like foliage. It was huge, almost the size of a domestic cat, and there was a knowing look in its eyes, as though it realised who had the upper hand here. And it wasn't Finn.

'Get out of here!' Finn cried, frantically groping in the car's footwell for something to throw at the rodent. His search yielded nothing at first except for an empty takeout cup, which he immediately discarded. He was reaching back into the footwell when his fingers brushed against the key ring swinging from the Torino's mangled ignition. The fob was heavy, too large really to hold just two keys, but it was a souvenir from a romantic weekend break he and Gemma had taken, and every time he saw the engraved name of their hotel on the shiny brass plate, it made him smile. He wasn't smiling now, though, as he snatched the key ring from the ignition and threw it with more venom than accuracy at the lingering rodent. The keys disappeared far into the dense foliage and so too, mercifully, did the rat.

Finn hauled himself closer to the shattered side window to check it had definitely gone and immediately jolted back as another streak of grey with an impossibly long pink tail scurried past the car. And then another. He was deep in the shadowy undergrowth of the gully, and this was the rats' territory, although to be fair, none of the creatures running past the car appeared to be interested in him. They seemed far more intent on moving as quickly as possible away from this place.

Finn was slow to connect the frightened rodents and the rumbling thunder with a new sound, which at first he couldn't identify. It rustled the leaves surrounding the car and pinged eerily on the Gran Torino's bodywork. He turned his face and felt something on the leather of the driver's seat that definitely hadn't been there a moment earlier. He lifted an exploratory hand to his cheek. It was damp. And suddenly it all made sense: the thunder, the fleeing rats, and the weird plinking noise on the car's metalwork. It was raining. No, more than that: it was pouring, and some of the deluge was managing to penetrate the foliage and reach the bottom of the gully.

He scarcely even noticed the new cuts and grazes he acquired as he thrust his arm through the broken window and into the dense undergrowth. Carefully, because a mistake now would be disastrous, Finn found a gap in the thorny foliage and wedged the takeout cup into it. Almost immediately he was rewarded with the satisfying plink of a raindrop hitting the bottom of the empty container. And then another. And another. He'd been desperate for a sign that he shouldn't give up hope, and now he'd got one.

The rain was going to save him.

31

The retro clock hanging in my kitchen had a tick like a metronome, but today it was playing a duet with the distantly rumbling thunder. The rain of the previous night had been almost biblical in its ferocity, but it looked as though we'd still not seen the last of Storm Edna. Despite the cloying humidity, I reached up and pulled the sash window to a close. Whoever had thought that giving storms cute names would somehow humanise them had got it completely wrong. Edna had capriciously flooded roads and burst riverbanks, and she wasn't done yet.

I filled my time clearing up broken crockery and making two cups of coffee, neither of which I drank. I also paced a lot, covering the chequerboard kitchen tiles like a zoo animal before my restless feet led me into the hallway and from there to my desk.

With a feeling of déjà vu I once again drew the Mushroom Cottage paperwork from the drawer. I slid my hand into the crevices of the folder, swearing under my breath as my fingers fastened on a rectangular business card which sliced a paper cut into my thumb. I drew out the card. A tiny drop of blood had fallen across the name emblazoned in flamboyant script across the middle. I wiped it clear. Amelia Holmwood. I thought I'd forgotten her name and practically everything else about her, but the memories were coming back now as though summoned at a seance.

We'd been laughing as we climbed back into Finn's car after our first visit to the estate agent offices, giddy with excitement at the prospect of becoming joint homeowners.

'I think you might have made another conquest in there,' I told him, nodding in the direction of the building we'd just left.

He turned to me with a mystified expression.

'Really? Who?'

I gave a wry smile. There had been only two employees in the estate agent offices that afternoon; one was the pretty blonde with the husky voice and Disney-princess eyes, and the other was a bespectacled, grey-haired secretary in her late sixties. Although, to be fair, Finn had the kind of charm that sliced effortlessly through age barriers, so it could have been either of them.

'The young, pretty one,' I replied.

Finn gave an easy shrug. 'I didn't notice.' And I could tell from his eyes that he truly hadn't. He leant across from the driver's seat to press a warm kiss on my lips. 'It doesn't really matter – wherever we go, I never see anyone but you. Miss Whatever-her-name-is could rip off her clothes and run round the office stark naked and I still wouldn't be interested.'

I could feel his love for me, as if it were a coat he'd slipped around my shoulders to ward off the chill. 'I'm fairly sure they only do that *after* you've exchanged,' I said, my lips twitching.

Finn's rumbling laughter had filled the car as we'd driven away.

That was a good memory.

The garage phoned just when I was on the verge of caving and calling them back myself.

'I have good news,' the manager began without preamble.

I made an inarticulate sound, which he correctly interpreted as 'Go on'.

'We still have the CCTV tape from that Friday night.'

'And did my fiancé's car come in for petrol?'

The manager sighed. 'I know this isn't what you want to hear, but I'm really not comfortable about revealing that kind of information,' he said.

I flopped back against the kitchen cabinets as though I'd been sucker-punched.

'Obviously, if the police want to view the tape, I'll willingly surrender it to them. In the meantime, I've locked it away for safekeeping.'

Tears of disappointment stung my eyes, but I'd worked in journalism long enough to understand the laws protecting identity and personal data. Badgering this man into revealing information he wasn't comfortable sharing would be stooping lower than I was prepared to go.

'I'm sorry I couldn't help you,' the manager said, speaking slowly now, his voice deliberate and careful, as though reading from a script. 'And I'll tell you something else. I'm sorry I wasn't working the late shift last Friday, because I used to be a really big fan of *Starsky and Hutch*.'

32

The sky had darkened to the colour of an angry bruise. Rain was hitting the ground with the velocity of artillery fire. Through the kitchen window, I saw people in the streets below scurrying for cover. They ran with jackets, bags and briefcases held above their heads, but their attempts to stay dry were all futile. This was the type of rain that took no prisoners.

Despite the downpour, I opened the window, relishing the instant drop in temperature, however short-lived it might prove to be. The kitchen window had a low, deep sill, and I perched on it now, with my back to the elements. I could feel the rain splattering against my T-shirt, but I made no move to escape it. There was something wild and primordial in the weather that suited my mood right then.

I knew what I had to do. I'd known it even before the garage manager had covertly confirmed that Finn had been in the Foxton area on the night before our wedding. It was the reason I'd pulled the folder from my desk.

I looked down at my hands; in one was my phone, in the other Amelia Holmwood's business card. I stared at her mobile number long enough for the digits to blur and dance. Rain was trickling down from the open sash above me. A few intrepid drops found the gap at the back of my thin black T-shirt and ran down my spine, but that wasn't why I shivered. Part of me wanted to tear the business card into symbolic, confetti-sized pieces. But the saner part of my brain advised me to do no such thing. What if she knew the answer to the question I'd been asking all week? Did this woman know where Finn was?

And could I find the courage to ask her, when the answer 'He's with me' would shatter my heart for ever?

You can do this, a voice in my head whispered.

My lip was trembling, and I bit down on it hard enough to hurt. The phone call I was about to make wasn't just a random shot in the dark. I had no idea how or why I knew this to be true, but there it was. Call it journalistic instinct, or pure feminine intuition. Both of those had served me well in the past, and I hung on to that thought as I began keying in the number. *This must be what it feels like,* I mused, *when you're standing at the open door of an aircraft and someone yells at you, 'Jump!' All you can do is trust that your parachute will unfurl correctly and save you.*

It rang four times before she picked up.

'Hello.' Her voice was low and throaty and exactly how I remembered it. In comparison, mine sounded like a poor man's impersonation of Mickey Mouse.

Even though I knew it was her, I bought myself a few extra seconds before everything in the world changed. 'Amelia Holmwood?'

'Speaking.'

I was breathing fast, as though the truth might even now try to sprint away from me. 'I'm not sure if you'll remember me...' I began, picking my words with care. There was just a chance, if she didn't recognise my name, that this really was just a terrible misunderstanding.

'My name is Gemma Fletcher.'

She gasped, and unless she'd been holding her breath too, I could only assume it was from shock. This was bad. Very bad.

'You know who I am?' It was more statement than question, because I already knew that she did.

'Yes, of course,' she replied, speaking slowly and drawing out every word. I could almost hear wheels within wheels spinning in her head. Whatever else I'd lost, the element of surprise had been all mine.

'I'm a bit startled to hear from you,' Amelia said.

I bet you are, I thought bitterly.

'I didn't think he was going to tell you yet. I thought he was going to wait for a couple more weeks.'

The assassin's knife slid straight into me. 'By "he", I take it you mean Finn?'

She laughed then, as though I'd said something truly funny. 'Yes, of course I mean Finn. I imagine it was quite a shock for you.'

Was this woman for real? How could she be so heartless?

'That's one way of putting it.' My voice was dripping icicles, but she didn't appear to notice.

'This is such an amazingly clear line. You'd never know you were calling me from the other side of the world.' I heard her words, I understood their meaning, but they made absolutely

343

no sense to me. 'There's not even a delay, is there? I always imagined there would be. Is Finn there with you?'

That had most definitely been *my* next question.

'There's a couple of things I should probably tell him. The electricians came today, so that's good, but I'm afraid you won't have internet until the end of the month.'

I felt like I'd been shoved on to a stage in the middle of a Chekhov play. I hadn't studied the script and I had no idea how to ad-lib my way out of it. 'I don't know what on earth you're talking about.'

'Mushroom Cottage,' Amelia Holmwood said, as though that cleared up everything.

'What does Mushroom Cottage have to do with anything?'

The line went quiet for a long moment. 'Shit,' Amelia said. 'Shit. Shit. Shit. I've ruined it, haven't I? He hasn't told you yet, has he?'

'Hasn't told me what?'

'About the sale of the property and its new owner.'

'Why would that have anything to do with me?'

'Because it's *you*,' Amelia said, sounding close to tears herself. 'The cottage is in your name. Finn bought it for you as a surprise wedding gift, and he's going to present you with the keys when you get back from your honeymoon, only now I've gone and spoilt everything.'

If I hadn't been sitting down, I doubt my legs would have been able to keep me upright. The weight of this much information was buckling me.

'Finn bought the cottage?'

'Yes. We completed on the sale just before your wedding.'

It was finally my turn to provide Amelia with some earth-shattering information. 'But there *was* no wedding.

Finn never showed up. He's been missing for the last six days.'

Ten minutes of rapid explanations later, and it was still hard to know which of us was the more shocked.

'I thought it was weird when I went there today to let the electricians into the property. Finn had made arrangements for me to oversee various tradesmen and whatnot, so everything would be perfect by the time you came back. Anyway, I'd left the keys for the house in a key safe for Finn to pick up, before you went off on your honeymoon. But today, when I checked the box, they were still there.'

'This is really important,' I said unnecessarily, because I was fairly certain Amelia had worked that out for herself by now. 'Was there any sign at all at the property that Finn had been there?'

'No,' she replied, emphatic in the way I hoped she would still be when Inspector Graham put this question to her very soon.

'The driveway is being redone, and it's really muddy at the moment. It gets churned up whenever a car arrives, but now that I think about it, the only tyre tracks I've seen on it over the last week have been mine and the electrician's. I can't tell you where he is, but I don't think Finn ever made it to the cottage.'

33

I was talking too fast. Each word was running into the one that followed, as though breathing was now optional and I'd simply decided not to do it.

'Slow down, Miss Fletcher – Gemma,' pleaded Inspector Graham. It was his fourth request for me to do so. I drew in a much needed gulp of air and forced myself to be silent. 'Okay, can you go back to what the manager of the garage said.'

My sigh was impatient. Every minute – every second – we spent on the phone was one less that could be spent searching for Finn. But this wasn't the right time to lose my temper, not now, when – finally – it looked as though something was going to be done. With a real effort, I forced myself to speak slowly and clearly as I answered each of the officer's questions.

'Is it enough?' I asked anxiously, speaking over the satisfying sound of his pen scratching on paper. He'd been making notes as I spoke. From the sound of it, a great many notes.

'It's not a lot,' Inspector Graham began. My dismayed gasp

was like a scythe, cutting down my hopes. 'But it *is* enough to get things started. Well done, Gemma. You've given me something I can work with now.'

Hot tears of relief stung my eyes. 'So what do we do next? What's the next move?' I glanced worriedly skywards as yet another enormous crack of thunder exploded overhead.

'*We* do nothing,' Inspector Graham said, giving me no chance to interject. 'But as soon as we're off the phone, *I* will start setting things in motion. We have procedures and protocols for these things.'

'And they are...?'

I'm sure we both heard the frustration in my voice. He didn't challenge me on it, and I certainly didn't apologise.

'First, we'll contact the garage and the estate agent, to see if there's anything more we can learn from them. We'll also study the CCTV footage. There may have been other customers at the petrol station who might have seen something useful.'

'That's it? Shouldn't you be out there, physically searching for him? Knocking on doors or holding a press conference?' No one likes being told how to do their job, but I was beyond caring. If being rude to a police officer was a criminal offence, then they'd just have to arrest me for it.

'Whoa, slow down, Gemma.' It would appear that, somewhere along the way, 'Miss Fletcher' had been permanently dropped. 'I'm going to be doing plenty. But there's one thing I definitely don't want to do. I don't want to have to worry about you going all Nancy Drew on me and trying to find him yourself.'

'Wouldn't you do that, if it was your partner who was missing?'

'That's different. I'm a police officer.'

'And I'm the only person who truly believed there was something wrong about Finn's disappearance. I have to do something.'

'There's only one thing I want you to do: stay home and let us do our job.'

'Like you've been doing for the last six days, you mean.' My criticism was a sword, and I wasn't above wielding it.

'I know how frustrated you must have felt this past week. But now's not the time for finger pointing. Now is the time to find your fiancé. I'm going to send a patrol car to the area and ask them to travel the route Mr Douglas would have taken that night.' He paused, and I could almost hear him looking for the right way to phrase his next request. 'And I want you to promise that you'll keep your phone close to hand and wait for news.'

My mouth opened and closed like a goldfish in silent protest. Did he really think that asking me to stay meekly in my flat was a reasonable request?

'This storm is going to make the search hard enough, without my officers having to worry about you as well. I'd much rather direct all of our efforts and resources into finding Finn.'

Bravo, excellently done, I thought with wry admiration. He knew the last thing I'd want to do was hamper the search. 'Okay. I'll stay by my phone,' I promised.

'Good,' said Inspector Graham, who might have known a great deal about police procedure but knew very little about women, as it turned out. 'I'll be back in touch as soon as I have some news.'

My finger was still on the icon disconnecting the call as I ran towards my bedroom and pulled a heavy wax jacket and a pair of waterproof boots from the wardrobe. Mushroom Cottage was a two-hour drive away, in normal weather conditions. But with luck I would get there by early afternoon. I assumed the patrol car would be starting their search from the petrol station, so it made sense to begin mine from the opposite end of the route.

My fingers drummed impatiently beside the call button for the lift before I abandoned it and headed for the stairwell. After a week of inactivity, I was suddenly driven by the need to keep moving. Perhaps it was the ominous weather conditions or the latent power of Storm Edna, but it felt very much as though time was fast running out.

I'd only got as far as the floor below mine when I rocked to a sudden halt. There was something I'd forgotten. I glanced upwards at the flight of concrete stairs, wasting a few more valuable seconds in debate, before swearing softly under my breath and turning around. I pounded back up the stairs I'd just run down.

I left my front door swinging open as I tore through the flat and shot into the bedroom, where I snatched up the item I'd come back for and dropped it into the deep pocket of my wax jacket.

I must have driven in the rain hundreds of times before, but never in a storm like that. The wipers, even at full speed, were hardly clearing the windscreen at all. Throughout the morning, the weather forecasters had been warning people to stay off the roads unless their journey was of vital importance. Looking for your fiancé who'd been missing for the last six days most definitely qualified as vitally important, as far as I was concerned.

I felt no guilt at doing the exact opposite to what I'd been instructed. 'And my phone *is* close at hand,' I assured Inspector Graham in my head as I glanced down at my mobile on the passenger seat beside me.

This wasn't the kind of journey where you played music, but I drove with the news channel on, turned up loud so I could hear it over the pounding rain and the constant spray beneath my tyres. The storm updates were frequent and far from encouraging. Many areas were flooded, some completely cut off. Power lines had been brought down by the winds, and whole towns were without electricity. It sounded apocalyptic. Storm Edna would go down in the history books.

I drove hunched over the steering wheel, peering intently through the wedge-shaped gaps in the deluge that were all the windscreen wipers were able to give me. The wax jacket was too stiff and uncomfortable to drive in, but I refused to waste even the minute or two it would have cost me to pull over and slip it off. I knew that time would prove to be either my enemy or my friend today, and it was disconcerting not to know which.

34

FINN

He'd known heavy downpours before – Australia was famous for them – but this storm was something else. The rain had been falling for hours and still showed no sign of stopping. *Thank God*, thought Finn as he closed his eyes to the satisfying sound of the cup slowly collecting it, drop by drop. The rainwater had taken an excruciatingly long time to filter through the heavy canopy of undergrowth, but finally the beaker had filled. Quietly congratulating himself, he'd carefully drawn the cup back into the car. It had been a brilliant idea – quickly followed by a totally stupid one. He should have known that his stomach would never cope with such a huge intake of water in one hit. His body had convulsed like a cat with a furball, unable to retain the water.

Swearing like a marine, Finn thrust the cup back out into the thorny bushes to begin the process all over again. His eyes had closed, and he'd drifted into the weird state straddling the boundary between sleep and unconsciousness that had become his new normal.

The dream was vivid. He was on a beach – Bondi, maybe, although he'd never known it that empty. With a surfboard beneath his arm, he'd run into the sea and paddled out. Everything felt so real: the heat of the sun on his back, the wax on the board where it stuck to his chest, the gentle lapping sound of water beneath him. He waited for the perfect wave, and when it came, he jumped to his feet and rode it to shore, hearing the echo of its roar as it crested behind him.

Finn's eyes flew open and for a moment the line between dream and reality remained blurred, for he could still hear the rumbling wave, still feel the splash of spray against his face. He turned his head just in time to witness the nightmare of a storm surge of water thundering towards him. The cracked rear windscreen was no match for the miniature tsunami. It splintered and imploded as dirty, debris-strewn floodwater filled the car.

It kept coming, and Finn struggled to haul himself clear of the rising water, finding a strength he'd thought had gone. The pain in his leg was like nothing he'd ever known as he pulled against the metal that was impaling him there. Huge grey dots clouded his vision, but he shook his head to dispel them. If he lost consciousness now, the game really would be over.

After what seemed like an eternity, the torrent finally slowed. The gully was filled with about three feet of water, and although it was no longer gushing into the car, it still posed a very real threat. The seat beside him was practically submerged. Had his car flipped the other way into the gully, it would have been the driver's side beneath the water, instead of the passenger one. Even now, the water was only a foot below his face. And it was still raining. Heavily. Unless it stopped very soon, the water level inside the car was just going to get higher and higher.

The rain was going to kill him.

35

After three hours of driving that were probably going to feature in my nightmares for years to come, I was finally only forty-five minutes from Mushroom Cottage. I had been diverted twice, had narrowly avoided a collision with an airborne wheelie bin, and had had to slalom around numerous branches that Edna had capriciously ripped from trees on her way past.

I should have been on the final stretch now, except a 'Police: Road Closed' barrier was blocking my way. I stared through the windscreen at the barricade while Google Maps plotted me a new route. Even though everything looked vastly different in the rain, I was pretty sure this was the same road Finn and I had travelled on twelve months ago on the day we'd first discovered the cottage.

The route my phone found for me would add an extra half an hour to my journey and would take me through some fairly remote hamlets and countryside. I sighed in frustration and executed a turn in the road that contained many more points than the three the Highway Code told you to use.

The signpost for the ford forced me to slow down. I looked down at my phone, which was still advocating that I should continue straight ahead. 'Really?' I asked it. I took its lack of response as an affirmative.

Way back when I was seventeen and being taught to drive by my dad, he gave me a stern warning about never driving through deep standing water. I recalled that now, as I brought my car to a stop in front of the ford. I didn't need the yardstick gauge beside the flowing water to know it was already at a level where only an idiot would decide to proceed. The ford, which in summer was probably just an elongated puddle, today looked more like a river. It was flowing fast and deep. It was dangerous. And it was also my only possible route to Mushroom Cottage.

I patted my steering wheel as though it were a horse I was encouraging to make an impossibly high jump.

'If you do ever have to drive through deep water, go slow and steady,' I could hear my father telling seventeen-year-old me.

'Slow and steady,' I muttered as I released the handbrake and crept, foot by foot, into the water.

36

FINN

'Finn. Finn, wake up. Open your eyes.'

Finn jerked. He'd slipped away again, and during that time the water had crept another few inches closer to his face. The passenger seat was now completely under water.

'Finn.'

The voice came again. He identified the source of the sound. It was coming from the back seat of the car. He turned slowly, tears already dripping silently into the water below him. It had been so long since he had seen his face or heard his voice.

'Hello, son.'

Curiously, his father looked no older. There was scarcely a discernible age difference between him and Finn. Finn's confused subconscious clearly hadn't been able to imagine what twenty-seven years would have done to his father's appearance.

'Dad.' It was all he could manage. Finn's throat had locked, and he really didn't want to break down in front of this man, even if he was only a creation of his imagination. He still wanted his father to be proud of him.

'I'll always be proud of you,' the man in the back seat said, somehow knowing what Finn was thinking. He rested his hand on Finn's shoulder, and it felt so unbelievably real that he couldn't help the anguished sound that escaped him. Was he close to the end, to be conjuring up an illusion this vivid? Were the failing synapses and neurons in his brain giving him one last opportunity to say all the things he'd never had the chance to say to his father in real life?

'It was all my fault,' Finn said on a rush.

Once again, his father was immediately on Finn's wavelength.

'Bullshit.' If Finn had needed further confirmation that this was indeed a hallucination, he had it now. His dad had never, ever sworn. 'What happened was an accident. A terrible, unavoidable accident. Just as this is.'

Finn shook his head. Noticing as he did so that the water had risen.

'I should have been braver. I should have jumped when everyone told me to. Then you'd never have gone back inside – and neither would Mum.'

The hand was back on his shoulder, squeezing it gently.

'Listen to me, son. Nothing and no one could have stopped me trying to get to you. Fifty firemen couldn't have held me back. You're my boy. *Of course* I was going to try to save you. You'll understand what I mean one day, when you have kids of your own.'

Finn looked around at the wreckage that was fast disappearing beneath the storm water. 'I don't think that one's on the cards for me.' He made a sound, halfway between a laugh and a sob. 'I always thought if I didn't have a family, then no child of mine would ever be left alone if anything happened to me. But who lives their life like that? I found this incredible woman who wants to share her future with me, to be the mother of my children – and I finally realised that that was what I wanted too.' His voice cracked. 'This time I found the courage to jump. But I waited too long to tell her, and now it looks like *Gemma*'s the one I'll be leaving alone.'

'Don't be so sure. You just hang on, son. You've got a hell of a lot to live for, and someone very special waiting for you.'

'I wish you could have known her, Dad. You would have loved her – it's impossible not to.'

His father said nothing. With a Herculean effort, Finn used the seat belt to haul himself up and look into the back of the car. It was empty.

The water found his right ear first, tickling it almost like a caress. He twisted his head away so that it lapped against the back of his neck. It crept slowly, like a thief, trying to cover his ears and steal away all sounds. He closed his eyes. It was said that drowning was a peaceful way to go. Finn guessed it wouldn't be too long before he found out.

When the time for words ran out, there were only four that Finn wanted as his last: 'I love you, Gemma.'

37

The car shuddered to a stop at the worst place imaginable. Right in the middle of the ford. Glancing down in panic, I saw that every light on my dashboard was on; it was lit up like a Christmas tree. The car had stalled, that much was obvious. But had water got into the engine? I wasn't much of an expert on cars, but I knew enough to be aware that if it had, this would be the end of my journey today.

I sat up taller in my seat and peered through the windscreen. There were no houses nearby to yell to for assistance, and certainly no other cars who'd been foolish enough to chance their luck by driving through the ford.

The car was rocking worryingly as the fast-running water buffeted it. It wasn't yet deep enough to reach the bottom of the driver's door, but if the rain kept falling, it soon would be.

I bit my lip and reached for the ignition key. I probably had just one shot at this before Inspector Graham's worst fears were realised and I became part of the problem rather than the solution.

'Please start,' I pleaded to my car, or to the patron saint of hapless drivers with missing fiancés.

I almost cried when, after a wheezy cough, the engine decided to forgive me for my bad decision-making and came back to life. Forgetting the 'slow and steady' advice, I pressed down hard on the accelerator and shot out of the ford like a stunt driver. Unable to believe my luck, I didn't stop but drove shakily forward, one hand on the wheel and the other brushing away tears of pure relief that wouldn't stop falling.

Amelia Holmwood had mentioned that various tradesmen had been hired to work on Mushroom Cottage, but understandably, given the weather conditions, none were there today.

I took one glance at the mud-furrowed driveway and decided not to press my luck. I'd escaped from the ford, but the sludgy drive might not be so forgiving. I flicked on the hazard lights and left my car in the lane. Even through the driving rain I could see that the cottage was looking considerably smarter. The front door was now a bright cherry red, and the window frames all looked as though they'd recently been painted. I skirted the quagmire of the drive, but the front lawn was almost as badly waterlogged. I could feel the ground sucking hungrily on my boots with every step I took. I walked quickly, pulling my feet free in a series of squelching strides.

I paused just once, beside the estate agent's signpost that was hammered into the lawn. I reached out and ran my fingertips over the diagonal 'Sold' sticker. I shook my head, still unable to take in the enormity of what Finn had done. I still didn't know *why* he'd changed his mind, but several missing pieces of the puzzle had fallen into place during my drive that morning. Finn's reluctance to hand over his passport hadn't been so that he could flee the country; I realised now that he must have needed it as proof of identity for the house purchase. And the money missing from our joint account had actually been used just as it had always been intended, as the deposit for the cottage. I was also willing to bet that Finn's missing belongings were either in a storage unit somewhere or already in the house. My house. I shook my head, because it didn't matter what the paperwork might say. This was our house, our home, and it always would be.

Amelia had given me the combination for the key safe, but I had no reason to enter the property. There'd been enough people milling through Mushroom Cottage over the last week for me to know that Finn wasn't inside. He wasn't lying injured at the bottom of the stairs, as Walter's daughter had feared her father might one day be. According to Amelia, Walter had been absolutely delighted that we'd changed our minds about buying his home. 'He said he could tell how much you and Finn loved the house,' she told me on the phone. She gave a nervous laugh. 'He also said that his wife had told him it was time for him to move on.'

With one hand gripping the hood of my jacket, I ran into the wind and towards the house. Edna whipped viciously at my clothes and threw broken twigs and leaves at my face as I peered through every downstairs window. I wasn't sure what I was looking for, but if it was for a sign that Finn had been there on the night he'd gone missing, there was none. What I did see were ladders, dust sheets and a great many pots of paint.

Finn had wanted so much to make this place perfect for us, and the thought that he might never see the end result cut me like a knife. There was nothing more to see there, and I ran back to my car with a sinking feeling that had nothing to do with the waterlogged soil.

There were, I realised, very few reasons why Finn might have mysteriously gone missing between the petrol station and the house. Once I'd eliminated the downright crazy ones, like alien abduction, every alternative filled me with dread. I ping-ponged between them, unsure which option was worst. Frankly, they were all equally terrifying: carjacking, kidnapping, mugging, amnesia. Every theory had holes, and yet as I drove along the rain-slicked lanes, I refused to allow the far more logical possibility to gain a foothold.

Could Finn have been involved in an accident? He was a good driver – far better than me; his reactions were fast, and he never took stupid risks behind the wheel, but still.

Through the deluge I could see a signpost up ahead, but even with the wipers at full speed it was impossible to read. I wound down the window and leant out, jerking back as the wind hit me like a slap. Blinking the raindrops from my eyes, I read the sign. Foxton was just seven miles away. Seven miles to the last place Finn had been seen. My chest tightened uncomfortably as I studied the narrow road, which disappeared into the distance like a spool of grey ribbon. It was deserted, because who but the most desperate of people would be out in these conditions?

Lightning flashed above me and even though I would have thought it impossible, it began to rain even harder. Seven miles from here there should be a police patrol car, dispatched by Inspector Graham, heading this way. I shivered and wound up the window. It felt like a race to find Finn, and I really didn't care whether the police won it or I did. Just so long as he was found.

The rear-view mirror confirmed the road was clear as I went to pull away, but out of habit, and because I hadn't forgotten *all* of my dad's driving tuition, I glanced at my side mirror. Something glinted briefly behind me, snagging my attention from the road. It wasn't enough to stop me from driving away, but it bothered me, and I'd travelled no more than a couple of hundred yards before I brought the car to a stop. I swivelled in my seat and looked over my shoulder. The rear wipers weren't as effective as the front ones and whatever I thought I'd seen was impossible to spot from this distance.

It's probably nothing. A trick of the light. Except there wasn't any light, not really. It was grey and gloomy and there *was* something back there. Something I was meant to see.

Even in good conditions I would have hesitated before reversing along a road this narrow, and today wasn't about pushing my luck. I paused to switch on my hazard warning lights again and reached into the glove box for a torch. Edna savagely ripped the car door from my hand as I stepped from the vehicle. I yanked it back, and after a brief tug of war managed to slam it shut.

The wind howled like a banshee as I walked into it, my body hunched forward. With every step I took, the elements tried to push me back. Leaves and fragments of branches littered the tarmac and swirled through the air as though magically levitated.

Without the signpost as a marker, it would have been easy to lose all perception of distance. The wind repeatedly whipped the hood from my head and eventually I stopped pulling it back up. My hair was plastered to my skull, my jeans flattened against my legs, and the boots that were supposed to be waterproof were definitely not.

The signpost shimmered in the rain like a desert mirage, but eventually I reached it, leaning heavily against it as I caught my breath. The distance I'd covered had been nothing, but I felt as though I'd walked for miles. My fingers were cold and numb as I fumbled with the switch on the torch. It took four attempts before I located the setting with the brightest beam. I shone it down the road, trying to recreate the line of sight I would have captured in my car's wing mirror. I was hoping that whatever it was I'd glimpsed would reflect in the beam of light. But had the mystery item been on the road, or in the undergrowth beside it? I had no idea.

Sweeping the torch beam left and right, I slowly walked along the route I'd just driven. After a few minutes, the certainty that I'd seen something had diluted to just a vague suspicion. I was at the point of giving up when I saw it, half buried in the overgrown weeds beside the road. A piece of twisted chrome – no more than a foot in length – was embedded in the earth. I crouched down beside it and pulled it from the ground. It broke free from the soil with surprising ease. Did that mean it hadn't been there for long? Perhaps for only six days?

I turned the length of metal over and over in my hands, no longer feeling the rain as it relentlessly pummelled me. Had this been torn from a car? More specifically, was it from Finn's highly distinctive Gran Torino with its gleaming chrome bumpers?

I got to my feet and began searching the surrounding undergrowth at the side of the road. I found no other pieces of debris; no tyre tracks, or flattened foliage, or anything else to suggest that what I'd found wasn't just another piece of roadside detritus. My search was hampered by the waterlogged grass, which was slippery underfoot, and I was all too aware of the deep gully bordering the edge of the road. If I lost my footing and fell into it, tumbling through the dense gorse and brambles, who knew how I'd find a way out. The thought felt like a well-aimed punch. It quite literally took my breath away. How deep were these gullies? Were they deep enough to swallow a person from sight? How about a car? Were they deep enough to conceal one?

I didn't stop to think, which in hindsight was probably a mistake. Dropping the piece of chrome to the ground, I slithered my way to the edge of the gully and cautiously began to climb down. My feet skidded away from me almost immediately and if it hadn't been for the network of exposed tree roots on the steep sides, which I grabbed as a handhold, I would have slipped beneath the foliage in an instant. But my passage through the brambles and gorse was treacherous and it wasn't long before my hands were scraped and bloodied as the prickly undergrowth did its best to resist intruders. I crept forward, inch by painful inch, hacking a pathway through the thorns with a length of branch and peering into the shadowy bushes for further clues.

I'm not sure when the folly of my actions began to dawn on me. Blood was trickling down my forehead from a particularly nasty cluster of thorns, and the deeper I went into the gully, the more worried I became that I wasn't going to be able to get back out. From somewhere below me I could hear the unmistakable sound of flowing water. The gully was beginning to fill, and if I didn't turn back there was a good chance that rather than helping Finn, *I* was going to be the one who needed rescuing.

And then I saw it. Hanging on a bramble branch a short distance ahead of me, looking for all the world like a Christmas tree ornament. The breath caught in my throat as my fingers tightened around the familiar key ring, with its fob bearing the insignia of a hotel where we'd stayed, and the keys for the Gran Torino.

'Finn!' I cried, raindrops filling my mouth as I screamed his name into the storm. I pushed through the brambles with renewed purpose, no longer feeling the cuts, scrapes and grazes. Fear and hope had tangled together in an impossible knot that was lodged somewhere in the middle of my chest, making it hard to breathe.

My first glimpse of red paintwork through the brambles below me felt like a gift. One I was almost too afraid to open. With one hand curled around a tree root, I leant over the abyss of thorns and saw the distinctive chevron stripe of the Gran Torino about six feet beneath me. The car was on its side and tilted upwards, with most of it buried beneath the foliage.

Against all the odds, I had found him.

I called out his name, but there was no responding cry from within the car.

Frantically, I looked around for a way to climb down to him, but there was nothing to hold on to. There was only one way to reach Finn's car. I was going to have to jump. Good sense did its best to remind me that I was neither athletic nor particularly agile, but I wasn't listening. Finn's car was lodged at a strange angle, and I would need to leap forward towards the middle of the gully if I had any hope of landing on it. If I missed, I would go plummeting through the thorns straight to the bottom of the gully.

I took just a moment to steady myself. From this angle the

jump looked unachievable, but I refused to allow doubt to sway me. It would be, in the truest sense of the phrase, a leap of faith. But faith had led me this far and I had to trust that it wouldn't abandon me now.

I landed in a crouch on the wing of the Gran Torino like a practised stuntwoman. It was an illusion that quickly disappeared as I slipped and slithered down the side of the tilted vehicle, calling Finn's name between desperate sobs. My eyes were fixed on the windscreen, which was a milky mosaic of shattered glass. I couldn't see through it. I couldn't see him.

And then suddenly I was beside the driver's door and finally, after the worst six days of my life, I saw him.

'Finn. Finn. Can you hear me?' I cried, reaching in through the broken window. My hands touched his face; his beautiful, precious, motionless face. But he didn't respond. His long dark eyelashes didn't flicker open, his dry, cracked lips didn't part.

'Finn, it's me. I'm here. It's Gemma. Open your eyes, baby. Please open your eyes.'

I reached into my jacket pocket where I'd stuffed the torch and shakily shone it over him. What it revealed was the stuff of nightmares. Finn's lower body was covered in blood. So much blood. And I couldn't see where it was coming from. There was twisted metal pinioning him in the wreckage, which I already knew I would never be able to move.

My fingers flew to his neck, but in my panic I couldn't find his pulse. Was it on the left or the right-hand side? I couldn't think straight. Was I too late? Had I found him, only to discover he was already lost?

'Finn, wake up, please wake up,' I begged, pressing my lips against his frozen cheek.

38

FINN

The darkness was complete now. His eyes felt heavily weighed down and he couldn't imagine that he would open them again. And why would he want to? Because in the dark shadows of his mind he had finally found her. He could hear Gemma's voice, more clearly than the hallucination when she'd sat beside him in the wreckage in her wedding dress. He could feel her fingers caressing his cheek, and if he had just a shred of strength left in him, he would turn his face and kiss her hand. But strength, like time, had run out for him now. He could hear the water so close to his ear that it muffled her voice.

She was talking now. Not to him, because the softness was gone from her tone. She was crying as she spoke, urging someone to hurry. 'Tell them to look for my car on the road. That's how they'll find us.'

Finn grappled with the words, but they made no sense to him. But then why should they? They existed only in his mind.

He knew he should be afraid; he knew that death was very, very close. He could feel its hot breath on him. But his mind had found him a safe passageway from this world to whatever came next. It had brought Gemma to him, so real that he could even smell her perfume, feel the brush of her hair on his face as she leant over him, and pressed her mouth on to his.

Just one last look at her beautiful face. That's all I need. Let me see her just one more time and then I will be ready to go. Everyone deserved one last wish, and that was his.

He opened his eyes.

39

Someone had draped a fresh, dry blanket around my shoulders. Like the two that had come before it, it would be saturated in minutes. They kept trying to persuade me to sit in one of the many emergency vehicles lining the lane – and there were certainly plenty to choose from. I could see at least three police cars, two fire engines and a bright yellow recovery truck. But I refused to move from my position at the edge of the road. If I'd had my way, I would still be down in the gully with Finn, although obviously that was out of the question.

The moment of pure joy when Finn's eyes had flickered open had been snatched away when I'd seen his glazed, unfocused expression. I kept saying his name and touching his face, and for a second or two I'd thought he was there with me, but then he'd given a small sigh, that sounded almost happy, before his eyes had closed again. I tried calling him back, but he was somewhere else now. Somewhere I couldn't reach.

Strangely, I didn't hear the first siren, even though it must have been deafening. I jumped in genuine shock when a pair of heavy boots landed on the Ford beside me and would have lost my footing on the slippery surface if the firefighter hadn't reached out and grabbed me. I was less grateful a few moments later when those same arms insisted on lifting me and passing me like a parcel to the outstretched hands waiting to haul me out of the gully.

Since then, a great many people, all of them wearing troubled expressions, had descended into the gully before eventually re-emerging. None of them had been Finn.

Finally, one of the blanket bearers had explained that the situation was too precarious for Finn to be cut free while the car was still in the gully. Frustratingly, they insisted that I wait even *further* down the road while a recovery truck manoeuvred into position and began the tricky operation of lifting the Gran Torino back on to solid ground.

I was desperate for an update on Finn's condition but was continually turned back whenever I tried to creep a little closer.

'Can you at least tell me if he's conscious? How is he doing? Is he in much pain?' I fired the questions like a round of bullets at a young police officer, who had neither the answers nor the experience to hide his shock when I told him brokenly: 'He's been trapped in that car for nearly a week.'

A hand had fallen on my shoulder then, and a voice I recognised had gently said my name. I turned around and for a moment I didn't even recognise the man whose number I had phoned repeatedly over the last six days. In the end, Inspector Graham had done more to find Finn than simply send out a patrol car, he'd joined the search himself.

'Wait here, Gemma, let me see if I can get you an update,' he said.

He strode off in the direction of the recovery truck, which was still blocking my view of whatever was happening in the gully beyond it. It felt like he was gone for hours, but it was probably only fifteen minutes before I spotted him in the distance, waving an arm in my direction. I set off towards him as though a starting pistol had been fired.

'Hey, you can't do that,' the young policeman protested as I sped past him, which was clearly incorrect, seeing as I'd very much just done it. He tried to catch hold of my arm, but I was too fast and too desperate to be stopped.

'It's okay,' a voice called out through the rain. 'Let her through.'

I have no memory of running the hundred yards or so that separated me from Inspector Graham. He gripped my shoulders firmly, bringing me to a bone-shuddering halt.

'Gemma. Stop. Listen to me. They've got him out. He's alive. Finn is alive.'

My knees tried to give way, but I wouldn't let them. I saw now that there were even more emergency vehicles lined up beyond the recovery truck. My eyes flew straight past the fire engines and police cars, focusing only on the ambulance and the team of paramedics who were busily bent over a stretcher.

I turned a horrified gaze towards the police officer and then to the mangled remains of Finn's car.

'He's badly hurt, but he's still alive,' Inspector Graham confirmed.

I was running again, faster than I'd ever done, past the sympathetic glances of the clustered emergency service personnel. I was calling Finn's name over and over, but the figure on the stretcher remained horribly immobile and silent.

I hadn't realised Inspector Graham was running right alongside me until I heard his voice calling out to the paramedics who were about to move the stretcher into the back of the ambulance.

'Hold up a moment. This is his fiancée.'

It was Finn, but it wasn't him. His eyes were still closed, blue veins visible through the alabaster skin. There was an oxygen mask covering his face, and his neck had been immobilised by a cervical collar. He was soaking wet. A heavily bloodstained bandage was wound tightly around an injury to his right leg, which one of the paramedics was attending to with a worried expression. There was scarcely an inch of Finn's body that wasn't covered in cuts or bruises, and his right shoulder and arm were at an angle that made me wince.

'Finn,' I cried, my voice not breaking but shattering as I looked down at his battered body. What kind of hell had he been through for the last six days? How had he ever survived?

'How is he?'

The paramedics didn't answer my question. 'We need to get him to hospital,' said one, and the fact that every second counted wasn't lost on me.

'How badly is he hurt?' I pleaded, reaching out and grabbing Finn's left hand. It felt cold, and for the first time ever, his fingers didn't curl warmly around mine.

'We really need to go. *Now*,' said the other paramedic to his colleague.

'Can he hear me?' I asked desperately, moving with them as they wheeled the stretcher closer to the ambulance doors.

'We had to give him something for the pain before the

fire service could cut him free. We really need to get going. He's lost a lot of blood and we're concerned about possible internal injuries. But you can follow us to the hospital.'

I looked around despairingly. My car was far in the distance. 'I'll drive you,' Inspector Graham said, his hand a comforting weight on my shoulder. 'Can she just say goodbye first?'

Someone must have agreed, for they stepped back momentarily, allowing me to place a single kiss on Finn's cheek. 'I'm here, Finn. I'm right here. Please hold on.'

Inspector Graham was attempting to draw me back from the stretcher, but before he could, my hand delved into the pocket of my wax jacket.

'Wait,' I implored the paramedics as I took Finn's wedding ring and shakily pushed the gold band on to the third finger of his left hand. 'Okay,' I said, stumbling back from the stretcher as though I was the accident victim, not Finn.

'Was he ever conscious?' I asked brokenly as I watched them slide the stretcher into the ambulance.

One of the paramedics looked up to answer me. 'Only very briefly when we first got here.'

'Did he say anything?'

The paramedic's voice was softer, kinder now, knowing the importance of his next words. 'Yes, he did. He said to tell Emma that he loved her.'

Beside me, Inspector Graham cleared his throat gruffly. 'I think you may have misheard him. It would have been "Tell Gemma I love her".'

I made a sound that was halfway between a sob and a laugh. 'Not necessarily,' I said, as they slammed the ambulance doors shut on the man who was my whole world.

And that's when I started to cry.

40

The next eight hours will live on in my nightmares for the rest of my life. After days of uncertainty, knowing that Finn was somewhere in the vast hospital labyrinth – even though they wouldn't let me see him – ought to have been a comfort. But the grave expressions on the faces of the medics warned me it was too early to feel relief. It seemed like good news when they told me they wouldn't be taking Finn into surgery straightaway, until they then explained this was because he was neither stable nor strong enough to undergo an operation.

Inspector Graham stayed with me for longer than I expected. I'd imagined he would simply drop me at the hospital doors, but he surprised me by insisting on accompanying me into the building. He asked more than once if there was anyone he could call to be with me, but I shook my head. Dad and Hannah had wanted to come straight to the hospital the moment I'd phoned them, and it had been almost impossible to deter them. My refusals had sounded clumsy and ungrateful, and I'm not sure either of them fully understood my reasoning, when even I could hear it was flawed. But I'd begun this journey being the only one who had kept faith, the only one who had never once stopped believing in Finn and his love for me. And it felt important somehow that I completed it alone. 'Okay, but I'm coming tomorrow,' Hannah had said, finally hearing the determination in my voice. 'And don't even think about trying to dissuade me.'

Dad understood better, perhaps because of Mum. In the final days, even a crowbar couldn't have prised him away from his solitary vigil at her bedside. 'Just promise you'll call me if you change your mind, Gemma. Even if it's the middle of the night, just call and I'll be there.'

I was sipping yet another cup of unpalatable vending-machine coffee when Inspector Graham got reluctantly to his feet.

'I'm sorry, Gemma, but I really have to go.'

To be honest, I was secretly relieved because his guilt had sat on the hard plastic seats alongside us like a palpable presence. I had a feeling Inspector Graham would be blaming himself for not having believed that Finn was missing long after I had eventually forgiven him.

He ran a weary hand across a jaw that sounded scratchy with stubble. He looked tired.

'When does your shift end?' I asked.

'About three hours ago,' he said with a rueful smile.

Perhaps forgiving Inspector Graham would happen sooner than I thought.

Before leaving, the policeman bent down and pressed something into the palm of my hand. I unfurled my fingers and stared down at my car keys as though I'd never seen them before. How distraught does a person have to be, I wondered, to forget they'd abandoned their car miles away, in the middle of nowhere?

'You're in the hospital multi-storey, on Level 2,' he said, turning to go and then pivoting on his heel to face me again. He held out his hand, and I was perhaps slower than I should have been placing my own within it, for a handshake that felt an awful lot like an apology.

'Keep me in the loop. Let me know how he's doing.'

I wasn't sure if that was a friendly request or an official command, so I simply nodded and watched him stride towards the exit.

At around seven o'clock that evening, a doctor I'd not seen before strode up to the desk and asked something of the two women sitting behind it. I didn't like the way their faces turned grave as they listened to what he had to say. They both scanned the waiting area, and I willed their gaze to pass me by. But it didn't. The elder of the two women raised her arm and pointed to where I sat. By the time the gowned surgeon had crossed the distance between us – quickly and decisively, as though every second counted – my heart was thumping uncomfortably against my ribs and my palms felt slick with sweat.

'Miss Fletcher?' the doctor asked unnecessarily. It was surely obvious I was the person he was looking for, as no one else had paled to the colour of chalk or swayed on their feet as they leapt from their chair.

'What is it? Is it Finn? Has something happened?' I asked

stupidly. He said nothing and I could feel the world slipping from beneath me. *No, no, no. Please, not that.*

The doctor cast his gaze around the largely deserted reception area and, in a surprisingly mellifluous voice, said, 'Shall we talk over there?' He inclined his head towards a corner of the room, beside an overflowing noticeboard and a fire hose. It was an inauspicious spot to hear something that could change the course of my life.

'As you know, we have been monitoring Mr Douglas's condition very closely over the last few hours,' he began with absolutely no preamble, 'in the hope of delaying his surgery for as long as possible, until he's more stable.'

There was a 'but' coming. I felt sick as I waited for it to fall like a swinging axe.

'But,' continued the surgeon, 'we have reached the decision that we cannot afford to delay any longer.'

'He's strong enough now for an operation?' I asked, my voice squeaky with hope.

The doctor's eyes looked troubled, and I didn't like the expression that flitted across his face.

'These situations are always a matter of weighing up the best possible outcomes. To begin with it was best to try to allow Mr Douglas—'

'Finn,' I interrupted. The man saving Finn's life should at least call him by his name.

'Finn,' corrected the doctor gently. 'We wanted to address Finn's severe dehydration before subjecting his body to further stress, but I am afraid the situation has taken a critical turn and we now need to balance the risks of delaying against the risks of surgery.'

'Do you need to get consent for this?' I asked, perfectly

aware that 'Next of kin' on Finn's hospital form was tellingly blank.

The doctor shook his head. 'Not in cases where an incapacitated patient requires emergency treatment to save their life. Then it becomes a medical decision.'

Suddenly, I was very glad of the wall I was leaning against. I'd known Finn's condition was serious, of course I had, but I'd had no idea that the threat of actually losing him was this close. Every dreadful moment of the last six days was suddenly eclipsed by this one.

The doctor's eyes flicked towards the wall clock and his sense of urgency was obvious.

'I'm sorry but I need to go. I will get word to you as soon as we have news.'

I watched the man who held Finn's life in his hands hurry away, before sliding slowly down the wall with a helpless cry.

Finn was in surgery for six hours, and I spent most of that time pacing the hospital corridors and then the perimeter of the waiting room I was eventually led to. I shared the space with two other families, and although we didn't introduce ourselves, I felt a bond with those strangers whose lives, like mine, had been put on pause as we waited for news of our loved ones. Outwardly, we had little in common, yet we tensed in unison whenever the door swung open and someone received an update. Eventually, both families got good news and left the room with sympathetic smiles that were tinged with survivor's guilt.

By 1 a.m., my phone had finally fallen silent. The endless stream of messages and texts from friends and family would no doubt resume in the morning, but by then I would hopefully have something to tell them. For now, I relished the quiet.

I trod a path to the nurses' station repeatedly throughout the night, desperate for news. But each enquiry was met with the same response: 'Mr Douglas is still in surgery.' Finally, too exhausted to stand, I lay down on the uncomfortable waiting-room chairs, my face turned towards the door. My eyes felt hot, gritty and dry, which was curious given the quantity of tears I'd shed.

I would have sworn I was too overwrought for sleep, but somehow it caught up with me anyway. My eyes drooped to a close, and the dream immediately reached out and grabbed me. The plastic seats beneath me became the twisted wreckage of the Gran Torino as my subconscious chillingly reconstructed the conditions Finn had endured. Floodwater was thundering into the vehicle, but, as hard as I tried, I couldn't reach Finn, for I was entangled in the folds of my wedding dress, which, bizarrely, I appeared to be wearing.

'I can't get to you,' I cried desperately.

'It's all right,' Finn replied with a quiet, almost eerie calm. 'I'm here. I'll always be here. I love you, Gemma. Please don't ever forget that.'

It sounded horribly like a goodbye, and my involuntary cry of protest was lost somewhere between slumber and reality as a sound jerked me awake.

The door to the waiting room was open and within its frame stood the surgeon from earlier, who looked every bit as exhausted as me. He was still wearing his surgical scrubs.

His eyes met mine, and I died a thousand times over as I waited for a sign that Finn's surgery had been successful. Finally, he nodded and slowly smiled. The green-gowned medic shimmered behind a fresh wave of tears, but this time they were happy and hopeful ones.

'It was a long and complicated procedure, and in the end we needed to remove his spleen.'

I had no idea what that even meant, but I nodded happily as if it were an entirely superfluous organ.

'The dislocated shoulder and fractured arm were an easy fix, but he might require further surgery on his leg. But the good thing is that we managed to save it.'

I gasped softly, realising how close Finn had come to having life-altering injuries.

'It'll be a slow road to recovery, but he's a strong and healthy young man. He should get there.'

It wasn't a conscious decision, but I suddenly launched myself at the surgeon who'd saved the life of the man I loved, hugging him so tightly he was probably fearful for his ribs.

'Thank you, thank you, thank you,' I gasped between hiccupping sobs.

He patted me awkwardly on the shoulder and I got the sense this wasn't the first time he'd been on the receiving end of such effusive gratitude.

'Someone will come along shortly to take you to him,' the physician said, gently extricating himself from my bear hug.

I was still thanking him as he backed silently out of the room.

I got to Finn's room before he did. It looked odd with an empty space where the bed was meant to be. There was a window that looked out on to a view I suspected was better by night than by day. The harsh grey contours of the multi-storey car park were softened by its lighting. I had no idea if Finn would be in hospital long enough to grow tired of this view.

A trundling of rubber wheels on linoleum had me spinning around from the window. Four people entered the room – five if you counted Finn, and, truthfully, he was the only one I was looking at. I was like a runner on the starting line, itching to race across the room towards him, but I forced myself to wait patiently as they carefully manoeuvred his bed into position and then ensured that the drips, monitors and other paraphernalia that had travelled with him were where they needed to be.

And then, finally, there was just one nurse left. She ran her hand professionally over Finn's forehead, but he didn't flinch or even react to her touch. She looked up and smiled at me across the room, where I was still hovering hesitantly.

'He's going to be sleeping off the anaesthetic for the next few hours. But you're welcome to stay here with him, if you like.'

If you like. The nurse had no idea. It would have taken an entire SWAT team to extract me from that room.

The nurse pulled a high-backed armchair closer to the bed. 'It's not the most comfy seat in the world, but maybe you can catch a few zeds while you wait for him to wake up.'

I took a step closer to the bed, suddenly scared of hurting him.

'It's okay to touch his face or hold his hand,' the nurse said, her voice softer now as she read the longing and uncertainty in my eyes. 'Just don't go climbing into bed with him, eh? Although you wouldn't be the first person to try it.'

She was still chuckling as she left the room.

For the first time in a week, it was now, finally, just Finn and me.

*

Even though I was exhausted and every single muscle in my body was begging for rest, sleep continued to elude me. I perched on the edge of the chair the nurse had given me, pulling it even closer to the left-hand side of Finn's hospital bed. I wound my fingers through his, resting my face against the familiar warm skin of his forearm. The fine hair tickled my cheek, and I rubbed against it, like a cat.

I steered clear of the right-hand side of his body, with his wounded leg and broken arm, but my eyes kept going again and again to his injuries. How he'd managed to get out of the mangled car alive was nothing short of a miracle. I had no doubt that's what they would be calling it on the internet and in the media tomorrow. 'They're going to say you must have had a guardian angel looking out for you,' I whispered softly into the darkness. 'But they'll be wrong, because I think you had three of them: your dad, your mum' – my hand came up to the diamond pendant hanging on its chain from my neck – 'and my mum too.'

Throughout the rest of the night, nurses slipped quietly into the room to take Finn's obs. I had only a layperson's knowledge of what was normal, so I read their faces carefully as they took his temperature and blood pressure and read the monitors that bleeped constantly in the background.

'Everything okay?' I asked, more times than I could remember. Thankfully, the answer was always a reassuring 'Yes'.

The kindness of the nursing staff wasn't lost on me.

Sometime before dawn, one of them brought me a cup of tea and a plate of hot buttery toast, which I was going to politely decline, until my stomach growled noisily in protest. But the best thing they brought me didn't come on a tray from the ward kitchen; it was delivered in an opaque white plastic bag, like the ones I used to line my kitchen pedal bin.

I took the bag from the nurse, speaking in a whisper that was probably redundant, for Finn still showed no signs of waking up.

'What's this?'

'It's Finn's clothing and personal belongings,' the nurse advised me, watching as I carefully unknotted the bag. 'I'm not sure if any of it will be salvageable. The paramedics had to cut off most of it before he got here. But his wallet and whatnot should all be in there too.'

I waited until she had left the room before delving into the bag. The clothes were all damp and less than fragrant. I held each item gingerly, noting with a shudder how many of them were covered in dark red bloodstains. Even his white trainers were now the colour of old rust, I saw, as I dropped them back into the bag. Absolutely everything was destined for the bin.

With a wrinkled nose, I removed Finn's wallet and house keys from the pocket of the jeans and set them to one side. I very nearly didn't bother checking anywhere else, but as I bundled his ruined jacket into the bag, I felt something stiff within the lining.

Like a reluctant pickpocket, I slid my hand into the garment and pulled out a slightly damp but still intact envelope. There was no addressee on the front, and the back flap was open.

I had absolutely no intention of reading the contents of the envelope until I went to place it with Finn's wallet and caught sight of a single handwritten line. It was a snippet of a sentence that I'd first seen four days earlier. Only then I'd been sitting on the lawn in Hannah's sunny back garden, surrounded by the contents of Finn's dustbin.

I'm sure there are people who would have been able to resist the tug of their curiosity; people who would have told themselves it was none of their business and who wouldn't have dreamt of pulling that letter from the envelope. But I wasn't one of them.

Gemma, this is without doubt the hardest thing I've ever had to write...

My heart began thumping crazily, in much the same way as it had done when I'd first read those words, in what I'd believed was a draft 'Dear Jane' letter. Only now I saw that I'd been wrong.

Gemma, this is without doubt the hardest thing I've ever had to write, because as much as I search for them, there are simply no words to express how happy I am today. I never thought I'd be fortunate enough to find someone as wonderful as you, and I still can't believe that out of all the people in the world, I'm the lucky one you chose to be your husband.

A single tear trickled down my cheek as I realised this was no break-up letter, as Hannah and I had first thought; it was the exact opposite, in fact. This was Finn's wedding speech.

I didn't read it properly, because I hoped that one day, not too far away, he would have the chance to deliver it the way he had intended. But it was impossible not to skim the neatly written paragraphs for the phrases that had sent us off in totally the wrong direction.

'Change of plans' didn't sound nearly so ominous when it was nestled within a sentence that read:

I thought I was destined to spend my life alone, but then one morning seven years ago two people tussled over a parking space and fate stepped in with a change of plans.

Seeing the underlined word 'disappointment' had filled me with dread when reading Finn's draft, but far less so now, when read in context.

My greatest disappointment is that my parents, Peter and Amanda, and your mum, Catherine, can't be with us today to share this wonderful occasion.

But the best line of all had been saved for Finn's closing sentences.

It's hard not to feel overwhelmed right now when I look into your eyes and see the love, faith and trust that you give me every single day. Gemma, yours is the face I want to wake up beside each morning for the rest of my life, and the one I'll forever hurry home to. You're the picture in my wallet of my unborn children's mother. You are, quite simply, my partner, my best friend... my everything. This is just the start of our love story and I promise you today, in front of all our family and friends, that I will never, ever let you down.

'And you didn't. You haven't,' I said, leaning over and kissing Finn gently on the lips.

Sleep must have claimed me with almost no warning. I woke up contorted like a pretzel, draped halfway between the chair and Finn's mattress. I could feel the waffle weave of the blanket pressing into my forehead, but I could feel something else too. Something that had woken me. There were fingers in my hair, moving tentatively among the tangled curls.

The mattress swallowed most of my overjoyed cry, but enough escaped for him to hear me.

'Hey, you.' His voice was hoarse. It rasped like a rusty tool that hadn't been used in a long time.

I sat bolt upright, unthinkingly jarring his arm and bringing a spasm of pain to his face. And yet somehow he still smiled through it.

It should have been the moment to say something deeply meaningful or memorable, but all I managed to come up with was, 'You're awake.'

'I am.' His eyes were bloodshot, and there was a horrible bruise darkening the brow above the right one, but they remained fixed unblinkingly on me. 'Unless this is just another hallucination. And if it is, I don't want it to end, because it's so unbelievably wonderful to see your face again.'

There was pain in his eyes, but not the physical kind, as he lifted his arm and traced the contours of my features with his fingertips, as though imprinting them on his memory.

'I never thought I'd get to touch this face again.'

And with that I was undone. I closed the space between us, covering his face with featherlight kisses. I wanted to kiss away the pain from every graze, cut and bruise, but there were deeper wounds that would take much longer to heal.

'I'm so sorry, Gemma. I can't imagine the hell you must have gone through.'

'It was nowhere near as bad as what you lived through. I was there, Finn – I saw the car, the gully...' My voice trailed away, the memory still too raw and painful. Perhaps it would always be.

'You know what the worst thing was...' Finn's list of injuries was so long, it was hard to know which one could be deemed the worst. 'It was knowing that you'd been there, at the church, waiting and waiting for me and thinking that I'd let you down.'

I shook my head so fiercely that the bones in my neck cricked in protest. 'Never, Finn. Not once did I think that.'

His hand slid gently behind my neck and brought my mouth down to his. In the years to come we would probably kiss thousands of times, but no kiss would ever match this one for love and tenderness, or for the sheer joy of being reunited.

We broke apart to the sound of running feet, followed by a laugh. The friendly nurse from the night before rocked to a squeaky halt in her rubber-soled shoes as she saw the reason for Finn's elevated pulse.

'Well, that explains your increased heartbeat,' she said to Finn, giving me a small grin. 'Welcome back, Mr Douglas. It's good to see you.'

Finn's grip felt stronger now as he wound his fingers through mine. 'It's very good to be here.'

★

They should probably have fixed a revolving door on Finn's hospital room to accommodate the constant flow of medics who came through it over the next few hours. I was pleased to see the surgeon who I'd met the night before, now looking considerably more refreshed and less concerned than he'd done straight after the marathon surgery.

Finn listened intently as the doctor explained each of his injuries in detail and then carefully outlined his road to recovery.

'As long as you take it steady, stick with the physio and don't give up, there's no reason why you shouldn't make a full recovery.'

'He won't give up,' I said confidently. My eyes locked on to the man in the bed, who I loved and had almost lost. 'Finn doesn't quit on things. It's not in his nature.' My words were rewarded with a smile worth treasuring.

The doctor paused at the door and turned around to face us again. 'What happened to you is one of the most incredible stories I've ever heard. It's like something out of a film or a book.' He shook his head and closed the door behind him, but his words lingered in the air.

'You always said you'd write a book if you found an interesting enough story to tell. I think this one might qualify.' Finn was dangling the suggestion like an enticing carrot, and even though it was too soon to think about it, I could feel the idea finding a quiet corner of my mind where it could germinate and grow.

★

Between the physical examinations and a hospital breakfast that Finn devoured as though it was a gourmet feast, I listened in horror as he gave me what I believe was a heavily censored version of the hell he'd lived through since the night of the accident. I wasn't sure if it was a blessing or a curse that we would probably never know what caused the crash. For now, it was enough to have him back.

When his breakfast tray had been pushed aside, he reached once again for my hand, as though every moment spent not touching me was a wasted one. He looked down at our linked fingers with a crooked smile that I'd never loved more.

'So, the surgeon didn't mention it, but I have to ask: am I suffering from amnesia?'

I felt a heart's skip of panic. His head CT scan had been clear; there'd been no serious cranial injuries.

'No. Why do you ask that?'

Finn's smile was broader now. 'I was just wondering how I managed to forget that we'd got married.' In explanation, he held up his left hand. The gold wedding band glinted in the sunlight streaming in through the hospital window. Storm Edna, having done her worst, had simply disappeared overnight.

'Ahh, that,' I said, feeling my cheeks grow warm. 'I slipped that on to your finger just before they put you in the ambulance.'

His eyes clouded, and I knew he felt bad that I'd witnessed first-hand the horror he'd lived through.

'I wanted you to see it the second you woke up. I wanted you to know that it didn't matter whether we'd had the ceremony or not. That we're just as married as it's possible for two people to be.'

'And if I hadn't woken up…?'

The sun was still shining, but it felt as though a dark cloud had passed across it.

'Then it would have been even more important that you knew how much I loved you and that in my heart I would always be your wife.'

'I wouldn't have gone too far ahead,' Finn said softly. 'In fact, I don't think I'll want to be separated from you ever again.'

He took my hand in his. 'I love you, Gemma Douglas.'

'Still can't get my name right,' I said with a smile, as he pulled me in for a kiss.

Acknowledgements

When I sat down to write these acknowledgements, I began by asking myself a question: '*Who could this book not have existed without?*'

Certainly not without the talented team of individuals at my publishers, Head of Zeus, and especially not without my editor Laura Palmer, who championed this book from the beginning and helped to make it so much better than I had ever dreamed possible.

I feel sure that *Six Days* – and in fact my entire career as an author – wouldn't exist without my incredible agent, Kate Burke, who has been with me since Day One of this amazing journey. Kate and the entire team at Blake Friedmann quite simply 'have my back' and I feel in very safe hands being part of their family.

Speaking of family, I need to acknowledge that this book would never have come to being without the insightful input of my daughter Kimberley, who aside from being one of my favourite humans, is also a very talented publisher. It was during one of our brainstorming sessions that Kimberley came up with the suggestion: *'How about a book that begins with a jilting?'* And just like that an idea I'd been playing with for some time suddenly found a home and all the pieces fell into place.

But finally, I realised that the most important group of people who are responsible for this book's existence is YOU: the readers, the book bloggers, and the reviewers who have loyally followed and supported me in ways too numerous to mention. Please know that every book you buy or download, every message you send, every Tweet you share, or review you leave is a gift that I will never take for granted. Thank you for following me as we dip in and out of other people's lives and stories. I hope you'll be joining me for many more in the future.

Sometimes we need to seek help from professionals, and I would like to thank Graham Skitt, ex Inspector in the Met Police and old friend, for his assistance in matters relating to police procedure in *Six Days*. Thank you, Graham, for allowing me to borrow your name – which you knew nothing about – and for your patience in the face of my many questions. If there are mistakes in those areas of the book, they are all mine and not his.

No acknowledgements would be complete without thanking some very special friends who I can always rely upon for advice, support, and laughter – the kind that makes your mascara run. Kate Thompson, Fiona Ford, Sasha Wagstaff and Faith Bleasdale, one of the best things about being an author is having found you all.

To the friends I've grown up with, the ones I've worked

with and the ones I've recently made, thank you for buying the books, for turning up at the talks and tuning in to the interviews. You're a great team of cheerleaders: Hazel, Annette, Debbie, Sheila, Kim, Christine, Barb and Heidi.

And to the authors, too many to mention, who generously support and promote books that aren't theirs, I thank you – with a special shout out to Ian Wilfred, who tirelessly goes above and beyond with his time and help.

And lastly to my family. Living with an author isn't easy (or so they tell me). We want to talk about our books – ALL THE TIME (allegedly) and are incredibly grumpy when things are going wrong and annoyingly chirpy when they are going right. Thank you, Ralph, Kimberley and Luke for being there for me. There's no better feeling than standing in front of an audience at a book talk and knowing that you're the ones clapping the loudest, whooping and cheering me on. I couldn't do this without you.